THE MILLIONAIRES' DEATH CLUB

by

Mike Hockney

Hyperreality Books

All characters in this book are fictitious, and any resemblance to any actual persons, living or dead, is purely coincidental.

ISBN: 978-1-84753-679-2

With special thanks to Carolyn Hewitson, Suzanne Newell, Ian Breckon, Ros Cook, Emma Hooper, Nikita Lalwani, Joachim Noreiko, Jules Williams, Penny Smith, Harry Bingham and Jonathan Lloyd.

The Millionaires' Death Club

It's the most secret club on earth. It provides exclusive access to the greatest pleasure mankind has ever known. There's just one problem. *Membership is fatal.*

'The trouble with the rat-race is that even if you win, you're still a rat.'
Lily Tomlin

1

The Invitation

In a few minutes, my middle-aged clients would arrive and I'd have to begin my performance. There was a time when I thought it was the greatest job on earth. Now everything about it depressed me. In fact, I was fed up with my whole life. It wasn't how you were supposed to feel at 23.

'Hey, Sophie, what do you think those weird guys are up to? I mean, they're missing something, aren't they? You know, that big powerful thing between their legs.'

I was barely taking in what Jane was saying. Why had I decided to meet my clients in Trafalgar Square of all places? It was mayhem here. Tourists kept bumping into me, and one of them, a snake-haired woman in a blue cagoule, apparently thought I worked for the Tower of London.

'The Crown Jewels are where?' she asked in some indeterminate eastern European accent. When I didn't reply, she squinted at my red military coat, black pillbox hat and knee-high black boots. 'You not Beefeater?'

Christ.

Obviously the Slovenians, or whatever, didn't appreciate high fashion.

Style, darling – some of us have it and some of us shop at Euro-Matalan, I wanted to say in a glamorously dismissive way, but all I managed to mumble was, 'I no speak English.' Hey, wasn't that supposed to be her line? I turned away fast.

'Some weird guys haven't got *what* between their legs?' I blurted to Jane.

'Motorbikes, dumbo.'

'Eh?'

'You haven't a clue, have you? You know, I could swear they're all staring at you.'

What was she blabbering about? A kid with a fat head who seemed determined to splash me with water from the fountain distracted me. Jane frowned and wandered off, saying she was getting an espresso from a street vendor.

'You look funny,' the kid grunted.

Not as funny as you, fatso, I thought. The boy stuck his tongue out at me and I stupidly tried to stare him down. 'Waaaant a photo, Mrs?' he shouted with the devastating sarcasm only eight-year-olds can pull off.

I retaliated by sliding my tongue out as far as it would go, trying to make it curl in the middle to add extra *yuk* factor. A gorgeous guy in a high-fashion pinstriped blue suit strolled past, giving me a sideways glance. Instantly, I tried to rearrange my tongue into a delightful *come hither* shape, but it refused to cooperate and lolled out as though I'd just emerged from a convention for astonished people.

The hunk shuddered, scrunched up his face and hurried away.

Jane, clutching her fresh espresso, rolled her eyes and tutted. 'For God's sake, Sophie, would you look around you.' She started pointing and turning at the same time. 'There, and there, and there…I've counted twenty so far.'

Dotted all around the square were men and women in black leathers and gleaming black motorcycle helmets, their tinted visors pulled down. Not a motorbike in sight, and they had to be sweating like hell in this heat. If I'd had anything more than a black mini-dress under my coat, I'd be burning up.

'Maybe it's you they're after,' I said feebly.

'Listen, babe, you're the only celebrity around here.'

'Ex-celebrity,' I corrected wearily. Ex-everything, really. Fame, boyfriends, money, even my family. It was four years since my parents disowned me. I hadn't planned to humiliate them but…God, *Monarch of the Jungle* – what possessed me? I knew all along it was the most lurid of the C-list celebrity TV shows, but that didn't stop me. I ran towards disaster with open arms, and a silly grin.

'Look, one of those crazies is coming this way,' Jane said. 'Just your type – tall, dark, and handsome. Well, it's about time you found yourself a new boyfriend. How long has it been?'

'That's a woman,' I replied. 'Besides, blond hair and blue eyes are what I go for, as you know perfectly well.'

As the motorcyclist approached, I didn't really believe she was heading for me, but she kept coming. I couldn't help thinking she had a good figure. Actually, breathtaking – slim, but not skinny, curvy but far from pneumatic, athletic yet highly sexual. That was exactly the sort of body I'd been trying to sculpt with my twice-weekly trips to the gym. OK, once a month. You know how it is.

Lots of blokes were gawping at her in that ridiculous male way of theirs. I wanted to be able to walk like that. What was the word? – *sashaying*, gliding along as if she owned the place. I wondered if her face were as striking as the rest of her. Pug ugly, I decided to console myself.

She stopped in front of me, and all I could see was my face reflected back in her gleaming visor. Reaching out, she placed a gold envelope in my hand. Without a word, she turned and left, male eyes still tracking her like the most sensitive radars ever invented. All around Trafalgar Square, the other motorcyclists turned and walked away. In seconds, they'd all disappeared.

Jane made a face and shrugged. 'A ridiculously early Christmas card?' She gestured at the envelope. 'Valentine's? Maybe you have a mystery admirer.' She gave up and implored me to get a move on with opening it.

My guess was that the motorcyclist was a courier sent by one of my many creditors to give me more bad tidings of discomfort and killjoy, but I was puzzled that she hadn't asked me to sign anything to confirm receipt. I held out the envelope in front of me and was amazed that it didn't have my name on it. Instead, in embossed black gothic letters was a bizarre sentence: '*How far will you go for ultimate pleasure?*'

'Wow, luxury, hand-delivered junk mail,' Jane said. She slapped me on the back. 'Maybe your magic bus has arrived.'

I laughed with worrying enthusiasm at that. At school, I'd fantasised about a bus with special powers that appeared whenever I was in trouble and whisked me to safety. Unfortunately, it hadn't turned up very often and never at the right time. I think its tyres were always flat.

I peeled open the shining envelope. A small white card was wedged in the corner. 'Sophie York – winner or loser?' it said, the words printed in elegant gold lettering. 'One-time opportunity. Tomorrow, 33rd floor, The Gherkin, 4 pm.'

Jane snatched it from me. 'Jeez, I've waited forever for one of these.' Her face beamed. '*An offer you can't refuse*.'

'Don't even start,' I said. 'I swear, the last place on earth where you'll find me tomorrow is The Gherkin.'

'Loser!' Jane hissed.

We stood, arms folded, staring at each other, knowing exactly what the other was thinking. The Gherkin might well be one of the architectural marvels of London, but there was something supremely comical about it thanks to its many nicknames. Take your pick: 'the Erotic Gherkin', 'the Crystal Phallus', 'the Towering Innuendo', 'the Dog's Dick.'

'I can't believe you're turning up your nose at a trip to The Gherkin,' Jane said. 'I mean, when it comes to glass towers shaped like penises it's the, er…*dog's bollocks*.'

We both cackled. I caught the cagoule woman staring at me, muttering to her husband then making some queer hand gesture at me. A Balkan curse, I decided. As if I didn't have enough trouble already.

I'd recently written to my bank to ask for a bigger overdraft or an additional loan and I was waiting for the reply. The odd thing was that they'd sent me several letters in the last month and I hadn't actually looked at any of them. I stuck them all in a drawer and hoped they'd vanish, taking all my financial woes with them. It frightened me how many unopened letters lay in that drawer. Maybe my whole life had unravelled and it was only because I hadn't read my mail that I didn't know.

The letter that had dropped on my doormat that morning was one I couldn't ignore. 'Urgent,' it declared. 'Immediate Attention Required.' The last couple had said that too, of course, but there was something different about this one. It included two additional words: *Final Notice*.

'But how did that motorcycle girl know who I was?' I asked. 'How did she know where to find me? Doesn't that spook you out?'

'Anyone who has an office in The Gherkin is rich,' Jane pointed out. 'They could easily afford private investigators. I think you have a wealthy admirer who's a bit shy. Maybe it's a potential new client with confidentiality issues.'

It was true I'd had my fair share of eccentric clients, but this was taking things to a new level. 'Or a stalker,' I said, futilely looking for a bin. I stuffed the card and envelope into my pocket.

A white stretch limo pulled up at the edge of the square: my clients. 'Wish me luck,' I said.

Jane gave me a hug.

'These guys are hotshots from Wall Street,' I mumbled. 'And they're all opera buffs. The only thing I know about opera is…'

'Don't you dare!' Jane interrupted. 'I must have heard that dreadful anecdote of yours a hundred times.' She pulled away and wagged her finger at me. 'And it doesn't improve with the telling, I can assure you.'

'Well, these guys won't be hearing it, that's for certain. Can you imagine their faces? They'd think I was some kind of…'

'Anyway, what's the plan?' Jane cut me off. 'Champagne bar, swish restaurant, West End show and then off to *Ballum-Rancum*?'

'Something like that.' *Ballum-Rancum* was old New York slang for a grand ball where all the honoured guests were thieves and prostitutes. I couldn't imagine a more fitting name for the seedy nightclub where I'd spent so many nights with fat cats leching after attractive girls. Strangely, my clients always loved it when I explained the name to them. It had become part of my routine.

'I bet you're praying these Yanks like the British Olympic synchronised swimming team as much as everyone else.'

I nodded. The swimmers' most famous routine was *Waving Not Drowning*, involving elaborate, orchestrated hand gestures. It was always a showstopper. Worryingly, I hadn't managed to get through to Cathy on her mobile phone. If she and the others weren't there tonight, forget the waving part of the deal…just scream for the lifeguard.

2

Synchronised Drowning

OK, where was I? Oh yeah, the operatic sex anecdote. God, how did it happen? One second I was talking about Nelson's Column. The next...I only had a single glass of champagne. It *was* just the one, wasn't it?

'I'm serious,' I heard myself saying. 'Yes, *the* Mario Lanza, the great opera singer.'

I couldn't believe it. I swore it wouldn't happen, but when I'm nervous I just sort of lose it. *The strange case of Sophie's runaway mouth* my father called it, in the days when he was still talking to me.

My clients were staring at me with either sympathy or contempt. It was hard to tell given their odd, unblinking eyes. Obviously, being from Wall Street, they were loaded. Since they were each paying me a thousand pounds per day, plus expenses, they had to be. For that, I'd promised them the night of their lives. The trouble was they were ugly, with paunches, ill-fitting suits, crap haircuts and, God save us, *brown shoes*. They worked for some high-powered merchant bank and whenever they tried to explain what they actually did, my memory went all goldfish on me. Thankfully, their names were easy to remember: Ted, Bill, Chuck and Greg. I smiled constantly to reassure them of how attractive they were, but my fake smiles were now sliding off the side of my face like rats overly acquainted with sinking ships.

If I continued with this anecdote, I was finished. I mean, I told it all the time to anyone willing to listen, but only to people who'd never heard of Mario Lanza. These guys unquestionably had and they might throw me out of the limo on the spot. I didn't even know if the damned story was true, or when I first heard it. At least Mr Lanza was long dead and couldn't sue. Even though the anecdote was spectacularly obscene, I hoped it was legit because then he'd be so cool.

My four distinguished international financiers had practically been ignoring me until now. They had begun to exchange glances. You know, *those* glances – *who is this stupid girl and why are we paying her so much? A night never to be forgotten; wasn't that what she promised us?*

Sure, I'd be thinking it myself if I were in their shoes. But now that my mention of Mario Lanza was sinking in, they were starting to give me their full attention. There's no cocktail more powerful than sex and celebrity gossip and that's exactly what I was going to deliver. Jesus, maybe I could pull this off.

'More champagne, gentlemen?'

'*Yes, please*!'

We'd been to dinner in *Tmolos*, one of London's most exclusive restaurants, and now we were on our way to an equally exclusive nightclub. I'd been using the mini-bar to serve as much alcohol as possible and I'd noticed that the men had begun to look at me in a certain way. They knew I was an 'entertainment consultant' but, as their alcohol consumption rose, they apparently had difficulty separating that from 'high-class hooker'. I hoped that meant they thought I was classy, beautiful and knew a good few sex tricks. Of course, as an entertainment consultant charging extortionate prices, it was my aim to be classy, beautiful and to imply I knew a good few sex tricks. You can see the problem. Was I a fake entertainment consultant or a fake high-class hooker?

I could get high on the power I felt at times like these. You know, when you've gambled and it's actually paid off. I was a bit like the Incredible Hulk, without all the going green and sprouting improbable muscles, of course.

'So, as I was saying, Lanza liked to stand naked in front of a pair of beautiful blonde models and ask them to remove their expensive designer high heels and place them in a neat row in front of him.' I paused for dramatic effect and all that. 'Then he'd urinate into their thousand dollar shoes.' Shock flickered over the men's faces before giving way to seedy smirks. 'No, I'm just making that bit up.' I laughed uproariously. They gawped at me and I liked to imagine they wanted to worship me in some vague way.

'So, no shoe pissing,' I said sternly, dominatrix-style. I've found that, for some reason, rich men really get off on the idea of being submissive; always fantasising about their stocking-clad young secretaries spanking them.

'No, what Lanza actually did was ask the blondes to strip naked, get on all fours and crouch over him on his bed.' I was gesticulating wildly, really bringing this thing to life. My clients were mesmerised. 'Then he'd push his hands through the models' legs and, with a vagina in each hand, place his fingers over their labia. While his buddies watched, he'd manipulate his companions', er, lips, while singing one of his top operatic numbers. His pals swore it was as if the vaginas themselves were doing the singing. Apparently, when Lanza hit the top notes, his beautiful blondes had simultaneous orgasms of the most sublime and multiple type.'

I was so good at telling the singing vaginas anecdote that I'd begun to believe I must have been the one who created it. It seemed wrong that it could ever have existed independently of me. The four men began to hee haw and it was obvious they'd be retelling it for years to come, boring everyone to death at their opera societies and golf clubs with sweet Sophie's tale of heavenly pussy music.

Now they were all staring at me in a certain way. It's sadly true that some of my clients are determined to get me to sleep with them, usually when it's five o'clock in the morning and I've taken them back to their hotel after a wild night of partying, or as wild as it can ever get with accountants. Their hands reach out to grab my bum, they tell me how much fun I am, how sexy my laugh is and how they'll give me a special bonus if…well, you can guess the rest. Above all, they plead with me to help them re-enact my operatic anecdote, and I always give the same reply: that they'll need years of singing lessons before that could ever happen.

As if.

The smile never leaves my face as I repatriate my clients' roving hands. I'm excellent at my job – well, some of the time – but I'm so fake that if I ever actually did go to bed with any of them my fake orgasms would probably be real. And, if you think about it, that's one hell of a trick.

Anyway, having got the reaction I wanted, I started to lay it on thick. I reminded the Wall Streeterati that the largest sexual organ is the brain and they were particularly well hung in this department. How they loved that! As we passed Grape Street, I said it used to be called 'Gropecunt Lane' because prostitutes used to congregate there. I mentioned there was a word in Portuguese that meant 'throw the woman against a wall and fuck her like a lizard.' I breezily proclaimed that this was the type of wild lovemaking I enjoyed. Chance would be a fine thing! Fortunately, none of them asked me what the Portuguese word actually was. I say fortunately because I didn't have a clue if there really was such a word. When I first heard of it – from a sleazeball footballer who'd just returned from a match in Lisbon – I didn't ask either. I tried to look it up in a Portuguese dictionary, but couldn't find anything that came close. I mentioned it to a Portuguese client once and he laughed so much I thought I'd have to call an ambulance. I hope the word exists; otherwise we'd all be lesser people living in a lesser world. Besides, I can't believe a dumb Chelsea player could have invented it.

I told the Wall Streeters that stunning babes would fall at their feet once they were in the nightclub, and I said it so skilfully that I think they believed me, and I half believed it myself. Of course, the reality was that they'd be forking out for 'professional' company, unless my ultimate secret weapon – the British Olympic synchronised swimming team – were in the club tonight, in which case it was the clients' lucky day, and mine too, because the heat was definitely off. Satisfaction well and truly guaranteed.

Ballum-Rancum really was once one of the most fashionable nightclubs in London. Now the action had moved on, but a faint smell of bygone glories lingered. A certain type of person still came to the club, unable to accept that no one had told them the party was over. Old paparazzi who couldn't hack it any more hung around looking for snaps of a has-been who *had* been in the days when they were still hungry for long-lens scoops. They lowered their cameras when they saw my clients emerging from the limo. I could hear them sighing and I imagined a faint wind blowing through cobwebs. That image entered my head whenever I thought of where my life was heading.

One of the paparazzi had second thoughts and half-heartedly pointed his camera at me. Now, the first rule for a successful entertainment consultant is that you must know where to stand when you're having your photograph taken. Actually, what I mean is you must know who *not* to stand next to. If you stand next to a fat or an ugly person, scientists say you will appear less intelligent, less attractive and less successful. My problem with this is that if I have my photo taken next to a woman more beautiful and thinner than I am then I'm convinced I'll appear fat and ugly in comparison, and that will make my companion seem less intelligent, less attractive and less successful etc – so we're not exactly doing each other any favours, are we? I guess that's why I appear on my own in most of my pictures.

The veteran paparazzo took the picture. He shrugged, and I shrugged back. Hey ho. I knew the picture would never show up anywhere, but I still wondered how I looked. Had I gone to seed? It was only four years ago that I was a regular in the magazines. Hardly anyone recognised me now even though I looked exactly the same, but I might as well have had a face-lift and a body transplant, or a face transplant and a body-lift, for all the recognition I got. Even on the rare occasions when someone remembered me they always said, 'Didn't you used to be somebody?' I'm only 23, for Christ's sake.

As I was about to enter the club with my clients, a smiling guy sprang out of a doorway. He was about my age, wearing a leather box-jacket, and a pork-pie hat. Green felt-tip-pen marks were scrawled on his left cheek. He handed me a badge advertising a band called *The Bleak Morts*.

'Never heard of them,' I said.

'They're hot,' he replied in a fake Cockney accent. I could tell it was fake because it sounded exactly like a male version of the fake Cockney accent I sometimes used 'Get in before the crowd,' he said. 'They've just signed a mega-deal.'

'Where are they playing?'

'Invitation only. When the time's right, I'll let you know.'

I smiled at him because I realised he was a phoney: there was no band, no gig, no mega-deal. He must have known I'd twigged him because he gave me a knowing wink. I contemplated sticking out my tongue in that uniquely seductive way of mine then thought better of it after my earlier disaster. Instead, I took the badge from him, pinned it on my lapel and said I was looking forward to the gig.

'What's your name?' he asked.

'I'm Sophie. You?'

He grinned mischievously. 'I'm Ligger.'

I had to laugh at that. 'You mean you hang around backstage, pretend to be the best friend of stars, and eat and drink all their goodies?'

'Sophie, you know me so well I want to marry you.' He took my hand and planted a romantic kiss on the back.

I felt myself blushing. There was something about him I really liked.

'I bet I can make you remember me forever,' he said. He leaned over and gently tugged one of my earlobes.

I stared at him, baffled – and quite turned on.

'That's called an anchor gesture,' he said. 'If ever you tug that ear in the future, you'll automatically remember me. You won't be able to help yourself. I'm in your life now and there's nothing you can do about it. Scary, huh?'

'Do you do this with every girl you meet?'

He smiled. 'No, you're the first, and the last. It's a one-time deal for the girl of my dreams.' He tipped his hat at me and I was sure a little part of me had just fallen in love. I thought of giving him a hug, but instead I snatched his hat and put it on.

'Well, that's *my* anchor gesture,' I said and sauntered off with my new headgear.

Inside the club, the staff were as professional as ever and, as I signed in my clients, we all nodded at each other in that comradely way we'd cultivated over many months. After all, we were all in the same game: faking away like there was no fake tomorrow, pretending our clientele were ice-cool in Alex, or something like that. We were so phoney we thought making phone calls was the ultimate phoniness, just because the words sounded the same. The girls were all dressed in Christina Aguilera leather chaps and tiny knickers à la her legendary *Dirrty* video. As for the guys, they were Latino hot in tight Mariachi outfits.

The club had four floors: a wine and champagne bar at the top, a spirits, cocktails and beer bar in the basement and two dance floors in between, one for 'classic' tunes and the other for contemporary stuff. I always took clients to the classic floor since most apparently believed time stopped, inexplicably, around 1981.

As we reached the dance floor, I was overjoyed to see the Olympic synchronised swimmers in the centre of the action, performing a dry-land version of one of their most spectacular routines to Abba's *Dancing Queen.* They were all wearing low-slung hipster jeans, showing off their sparkling gold thongs, which matched their twinkly bikini tops. Of course, things being the way they were, they were not real Olympians, had never been near a synchronised swimming event and, quite possibly, had never even been in a swimming pool.

A year ago, Cathy, their leader, was bemoaning with her three friends why they could never attract wealthy men who would treat them to the finer things in life. The problem, she realised, was that they had no unique selling point. The remedy, naturally, was to fake one. Perhaps synchronised swimming wasn't the most logical choice but it seemed to tune into something deep in the male psyche. Men, somehow, couldn't resist the allure of synchronised swimmers. Perhaps they imagined four naked, beautiful girls with gorgeously toned and tuned bodies, performing elaborate synchronised sexual manoeuvres. And what better than Olympic competitors? The biggest lies are so much more believable than the small truths. I think Hitler said that.

The girls swept their hair away from their faces and tied it back in ponytails, vaguely making them look as though they were wearing swimming caps, and somehow that was sufficient for them to look the part. So, rich men were now falling over themselves to seduce them.

Cathy and her friends weren't strikingly beautiful; their bodies were shapely but not exactly athletic; their personalities were nothing remarkable. But, in the fake world, who was looking, and who cared? In the fake world, they were the most desirable of women because they were members of the British Olympic synchronised swimming team. They had learned that the only way to become who you want to be is to fake it. Personally, I think Cary Grant summed it up best when he said: *I pretended to be somebody I wanted to be until finally I became that person. Or he became me.*

Recognising a kindred spirit, I befriended Cathy and arranged to steer a constant supply of my rich clients in her direction. Now, I pointed my Wall Streeters her way, knowing everything was going to be fine. I could relax.

Yeah, right.

3

Conning the Conmen

Glancing up, I saw Teri Flint and Tamsin Creswell heading towards me across the dance floor. My direct competitors, they were trying to squeeze me out of the entertainment-consultancy business, but I was determined not to let those peroxide bitches beat me. I stared at their spooky, Botox-assisted faces with their frozen smiles that looked as though they'd been transplanted from the undead, and their overdone red lipstick from the Coco the Clown school of make-up, and tried to find my most nonchalant expression.

'Hi, Sophie,' they said, in that completely phoney way of theirs. They were wearing identical designer dresses – silver creations that hung in an odd, lifeless way.

'Hi, Teri and Tamsin,' I answered with equal phoniness.

'Hey, nice coat,' Teri said. 'Has the season at Butlins ended now?'

They did a twirl for me, revealing that their dresses were backless and plunged all the way down to their bums; in fact, several inches lower. Neither of them was wearing even a hint of underwear. Jesus, they must have been at least 29. Mutton, lamb etc.

'Still pulling that dreadful synchronised swimming scam?' Teri said.

'We don't see you around too much, these days,' Tamsin chimed in. 'Business not so good?'

'At least I can still afford knickers.'

'Let me guess,' Tamsin retorted. 'White lace with stretch. Three for a tenner from M&S.'

Damn. I couldn't believe I'd had to stop shopping at *Agent Provocateur* as part of a feeble economy drive.

'Look what I picked up.' Teri brandished a copy of the brochure that I gave to potential clients. 'Do people actually swallow this?' She flicked to the introduction and started reading my blurb aloud in a mocking, squeaky voice:

'Hi, I'm Sophie of Beauté du Diable and I'm here to make sure you have the best time while you're on vacation here in sensational London. I'm the princess of pleasure, the queen of quality, the empress of ecstasy. I'll arrange all your fun for you; open those secret doors that only the connected can access. In no time at all, you'll be in the centre of the hottest action,

surrounded by the rich and famous, rubbing shoulders with the brightest stars. My many satisfied clients know exactly what I offer – the most unforgettable night of your life.

'Don't worry about the party list – with me by your side, you're already on it.'

'The princess of pleasure,' Teri repeated with a witchy cackle.

'Who in their right mind calls their company *Beauté du Diable*?' Tamsin said. 'I don't even know what that means.'

'*Devil's Beauty*, actually.'

'Black magic orgies, right? Is that your secret ingredient?'

'You wouldn't understand.' I resisted the temptation to stick my tongue out at them.

They smirked, started doing synchronised swimming gestures with their hands and went away giggling, breast-stroking their way through the throng of dancers.

A few minutes later, my night had managed to get worse. A fat guy with a small head, red bulging eyes and creepy little chalk-white hands cornered me.

'Hey, Sophie York,' he said.

'Yeah?' I replied. He stared at me too long, so I switched on my bullshit detector.

'I'm, uh, an old acquaintance.'

'Sure you are.' I tried to work out his angle. A conman? A stalker? Did almost-forgotten C-listers get them?

There was a curiously pained looked in his eyes, as though I'd offended him. 'OK, I'll come clean. I'm a journalist.' He didn't look anything like a journalist, but what did they look like anyway? Apart from the rancid black hearts, obviously. 'I'm doing a piece on…'

'Let me guess – the London party scene.' Six months ago, I'd been interviewed for an article for the lifestyle section of *The Sunday Times*. The article was called, 'Extreme Pleasure: the Search for the Perfect High. (Adventures of modern city girls seeking their personal Xanadu.)' I said to the journalist that everyone I knew was dissatisfied because they were certain others were having more fun. My 'solution' was to try as many exotic experiences as possible. Then at least you could feel you hadn't missed out on anything. Trouble was, missing out was precisely what I was good at these days.

'Nothing to do with that,' the journo replied. 'It's your appearance on *Monarch of the Jungle*.'

Shit.

Everyone has done something they regret. For some, their regret is epic. I was invited onto the show because…well, I liked to call it a long story, but it was actually rather short – I shagged a boxer the night before his title fight, and when he proceeded to lose before the bell rang for the end of the first round, he had the cheek to blame me: *the meaningless, rubbish bonk that cost me the heavyweight title*, as he later describe it. So, instant infamy for Sophie. Anyway, I was too keen on the alcohol lavished on us by the producers and I stripped off and did a stupid disco dance in the middle of the jungle on a live broadcast. Being surrounded by long-tailed monkeys pulling down my skimpy shorts as I gyrated like a Bratz Doll on speed ensured I was tabloid front-page news the next day and for many days after. It was a slow news period, obviously. *Ex-public-schoolgirl discovers where the monkeys hid their nuts*, one caption read, rather cryptically.

'I don't like talking about *that*,' I said.

'I'm sure you don't. A lot of people didn't know why you were on the show in the first place. I mean, what had you ever done? If I remember right, you got expelled from Roedean, screwed some loser-man boxer and showed up at lots of parties. I don't think that even qualified you as F-list.'

'For your information, Leroy fought for the WBC world heavyweight title.'

'Yeah, but he was knocked out in the first round and vanished without trace. You dropped him like a brick – or is that *prick*? – straight afterwards, didn't you?'

'Leroy and I had a difference of…' I stared at this obnoxious little man. 'It's none of your business.'

'If I were you, I'd co-operate. You know what happens otherwise.'

In my boots, I was taller than he was, so I tried to look down on him as much as I could. 'You people are scum. I don't know how you can live with yourselves.'

'Look who's talking. All you do is take gullible bankers for a ride. With the prices you're charging, you'd think you'd be offering something a lot classier than this dive. It was fashionable two years ago, but nowadays…'

'*Screw you.*' I was confident that no one had ever nicknamed this guy *Funderella*, and just as certain that nobody had hugged and kissed him after joyously announcing that he provided London's best full slipper service after midnight. OK, I didn't know what that meant exactly when a client said it to me, but I appreciated the thought anyway (I think!).

He had a copy of my brochure and started waving it in the air. I was a parasite, he said, a rip-off artist, a snake-oil saleswoman, a 24-carat freeloading fraud.

I knew what this bastard was really up to. He was doing one of those mocking articles about what happened to such and such non-entity after their brief spell in the spotlight ended. What sad, pathetic life did they fall into?

'I'm not playing your dumb game. Print whatever you like.'

Minutes later, I was sitting in the centre cubicle of the big loos in the foyer, having an imaginary cigarette. I couldn't stand actual cigarettes, and, hey, they were banned in public places now anyway, but I found that holding two fingers in front of my mouth as if I were smoking was oddly relaxing.

Fucking journalists.

It took me three fantasy cigarettes to calm down, but the imaginary smoke made my eyes water. I *was* a conwoman, a horrible cow in every way.

The main door opened and I heard the click clack of stilettos. Two voices – unmistakably Teri and Tamsin's – boomed out.

'She's just so vulgar, darling,' Teri brayed. 'I mean, you'd think she'd have some class, being a Roedean girl and all that, but she's such an oik. Her clothes are ghastly, her make-up awful, her sense of style – how shall we say – more *Primark* than *Prada*.'

'Well, her sister was the special one, of course. Such a tragedy. Ophelia would have been so embarrassed by how her little sister turned out. If she'd still been around, she would have taken Sophie in hand and sorted her out, made her one of *us*.'

'Absolutely,' Teri agreed. 'It's the one thing that makes me feels sorry for Sophie. Otherwise, I wouldn't give her the time of day.'

I stubbed out my non-existent fag and started to stew. I couldn't believe I was having to listen to this toxic tittle-tattle. Should I storm out of my cubicle and stop the bitch fest in its tracks? But I was too gutless. To top it all off, I loathed hearing about my perfect sister, and, even worse, I missed her so much. Would she really have been ashamed of me? I could never live up to Ophelia. I'd always be in her shadow, smothered, blotted out, *erased*.

I waited for Tweedledum and Tweedledee to leave, and tried to think positive thoughts. Unfortunately, all I got were negatives. I was particularly dreading the meeting with my bank that they'd insisted on scheduling for nine am the next morning. *9 am*? Did such a time really exist? Their letter said lots of other things, but I couldn't bear to read it all. At least I didn't have to worry about my clients. Cathy and her crew wouldn't let them stray far.

Conning the Conmen

I left the cubicle, touched up my makeup, tipped up my chin, and sauntered into the main foyer with magnificent fake nonchalance. I stood in front of the club's proudest memento, a large photo of Hollywood heart-throbs Sam Lincoln and Jez Easton opening the club. It was thanks to them that the club became the place to be seen for a few vital months. Even though that was almost two years ago, the club still traded on its link with the two superstars.

I always stopped to stare at the photo because it was so exciting to think that Sam was once in this club, standing right here. He was my number one fantasy hunk. Well, every woman's, I suppose, given that he was Hollywood's hottest star. I had been a fan ever since I saw him butt naked in *The Eye of Sumatra*: me and three billion other women, I guess. It was love at first sight for all of womankind. It didn't do any harm that he had no kit on, of course. Talk about a perfect body; slim, athletic, a six-pack, just the right amount of muscle, buns to die for and a swinging dick that didn't scare the horses, but made you tingle in all the right places.

Having A-list stars like Sam as my clients would answer all my prayers, but, right now, I had more chance of making the two Ts' frozen foreheads wrinkle than of getting anywhere near a god like Sam.

'I've met him,' a voice said.

I spun round and found myself in the company of a tall, skinny man with a shaved head, wearing a beautiful navy-blue Italian suit and an open-necked black shirt. He smiled and introduced himself as John Adams, head of *Captain Toper Records*, a major independent label with a track record of spotting new talent.

'So, is he divine?' I loved hearing snippets about Sam.

'He's a cunt.'

I was momentarily stunned. How dare he talk about Sam like that? 'What do you mean?'

'I'm sure you know all about cunts,' Adams said in a way that I didn't like at all. 'I met Lincoln at an MTV awards ceremony. He didn't have a clue about music. Spent the whole time saying he was fed up, and moaning about how nothing got him juiced any more. Like I say, a real pain in the arse.'

'Yeah, I hear he speaks highly of you too.'

'I'm not the only one he's pissed off. Word is there's a contract out on him.'

I stared hard at Adams' face to spot any telltale signs that he was having me on, but he actually seemed serious. 'You mean the Mafia's going to bump him off just because they think he's a jerk?'

'Oh, nothing so crude. This is a unique contract. There are no gangsters involved. Quite the reverse.'

'In what way?' This baffled me. A contract where no one got hurt, was that what he was suggesting? By people who were the reverse of gangsters? *What*?

He smiled in an odd way. 'Ah, that would be telling.' His smile grew even creepier. 'Of course, if you want to get near Lincoln you have to get past the biggest bastard on earth – Mr Harry Mencken.'

I didn't like this Mr Adams at all. I pointed at my badge for *The Bleak Morts*. 'Here's a hot tip for you,' I said. 'These guys are sensational. A&R men are all over them.' I took it off and pushed it into his palm.

'Hey, thanks, I'll check them out.' He wouldn't let go of my hand. 'One good turn deserves another. I have a very special tip for you. Mencken is having a soiree in The Gherkin tomorrow. You never know who might be among his guests.'

For a second I was taken aback, then I stuck my hand in my pocket and brought out the card the courier gave me in Trafalgar Square.

Adams glanced at it and shrugged. 'Oh, you already have an invitation.'

'So, this is *kosher*?'

'You must have friends in high places. Those things are like gold dust.'

'You know me,' I answered, but I was baffled.

'Careful what you wish for,' he said, peering at me. 'If you don't know what you're looking for, you never know what you'll find.'

Asshole, I muttered under my breath and made my escape, clutching my card. To think I'd almost thrown it away. Now I was seriously intrigued.

When I reached the top-floor bar, I was delighted to see the synchronised swimmers and Wall Streeters in happy union. They were sitting at a circular table – swimmer, banker, swimmer, banker, all the way round – with bottles of Krug scattered between them. That meant my evening was over, bar the goodbyes and arranging for hooking up tomorrow for the fond farewells – and large tips, hopefully – at the airport.

I went over and spoke to my clients and they gushed all over me, saying how wonderful the evening had been and what amazing luck it was to find the British Olympic synchronised swimming team here.

Cathy winked at me and I could tell she wanted a private word. I leant over and she whispered, 'Hey, are you having a reunion?'

'I beg your pardon?'

'Come on, Sophie – I saw you talking to Tommy Miller earlier.'

'No, I was speaking to John Adams.'

'Who? I'm talking about the guy you were chatting with before you went to the loo.'

'You mean the journalist?'

'Journalist? Oh, Sophs, you've let him do another routine on you, haven't you?'

'*Tommy Miller*?' I repeated. The name still meant nothing to me, but slowly…bloody hell! Tommy Miller was even more of a nobody than I was. One practical joke at a Manchester United game when he managed to sneak onto the pitch disguised as the referee was his sole claim to fame. Somehow, that got him onto the *Monarch of the Jungle*, but it didn't save him from being voted off on the first day. If I were F-list, he'd be lucky to make row Z of the why-the-hell-is-this-person-famous parade. I was amazed Cathy actually remembered him. After all, I was on the same show and I'd completely forgotten him.

I'd been outfaked by a bigger fake than I was. Jesus, were there no real people any more? Then I realised something else. The mystery card must be a fake too. Adams and Miller were probably in on it together. In the kingdom of fakes, anything that's not fake isn't just unlikely: it's impossible.

4

The Debit Side

'Miss who?' the receptionist said. 'OK, take a seat, someone will be with you shortly.'

I wondered how I'd come to be in an industrial estate in Hounslow, one of the shabbiest parts of London. I was wearing high heels, a white blouse, a black pencil skirt with matching fitted black jacket, and was feeling far too power-dressed for this kind of place. The letter I received the previous morning said if I failed to present myself at the offices of *Far Havens Financial Services* at the appointed time 'serious consequences will follow.' So here I was, coping as best as I could with the strange world of 9 am.

I'd travelled here by Tube and was amused to see stickers for Ligger's band *The Bleak Morts* plastered everywhere. I'd smiled when I found myself tugging my ear – Ligger had well and truly anchored me! But I wasn't smiling now. I cursed my former business mentor Peter Henson for condemning me to this Hounslow hell. Several months ago, Henson abruptly sold his business interests to *Far Havens* and left the country, though one gossip column said 'fled' might be more like it. All I knew was that his little empire was now in much less well-scrubbed hands. My quarterly meetings in prestigious offices in Regent Street were well and truly over. The VIP treatment had been replaced by anonymous, computer-generated, urgent summons to this grim, pre-fabricated block of concrete, or plastic or whatever.

The walls were covered with timeless slogans such as *Get it right first time every time*; *There is nothing permanent except change*; *Not revolution but evolution*; *Total Quality Management*; *We respect each other*; *We are creative*; *We are loyal*; *Our vision is*…blah blah; *Our mission statement is*…snore. Best of all was: *We are always happy*.

Bring back Peter Henson! I didn't care if he was a crook. I first met him when he came to one of my parties. He told me he was a venture capitalist running an incubator business. I'd looked dozily blank and he'd laughed and explained that it was a collection of small start-up companies that he'd taken under his wing. He was nurturing them until they could be floated on the Stock Market to generate a whacking great profit for him. Now he was looking for a business in the luxury entertainment field. He wanted a charming service, emphasising the personal touch, that he could recommend to wealthy clients. Ultimately, he wanted to replicate the service in every British city. It sounded good to me and three months later, thanks to the business plan he put together for me, *Beauté du Diable* was up and running.

'Miss, er…please come this way.' A man in a shiny grey suit stood at the far doorway and beckoned me through. He had a face that appeared to lack the muscles necessary for smiling.

It depressed me how few people recognised me these days. For a few weeks back in my *Monarch* glory days, everyone knew me. My face was plastered over every tabloid, albeit usually accompanied by asses' ears, a dunce's cap, or assorted comical vegetables. Now all that attention had gone. I was anonymous, a nobody, a big fat zero. It's funny but if everyone else ignores you, you sort of start to ignore yourself too.

I got up and followed the shiny-suit man into a small office. In front of him was a framed photograph of, I assumed, his wife and two children standing outside a dreary church. *Yuk*!

'Well, Miss Yoker, I've gone through your accounts and…'

'It's Miss York, actually. Sophie York.'

He looked at me as though he'd just discovered I'd burned his house down.

'You're not Miss Jenny Yoker?'

'I just told you.'

'So what are you doing in my office?'

'But you…'

'We all have to take individual responsibility.'

'*What*?'

'You're here about arranging a loan for quarter of a million pounds, using your holiday home in North Wales as security…'

'No, I'm here about arranging an extra fifty thousand…'

'Why didn't you say? I never deal with anything below a hundred.'

'But I…'

'Remember, Miss Yoker, personal responsibility. It really isn't good enough.'

I stood up then stomped back to reception and explained there had been some mistake.

The receptionist gazed at me for several seconds before muttering, 'Not Miss Yoker?' several times as though it were some religious chant. 'Are you sure?'

I breathed in hard.

She got up and sauntered out of the front door. For a moment, I thought she'd abandoned me and gone for lunch in a nearby Grotsville café. A few seconds later, a man came in and sat down in her seat.

'Who are you?' he asked. He had a narrow mouth that looked painted on. 'I have no record of any appointment.'

'I have the letter right here.'

He glanced at it then handed it back. 'Let me look you up on the computer.'

I waited expectantly, but all he did was glare at me.

'Your appointment was with Debt not Loans,' he said eventually. 'You've been sent twelve letters in the last three months. Debt is through the main doors and on the right. I should point out that this organisation does not appreciate time wasters.'

When I followed his directions, I found myself in a vast call centre filled with scores of bland, featureless little booths sectioned off by clip-together partition walls in a dreary blue-grey colour. An army of people dressed in 1970s disco gear populated the booths. They were yelling at each other in what sounded like Polish or Russian, or perhaps it was just estuary English. Every now and again, someone screamed and squeezed a klaxon horn, making everyone else stop to clap.

In one corner, several of the staff were dressed in an assortment of revealing nightwear and were playing a game that looked like it might degenerate into an orgy at any second. I'd heard about a new craze among schoolchildren called daisy chaining whereby each kid had to connect with the genitals of the person next to them in the circle while each schoolgirl chanted, 'He loves me, he loves me not.' I think these grown-ups were trying to keep up with the latest craze, but they kept falling over in a heap.

Someone tapped me on the shoulder. When I turned round I encountered a middle-aged man with a serious dandruff problem, but that was the least of his worries – he was dressed as John Travolta from *Saturday Night Fever*.

He shot me a furious look. 'Come off it, the memo said *everyone*. You know what happens to non-team players.'

'I…er…I'm looking for Debts.'

He shrugged. 'I shouldn't be helping you since you're not playing the game, but it's in the corner over there.'

I hurried away before he tried to make me join in and soon found myself in another reception area, this time unstaffed. An electronic sign said, 'Please take a number. Do not enter until your number is shown.'

The Debit Side

Irritated, since no one else was waiting, I snatched a ticket from the dispensing machine, sat down and picked up an internal company magazine. The first article gave the history of *Far Havens Financial Services*. Apparently, it began as a debt recovery agency then rapidly expanded by buying up a psychic TV channel, a soft-porn premium rate chat line, a lap-dancing club, a Lithuanian bank, a Latvian estate agency, a Russian 'Protection' firm and, last and definitely not least as far as I was concerned, a small portfolio of businesses collected by one Peter Henson. Although I liked to call *Far Havens* a bank, I think that was rather stretching things.

Number 61 flashed up on the board and at last I entered the Debt department.

The office was large and modern. The man sitting behind the maple table wore a designer black suit and a pink shirt with crimson tie. Beneath his early-stage comb-over, two black eyes stared out with all the compassion of a Great White shark.

'I'm James Graveson,' he said. 'Your business is one hundred thousand pounds in debt.'

'I'm Sophie York.'

'Do you think we don't know who our customers are?'

'There's no way I'm in that amount of debt.'

'We've been sending you weekly statements. The last time you met your scheduled repayment was over six months ago.'

'It's a bad time,' I said feebly. 'The terrorist scares and…'

'Your apartment in Mayfair costs seventeen hundred pounds per week,' he interrupted. 'You have a Renault Clio V6 255 sports car. Then there are your well-used accounts with Harrods, Harvey Nichols, and Versace, to name just the top three. Your accounts show that you have a surprising number of "business contacts" on monthly retainers.'

'Those are my spotters. I need good lookouts in the big hotels and top bars to get my share of the juiciest clients arriving in London. It's a business expense.'

'Right now, Miss York, you scarcely have a business.' He picked up a summary sheet, licking his lips with all the creepiness of Dracula's most loyal attendant. His face wrinkled, as if he'd sucked on something sour yet strangely delicious. 'I see you're one of the clients that the reputable Mr Henson bequeathed to us.'

He started talking about break-even points and business projections and blah de blah. I wasn't following, but I think he said my apartment was costing £100,000 pounds a year, all told. My total annual outgoings were…did he actually say a hundred and fifty grand? Had they reinvented maths on the planet he lived on? I was apparently supposed to have an average of three or four clients per week to stay afloat. Come to think of it, wasn't that what Henson told me too?

'Mr Henson anticipated that you would have fifteen to twenty clients per week, bringing in a healthy profit and allowing you to expand, but…' Graveson squinted at his sheet of paper. 'Your total number of clients for the whole of this year has been – let me see now – a veritable legion of, ahem, thirty-seven.'

I rolled my eyes. Entertainment consultancy wasn't some baked beans production line. It was *art*. Someone like Graveson could never understand. My business revolved around pleasure, extravagance, dreams – the things that no doubt sprinted fast in the opposite direction whenever he showed his tedious face. I felt like telling him to get the express plane back to his ancestral home in Transylvania.

'You suffer from SSS,' he said.

'What?'

'*Spontaneous Spending Syndrome*. It means you're psychologically unable to save. You live for today and ignore whether or not you can fund your lifestyle. When times are good you spend freely, refusing to save a penny. When times are bad you spend just as freely. These considerations have had an inevitable consequence.'

'Which is?' My voice had become reedy.

'You've been placed on our high-risk register.'

High-risk register? 'OK, this year hasn't been great. Things are slow right now, but the summer season's only just started. I could…' Truth was I needed a big hit soon. There was no disguising that business was dire and I had a scarily big overdraft. My luxury Mayfair apartment was the real killer but a move to the sticks was unthinkable. I couldn't function without a prestigious address. I often used my apartment for introductory drinks and little soirees. The notion of dragging clients out to some godforsaken place like Hammersmith…the very thought!

Graveson stared at me. 'Do you really believe you're cut out for this kind of job?'

What was he on about? I was presentable, I had a nice accent, I'd been to Roedean. I was even an ex-celebrity.

'You strike me as strictly second division,' he said.

I couldn't believe I was stuck in Hounslow in an industrial rabbit hutch full of ageing disco stars listening to the cheerleader of the undead telling me

I was second division. I guess when you're sitting in the losers' lounge the last thing you want to do is admit it. I once crossed paths with a depressing IT Director who said 'snafu' all the time. *Situation normal – all fucked up*. That pretty much summed it up.

'I can't see any big star ever asking for your services,' Graveson said. 'Can you?'

Well, I dreamt about it every night. Wasn't that good enough?

'Miss York, you have a fortnight to pay off half your debt. If you fail, we're pulling the plug. No further monies will be advanced to you by *Far Havens Financial Services* and your situation will be passed over to our Recovery department for appropriate action.'

I think he could see that his words had bounced off my head, hit the ceiling and scattered meaninglessly around me. If it had been someone else, I might have thought he was putting me on, but Graveson plainly wasn't the joking type.

'Frankly, I have little doubt you will be declared bankrupt within weeks. To be clear, your landlord will evict you, the bailiffs will seize any goods that can be sold, and the only shopping you'll be doing from then on will be strictly of the window type.'

My body temperature was plummeting. So, shitcreek had finally arrived. In a matter of days, I'd be surrounded by discarded pizza boxes and empty bottles of gin as I stared forlornly at the poster of Sam Lincoln in my bedroom. My life was disintegrating. I had two weeks to find fifty grand or I'd be drinking *snafu au lait* in the losers' lounge for the rest of my life. And gorgeous Sam definitely wouldn't be joining me there.

5

Stick 'Em Up

'I've got it – a *heist*! That's the fastest way to get the big bucks you need. We could wear Bonnie and Clyde gear. I'd look great in a beret and a maxi-skirt, with a Tommy gun slung over my shoulder.'

Jane, apart from being my closest friend and a worryingly enthusiastic fan of gangster movies, was also my self-appointed career adviser. She could be relied on for less than practical suggestions, but at least she always gave me her shoulder to cry on. It was just as well she had a job in PR because that meant that after hearing my meltdown news she'd been able to leave work early ('Work? – what's that, *dahling*,' as she liked to say in her best Marlene Dietrich accent) and take me to our regular wine bar to drown my sorrows in the traditional liquid manner.

She was wearing a blue tartan outfit that made her look like a Scottish airhostess. Tall, slim, big-busted with flowing auburn hair and large green eyes, her main feature – according to her – was a set of pouting lips that men found irresistible. We'd known each other since schooldays but I'd never personally observed this lip effect. Breasts yes, lips no.

Unfortunately, Jane had managed to drag along one of her tedious colleagues. Becky Rogers – a mousy creature with fat ankles – was a shrill Sussex girl with a penchant for Burberry. Today, she sported a Burberry jacket with matching mini-skirt, high heels and handbag. When she uncrossed her legs, I was unfortunate enough to glimpse Burberry knickers. Well, at least she wasn't commando. Small mercies, I suppose.

'Gangster chic is brill,' Becky announced. 'We could be Reservoir Bitches and go on a robbing spree all over the South-East.' As she started to bray hysterically, she attracted the attention of two City types standing at the bar drinking tequila, vodka and Red Bulls. Jesus, TVRs – so passé.

I glanced around in irritation. The bar – *The Last Reel* – was a converted warehouse with cherry-wood floorboards, rough brick walls and stylish furniture in assorted chocolate, plum and raspberry. I always felt like having fruit salad and ice cream when I came here, but not today. Graveson had ensured I was on a major downer.

I couldn't believe Jane had given her colleague a full briefing on my financial woes. It wouldn't have been so bad if Becky could offer constructive advice, but the only helpful thing she'd done so far was buy the first bottle of white wine. The alcohol had gone straight to her head, judging by the way she was giggling and throwing flirtatious hair-flicks at the two City Slickers, or Shitty Lickers as I preferred to call them on account of their well-known feeble sexual technique.

'Magic bus time again, huh?' Jane said.

She was right – my mythical bus was exactly what I needed now. Fifty grand in a couple of weeks? Impossible.

'I've got it,' Jane said. 'You could do an outrageous novelty act that people would pay thousands to see. How about your own version of the singing vaginas? We could team you up with one of those hunks from that pop-opera group from *X-Factor*.'

I smiled indulgently.

'*The singing whats*?' Becky spluttered.

As Jane explained, I couldn't help fidgeting. I had a nagging feeling there was something important that I ought to be thinking about. Too much damned alcohol had frazzled my brain.

'Gross,' Becky said, making a gagging gesture as Jane finished off the anecdote.

What had I forgotten? A get-out-of-jail card hopefully.

'Sophie, won't your parents lend you some money?' Becky said. 'They must be rich if they could afford to send you to Roedean.'

Images of my schooldays drifted into my mind like rolling fog. Ah, dear, sweet Roedean. My parents had decided that because the school was in such a beautiful location on the Sussex Downs, it was the perfect setting for a 'genteel' young lady. Not so perfect when I was expelled at 16, of course.

I still remembered the letter sent by the head teacher to my parents. It said I'd fallen under the spell of a troublemaker and was naïve, gullible and suggestible to a dangerous extent. I apparently had no moral backbone and was easily led astray by more dominant personalities. That wasn't the end of it. I was allegedly fascinated by the wrong side of the law, naturally aligned myself with undesirables and had amoral tendencies. I dreaded that they might mention what had happened to my sister as a mitigating factor, but there wasn't a word about it. I couldn't have stomached her being dragged into it. The *comparison*.

'Sophie still maintains she did nothing wrong,' the letter concluded. 'She hasn't cooperated with our investigation. This is unacceptable to the governors of this school. Therefore we have no option but to expel Sophie.'

It seemed a bit harsh when my only offence was helping my best friend get in a bit of bonking with her fit boyfriend. Jane had embarked on a major pash with a farm-boy from a local village and it was my job to help with the cover-up. I still didn't know how we were rumbled. Anyway, what did I do that was so wrong? OK, I secretly watched a few times but that hardly made me amoral; more of a voyeur.

Strangely, my dad told me he was proud of me for not betraying my friend, even though I could have saved myself if I had.

'Don't forget, the world hates a snitch,' he said. 'People of good breeding never break the bond of honour with their friends.'

I think that was the last time he was ever proud of me. He didn't like it that after educating me so expensively I ended up as nothing better than an office temp. Partying was all I was good at and that's how I eventually came to the attention of the tabloids, especially when I had my brief liaison with Leroy. Some of them called me an *IT* girl. Often, they changed that to SH-*IT* girl and claimed it was a spell-check error.

'Er, Roedean's a touchy subject,' Jane whispered to Becky. 'Let's just say Sophie doesn't see much of her parents these days and leave it at that.'

Much? Not at all. They were distinctly unimpressed with my party antics. My mum was in the WI and my dad was well connected with the local church, playing the organ at the weekly Sunday bore-a-thon. I'd become a permanent embarrassment to them. *Monarch of the Jungle* was the final straw. So, the answer to Becky's question was that the family money trough had long since dried up.

In the circumstances, there was only one thing to be done. 'Champagne,' I said, frantically waving at the nearest waiter.

I reached into my pocket for my purse. As I took it out, something fell on the floor. In a flash, Jane snatched it up. It was the card I was given at Trafalgar Square.

Jane read it aloud: 'Sophie York. Winner or Loser? One-time opportunity.'

Winner or loser? According to Graveson, there was only one answer to that.

'It's a fake,' I announced. 'That bastard Tommy Miller set it up. I bumped into him last night. He's on my case for some reason.'

'Tommy Miller doesn't have the class,' Jane answered. 'This card is really high quality. It's bona fide, I'm certain.'

She handed it back to me, and I held it up to the light. The gold letters were entrancing. They seemed to be genuine gold leaf. There was no question it was beautifully crafted. It did seem improbable that Tommy Miller could have produced something so stylish, and I'd never totally convinced myself that he and the Captain Toper guy John Adams knew each other. But did that mean it genuinely *was* an invite to a soiree thrown by a Hollywood big shot? Maybe, somehow, I'd come to the attention of the right people and I was being welcomed into the in-crowd. My magic bus arriving at last?

'You can still make it to The Gherkin,' Jane said, glancing at her watch.

I wasn't surprised the card appealed to Jane with those gangster instincts of hers, but I hadn't signed up with her criminal fraternity just yet. Besides, I'd told my American clients I'd see them off at Heathrow. I didn't have to, but it was bad form not to, and, besides, what about the tips?

'I'm picturing the guy who sent you this,' Jane went on. 'He's an eccentric millionaire, a recluse who suddenly wants to party. One of your clients told him how fabulous you are.'

'It's probably from a crank,' Becky said sniffily, taking the card from Jane. 'It might even be a kidnapper. Who knows, maybe a serial killer?'

Gee, thanks.

'Come off it, Becks,' Jane said with a snigger. 'Since when did serial killers work in The Gherkin? She slammed back the rest of her champagne and smacked her lips with satisfaction. 'Emphasise the positive, Sophs. Here, I'll give you another theory.'

Sitting back, she cupped her chin. 'He's a distinguished older man, rich and self-confident, someone who gets off on pulling people's strings, always looking for new blood for his glamorous operations. He's an A-lister who deals only with the best. He wants to find out if you're the right stuff.'

'What about a Hollywood producer?' I ventured.

'You can't be serious,' Becky spluttered into her wine.

I was sure she was weighing up whether she should sneer openly at me or try for a more subtle form of contempt.

'No offence, Sophie,' she said *offensively*, 'but the idea of anyone from the A-list being seen dead with someone like you…I mean it just couldn't happen.'

Bloody hell, what was so wrong with me? I'd tell Mr Hollywood my singing vaginas anecdote and he'd use it on the Jay Leno show. Just wait and see.

'Why don't you come out and say it,' I said. 'You think I'm second division.'

'Are we talking football now?'

'You don't think I can hack it, do you?'

'Well, if this is legit, why is this person, or these people, being so secretive? What have they got to hide?'

'Don't be a misery, Becks,' Jane intervened.

'But Becky might have a point.' Jeez, I couldn't believe I was agreeing with her. I just didn't trust that invitation though, nor John Adams, nor Tommy Miller.

'Sure, Sophs, do nothing and you'll be safe,' Jane said, raising her hand as though she were stopping traffic, 'but you might have missed the best thing ever. Could you ever forgive yourself? Besides, after what that dreadful little banker told you this morning, do you have a choice?'

Graveson's words flooded back in blood-spattered Technicolor. I had to raise serious money fast and I didn't have a clue how to begin. Now I had this mystery invitation promising me a one-time opportunity.

Jane glanced at her watch again. 'Well, babe, if you're doing it, you have to do it now.'

6

Finding the Devil

I wondered why the glamorous secretary with a 1950s beehive hairdo was studiously ignoring me, despite obviously having absolutely nothing to do. She spent all of her time texting on her mobile and occasionally staring appreciatively at her well-groomed fingernails. The Gherkin's 33rd floor reception area was easily big enough for a party, but there was no sign of any A-list soiree.

I was already shaken up having spent ten minutes in the lobby explaining to a security guard that I had a genuine appointment. There was no mention of me on the clipboard that he was clutching to his chest as though it were the Ten Commandments, and that meant I apparently didn't exist – *not anywhere*. He kept looking through me as if expecting me to vanish, thus resolving his clipboard issue. Eventually one of his colleagues rang reception on the 33rd floor and I was finally allowed through. Now I was enduring the secretary from hell or, more accurately, Sheffield.

Her phone rang and she leisurely answered it before putting it down again with well-rehearsed slowness. Staring out of the window, she said, 'Mr Mencken will see you now.'

'So it really *is* Harry Mencken?'

'You don't expect me to know clients' full names, do you? The agency would have to pay me twice as much for that kind of thing.'

God, a bona fide slacker. She seemed so lazy that I felt on a par with some Polish labourer working sixteen hours a day. I walked past her, turned the corner and discovered a sleek black door with a shining silver nameplate. 'Harry Mencken,' it said. 'Producer.'

I stared at the words. *The* Harry Mencken – who, according to John Adams, might well be the Devil Incarnate. I didn't know whether I should be running for my life or falling on my knees in grateful prayer. A movie producer was the real deal. And he knew Sam Lincoln…

Sam *Sex God* Lincoln.

Christttttttt!!!!!!!!

Got to play it cool. I had to act as if I met A-listers all the time, as if it was second nature for me to mix with movers and shakers. If I could pull this off I'd be made, but how could I show a movie boss a good time? It's one thing putting on a show for accountants, but showtime for Hollywood's finest has a degree of difficulty of ten. It's a toe loop, followed by a double klutz and triple salco. Double klutz? *Jesus.*

I fled to the loo – conveniently positioned next to Mencken's office – but only managed a dribble when I got there. Then it was time to face the mirror test. Instantly, I regretted what I'd chosen to wear.

Because it was such a nice day, I'd grabbed a red tartan miniskirt from my wardrobe (which would allow a flash of skimpy, see-through knickers if circumstances permitted, I'd thought in my lunacy); a black printed T-shirt showing Audrey Hepburn looking impossibly cool in the party scene from *Breakfast at Tiffany's*, a silver necklace and black leather biker boots with three inch heels – taking me to an impressively leggy 5'10". Urban chic was how I liked to describe my look. My dark brown hair, with a few red highlights, was trendily messed up with putty, and eye-drops were making my hazel eyes gleam. Best of all, I'd lost a few pounds lately and was looking quite slim at just under nine stones. I decided to give myself an overall score of 7.5 out of 10.

I came out and stood in front of Mencken's door once more, geeing myself up for the best client presentation of my life. Two maintenance men sauntered past and started sniggering. One of them extravagantly patted his backside. Flustered, I moved my hand down the back of my skirt, gingerly checking that all was in order. My hand came to a stop. Things were definitely *not* in order. My skirt was tucked beautifully into the back of my knickers. I turned away in horror, convinced my face had managed to define new shades of red: a perfect ten on the embarrassment Richter scale.

'Give the guys a wave,' one of the guys said, pointing up at a CCTV camera.

I desperately sorted myself out, fumbled open Mencken's door and almost fell into a palatial, air-conditioned office with a glistening, black-tiled floor. Light flooded in through vast, spectacularly curved windows. There were several exquisite pieces of furniture, including an arctic-blue leather sofa. And there was Harry Mencken himself, sitting at a mahogany table with an expensive silver laptop, with a trio of golden statuettes on a thick marble shelf behind him. *Three Oscars!* Wow. I was scarily impressed.

Mencken had a perma-tan and swept-back, thick dark hair with flecks of grey. Dressed in a cool, designer linen suit, he had a chunky gold bracelet on his left wrist. Fit and trim, he was one of those men who was probably over fifty but managed to look twenty years younger. A country club type. He was more than just handsome for an older man. He positively glowed. With a flick of his wrist, he motioned to me to sit down.

'Impressive receptionist they assigned to me, huh?' he said in a soft Californian accent, a bit like Jim Morrison's. 'I've hired this whole suite for two weeks at their top rate. You'd have thought they'd give me the best. If we were in the States, they'd hear all about it. But when in Rome, right?'

He didn't look or sound anything like the monster Adams had portrayed.

'We're not all like that,' I said then quickly shut up, fearing he might have caught sight of my incriminating CCTV footage.

A framed picture of Sam Lincoln hung on the wall behind him. I couldn't help smiling and felt myself relaxing. In the photograph, Sam's hair, a little longer than usual, was styled just so. He was standing on a beach in front of a beautiful turquoise sea. He had on khaki shorts, and a gorgeous black shirt that made his misty blue eyes seem bluer than ever. With a sexy trail of stubble, an immaculate jaw-line and a cute nose that made him look boyish, he was achingly hunky. Whenever I saw him, my favourite novel came to mind. *The Great Gatsby* was the only literary book I studied at school that I actually finished. I just loved all those Jazz Age flappers and their fabulous parties. Above all, Jay Gatsby was the most gorgeous and romantic man imaginable. When I first saw Sam clean-shaven, with his hair groomed, I thought he'd been stolen from my imagination: he was *exactly* how I pictured Gatsby.

'That was a pretty impressive courier you sent,' I said. 'But why did all the others have to come with her?'

Mencken gave me an odd look. 'Others? The courier was called Ted: one of those rent-a-mouth Cockneys, if you know what I mean. In his forties, I think. I gave him the envelope myself and told him to deliver it to the address shown in your brochure.'

'But it was some statuesque motorbike chick who handed it over, and she found me in Trafalgar Square.'

'Really?' Mencken shrugged. 'Well, who cares? You got it and here you are.' Standing up, he motioned to me to follow him. 'Come on,' he said, 'let's go to the lounge on the top floor. Not even my office in LA has views as good as these.'

****

The view was as breathtaking as Mencken promised: an uninterrupted 360-degree panoramic view of London, according to a tourist leaflet I picked up. I imagined I was in a sci-fi movie as I walked around, my jaw suitably slack. Up here, you could imagine you lived in the clouds, with the stars for company. I was so close to being where I wanted to be, with the type of person I'd always dreamt of. I'd die if I blew this.

'Two Black and Blues, Misha,' Mencken said to a pretty Asian waitress with blonde streaks in her raven hair. We sat down at a beautifully elegant, tinted glass cocktail table next to a wide window giving us a terrific view of the London Eye.

Misha returned moments later, carrying the drinks on a gleaming silver tray. She put down the tray, smiled flirtatiously at Mencken then lovingly handed him his drink, tenderly brushing his fingers. As for me, I was the beneficiary of an icy stare as my glass was thumped down in front of me.

The drink, unlike the service, was impressive – a layer of black vodka floating on top of blue curacao – but I was slightly irritated that Mencken hadn't offered me any choice. 'You didn't just bring me up here for a drink,' I tried to appear sophisticated and sound confident.

'You're here because I have a problem.' Mencken leaned back in his seat. 'What do you think my shrink says my issue is?'

'I'm afraid I have no idea.'

'Not the guessing type, huh? Well, let me run this past you. My wife left me twenty-five years ago to move in with a plumber. According to my therapist, I've been traumatised ever since. I mean, what does it say about me that a plumber's a better option?'

I'd picked up somewhere that whenever someone talks weird stuff, you should reply with an open question. 'What do you think of your therapist's analysis?' I asked.

'I've told virtually no one what I've just told you.'

'Why did you?'

'Who cares? It's just talk, isn't it?'

I couldn't work out if this man was the biggest fake I'd ever met, or the least. That's the most dangerous type, of course. I sat back in my seat, crossed my legs and wondered if I was showing too much leg or too little. It was easier thinking about that than trying to work out Mencken.

He set in motion a Newton's cradle positioned in the middle of the glass table. 'They say that life isn't measured by how many breaths we take, but by how many moments that take our breath away. Some people will pay any price for those breathless moments.' Reaching out, he stopped the pendulum. 'I'm one of those people.'

I didn't know how to react and just smiled.

'I have the wealth to take my search anywhere.'

I didn't doubt it, but how did he think I could help? Sure, I was an entertainment consultant, but not for people like him.

'What do you think the most important thing is for the rich when they have all the money and status they could ever desire?' he asked.

I couldn't think of anything.

'Ultimate pleasure,' he remarked. 'That's what everyone wants. The difference is that some people are for real. They mean it, they want it, they'll fight for it. Some of us are prepared to do anything to get it.'

'You really mean *anything*, don't you?'

'People like me must have pleasure, Sophie. Simple as that.' He stared out of the huge windows. 'My therapist says I'm an obsessive. I take everything to extremes. I say I've never met a successful person who wasn't all of those things. She says I'm not happy. I say I'd be miserable if I were poor and a failure.'

'So, how's she helping?'

'I'm not looking for help. I'm seeking fellow travellers.' He ran his finger round the lip of his glass. 'I can't bear thinking that there's something out there – maybe the greatest experience of them all – and I'm not getting my share. Shit, I could die and my last thought would be that I'd been robbed of that priceless thing.' He sat back. 'When I was last in London, I read that newspaper article you featured in, the one about extreme pleasure. That's what got you on my list.'

At last, something that made sense. 'True,' I said, 'I want pleasure, as good as it gets.'

Mencken nodded. 'That's right. *As good as it gets, and even better*.'

Was I making a good impression? I felt things were going OK, but there was a peculiar undercurrent.

'I noticed you looking at my picture of Sam Lincoln earlier,' Mencken said. 'Do you know how much his Oscar goodie bag was worth when he got his nomination for best supporting actor last year? *One hundred and fifty thousand dollars*.' He whistled. 'Not bad, huh? Here's another interesting fact about him – he's insured for a hundred million dollars per movie. If he died during film-making, that's how much I'd collect.'

This conversation was off the main road and I wasn't sure where it was heading. I loved hearing stuff about Sam, but not how much he'd be worth dead.

'Do you know what Sam's most famous catchphrase is?' Mencken asked.

Everyone on the planet knew the answer to that. I sometimes used it myself. 'All the way,' was Sam's response to the question, 'How far are you going?' It featured about twenty times in the hit road-movie *The Ends of the Earth* about the adventures of a conman – played by Sam – who hitched rides from various gullible tourists as he made his way from New Mexico to the southernmost tip of Chile in search of a mysterious flower called *Kalukas* that supposedly reversed the ageing process. I repeated the catchphrase to Mencken.

'*All the way*,' he echoed then took another sip of his drink. 'That's how far I'm going.' His face had become hard, almost sinister. 'In or out, Sophie York?'

****

I sat looking at the black bar of soap in front of me. When I'd said *yes* to Mencken, he'd reacted by taking out this small soap bar, covered in scented tissue, from his pocket and placing it in the centre of the table. Then he just stared at me. That was over a minute ago.

'What's going on?' I asked when the silence had become creepy.

'Do you know how to keep your mouth shut?' Mencken said. 'Accidents can happen to people with big mouths. Capiche?'

John Adams' warning leapt into my mind and I suddenly felt a desperate urge to pee.

'Ask around,' Mencken said. 'Fucking with me isn't a smart career move.'

The pressure in my bladder built incredibly rapidly. I thought I might have an 'accident' at any moment. I was actually in quite serious pain.

Mencken gestured at the soap. 'A fat guy messed me around once. Let's just say he's thin now.'

I didn't understand. I didn't think I wanted to.

'Have you ever seen a liposuction operation?' Mencken said. 'It's amazing what they can do with the fat they extract.'

I stared incredulously. Does it say in the small print that every dream trip must take a jeepers-creepers detour to hell? I had to get to a toilet. I didn't care if Mencken was a fully paid-up member of Serial Killers Anonymous, I was going.

'You're finding it hard to take in, right? Don't worry about the details. Just know that things like this can be done and people like me can do them.'

'I need to, uh,' I said like a little girl, squeezing out each word. I prayed it was obvious I was referring to the loo because I couldn't say another thing. All my energy was focused on controlling my bladder for a few more vital seconds.

'It's on the left.' Mencken gave me an unsettling smirk.

I scuttled away, reached the loo, slammed the door behind me and did my business, almost dying with relief. Then I sat there, numb. What in God's name had just happened?

I breathed in hard and tried to compose myself. The loo was on an epic scale; all marble, mirrors and every luxury trapping imaginable. I prayed there was an alternative exit that led to anywhere other than back to Mencken, but that was the one feature it lacked.

'Come out.' Mencken pounded on the door.

Jesus, he'd followed me. 'I'll be there in a moment,' I mumbled. Did I have any choice?

'Make sure you wash your hands,' he said.

I wanted to throw up. Had he really turned a rival's fat into a soap bar? I went through the motions of tidying myself up, washing my hands – minus soap (yuk!) – splashing water on my face, combing my hair. Then I opened the door, wondering what would happen if I told Mencken to stick his freaky mind-game up his arse. Would I just call for a cab as though nothing had happened?

'I'm on the trail of something unique,' Mencken said.

I was amazed that he was acting as though everything was normal. If this was how he treated his ex-wife, no wonder plumbers were so irresistible.

'I'm leaving,' I said. 'I think you'll need to arrange a few extra sessions with your therapist.' I turned towards the elevators, but Mencken blocked my path.

'OK, that was a shitty thing I did.'

I thought he was about to deliver a grovelling apology, but it didn't arrive.

'I misjudged you. I should have realised you were a businesswoman. You need celebrity endorsements, right? I can get those for you. I'll open the doors that have always been closed to you.' He held out his hand. 'Are we cool?'

Cool????? I was dumbfounded but I saw my hand reaching towards his. I wanted to tell this creep where to get off, but my treacherous hand was prepared to do the precise opposite. 'I guess so,' I heard myself saying as my hand gripped his. What had just happened?

'So, what exactly are you looking for?' I barely recognised my own voice.

'It's called NexS.' He spoke as though the word had incredible meaning.

'I've never heard of it.'

'I only found out about it a week ago at a party in Beverley Hills. I met a student who'd hooked up with the entourage of a hot new English director. He was real intelligent, a good-looking kid with one of those plummy accents, like yours. Said he went to Oxford University. He claimed a bunch of people at Oxford had discovered the secret of ultimate pleasure. They're an elite club and they go somewhere in London each summer to perform a weird ceremony. A woman – a goddess, according to him – is behind the whole thing. The guy started rambling, but I remember he said "NexS" repeatedly. He refused to tell me what it was and the party broke up. Next morning I tried to find him, but he'd gone. I never found out his name.'

So, Mencken wanted me to discover if there was any truth in this urban legend. Mr Obsession had another obsession to pursue. I shook my head. 'I don't see how I can help.'

'You're perfect for this job. You're an attractive girl, you're connected and you know the London party scene. If NexS exists, it will find you, and when it does I want you to give me a call.' He reached into his breast pocket and pulled out a neatly folded cheque. 'You'll be fifty grand richer. That's sterling, of course.'

I blinked in amazement. Fifty Gs? *Deliverance*.

'Oh, and two others will be involved with the project.' Mencken unwrapped a mint sweet and popped it into his mouth. 'They're both well known.' A curious grin flickered over his face. 'In fact, they're two of the most famous men in the world.'

Hundreds of celebrities' faces spun on reels in my mind, like in a Vegas slot machine. 'Who?' I blurted.

'You'll find out soon enough,' Mencken answered. 'They need their privacy. That's why I needed to make sure you wouldn't go opening your mouth.'

'I understand client confidentiality.'

'I'm sure you do, but you've never had clients like these. It's my job to keep shysters away from them.'

'I'm not a shyster.'

'You'd better not be. I'll be introducing you at the Sargasso hotel tonight. Do you know it?'

'Sure, I live ten minutes from there.'

'OK, see me in reception at eight o'clock.' He stared at my miniskirt and frowned. 'Get yourself glammed up.'

'I like you, Sophie, but I'm not convinced yet,' he said as he escorted me towards the elevator. I'm going to ask you to do something tonight, a final test.' He glowered, using one of his finest *Hammer Horror* stares. 'Something potentially embarrassing.' The elevator doors swished open. 'If you pull it off, I can promise you the ride of your life.'

****

I must have been in shock when I stepped out into the lobby. For a minute, I didn't get why all the security men were glancing at me and chuckling into their sleeves. The clipboard guy who'd hassled me earlier pointed at one of the security monitors as it replayed some recent footage.

'Nice arse,' he said.

Then I remembered.

7

The Silent Treatment

A cab dropped me at the Sargasso. As Mayfair's newest five-star hotel, it was creating a buzz. Its façade, designed like a huge metallic butterfly, was spectacularly bathed in evening sunlight. As I entered reception for my meeting with Mencken and his two mystery companions, several men leered at me. Oh well, a positive sign, I suppose. I wondered if my parents would be proud if they could see me now. I was kidding myself, wasn't I? They thought everything I did was an insult to the memory of my sister.

I searched for a mirror. I'd taken Mencken's advice and dressed to impress. My backless designer dress in a beautiful shade of burgundy definitely fitted the bill. I'd bought it that afternoon on a credit card that hadn't maxed out just yet, though it was teetering. While I was trying on the dress, a couple of girls stared at me as though I was a movie star they didn't quite recognise. When that happens often enough, maybe you start believing you're the real thing. These days with all the Reality TV shows, it's hard to know where fake celebrities end and real ones begin. Fake's the new real, I guess.

Gazing at myself in an elegant, full-length Louis XIV mirror, I wondered if the hotel deliberately used a distorting mirror for the 'comfort and convenience' of its patrons because I was looking slimmer and more glamorous than I ever had.

When I found Mencken, he was relaxing on a white leather sofa. Rising to greet me, he leaned forward for a kiss, but I shrank back. I'd never be comfortable with him again.

'You're looking beautiful.'

'Thanks,' I mumbled.

'I have to give you some ground rules,' he said, inviting me to join him on the sofa. He told me that at all times I must be good fun and ignore any bad behaviour by the two men he was about to introduce me to. I was to keep my mouth shut about everything I witnessed. He also produced a confidentiality agreement for me to sign. 'Come on,' he said after I'd scrawled my signature, 'time to earn your daily bread.'

He guided me towards the hotel's main bar. With its bamboo floor and camphor-wood walls embellished with Art Deco designs, it was pure style. The perfect place for a civilised drink.

The Silent Treatment

Clusters of hotel guests were whispering and pointing; a couple of fat women surreptitiously filming with their camcorders. Ahead of them stood an entourage of advisers and bodyguards.

'You know the number one rule of PR,' Mencken said, 'You don't get a second chance to make a first impression.'

My heart was thudding so hard I could hear it inside my head. I was dying to know who the two celebrities were. Was one of them Sam? Jane would need to book herself on a jealousy management course for a month of Sundays if she ever heard I'd met Mr *Eye of Sumatra* himself.

'I think I need to go to the loo,' I said. I thought Mencken would snarl at me and fish out a fresh soap bar, but instead he was surprisingly nice.

'You can do this, Sophie.' He gripped my hand then steered me to the rear of the bar where there was a quiet booth, almost out of public view. As I turned to face the occupants, I closed my eyes. When I opened them again, my knees nearly buckled.

Slouched over a table, with bottles of Belgian beer clutched in their hands, were two guys wearing dark trenchcoats and identical black baseball caps. Metallic-red shades lay in front of them. For a second, I thought I'd walked onto the set of *The Matrix*. I had to hold the table to steady myself.

Them – the highest paid actors in the world, stars of a dozen mega-blockbusters between them. They always topped the polls as the men most women wanted to sleep with.

You could smell the money, the success, the attitude. There, on the right, was Hollywood's top black actor Jez Easton. Beside him…

Not only had my jaw gone slack, my whole body was sagging. Just feet away from me was the brightest star of them all, my very own Jay Gatsby.

A friend once told me that whenever she wanted to stretch out a beautiful moment, she popped an LSD pill because it slowed down time perception. I wanted to grab how I felt right now and make it last forever. This was a magic bus moment, when the driver arrived right on time and took me to exactly the right destination.

The latest gossip on the girlfriend-ometer was that Sam Lincoln was currently single. Not even a sniff of a vaguely serious belle. Therefore, opportunity beckoned for sweet Sophie. But Jez Easton too? That made no sense. Jez had spectacularly fallen out with Sam at an MTV awards ceremony eighteen months ago. Most people thought it was hilarious when, instead of jointly presenting an award to a hip-hop star, they began throwing punches at each other because, so Jez claimed later, Sam made some under-the-breath insult that wasn't picked up by the microphones and had never been revealed to this day. Now it was hard to find a magazine where the two men weren't goading each other. *I'll piss on his grave*, Jez infamously declared. *I'll ram sticks of dynamite up his ass*, Sam had retaliated.

If Mencken had talked them into putting their differences aside, he was a genius. Movie fans everywhere would queue for months to see Sam and Jez in a film together.

'Here she is, guys,' Mencken said. 'Our very own English princess.'

Oh God, Sam Lincoln is looking at me.

'Hi guys, I'm Sophie.' I gave them my most endearing smile and held out my hand expectantly. Would Sam kiss it? It dangled there for a few seconds, unwanted. There was complete silence.

'The guys don't shake,' Mencken said.

Sam scribbled something on a yellow Post-It note, tore it off the pad and passed it to me. It was surreal to be receiving a piece of paper from someone so famous. In a childish scrawl, it said, '*You're fired.*'

The words started to swim in front of my eyes, twisting themselves into sharp, taunting little shapes. Mechanically, I began walking away. My head was all over the place.

Mencken came after me and stopped me. 'Come back, Sophie.'

Numb, I allowed him to lead me back. Sam was showing Jez his note and they both laughed, their bodies crumpling and contorting, but neither let a sound escape. They gave each other a high five, doing a decent impression of being best buddies.

Now it was Jez's turn to write something on a Post-It and parade it in front of me. When I tried to take it, he jerked his arm back. Again, he and Sam dissolved in silent laughter. This time a low five was exchanged under the table.

I grabbed the Post-It. 'You're still fired!' it said.

'Fuck you!' I tottered away on my high heels. I'd blown it so much that I felt like El Ninõ, and I wasn't even sure what that was.

An arm reached out and restrained me.

'Congratulations,' Mencken said. 'They loved you.'

What?

'Oh, don't worry about all that weird stuff. They're always messing around.' He explained that the actors were having a ten-thousand-dollar bet about who could keep quiet the longest, hence the Post-Its. 'My limo's waiting outside.' He glanced at his watch. 'It's time for your final test.'

****

How ever rich they are, no matter what job they do or where they come from, men always end up in a sleaze-joint leching after young female flesh. It's the No.1 law of nature, isn't it? That's why Mencken had brought us to *Sin 6,* a new lap-dancing club off Piccadilly Circus. It was gloriously kitsch, designed to look like an idyllic scene from the Garden of Eden.

We were in the best seats directly in front of the stage and must have looked peculiar with Sam and Jez still in their *Matrix* gear on such a humid night.

When a waitress brought the champagne we'd ordered, Sam brandished a Post-It saying, 'BOTTOMS UP.'

I wanted to smile but my facial muscles seemed to have locked in the misery position. I'd spent most of my life dreaming of a situation like this but now that it was actually here, I couldn't handle it. We clinked glasses and I took a long sip of Krug. Thank God for champagne because it's the ideal drink for absurd occasions. Marriages, divorces, births, deaths, triumphs, disasters – I've drunk champagne at all of them. You'd think there would be different drinks for highs and lows, but champagne always fits the bill.

Maybe something else was stopping me from smiling. This silence thing was appalling. I couldn't impress Sam with my personality, such as it is, and right now it was performing the amazing shrinking routine.

When I first went to Roedean and met all of these incredibly bright and confident girls, I didn't think anyone would ever become friends with me. I wasn't sporty, academic or good at anything in particular. I was gauche and had a reputation for being a bit of a clown. At first the other girls sniggered at me, but as I became prettier and started wearing more stylish gear, everything changed. Before long, I was one of the most popular girls in my year. Somehow, I'd made it to coolness. But I didn't feel cool. I'd accidentally got a few things right, that's all. I was a fake then and I still was. So, I've played that game of faking it ever since, and mostly it works. The question was whether I could be a good enough faker to get Mr Sam Lincoln to warm to me.

As we watched a succession of gorgeous dancers performing their routines, Sam tapped me on the arm and passed me another note. 'What are my two most famous catch-phrases, Brit babe?' it asked.

For an instant, I didn't care about anything other than being called a babe by Sam. Luckily, his question was easy, the same one Mencken had asked. Did they use it as some sort of test?

'All the way,' I said, giving the more famous of the two. As for the second, it came from one of my all-time favourite movies. In *The Out Crowd*, Sam played a young snob from Harvard Law School who was obsessed with being in the loop, until he fell in love with a young woman who definitely wasn't. The story of an arrogant jerk being brought to heel by Sally, an ordinary Wal-Mart shop worker, was, oddly enough, the one that made Sam a superstar. I snapped my fingers, trying to impersonate Sam's famous gesture from the movie. 'If you're not in, you're out,' I said.

Sam smiled half-heartedly, but I wasn't getting a friendly vibe from him. He and Jez were sinister sitting there in their trenchcoats, hats and shades. People were staring at them and whispering.

I glanced away then noticed a young guy in white trousers and a white linen shirt heading straight for us. I'd clocked him earlier because he resembled a blond-haired Elvis Presley. He swayed drunkenly, stumbled, then pitched forward into Sam. From his seat, Sam pushed him back and he went reeling into Jez, knocking over a half-full champagne glass.

'You think *these* girls are sexy?' the drunk slurred, waving towards the stage. 'I could tell you about a goddess. I swear to you, if you ever met her…' He swayed back and forth. '*Look on her works, ye mighty, and despair…*'

I was startled to hear a drunk in a strip club quoting from my favourite poem. We were told at school that Shelley's *Ozymandias* was all about how short-lived earthly glory was. For me, I thought that having poems written about you thousands of years after you died was about as glorious as it got.

Jez obviously didn't appreciate poetry. He got to his feet and shoved the man away. 'Prick,' he barked as the drunk staggered in the direction of the toilets. Instantly, an accusing finger stabbed out from Sam, directed straight at Jez's mouth. Even Mencken turned round.

'That's a ten grand noise you've just made, loser-man.' Sam jumped out of his seat, grabbed Jez and thumped him on the back, but his triumphant smile vanished as quickly as it had arrived. He sat down again and glared at the blonde dancing on stage. 'Hey, fatso, have you never heard of Atkins?'

The manager appeared from nowhere. 'Is there a problem?' he asked.

'We didn't pay good money to watch fucking Weight Watchers work out,' Jez said.

'Where's the talent in this crummy joint?' Sam swept his hand dismissively towards the regulars. 'And stop the Eyes staring at me. It's pissing me off.'

Mencken led the manager away a few steps and whispered something. The manager's eyes lit up and I thought he was about to kneel and kiss Mencken's feet. They spoke briefly then Mencken came back, grinning.

'They want to show us their "special" service.'

'Now you're talking,' Sam grunted.

Mencken whispered to Sam and Jez, and their faces beamed.

'*Sweet.*' Jez laughed in a deeply unpleasant way. 'Princess Diana,' he cackled. 'That's real sick, but I guess it's true.'

'What's going on?' I asked Mencken. He seemed to be struggling not to laugh.

'I'm surprised you don't know about this place. Your clients would love it here.'

'It only opened a month ago. I haven't had a chance to check it out.'

'That's not good enough.'

I nodded glumly.

'At least you took it on the chin. It's how we react to our mistakes that makes us winners or losers.'

'Please, I'll do whatever it takes.'

'Don't get so worried,' Mencken said, 'I doubt I'd get too many soap bars out of you.' He pointed towards a staircase. 'This club has an upstairs area for high rollers. The strippers up there are all look-alikes of famous beauties.' He handed me a list the manager had given him featuring names such as Marilyn Monroe, Madonna, Jennifer Connolly, Keira Knightley, Beyonce, Halle Berry, Cindy Crawford, Grace Kelly, Angelina Jolie, Aishwarya Rai, Louise Brooks, Isabelle Adjani, Paris Hilton.

'Lap-dancing is five times more expensive with these girls, but apparently they're worth every penny.'

'I heard Jez say something about Princess Diana. Surely there isn't…'

'There is! They haven't put her name on the list because it would be tasteless, but the manager tells me American clients always ask for her. She's so popular that the club has supplied five Diana look-alikes.'

I felt as queasy as I did the night I watched David Cronenberg's movie about people getting orgasmically turned on by car crashes.

'Sam and Jez have asked for all of the Diana look-alikes,' Mencken said.

Gross. I tramped upstairs behind the others, wondering why I was hanging around with these perverts.

We were shown to a private suite where another conference took place between the manager and Mencken.

Mencken returned and announced that the Princess Dianas were otherwise engaged at a special function at the American Embassy. The only multiples available were Madonna and Paris Hilton, four of each.

'OK,' Sam said, 'we'll have all of them.'

A minute later, we were gazing at a line of beautiful girls, the Madonnas in cowboy hats and chaps, the Paris Hiltons in sheer black stockings and suspenders.

One of the Madonnas looked at me with a puzzled smile. 'Who are they?' she mouthed, making eyes at the disguised actors. I pretended not to understand.

Sam nudged Jez and said, 'Watch this. I picked it up from a movie about Vegas showgirls.'

He walked along the line then made them all turn round and bend over for him. When they faced front again, he pushed one of the Paris Hiltons in the shoulder and said, '*See ya*,' as nastily as he could.

I'd never seen anything so rude, and I couldn't work out why the girl had failed Sam's test. Too skinny? Not blonde enough? Too few piercings?

Sam tugged at the G-strings of the others and had a good look. One of the Madonnas now got the 'see ya' treatment.

Weird.

I once had a boyfriend who was obsessed with pubic hair. He was always going on about Hollywoods, Brazilians, Tiffany Boxes and so on. For Valentine's Day, he wanted me to dye my pubic hair red and shave it in the shape of a love-heart. I guessed Sam had the same sort of fetish. Would I have passed his test? I was normally a Brazilian, since most men I knew preferred it, but I'd now decided to whip it all off and go full Hollywood in Sam's honour. I hadn't got round to getting a piercing in the action zone but that was on the cards too. I already had my tongue pierced because men swore it made blowjobs much better. One of these days, I was hoping to meet a pierced-tongue man to reciprocate the favour. Fat chance.

'I've got rid of the dead wood,' Sam announced to Jez. 'They ought to be glad I didn't ask them to bend over and spread their cheeks to show us what they're really made of. That's usually the best way to see who's up for it and who isn't.' He gave a sleazy grin. 'Well, you can finish up.'

Jez now inspected the line and got rid of another Madonna before signalling to a waitress. 'Cristal,' he shouted. 'Ten bottles.' He started telling a story about doing lines of coke on a supermodel's super-smooth, newly waxed pussy, after eating her edible, strawberry-flavoured knickers. *Yukeo.*

I had to make a visit to the loo and was glad of a moment's respite. After seeing Sam in action, I was rapidly reformulating my opinions. Forget hunky dreamboat god. A pig-ignorant sleaze-bag was more accurate, with Jez a short head behind.

I locked the cubicle door and slumped onto the seat. When I'm running from hassle, I always end up in the loo. Is that all life is – a succession of bad toilet trips? As a kid, I liked building snowmen and watching them melt. I found it fascinating the way there was something and then nothing, just a puddle on the ground. I felt a bit like that now, watching my illusions about A-listers vanish.

After, when I looked in the mirror, my face was blotchy and my mascara smudged. Not a sexy look. I wanted someone normal to hug me and tell me everything was going to be OK.

When I returned to the suite, Sam and Jez had removed their coats, hats and shades. Nirvana's *Smells Like Teen Spirit* was blaring out while naked Madonnas and Paris Hiltons did a cheerleader routine, with the actors freely pawing at them. Everyone knew that was totally against the rules. I guessed the girls weren't objecting because, now that they could see who they were with, they were starstruck.

Sam filled a glass of champagne to the brim and drank it in one. He gave me a wave. 'See, English, I always get what I want. ALWAYS.'

He was wrecked and obnoxious, but I couldn't take my eyes off his face. Tanned, with his perfect white teeth and his neat blonde hair, he was fantastic eye candy. Those blue eyes of his were mesmerising. He was well and truly back to his ultra-smooth Jay Gatsby look. He got up from his seat, came over and stood beside me. I had to concentrate hard to avoid drooling.

'No woman ever turns me down.'

I didn't doubt it.

He grabbed my hand. 'Am I a jerk?' Just as quickly, he let go. 'But you'd never tell me, would you? No one ever speaks to me. They see someone called Sam Lincoln, *Hollywood Legend*. The real me is right here but no one's listening. No one ever tells me the truth.'

Well, you just didn't, did you? Not with A-listers.

'You *all* fucking bore me.' Raising his right hand, he formed his index finger and thumb into the shape of a gun then began silently shooting everyone, mumbling *you're dead, fucker* each time. 'Why can't one of you do something interesting?' He slumped into his seat. 'Just once in your pathetic lives.'

One of the Paris Hiltons climbed onto his lap and ground herself against him, pushing her breasts into his face.

'You're doing it all wrong.' Taking a swig of champagne from the bottle, Sam pushed the girl to one side, struggled to his feet and made her sit down.

'Man, have I got to teach you how to do it?'

The girls giggled as Sam stripped off. Soon he was naked apart from tight white boxers. He began gyrating crazily, like a drunken rodeo rider, whooping and hollering. Jez stripped off too, as the girls clapped and cheered. Both men were super-fit, in perfect condition. I could see that the other girls were highly appreciative of the view they were getting. Who wouldn't be?

I lost track after a while. Too much champagne, I guess. Everything became blurred. I seem to remember that someone slapped my bare bum. It must have been Mencken. 'Time for your test,' that's what he said, wasn't it? I think he made me join in with the dancing. Did I take all my clothes off?

A pilot once told me that in aviation circles there's a term known as 'time of useful consciousness.' If I remember right, it's the time the body can cope without oxygen, and it diminishes rapidly with altitude. Very high up, you only have seconds to save yourself before you become unconscious. With me, I think of it in terms of alcohol. I know that by the end of my eighth glass of Cristal there's precious little consciousness left.

What was certain was that I passed out. I know that because when I came to I heard the sound of a vacuum cleaner. The dimmer lights in the room had been turned up to maximum and the manager was talking to one of the cleaners over the noise of someone snoring. I looked down, and there, his head resting on my stomach, was Sam. What was he doing down there? What was *I* doing down here? Jez was just as bad, stretched out on one of the sofas.

I was wearing only my knickers. Where was my dress? I pushed Sam's head away, then got to my feet and searched for my stuff.

Sam woke up and vomited. I winced, imagining if he'd done that seconds earlier.

'What happened?' he moaned.

I found my dress lying on one of the seats, snatched it up and retreated to my usual refuge. I sat in the loo for five minutes, doing nothing but sobbing. The night of my life? *Christ.*

When I emerged from the loo, I'd got rid of most of the signs that I'd been crying. It took me ten minutes to get Sam and Jez in a fit state to leave. I didn't want any stray paparazzi getting a money shot, so I made sure the actors were disguised as well as possible. The manager called a cab for us and we headed back to the hotel. Sam passed out in the back but Jez managed to stay awake.

We helped Sam to his room and threw him onto his bed. As he hit the mattress, something flew out of one of his pockets.

'What's this?' Jez picked up some sort of business card.

Puzzled, I took it from him. It was a coal-black card embossed with a terrifying holographic skull.

'Congratulations,' it said in silver writing. 'You have been selected by the Millionaires' Death Club.'

8

Star Map

When I woke the next morning, I was back in my apartment. I wondered why I was so uneasy. God, *that* card. I hurried to the Sargasso but there was no answer when I knocked on Sam's door. Jez wasn't around either. I went down to reception and asked if anyone had left a message for me.

The receptionist made me produce my credit card to prove who I was then handed over a slim package.

'You're so lucky,' she said. 'I'd give anything to be able to spend time with Sam Lincoln and Jez Easton. They're such funny guys. You should have heard the jokes they were cracking this morning before they went out.'

Jokes? I couldn't understand why they were treating that chilling card so lightly. Then again, perhaps this sort of thing happened to them all the time. Maybe the Millionaires' Death Club was just a tasteless prank – probably by one of the Madonna or Paris Hilton look-alikes that Sam cruelly rejected.

So, I chose to worry instead about what I did or didn't do at the club. Lurid images jumped into my mind. The lap dance Mencken made me do was full on naked, wasn't it? I'd practised on Jez then tried, pathetically, to do a professional job on Sam. I think I fell off his lap half way through. I seemed to recall that Mencken took pictures. Was he intending to blackmail me if I didn't do things his way?

'You can view it over there,' the receptionist said, pointing at a TV.

'View?'

'Don't worry, there's a DVD slot. The remote control is on the left.'

I went over to the TV and unwrapped Mencken's package. It was a DVD showing Mencken sitting on the upper deck of a tourist bus as it made its way around Hollywood. He was clutching a star map and writing obscenities next to the names of various stars as the bus swept past their luxury homes. Each time, he held up the map to the camera to reveal what he'd written, libellous every time.

When the tour guide announced they were about to pass Mencken's own residence, all the tourists booed loudly, gave the finger then twisted round en masse and waved at the camera. Sam and Jez were amongst them. I realised it was probably Mencken's film crew on their way to a location shoot.

Mencken's home was a leafy mansion in a prime location on Mulholland Drive, with a large swimming pool and iron gates patrolled by fierce, lean black dogs. Why didn't that surprise me?

'You see, Sophie,' Mencken said, gazing into the camera. 'I always knew you were one of us.' He held up a newspaper and pointed at the date. It was four days old – before I'd ever heard of him.

I winced. I didn't like thinking my life was being remotely controlled, and I hated being so predictable.

Mencken glanced at Sam who was concentrating hard on a playstation game.

'It's a soccer World Cup game,' Mencken whispered. 'He knows nothing about soccer but he'll play the game until he wins, no matter how long it takes. That man just doesn't know when to give up.'

What was he suggesting? That Sam had obsessive-compulsive disorder? It seemed you couldn't be a celebrity nowadays if you didn't have a trendy affliction to win the sympathy vote.

Gesturing towards both actors, Mencken said, 'These guys have partied hard in every big city on earth. They've tried everything, so it takes a lot to get them juiced. I've promised you'll show us something extraordinary in London. Don't disappoint us.'

Extraordinary? What could I offer these guys that they hadn't already done ten times better already? Entertaining people was my business, but it suddenly seemed such a difficult thing. How can you entertain the entertainers? It's like bullshitting the bullshitters. *Impossible.*

'Forget your normal tourist routine,' Mencken reiterated. 'Something way off track, check?'

Pass me a lifebelt, someone. I was so out of my depth, I doubted I'd ever see the shore again. I hadn't even started and already my confidence was evaporating. I felt like a snake charmer lacking both the snake and the charm. Even the way Mencken peered at the camera – into my soul, I thought – made me nervous. Showing these three around London would be the most stressful thing I'd ever done. Normally, I could control my clients. With their personality quadruple bypasses and complete ignorance of the world of glamour, my customary middle-aged bores were easy to fool. Not these three, though. When I was with them, I'd be like brittle glass, one vibration from shattering.

Mencken said that he'd given the actors a gift of £25,000 each. 'Walking around money' he called it. I wished I could walk around with that kind of money. He hoped that the two actors would spend their time in London 'bonding' and he wanted them to be on best terms by the time shooting began in earnest on his new blockbuster. It was part of my task to make that happen. I was to be paid my top rate of £1000 per person day, plus expenses, to keep the actors and Mencken entertained during their stay in the capital.

'Meet us tonight at eleven pm in reception,' Mencken said. 'Here's one thing that might get you some bonus points. Jez is looking to be fixed up with a woman whose name begins with the letter Y. Sam's looking for a Z.'

He wasn't talking about what I thought he was talking about, was he?

'Remember that big punch-up they had at the MTV awards?' Mencken went on. 'I managed to persuade them to settle their differences by having a special bet to prove once and for all which of them is the numero uno.' He winked at the camera. 'Alphabet Love – have you ever played it?'

9

Bad Therapy

I met Mencken and the actors in reception as arranged. Sam and Jez proceeded to ignore me while Mencken asked a few polite questions about what I'd been up to during the day, then spent the next ten minutes on his mobile phone. Were they deliberately trying to make me uncomfortable?

Sam wore desert-style combats and a black hoodie. As for Jez, he had on low-slung baggy blue jeans and a white T-shirt, and he was sticking with his combination of black baseball-cap and red shades. Despite their grungy style, both actors still managed to have film-star presence, but I doubted anyone would recognise them, not least because no one would expect to see them within a mile of each other. As for Mencken, with his white designer chinos and a black cashmere jumper, he had an unmistakable aura of success.

He'd told me in The Gherkin that Sam and Jez look-alikes were coming over from the States. Bogus events had been set up to keep the media occupied while the real Sam and Jez hopefully went around unnoticed. I prayed the trick worked: I didn't want to be mobbed all day long. I was certainly glad Sam was wearing a hoodie. When he pulled it over his head, he could be a Jedi Knight for all anyone knew.

Mencken's limo dropped us off at Leicester Square's cheesy super-disco, *The Moulin Rouge*. It was crammed with smiling tourists paying a fortune for an inauthentic London night out involving a fake celebration of nineteenth century Paris amongst hordes of non-Londoners. How ludicrous can you get?

The nightclub was one of those two-level cavernous monstrosities, the size of an aircraft hangar. I guessed it could hold anything up to 2000 people. *Ghastly*. It was supremely tacky, with the cheapest of glitter balls hanging from the ceiling, gaudy décor throughout, and appalling Euro muzak blasting out from a bad sound system – a genuine dump, the sort of place I'd never let my clients stray into, even by accident.

Mencken led us to a bar on the upper level and, thankfully, it was almost deserted, with only a couple of bemused Spanish tourists lurking around. Mencken announced that he'd buy us all a drink, but there would be no choice – we had to take whatever he put in front of us. Sam and Jez shrugged. They seemed incredibly respectful of Mencken. Maybe they'd had personal experience of a good clean down with his own-brand soap.

Mencken ordered absinthe. It was my least favourite drink and I thought of telling him to get stuffed, but some masochistic part of me wanted the whole, undiluted experience.

'What now?' Sam asked as Mencken distributed the drinks.

Mencken laughed. 'Why, you have fun, of course.' He slammed back his absinthe and walked away.

Sam shot a puzzled glance at Jez. As for me, I had no idea what was expected. Was I supposed to leap into action to entertain the actors? My nerves already felt as though they'd been slung across the Grand Canyon and a tightrope walker was treading on them, about to do a death-defying headstand. I followed Mencken's example and drank the absinthe in one. *Vile*.

An hour later, I was on my fourth absinthe – 'the devil in a bottle' as I think someone once referred to it. My head was spinning and I didn't feel well. I was standing on my own on the upper balcony, gazing down at the bobbing heads of the clubbers on the crowded dancefloor. I had no idea where the others were.

When Jez materialised beside me, I was startled and let out an embarrassing squeal.

'So, how will you find NexS?' he asked.

The question took me by surprise since I'd never talked about it with him, even though I realised he must have discussed it with Mencken. 'I have one or two ideas,' I mumbled, but I didn't have any.

'If ultimate pleasure's out there, I want my slice,' Jez said.

'But someone like you – don't you have a great time every day?'

'You have no idea. Sometimes I think if a boxer slugged me in the face, I wouldn't know it. I can't *feel*. Sam and I are bored the whole time. NexS isn't some distraction for us. We're praying it can make us feel again. Something, anything – it doesn't matter what.'

He massaged his temples. 'We both have recurring dreams. Isn't that weird? We're both seeing psychotherapists and neither of us thinks it does any good, but we keep going back.'

'So, what's your dream?'

I didn't expect an answer, but he showed no reluctance.

'I have a harness round my neck, and I'm dragging a boulder behind me. I can never get free of it. My neck, my shoulders, and my whole body ache as I pull this thing around.'

'I bet I know what your therapist says – the boulder is fame.'

'You're good,' Jez said, 'but wrong.' He shook his head. 'If I lost my fame, I'd be a nobody. I couldn't bear *that*.'

I didn't know if I loathed Jez for being so self-pitying or pitied him for being so self-loathing. I wasn't looking forward to the next few days. It seemed these guys were expecting NexS to bring them back to life.

Jez nudged me. 'Hey, watch this.' He nodded towards the loos.

I wasn't sure what I was supposed to be looking at, then I noticed Sam with a production-line gorgeous blonde just outside the men's loo. She slipped a note into his pocket.

'Did you see?' Jez said. 'Happens all the time. Sometimes when I'm taking a dump, women follow me into the toilet and pass their phone number under the cubicle door.' He rolled his eyes. 'Sex on a plate. It's so fucking easy.'

'You really are bored, aren't you?' I never thought I'd hear myself saying that to an A-lister.

'That's why I gotta have this NexS.'

I didn't think NexS would be providing any answers for Jez and Sam. I suspected it was nothing more than a clever party story by a druggy Oxford student trying to impress rich Americans, but I needed the fifty Gs Mencken promised and that meant I'd try my hardest to find the damned thing. I'd even had a half thought of faking it, using some cocktail of party drugs, but Mencken would no doubt be on the phone to place an emergency order with the local horse-head remover if he found out, so I dropped that plan.

Sam read the blonde's note, took her by the hand and pulled her into the toilet.

'He's in for a surprise.' Jez was almost gloating. 'I've met that lady before. She was the air hostess on our flight over.'

I wondered what he was driving at, but he chose not to enlighten me. Seconds later, the toilet door flew open and Sam hurried out, scowling. The airhostess appeared shortly afterwards, apparently bewildered. If they'd been having a liaison, it hadn't worked out, or had been incredibly premature.

Jez strolled away, sniggering.

I went to one of the lounges to sit down and get my head straight. I'd only been there for a couple of minutes when someone ahemmed.

'Oh, sorry,' I said, I didn't see you.'

'As stealthy as a Ninja.' Sam plumped himself down beside me. 'You seem like a nice girl. Why are you hanging around with people like us?'

My mouth opened but nothing came out.

'You'll only get hurt, you know. We're bad news.'

'Uh, didn't I see you with a blonde a few minutes ago?' I gibbered.

Sam amazed me by actually responding. 'Yeah, just when we were about to get down to action, she stopped and asked me to sign the back of a photo of her frigging baby. Can you believe it? Did no one ever tell these bitches that showing me a picture of their baby is like showing me a miniature version of one of the jerks who screwed them? Christ, it makes me want to vomit.'

I tried not to be shocked, but I failed.

'What are you looking at me like that for?' he said.

'You don't have dreams about babies, do you?' I asked, recalling what Jez had said.

'How did you know?' Instantly, he started telling me the story. I couldn't believe how anxious these superstars were to share their psychological hang-ups. Had their therapists told them to get it off their chests at every opportunity? They had so much in common. It was easy to understand why they'd been such good friends, and just as easy to appreciate how they'd fallen out so badly. Like brothers.

'In my dream, I'm eighteen years old,' Sam said. 'I'm holding a baby and the crazy thing is it's got my exact face. My therapist says it symbolises that I want to start my life again. Maybe that's right, but maybe something else is true. None of it changes the fact that I don't like babies.'

I tried, feebly, to feign sympathy.

'You don't have any brats, do you?' Sam asked fiercely.

When I shook my head, his hand shot out and rested on my knee. Without thinking, I brushed it away.

He rolled his eyes. 'Oh, get over yourself. I've seen everything you've got. You're nothing special.'

The words tore through me like bullets. I tried not to cry. I listed every fault I had. Bum too big, breasts too small, hips too wide, legs not long enough if unaided by heels, hair too lank, first traces of cellulite, tummy sticking out too much. God, I was a walking Gorgon, turning people to stone if they so much as glimpsed me. I must have been insane to think a Hollywood hunk could ever fall for me.

'You'd better find NexS for us,' Sam spat. Then he stood up and walked away.

I didn't know what to say and stared miserably at my absinthe glass. I pathetically raised my eyes to watch Sam as he strode off. He looked fabulous in his low-slung combats, his Calvin Klein boxers tantalisingly peaking out, practically beckoning to me. Whenever I watched his body move, I couldn't help imagining snuggling up to him in bed. I knew he was a complete git, but, my God – those gorgeous blue eyes when he looked at me. I fancied the arse off him, and it was unbearable. Why was he so mean to me?

I headed for my one place of refuge – the loo – and went through the motions of re-applying my make-up, and trying to keep my chin up, or at least prevent it dropping through the floor. As I came out, Mencken was emerging from the gents' toilet.

'Hey! How are you getting on with the guys?' he asked.

'Things could be better,' was all I could say, and that was *way* too much of a positive spin.

'You know, I've seen the way you look at Sam.'

I didn't reply, but I was sure my face was reddening.

'Maybe you won't believe me,' Mencken winked, 'but there's a nice guy in there struggling to get out.'

'I'll take your word for it.' As far as I was concerned, Sam was a complete arse – but *what* an arse! He made me as horny as hell, but that was just mega depressing since he'd made it insultingly clear he was totally unimpressed by my body and never going to reciprocate. *Ever.*

'Are you all set to track down NexS?' Mencken asked.

'I'll phone round, find out if anyone's heard anything. Maybe I'll get lucky.'

Mencken nodded. 'OK, tomorrow night, pick the boys up at nine and take them somewhere interesting.' He explained that he wouldn't be able to come himself because he had business to take care of.

'Can I ask why you brought us here tonight, Mr Mencken?'

'Don't be so formal, Sophie. Call me Harry.' His eyes gleamed. 'I wanted to show you how desperate Sam and Jez are for something different – a whole new experience. It won't be easy, but you're an imaginative girl.'

****

I found Sam at midnight in the lounge overlooking the dance floor. He was on his own, with a bottle of Bud in his hand and his hoodie pulled over his head. When he turned towards me, he seemed surprisingly excited.

'Hello!' I said. 'Why so happy?'

'Oh, I have a unique happening lined up.' He glanced at his watch then made sure I was standing next to him at the edge of the balcony overlooking the dancefloor. He signalled towards the DJ's booth. The music stopped, prompting a groan from the clubbers.

'Listen up,' the DJ announced, 'we've had a special request. Normally I would have told this guy to fuck right off but I took one look at him and, I swear, in my whole life I've never seen such a dead ringer. You have to check this guy out to believe it. We're going to put a spotlight on him so you can see what I mean.'

As the DJ spoke, a spotlight tracked along the balcony. When it reached Sam, he threw back his hoodie, raised both of his hands and waved at the crowd.

'After three,' the DJ said, 'who does that guy look like? One, two, three…'

'Sam Lincoln,' the crowd roared.

The DJ chuckled. 'You won't believe the nerve of this guy. He actually said he was better looking than Sam, and he said it in an American accent that I swear was identical to Sam's.' He pointed at Sam. 'Hey, man, you have to get yourself a job as a Sam Lincoln impersonator. It's what you were born for.'

It was obvious Sam was finding the whole thing hilarious. I couldn't help giggling too.

'So, could all of the boys please leave the dancefloor,' the DJ said. 'This is a girls-only event.' He told the girls to arrange themselves into ten parallel lines taking up the whole length of the dancefloor. 'Link arms,' he said. 'When the music starts, I promise you'll have no difficulty knowing what you have to do. I want you all to look at our Sam Lincoln look-alike and feel yourselves getting moist. Hey, I fancy him too and I'm a bloke!'

That prompted a huge jeer from the watching boys, but the opening bars of an extremely familiar tune – the cancan – cut off the booing. The girls let out a whoop and, with their arms tightly linked, started high kicking. The men alternately wolf-whistled, cheered and clapped along.

I watched in amazement as hundreds of girls kept their high-energy dance going for a good couple of minutes. At the end, all of them turned round, bent over and lifted up their skirts. Most of them were wearing thongs, but many had nothing on at all. The lecherous roar from the boys had to be heard to be believed, a kind of primal sexual howl.

'Wow,' the DJ shouted, 'was that something special, or what? I think I'm going to make that a regular event. We have one person to thank, of course – Mr *not-quite* Sam Lincoln.'

Sam, picked out once again by the spotlight, gave a bow.

The DJ put on Madonna's *Hollywood.*

Sam turned away and aggressively pulled up his hoodie again. 'Jesus, just by pretending to be me, I can get these people to do anything. It's fucking pathetic.'

Talk about mood swings! For the rest of the night he stayed in the same bad temper. Jez wasn't much better. As for Mencken, he had vanished completely.

I hung around all night, buying drinks, making inane jokes that neither actor laughed at, and tried to fill the frequent long silences with small talk. The men were clearly bored stiff. I contemplated trying out the singing vaginas anecdote on them, but all my energy had drained away. I felt pathetic, the least appropriate person on earth to be an entertainment consultant.

We carried on that way until 3 o'clock in the morning. We were all leaning against the balcony, trying to stifle yawns. Just as the last dance began, a group of people dressed as City Slickers appeared from nowhere and barged their way onto the dancefloor, where they grabbed partners for the slow dance. In dark trousers, blue pinstriped shirts and red braces, with slicked-back hair, they all looked like men but, as I peered hard, I realized some were women. There was one particular woman causing a lot of commotion. Men were surging around the figure, gawping. From up here in the balcony, I imagined I was watching people being sucked into a whirlpool. All the men in the room seemed to be trying to ogle this person. Their tongues were practically hanging out.

I couldn't get a good look. The woman had her back turned to me the whole time and all I could see was the feverish reaction of the men around her. If my eyes weren't tricking me, she had a gold-tipped swagger stick and was jabbing it into her admirers' genitals if they got too frisky. She was like the queen bee in the centre of a hive, surrounded by slavering drones.

When I glanced at Sam, he was leaning right over, staring even more intently than I was.

'I have to check this out.' He headed for the staircase and seconds later he appeared on the edge of the dancefloor and tried to push his way through the throng to get near the woman, but he didn't make any headway.

The last song ended and the house lights came on. All of the City Slickers broke off from their partners and headed for the exit. In seconds, they were gone. I was oddly impressed. They had been and gone in about five minutes flat, causing complete mayhem.

Sam, looking up at me from the dancefloor, obviously wasn't happy. What had he been expecting – for that gorgeous woman to see him and just leap into his arms? She and her City Slickers had certainly put on quite a show. What had it all been about? Maybe they were blowing off steam after getting their annual mega bonus.

I noticed someone standing behind Sam. The man was gazing hard at the back of Sam's head. He seemed to become aware of me and looked up in my direction. Startled, I stepped backwards. After a couple of moments, I sneaked back to the balcony and had another peek. The man was still there. I was certain I recognised him – the blond Elvis from the lap-dancing club.

He caught my eye and slowly, with a slight smile on his face, drew his finger straight across his throat in an unmistakable gesture.

10

Das Hexenhaus

When I dragged myself out of bed the next morning, I was haunted by a bad dream – with those strange City Slickers playing the starring role. In the dream I was stark naked and the Slickers had formed a circle around me and kept pushing me from one to another, laughing at me and pointing out all my faults. Their queen, with her gold swagger stick, kept her back to me the whole time. I had a terrible fear that if I ever glimpsed her face it would be my dead sister.

Someone else featured prominently in my dream – *Elvis*. Was he a stalker? A journalist? Why did he make that terrifying cutthroat gesture? Maybe I'd misinterpreted, or my eyes had played a trick. I'd become so edgy lately.

I made a strong black coffee then went through the address book on my BlackBerry. I phoned every friend and business contact I thought might be able to help me with NexS. No one had heard of either it or the Oxford students Mencken had mentioned.

Jane phoned and I gave her my carefully concocted cover story that the mystery man I'd met at The Gherkin was a reclusive financier and I'd be keeping a low profile for the next few days as I took care of his requirements. Miraculously, I managed to keep to my story and avoid blurting out a single thing about what was really going on.

At least I didn't have to make any enquiries about Alphabet Love. The rules were simple. You had to sleep with twenty-six partners, starting with someone whose name began with 'A' and making your way through the alphabet in the right order until you got to someone with a name starting with 'Z'. Strictly speaking, you weren't supposed to have sex with anyone who wasn't part of the game, but that rule was often conveniently ignored. I actually had a few male acquaintances playing it, though they'd probably be searching for compliant Annes, Alices and Annabelles for decades to come.

In the afternoon, there was nothing more I could do, so to relax myself I watched my well-worn DVD of *Dr Zhivago* for the umpteenth time. It was my all-time favourite romantic movie. The Machiavellian character played by Rod Steiger reminded me of Mencken, but I couldn't find any role for Sam. To me, he'd never be anyone but Jay Gatsby.

For going out that night, I changed into my outfit that guaranteed maximum male attention. It consisted of a white whalebone basque, a black satin skirt and thigh-high black Gucci suede boots with the zip on the outside of the leg. With six-inch heels, the boots weren't designed for walking much further than the bedroom. So, totally fit for purpose, as Jane always liked to tell me.

I collected Sam and Jez in reception at the Sargasso. They were wearing similar gear to what they'd had on last night. Just as we were getting into a cab. Jez said, 'Not too many Eyes, right?'

'Excuse me?' I remembered that Sam had used the same expression in *Sin 6*.

'You don't know, do you?' Jez glanced at Sam. 'Eyes are, uh…'

'Fans,' Sam intervened.

'Yeah, fans,' Jez repeated, with a snigger.

'Of course,' I said, nodding. In my line of business, the illusion of deep understanding of my clients is essential. Usually it works, but every now and again…

Sam gave me a sly look. 'You don't have a clue what we're talking about, do you? You're winging it.' His voice was unpleasantly aggressive. 'Come on, Sophie, tell us why we call fans *Eyes*.'

He was dead right. I was clueless. *Eyes*? Hollywood freak talk as far as I was concerned.

'We're waiting,' Sam persisted.

I realised he intended to push it all the way. 'One of my other Hollywood clients told me,' I said eventually, pretending I frequently dealt with A-listers. The words flowed after that, bullshit mixed with concentrated blag. 'He said that when he arrived at the Oscars ceremony, all he saw was a sea of eyes gawping at him. "Eyes," he said, "that's all fans mean to me."'

I had no idea if I was talking crap or digging gold.

Sam exchanged a glance with Jez. 'Let's get going,' he said.

I'd passed the test, I think. But why had Sam got so ratty in the first place? It wasn't a good sign. He was such a hard guy to figure – switching between nice and nasty in a heartbeat.

I hoped things would improve once I took the actors to my favourite bar. Maybe its spooky history would jolt a positive response from them. Local legend had it that two German witches once lived on the site, so the present-day owner called it *Das Hexenhaus* – The Witch House. The bar was gothic, everything in matt black and gloss red. Even the toilet rolls in the black marble toilets were black, and quilted for extra comfort. As for the staff, they wore fashionable black uniforms with bellboy-style red caps.

The bar's quirky style had made it one of the trendiest spots in London, at least at weekends. But tonight was a quiet Wednesday, so few trendies were here. Instead, it was populated by a sad cast of C-listers and worse: 'mortgage' actors stuck in the same West End shows for years, soap-opera stars whose shows had long since submerged beneath the foamy bubbles, one-hit pop stars, comics who'd told their last gags years ago. Some of them were even less famous than I was. Nevertheless, I liked to tell Japanese, European and American clients that they were mingling with the biggest and best of Britain's showbiz stars. It seemed to keep them happy.

The Brit 'stars' mostly stayed in the VIP Room, though some preferred slumming it in the public bar. I wasn't sure which bar was riskier. Would VIPs be more likely to recognise Sam and Jez than ordinary punters? I couldn't decide.

I eventually chose the VIP bar, simply because it was visually more appealing. I found three luxury red leather seats for us near the horseshoe bar. I wondered if the actors liked the bar's red-painted oak panelling or the reproductions of Goya's paintings of witches. It was impossible to tell. They sat in silence with their legs wide open, vaguely staring at each other. They were so statue-like, I wondered if they were having another of their bets: a thousand dollars for who could do the best impression of a showroom dummy.

I asked if they fancied some Cristal and they both nodded stiffly. I signalled to one of the roving barstaff – Gary – one of my network of contacts. I once jokingly promised to put ice cubes in my mouth and suck him off for the coolest, or coldest, sexual experience of his life if he made sure my clients were always treated like royalty. He never gave up trying to get me to make good on that particular promise.

'Who are the dudes?' Gary whispered. When I smiled in a particular way, he responded with a knowing nod. 'So, full tongues?'

'In whatever orifice they prefer,' I replied, winking.

'Oh, by the way – bitch alert. Teri and Tamsin are round the corner with a group of Danish businessmen, spending shitloads.'

Christ, as if I didn't have enough to worry about.

'Thanks for the tip-off,' I said. 'Two bottles of Cristal and bring those new fluted glasses, please.'

'On your account?'

I nodded. 'Make sure you're taken care of.'

'Pay me tomorrow.' Pushing his finger into the side of his mouth, Gary made a disgusting plucking sound. 'In full, of course.' He smiled lecherously. 'On the rocks, just like we agreed.' Luckily, I could tell he was being only thirty-three percent serious.

I did the honours of opening the first bottle. It was almost a sexual pleasure to undo that translucent gold wrapping and slide out the elegant bottle. Jane never tired of pointing out that Cristal was once the champagne of choice for Russian tsars. Of course, American rappers were its top patrons these days. They ain't sippin' if it ain't Cristal, right? I popped the cork, skilfully avoiding too much spray, and poured the champagne. Then I held up my glass for a toast.

'To ultimate pleasure, right?'

'Ultimate pleasure,' the actors grunted, raising their glasses.

The champagne was as delicious as ever. For a moment, I forgot everything and just sat back and surrendered to the taste. But as I looked around the bar and watched Sam and Jez sulkily sipping their drinks, I started to panic at my list of duties and the ticking clock of the timescales involved. The Holy Grail was NexS, but where would I find it? As for Alphabet Love, I didn't know any woman whose name began with a Y, apart from Yvonne whom I hadn't seen since Roedean. Z? – forget it. I'd heard of a Zelda, a Zoe and a Zadie, but I'd certainly never met one.

I finished my Cristal and was busy pouring a fresh glass when Teri and Tamsin appeared. I thought I smelt sulphur, but it was just their ghastly *Inferno* perfume. They were dressed identically in trainers, jeans, and waistcoats that didn't cover their tummies. Most ludicrously of all, they were sporting silver gaucho hats. Their plastic smiles were so deeply ingrained it would probably take an elite demolition team to remove them. They spotted me and slithered over. I could see them studying Sam and Jez, trying to work out who they were. Sam's hood was drawn right over his head now, while Jez's baseball cap was firmly pulled down.

'Hi, Sophie,' they chirped in unison.

'Hi, Teri and Tamsin.' The usual fake bonhomie. Why did we bother?

'Aren't you going to introduce us to your mysterious friends?' Teri said.

There wasn't so much as a flicker from Sam and Jez.

'They don't want to be disturbed.'

I could see that Teri and Tamsin were intrigued. Only A-listers behaved as eccentrically as this.

Teri leaned over and said, 'Did you know that because of last year's heat wave, the French think that this season will yield only twenty percent of the normal amount of truffles. The price has already gone up to two thousand pounds a kilo.' Her eyes glinted. 'They're more expensive than opium.'

Tamsin joined in. 'Did you know that the truffles of Perigord are known as black diamonds because of their value and scarcity?' She shot a flirtatious look at Jez. 'Believe me, there's nothing quite like rooting around for black diamonds, and using your tongue to polish them.'

Teri nudged her friend. 'Yes, but the most elusive and expensive truffle of all is the white truffle of Italy.' Then a long, lingering stare at Sam.

I couldn't believe it. The bitches were trying to steal my guys right in front of me.

'Truffles aren't our thing,' I said dismissively, relishing my moment of triumph. Teri and Tamsin were the ones who once told a reporter that I had a tattoo of 'I luv Essex' on my bum, just because I was born in Billericay. Very bloody funny. It's actually a picture of the Japanese rising sun on my left buttock, and it's absolutely not tacky.

The two Ts scowled and went on their way to the loo, glancing over their shoulders to see if the boys were checking out their bums. Thankfully, they weren't. I was delighted to note that the BFI – the *Body Fascism Index* – was beginning to catch up with the two women now that they'd almost entered their thirties. Some feminist once said that every woman must beware the 'male gaze'. I chuckled, thinking the male gaze might soon be the last thing these two had to worry about. OK, I was being a bitch, but they deserved it.

'You were wrong by the way,' Sam said as we moved onto the second bottle of Cristal. 'We call fans Eyes because they can look but never touch.'

'Yeah, but your version was much better,' Jez laughed.

The smile I rustled up was so weak it barely registered. I'd got away with it, *just*. The two Ts would be burnishing their broomsticks and throwing a toad in the pot for extra flavour if they could see how shaky things were for me.

'So, where's the off-road fun Mencken said you'd give us?' Sam asked.

Fact was, no inspiration had come to me. I couldn't think of a solitary thing that was weird or imaginative. I mean these guys were just so huge and had done so many spectacular things. I felt totally inferior. My sense of humour was vanishing too. Normally I filled silences with anecdotes and jokes, but I felt about as funny as the Orthodox Jewish comedian at the Hamas convention, as a broadsheet journalist once said about me. I was a comedy vacuum.

I'd begun to dread that a spotlight would pick me out and a sneering voice would say, 'She thought she could entertain the brightest stars with her hick operation, thought she could fool the Hollywood Gods but, Sophie York, it's time for your news flash: Sam and Jez knew all along that you were a low-class loser and now they're going to walk out on you and tell the whole world what a fraud you are.'

As I sank deeper into my seat, laughter erupted from the public bar. Instantly, I wanted to be there, surrounded by people capable of having normal fun. 'Come on,' I said.

When we went into the other bar, a man in a black top hat, frock coat and an elegant cape lined with red silk was standing in front of two tall companions dressed as butlers, each holding a tray heaped with delicious-looking cream cakes in Harrods' wrappers: strawberry tarts, raspberry pavlovas, pineapple and peach cakes, profiteroles, slices of black forest gateau, cream slices, chocolate éclairs, custard tarts, fruit flan, creamy chocolate meringues.

I instantly labelled the man 'Jack' because he resembled the bad guy in any *Jack the Ripper* movie you cared to choose. He even had a sinister gold-tipped cane.

The trio, none of whom seemed older than about twenty-one, approached each person in the bar, one after the other. Jack whispered something, there would be a puzzled look, and then either Jack or the person he'd spoken to would take a cream cake from one of the trays and eat it. I glanced at the actors to check their reaction. I thought I detected signs of interest.

After a couple of minutes, Jack sauntered over to me, followed by his helpers.

'Ah, young damsel,' he said in a much posher voice than I expected. 'Can you help a poor man?' He explained that the expensive cakes his companions were carrying were his last possessions on earth. His voice dropped. 'I won't be needing them where I'm going.'

When I looked into his eyes, I saw something strange there, like a shadow. I was uncomfortable, despite the giggling going on all around me.

He must have noticed my reaction because he broke into a pleasant smile, but it didn't last long. Taking a step forward, he came unnervingly close to me and I found myself backed up against a wall.

'Are you willing to risk everything?' he whispered.

The question startled me. 'Er, what are we talking about here?'

'Curiosity killed the cat.' He reached out and gripped my arm. 'Did no one ever tell you: the last thing you should ever be given is what you most desire.'

I must have looked alarmed because he retreated and his soothing smile reappeared.

'I'm offering a luxury cream cake to everyone in the bar,' he said in a different tone. 'Each person can either accept or decline. If they accept then obviously they eat the cake. If they decline then I have to eat it myself. Those are the rules.' He peered at me. 'So, what's it to be? Will you help me with this burden?'

I noticed him glancing at Sam and I had the distinct impression he knew exactly who it was even though Sam's hood was pulled right over.

'What should I do?' I asked Sam.

'Eat the goddamn thing.'

'Sorry, I'm just not hungry,' I replied to Jack. I was infuriated.

Jack took off his top hat and bowed. 'I understand.' Then the hat went back on and he turned and selected a strawberry tart from the tray. 'This will be my tenth. I confess the exercise is becoming somewhat tiresome.' He popped half of it into his mouth. A quick chew then he finished off the rest.

'An Atkins variation?' I asked, grinning.

'In what spirit is that remark made? One of mockery?'

'It was just a joke.'

'If only you knew.'

'Knew what?'

'I'm not here to expound my philosophy, just to distribute these cakes.' He turned towards the boys and gave them the same spiel he'd tried on me. Unlike me, they didn't hesitate. Each took a cake and devoured it.

Jack removed his hat and bowed. 'You are noble gentlemen, quite the best of Samaritans.'

He went on his way with his two butlers, approaching others in the bar in the same methodical manner.

'I want to watch this,' Sam said, nudging Jez. 'Is Heineken Export OK?'

Jez nodded and Sam then had the cheek to point me in the direction of the bar.

I was furious at being treated like a skivvy, but I didn't want to argue. I went to the bar, got three bottles of Heineken, and took them back to the table Jez had found for us. None of us spoke. We sat staring at Jack and his butlers as they went right round the bar performing their peculiar ceremony.

Usually, people accepted the cake they were offered. It took Jack about twenty minutes to get rid of all the cakes. Everyone in the bar was peering at Jack, trying to understand what was happening. The consensus around me was that it was some Rag-Week stunt by UCL medical students. I wasn't so sure, and I certainly couldn't forget the odd look I'd seen in Jack's eyes.

Whatever the three men were up to, they'd put on some show and I was disappointed when they left. It had been a relief not having to think up more small talk to keep the actors distracted. I groaned inwardly, thinking I'd be back on duty. I was supposed to love this job or at least be able to make it look like I loved it, but I was struggling hard to sustain my act.

When Jez tapped my arm I assumed he wanted me to get some more Heinekens.

'We're following those dudes,' he said.

Before I could respond, he and Sam were heading towards the door. I hurried after them, into the humid, dark night. It was five to eleven and the streetlights were on. Jack and his butlers walked at a brisk pace, heading in the direction of Green Park. Jez and Sam set out fast after them. With my high-heeled boots on, I couldn't keep up. I had to take them off and carry them. The pavement was hard and painful against my feet.

We passed the Ritz Hotel then arrived at Ritz Corner. Ahead of us, the three men made their way down Queen's Walk on the eastern edge of Green Park, heading towards St James's Park and Buckingham Palace. If they were aware of us following them they hadn't shown any signs. They went past a block of luxury apartments, turned to the left and…

Gone.

The properties in this area were ultra expensive, hidden behind large iron gates and thick foliage to keep out prying eyes. Peeking through the spikes of one iron gate, we glimpsed the trio. They were standing outside the entrance of a breathtakingly elegant white-stone mansion that looked like a cross between a Greek temple and an 18th century stately home. Lights picked out its Greek columns, grand windows and the scores of ornate features that decorated its façade. On the mansion's roof stood seven sculptures: three beautiful angels flanked by four hideous gargoyles.

In front of the mansion was an enchanting floodlit lawn neatly edged with eye-catching black tulips branded with a broad blaze of golden orange at the petal edges. A stone path led to several wide steps and up to a terrace, where the three men were waiting to be admitted.

The mansion looked like it once belonged to some great lord, perhaps even a member of the royal family. From what I knew of the property prices in this area, it had to be worth a fortune, maybe seventy-five to a hundred million pounds. Were these guys unbelievably rich? I wasn't even sure Sam and Jez could afford a place like this.

Jack tapped on the black-varnished door with his cane. When it opened, he took off his top hat and gave a theatrical bow.

A party of glamorous twenty-somethings in tuxedos and ball-gowns filed out onto the terrace and formed two lines, the men on one side, the women on the other.

One face stood out immediately – blond Elvis! I shuddered. Did that mean these others were the City Slickers?

All the attention was on Jack. After retreating a few steps while the two lines were being formed, he now walked forward with the proud bearing of a soldier. His two butlers patted him on the back while the others clapped and cheered as he made his way past them and into the mansion. It seemed to be some kind of honour parade. They all went inside and the door was firmly shut behind them.

'What's going on?' Sam asked. He and Jez started firing theories at each other – freemasons; street performers; a secret society of eccentric gay men and lesbians; a training facility for butlers or a finishing school for eccentric young gentlemen and ladies. A spy academy?

They stopped jabbering and Sam turned towards me, snapping his fingers.

'You're some piece of work. That was good…the best.'

For a second I considered playing along and try to steal the credit but I knew I'd never get away with it. I shook my head. 'Sorry, guys, nothing to do with me.'

'No?' Sam seemed surprised. 'Well, I know one thing, I swiped this from that dude's pocket.' He brandished a card in front of us and held it up beneath a streetlamp to let us see. 'I picked up a few tricks when I did that remake of *Oliver Twist* as a kid,' he remarked with a wink.

We all leaned in to see the card. It was eggshell white and embossed with gold letters. It said: 'Lawrence Maybury, One Button. The Top Table.' Then, in italics, '*Neither by land nor by sea shalt thou find the road to the Hyperboreans.*' Underneath was a phone number.

We looked at each other and shrugged.

Jez took out a silver Vertu mobile phone, so sleek and slimline I wanted one immediately, but I seemed to remember that they cost two and a half grand. He keyed in a number and handed the mobile to Sam while it was ringing.

Sam listened for a moment before saying, 'Uh, nothing.'

'You got burned, asshole, didn't you?' Jez sneered.

'A guy answered,' Sam said, 'and he asked, "What ails you, friend?" At least, I think that's what he said. I couldn't think of anything smart to say, then the line went dead.' He stared at the mansion. 'Man, I want to know what's going on in there.'

Jez nodded.

'Five hundred bucks says you don't go and find out,' Sam said.

'Candy from a baby.' Jez took off his skip cap and shades and walked over to the iron gate. He pushed it open – no attempt seemed to have been made to lock it – and walked right in. He sauntered along the path, up the steps and onto the terrace. When he got to the door, he rang the bell. It opened a moment later and a tall man with floppy dark hair appeared.

'Hey, guess who I am?' Jez said loudly. The door was instantly slammed in his face. He seemed confused when he came back. 'Er, do I win the bet?'

Sam shook his head. 'So, our mysterious friends don't want to party.'

'I guess we've had our fun,' I said. 'Want to do something else? It's still early. We could go to a casino. I know a private one just round the corner. Only millionaires are allowed to play. Their poker games are a legend. If there's anything else you want like, er, you know, high-class company, I can make the arrangements. If you're looking for backstage passes for anything…'

Jez laughed. 'Did you hear that, Sammy boy? Our English princess thinks we have to pay for sex.' He patted my head then instantly checked his palm, no doubt to see if anything revolting had been transferred. 'And she thinks we have problems getting backstage invites. Newsflash, honey – we're the first names on the guest-list. No one ever shuts doors in our faces.'

'Until now,' I said, unable to resist.

Neither man reacted. It was as if my comment had dissolved in the air.

'Like the man says,' Sam growled, 'no one ever closes the door on us. We're getting inside that joint. *Whatever it takes.*'

11

Death Wish

When I went to the Sargasso the next morning, my mind was flitting between the bizarre events of last night and my mission. What could I do to find NexS? As I walked into reception, I found Mencken reading a newspaper. I thought of turning round and going straight back out again.

'So, how are things going with the biggest whales in the ocean?' he asked. When he realised I hadn't understood, he said, in a ridiculous Mexican accent, 'You no understand the lingo?' Smiling slyly, he reverted to his normal voice. 'You've got Moby Dick on your hands.' He winked. 'Dicks, to be more exact.'

I continued to stare blankly.

He explained that a whale was a Hollywood term for a major celebrity. A Moby Dick was one of the top ten actors on the planet, a megastar who could open a movie and turn even shit into gold. 'Well, aren't Sam and Jez a brace of dicks?' He obviously knew I wasn't in any hurry to disagree. 'Word is they came back excited last night. Did you treat them to a Sophie special?'

'It was a night to remember, that's for sure.'

'You should be ecstatic. You've made it.'

'What do you mean?'

'Jez says you're a cool chick and Sam told me you were hot. If you've impressed them then you're in the fast lane in your Ferrari flicking ash from your Havana cigar, aren't you?'

Sam said I was hot? No way. 'I don't think so,' I said. 'Where are the gruesome twosome?'

Mencken grinned and nodded towards the restaurant. 'Try the reserved area in the breakfast room. I had a chat with them earlier. Like I said, they were excited. You're right, though – they didn't mention you at all.'

Well, cheers. As I turned, Mencken reached out and clasped my arm.

'NexS,' he said. 'Any news?'

'Nothing yet.' I freed myself and hurried away.

Approaching the breakfast room, I noticed Mencken's decoy versions of Sam and Jez eating their sunny-side-up fried eggs. Their bodyguards were fending off anyone who ventured too close. As ever, there was a buzz of whispering and gossiping, accompanied by a forest of pointing fingers as people hyperventilated at the presence of Hollywood superstars. It cheered me up that there were so many dumbos falling for the old doubles trick.

When I reached the reserved area, I soon saw the real deal – Sam looking gorgeous in black jeans and a sleeveless white T-shirt, Jez in baggy hip-hop gear. Their baseball caps and shades were lying on the table in front of them, ready for a quick cover-up.

They were engrossed in whatever was on TV. Sam noticed me and motioned to me to come and join them. I knew I was expected to say nothing and just look at the TV. As soon as I did, I knew why.

A photograph of a handsome young guy flashed onto the screen. I watched, wide-eyed. It was Jack from last night. I started to say something but Jez put his finger to his lips and turned up the volume with the remote control.

'Lawrence Maybury's body was discovered at seven am by the Thames river police,' the newsreader said. 'It lay in a black gondola that had drifted down the Thames for several miles before coming to a halt in a reed bank. Numerous sightings of the gondola were reported as it made its way downriver. Two unopened bottles of rare champagne were found next to the body.

'Mr Maybury was twenty-one years old and single. A brilliant philosophy student at Oxford University, he was tipped for a glittering academic career. The only child of Lady Northgate, he was heir to an estate estimated at fifty million pounds. His father was Earl Mansfield, a leading member of the nobility. The earl killed himself when Lawrence was five years old.

'Lawrence's family gave the police permission to disclose the contents of a letter found on the body. It said:

"I've always been haunted by my father's death. He was just twenty-six, a brilliant composer, already being hailed as a genius. Finishing the final note of his first symphony, he knew it was a masterpiece. He put down his pen, picked up a razor and slit his throat. When the music was played in public for the first time, it was at his funeral. His blood was still visible on the score. It has never been played since.

"I can't think of that music without weeping. Music to make you cry, music to make you die. Why did he do it? He had everything ahead of him. Then I went to the Lazar House and found NexS. At last, everything made sense. When the supreme moment of your life has come, why go on? NexS is perfection. It delivers your once-in-a-lifetime moment – *your death.*

"Lacrimae rerum."'

The newsreader paused. 'That's Latin for *the tears of things.*'

The picture cut away to a reporter on the bank of the Thames interviewing various people, but I was already playing back what the newsreader had said. A single word stuck out: NexS. I couldn't believe it. So, those people at the mansion were Mencken's Oxford students, and, judging by what the note said about it, NexS more than lived up to its billing.

I remembered Lawrence Maybury so vividly, especially that remark he made: '*Where I'm going, I won't need it.*' Did that mean he was thinking of suicide all along? But in that case why was he so cheerful at the mansion? Why the honour parade? The more I thought about it, the less things stacked up. I'd never heard of this Oxford gang and I hadn't found out anything about them from my contacts, yet they'd fallen into our lap on the very first night. Now one of them was dead and making national headlines.

On the TV, a police spokesman announced there were no suspicious circumstances. He said it appeared to be a clear case of a troubled young man committing suicide, using the tragic example of his own father. The precise cause of death hadn't yet been ascertained and an autopsy would be held. He said he was as yet unable to shed any light on the meaning of 'Lazar House' or 'NexS'.

Sam lowered the volume and turned towards me. 'Amazing, huh? Mencken promised us NexS and, kazam, here it is.'

'Yeah, hard to believe,' I said quietly. A young man with his whole life ahead of him was dead and NexS suddenly seemed more like poison than pleasure.

'So, NexS delivers your once-in-a-lifetime moment,' Sam said. 'What do you know – maybe Mencken has hit the jackpot after all.'

'That was one grand exit,' Jez commented callously as he pointed at TV pictures showing the black gondola the body was found in. He nudged Sam. 'If you were checking out, how would you do it?'

It was a revolting question and I expected Sam to ignore it, but he answered straight away.

'I'd like to drown in a pool of women's tears.'

'What?' Jez bellowed. 'That's some freaky shit, man.'

I looked at Sam to see if he was joking. Was he putting on an act? OK, we scarcely knew Lawrence Maybury, but we'd been talking to him within the last twenty-four hours. Anyway, it would take a hell of a lot of tears to fill a pool. Maybe he meant he wanted a tide of womanly emotion to wash over him as he died. After all, he was always surrounded by female hysteria.

'Come on,' I said, 'we need to let Mencken know about all of this.'

He was on his mobile phone when we caught up with him in the foyer.

'NexS,' Sam said. 'It's been on the news.' He explained the whole story; what had happened in the Hexenhaus bar, the mansion in Green Park, the students' honour parade, the suicide of Lawrence Maybury, the reference to NexS.

Mencken nodded. 'Small world, huh?'

'What's the plan now?' Jez asked.

Mencken turned to me. 'Any ideas, Sophie? You're the one with the local knowledge.'

'I've never hung out with any Oxford students,' I admitted.

'I need to think about this,' Mencken said. Luckily, he didn't seem too bothered that I couldn't help. 'I have some business meetings today, but let's hook up tonight and decide how to play this.'

'What about us?' Sam asked.

'Sophie has something lined up for you,' Mencken replied.

'It will be good to see you guys in top hats and tails,' I declared. I found myself easily faking a smile, even though I was still shaken up about Lawrence Maybury. I tried not to worry too much at how I was such an effortless fraud.

The boys looked at each other. 'Top hats and tails?'

'This had better be good,' Sam said threateningly.

12

The Royal Enclosure

My choice for the day's main event wasn't exactly original, but since Sam and Jez liked a bet I was sure they'd love a trip to a horseracing event. Not just any old horses – we were on our way to Royal Ascot to watch the Gold Cup. Mencken said he wished he could come too, but couldn't get out of his business meetings.

We left before noon, travelling in a fabulous old car: a 1929 yellow and black Franklin convertible coupe with gleaming nickel fittings. Gary from the Hexenhaus bar had organised the car – through a friend of a friend – and it came with a chauffeur in a bottle-green uniform. I mentioned to Sam and Jez that *The Great Gatsby* was my favourite American novel and Gatsby drove a swanky car just like this.

'I know all about it,' Sam commented gruffly.

The idea of Sam reading *The Great Gatsby* seemed far-fetched. I guessed he'd seen the old movie starring Robert Redford.

Sam sat in the front with the driver while Jez and I made ourselves comfortable in the back. I was looking forward to a glamorous occasion, especially since I had managed to swing privileged access to Ascot's Royal Enclosure. That meant I had to persuade Sam and Jez to fall in line with the strict dress code, hence the request that they wear top hat and tails. Surprisingly, once they knew what it was for they gave me no trouble and were now sitting in smart grey morning suits, hired for the day. With their elegant gold waistcoats, gold ties, crisp white shirts and yellow carnations in their buttonholes, I think even they were impressed by how classy they looked. Of course, they couldn't resist a little touch of Hollywood, so they were both sporting designer wrap-around shades in a garish metallic orange. They didn't blend in with the refined look of their outfits, but I didn't object.

As for me, I was the lady in red: red stilettos, a gorgeous red fishtail dress and a beautiful wide-brimmed red hat like the sort of thing Audrey Hepburn wore in *My Fair Lady*. Jez said I was looking 'mighty fine', but it was Sam I wanted the compliments from and I didn't get any.

When we reached the racecourse, Sam and Jez soon attracted attention. I think the top hats and sci-fi shades combination looked decidedly cranky, but at least it made it difficult for anyone to recognise them.

The actors were clearly impressed by the parade of gleaming Rolls-Royces, Bentleys and assorted limousines lined up on the lush turf. Lords and Ladies were wining and dining from luxury wicker hampers.

Sam and Jez sucked in the spectacle – the crazy haute couture hats and glam outfits, the eccentric aristocrats with their braying voices, the hordes of ordinary punters, the paparazzi stalking suitable prey. Luckily, everyone's attention was focused on a cackling of WAGs, tastelessly flaunting their fake breasts, garish hats and limitless bling. You have to hand it to the WAGs – even by my standards they're supremely vulgar. They make everyone else feel classy.

A woman pushed a pram past Sam and one of its wheels collided with his shoe. He gave the woman a furious look and I thought he was going to shout at her, but he managed to control himself.

'Catch a baby by the toe and when it squeals don't let it go,' he said in an odd tone.

He was one weird bloke. Avoiding a discussion of his baby phobia, I glanced at my watch. Almost 2 pm. I explained that it was the custom for the Queen and other members of the royal family to parade in an open carriage along the racecourse to signal the start of the day's competition.

The boys were unimpressed. 'I hate royalty,' Sam snarled. 'Who the fuck do these people think they are?' He prodded me in the tummy. 'You English folks can bow and grovel to them all you like, but they can kiss my ass.'

An explosion of clapping signalled the Queen's arrival, but after what Sam had just said, I thought it smart to lead Jez and him in the opposite direction.

'No, let's watch the old crone,' Sam said.

The royal procession entered through Ascot's golden gates and made its way along the course. There were four open-topped black carriages interspersed with a column of outriders in magnificent red tunics, seated on white horses. The Queen and the Duke of Edinburgh were in the first carriage while assorted hangers-on rode in the others. Shining, polished attendants with glittering gold braid on their red uniforms sat on the tailgates of the carriages.

The Queen wore her customary hideous outfit, reflecting the dress sense of a granny losing her wits and a bag lady who'd just wet herself. It always amused me that people would actually bet on what colour of hat she was wearing for the procession. This year it was an awful indeterminate colour and a few people behind me cheered when it was eventually officially confirmed as white for the purposes of the bet.

The Royal Enclosure

The national anthem struck up as the procession neared the winners' enclosure, en route to the royal box. Everyone took off their hats – except Sam and Jez who turned their backs. For a second, I thought they were going to drop their trousers and moon, but thankfully they spared me that.

With that ordeal out of the way, we made our way to the Royal Enclosure and navigated our way past the bowler-hatted gatemen without too much difficulty, though they stared disapprovingly at the boys' shades and made sure they hadn't broken the rule forbidding brown shoes.

Inside, hordes of men in morning suits, with binoculars slung round their necks, jostled past us to get the best vantage points to watch the horses crossing the nearby finishing line. Pushing through them, we went to the catering area. I was amazed that so many women were wearing miniskirts and showing off bare shoulders. For some reason, the traditional dress code seemed to have been suspended today. There were plunging necklines galore, exposed belly buttons and bare legs way past the modesty level of former years.

Sam and Jez's heads swivelled around as they stared at micro-minis, slip-dresses, lace-trimmed camisoles and an abundance of assorted corsetry. It was a fashion spotter's paradise. I suddenly felt boring amongst the acres of naked flesh.

After the skin fest, Sam and Jez concentrated on their stomachs and were soon enjoying strawberries and cream, washed down by champagne. I stuck with sparkling water. Twice before, I'd thrown up in the Royal Enclosure after getting wrecked on champagne within hours of arriving at the course.

The boys seemed fascinated by the gestures and signals of the tic-tac men and Sam announced that he and Jez intended to make £1000 bets on each race. Their way of choosing a horse would be simple. They'd approach the nearest beautiful woman, but only if she were wearing a ridiculous hat, and ask her, in their most ludicrous version of a Cockney accent, what she fancied in the next race.

I was happy enough with the way things were going. I just wished Sam would pull himself out of his sour mood when he was with me. While Jez chatted freely, I hardly got a word out of him.

After the third race, Jez disappeared. I said to Sam that I should go and look for him, but he told me not to bother. A few minutes of self-conscious silence passed until I decided I wouldn't let the strained atmosphere between us continue any longer.

'Are you enjoying yourself, Sam?' I said, taking his arm in mine. 'We're having a nice afternoon, aren't we?'

Sam sighed. 'It's been a long time since anything juiced me up. That guy with the cakes last night…that was the first time I've been intrigued for years. Then he shows up dead this morning.' He gazed past me. 'You know, I kind of relate to that note he left. Life isn't about how many breaths you take but how many moments that take your breath away.'

I stared at him. Mencken had said that exact same thing.

'I've not had moments like that lately,' Sam went on. 'I need some or I'll go crazy.'

It sounded as though he'd burned out his pleasure circuits. He and Jez were terminally bored as far as I could make out. The price of having everything, I guess.

There was a rippling movement in the crowd as though lots of people were moving at once, and some people began to snigger. Next thing, everyone was laughing. *Everyone*. The Queen, too, for all I knew. People were applauding and cheering. There were even some wolf whistles. Jez was walking through the crowd with a sandwich board round his neck. The board said: 'Hunk, fabulously wealthy, GSOH, seeks hot babe. First name must begin with Y.'

I nudged Sam. He was half-grinning, half-scowling.

'So when did you start playing Alphabet Love?' I asked.

'You heard about the punch-up at the MTV awards?'

I smiled. 'Yeah, I saw it on cable. The story I heard was that a third party intervened and managed to patch things up.'

Sam nodded. 'The third party was Mencken. He's the only guy who can smooth things between Jez and me. He told us Alphabet Love would prove which of us was the head honcho. We shook hands on it and here we are.' He took off his top hat and scratched the side of his head as he watched numerous women bustling around Jez. 'That jerk will never beat me.'

'What's the prize? Are you allowed to say?'

'Sure. It's a week at the Burj Al Arab seven-star hotel in Dubai.'

I knew the place he was talking about – the spectacular hotel that looked like a silver sail set in the surf. It had an underwater restaurant reachable only by submarine. *Nice*.

The prize had a part two, Sam explained – the loser had to spend a week in a one-star motel in Cleveland, Ohio, with someone nominated by the winner. One could only imagine the dreadfulness of the guest likely to be chosen.

'How do you prove who you've slept with?' I asked out of curiosity.

Sam said that each woman had to pose for a picture holding that day's newspaper to prove the date. She was required to write her name clearly on the bottom of the photo, accompanied by a phone number for verification in case of doubt. Cheating – particularly the use of a false name – would result in instant disqualification and the automatic loss of the bet. Sometimes, a woman didn't play ball and that liaison had to be written off.

'The game's easy most of the time,' Sam said, 'but there are some crappy letters. Q was sticky. I got lucky when I met Quira from Kenya. Xanthy was my X and Yasmine my Y.'

He pointed towards Jez. 'If Jez gets his Y it's going to be a photo finish. First one to nail a Z wins all.'

Part of me felt depressed that Sophie, ungratefully, refused to begin with a Z, while another part was outraged by how meaningless sex would be if all that mattered was the initial of your first name. What was wrong with men?

'Got to hand it to Jez, I suppose,' Sam said. 'He's going down fighting.'

The glamorous women clustered around Jez were giggling, flirting and pawing at him. A couple handed him notes.

'Winning Alphabet Love means a lot to Jez, doesn't it?'

'Did no one ever tell you? – second is the first of the losers,' Sam responded sharply. 'As we say in America, "Winning isn't the important thing, it's the *only* thing."'

There was another commotion and we turned to see what was going on. A gang of young men and women were rudely pushing through the crowd, ostentatiously sipping pink champagne as they went. The men wore old-fashioned grey morning suits and absurdly high stovepipe top hats; as for the women, they were dressed in beautiful rose-pink dresses and matching wide-brimmed hats. Crazily, all of their faces were covered with solid white make-up so that the women looked like Geisha girls and the men mime artists. Or maybe they were supposed to resemble ghosts. Everyone was staring at them and whispering.

Sam nudged me. 'Hey, aren't they…'

'How can you tell?'

'I've just got a feeling.'

I didn't need any feeling. One of the men had removed his hat – it was the guy with the blond Elvis quiff. This was getting ridiculous. The group passed close to us. Before I could react, Elvis pushed into Sam before swiftly moving away. Sam started patting his pockets.

'Nothing's missing,' he said after a moment. 'I've seen that guy before. *Sin 6* wasn't it?'

I nodded. I told him that the man had also been at *The Moulin Rouge* nightclub and that I'd seen him last night at the mansion.

'You're saying he's following us?'

'Not just him: the whole lot of them.' I noticed something sticking out of Sam's breast pocket. Reaching across, I snatched it out. It was a glossy black card stamped with a holographic skull, exactly like the one from the lap-dancing club. As I passed it to Sam, my hand trembled.

It said, 'The Millionaires' Death Club has accepted your application to join.'

13

Sexual Politics

On the journey back to London, Sam sat beside me in the back of the car, staring into space. He refused to talk about the skull card, but he was obviously rattled. We'd both seen Elvis bumping into him and that must have been when the card was planted. But Elvis's whole gang were in on it, weren't they? *They* were the Millionaires' Death Club.

As for Jez, he'd vanished and I couldn't reach him on his mobile. Sam told me to leave a message saying we were leaving and that he'd have to make his own way back.

As we reached the outskirts of London, Sam said, 'What if that guy Lawrence Maybury didn't commit suicide?'

'What do you mean? The police didn't mention any suspicious circumstances. There was a note.'

Sam shook his head. 'Something's going on. Those students...'

'Like the Manson family, huh?' I wasn't joking. I knew next to nothing about them, yet they spooked me. 'Should we tell the police about that skull card?'

Sam shook his head. 'I'll handle it.'

'But don't you think it's some kind of death threat?'

'They're rich students. How could they be a threat?' The more he talked, the less worried he seemed. 'It's a stunt,' he said. 'A bad joke, that's all.'

I wondered if I should tell him about the contract John Adams mentioned, but it seemed too freaky. 'Where do you think Jez went?'

'Screwing,' Sam retorted. 'He's found a Y.'

I laughed and that set Sam off. Maybe it was a release of tension, I don't know, but we just kept laughing. It went on for a good couple of minutes, tears-to-the-eyes stuff. When we were done, Sam bent forward, as if he were about to throw up.

'I was laughing,' he said, 'really laughing.' He sounded amazed. 'I'd love to meet people who didn't care who I was.' There was such a sad note in his voice. 'I wouldn't mind if they hated me. At least it would be real.'

'You can be yourself with me. I hope you know that.'

He gave me a smile and I was thrilled by just how warm it was.

'Why don't you join me for dinner tonight?' he asked.

I couldn't work him out, but one thing I knew was here was an invitation I didn't have to think twice about.

'I'd love to.'

'OK, I'll see you at eight.'

We spent the rest of the time talking about my business. I showed him my brochure, praying he wouldn't be as contemptuous of it as Teri, Tamsin and Tommy Miller. He grabbed it, glanced at it for a few seconds then took out a pen. He went to the contents page and started scribbling. Thrusting it back at me, he chuckled. Next to every item, he'd written, alternately, 'Horseshit'; 'Bullshit'. At the bottom of the page it said, 'You gotta have more than this, Limey chick.'

But I didn't. I needed a bigger vision, better events, better clients, better everything. Yet I started giggling and, crazily, it felt great.

Soon we were back in London and in all the hectic bustle of the capital my worries about the Millionaires' Death Club seemed idiotic.

As he got out of the car, Sam leaned over and kissed me on the cheek.

Reflexively, I put my hand up to where his lips had touched. I was dumbstruck for a moment. I realised I was grinning like a lunatic.

****

That evening, I put on my most expensive dress – a champagne-lace, floor-length gown. I'd gone heavy on the make-up and thought I was looking particularly glam. In the taxi on the way to the Sargasso, I wondered what sort of mood Sam would be in. I hoped Mencken and Jez were elsewhere so that I could be alone with him.

Reaching the hotel, I encountered a pack of paparazzi. Doormen were struggling to hold them back. Stepping forward, I was shocked to find myself the centre of attention with photographers wildly snapping my picture.

People were shouting things at me but I ignored them. The doormen had a list of approved names and said there was a private party going on. I relaxed, thinking that was why the paparazzi were here. Apart from those attending the party, only hotel residents, and people invited by them, were allowed in. I was impressed to see my name near the top of the list. Well done, Sam.

Inside, I took a deep breath. Lots of people were hanging around in reception and I wondered who was having the party. I headed for the restaurant and, as I walked in, I was greeted by the maitre'd who directed me to a quiet corner table. Annoyingly, Jez had resurfaced and was sitting there with Sam. He was laughing and brandishing some piece of paper in Sam's face.

Jez looked up at me, grinned then thrust the item into my hand. It was a digital print of a beautiful naked woman holding today's edition of *The Times*. I flipped it over and immediately saw that it was signed, 'Love, Yvette.' A line underneath said, 'Give me a ring anytime, you sexy beast.' And then a mobile phone number.

I smiled weakly. 'So, just Z to go for both of you.'

'Damn straight,' Jez said. 'It's the showdown now. Mano a mano. Last man standing wins. I've got the big M.O. behind me and Mr Lincoln here is shitting himself.' He glared at Sam. 'That's right, Sammy boy, isn't it? You're a busted flush.'

'I don't hear any fat ladies tuning up, let alone singing. I'll get my Z before you do.' Sam banged down his wineglass. 'You can bet on it.'

Dinner went on for two hours. The food and wine were delicious, the conversation less so. It was mostly taken up with Jez reminiscing about his various Alphabet Love conquests and making it clear he was going to win. He planned to choose a morbidly obese woman with a giant fat ass for Sam to hook up with in Cleveland. He made a stack of comments about what the weather was like in Ohio at this time of year and what kind of postcards Sam should send to Dubai.

Sam hardly retaliated. He seemed relieved when dinner was over and said he wanted to go back to his room to wait for Mencken.

'No, you're coming to the bar with us,' Jez said. 'Sophie's our guest tonight.'

'I should go,' I said, feeling awkward. 'I don't think Mencken will show.'

Jez held my arm. 'No, gal, we're here to have fun. Come on, I've discovered a great new cocktail.'

I looked at Sam and he shrugged. We went to the bar and Jez bought three Black Velvets. It might be new to him but it certainly wasn't to me. Half Guinness to half champagne, it was a drink I found distinctly sickly. Even the gold flakes sprinkled over it didn't increase its appeal.

Sam liked it though and I thought he was cheering up. He asked me if I ever got any interesting clients. No one in his league, that was for sure. As for Jez, he was keen to find out about my love life; if I was hooked up with anyone and, if not, then why not. I didn't want to divulge too much about romance in front of Sam. Not that there was much to tell, not for the last six months or so anyway. My love life had consisted mostly of less than brilliant one-night stands and two semi-serious relationships that fizzled out, one badly, the other so quietly that it was as if it never existed in the first place.

An hour passed pleasantly enough, though it was still a no-show from Mencken. I called him on his mobile, but it was switched off.

I went to the loo and was suitably impressed by all the marble and gold fittings. A good loo is close to every girl's heart, of course, and makes all the difference between a five star rating and a washout.

I came back out, smiling and feeling fresh. Then – *oh fuck* – I saw Jane. For a second I wondered how she'd got past the doormen, but a PR person with her big mouth could blag her way past anyone, couldn't she? She was wearing an almost-transparent black dress and gave every impression she was on a serious mission to pull, with her make-up applied at 'glam-max' level. I knew she *knew* and I tried to work out where I'd slipped up.

'You!' she bellowed when she caught me trying to slink past.

'OK, how did you find me?'

'Bloody hell,' she snarled, 'even Inspector Clouseau wouldn't have had any trouble.' She snatched a spare copy of *The London Evening News* from a table, turned over the first page and thrust it at me.

'Didn't you wonder why the paparazzi were camped outside? Doh!'

I took the newspaper and stared at the colour picture on page three. There I was – pictured at Royal Ascot earlier in the day – with Sam on one side and Jez on the other. Under a headline of *Who's That with our IT-girl*? there was speculation about who my 'mysterious' companions were. The consensus of five celebrity watchers was unanimous…

Posh Totty Sophie York – remember her? (Don't worry, we didn't either) – snares two Hollywood megastars, the article proclaimed. *She may have been expelled from Roedean girls' school, got sozzled on cheap plonk, stripped naked on live TV and jungle-jived with monkeys, but our Sophie sure knows how to make a Yankee Doodle Dandy*, it went on. In horror, I read the rest. *Old London Town has just received a visitation from on high. Two 24-carat überstars have checked into town and are looking for serious high roller action. Our expert panel of star spotters know that Hollywood's two baddest boys are holed up in luxury suites in the super-swish Sargasso hotel in Mayfair. Legendary as Hollywood's top party animals, Sam Lincoln and Jez Easton are responsible for so much hell raising that the Devil has probably sent them a letter of complaint, pointing out his vertigo issues. It seems they've turned to 'entertainment consultant' Sophie to discover what the capital has to offer. We wonder if any other young fillies caught their attention at Royal Ascot on Ladies' Day. One thing's for sure – their feeble attempt to disguise themselves fooled no one. It was probably Sophie's idea to make them wear 'look-at-me' shades. Do you think she's been lined up for a part in the new movie the actors are about to start filming? Maybe she'll play the mastermind of a heist. No, we didn't think so either.*

'Well?' Jane demanded, tapping her foot. 'I want an intro to Sam Lincoln. I can't believe you haven't told me what's been going on.'

I *did* feel guilty for not saying anything, but Jane was a notorious motor-mouth who could never keep anything secret.

Come on, Sophs, we're a team,' she whined. 'Share and share alike, and all that.'

'Sam's mine,' I snapped.

Jane gave me one of her knowing smirks. 'Of course you want Sam,' she said in that familiar patronising tone she adopted whenever she wanted to get her own way. 'But what does *he* want? We have to think of what's good for him. These Hollywood guys are always looking for something extra. Usual stuff is for usual people. Stars want the under-the-counter menu.' She paused, her eyes twinkling. 'He doesn't want you and he doesn't want me – he wants *both*. A tasty ménage `a trois with two Roedean girls; it's every Yank's dream, isn't it? We can both whisper filthy things to him in our posh English accents. Then we'll treat him to a Roedean spit roast. It'll blow him away.' She giggled. 'So to speak.'

I didn't know quite what to say to that. Frankly, I was well aware of Jane's sexual preferences. She was up for just about anything. Hell, she might even be right about Sam, but there was no way I was sharing.

'Keep your hands off Sam. You can have Jez if he's interested.'

Jane looked at me and pondered. She preferred Sam but I was betting she didn't really care. She just wanted to shag a Hollywood megastar and one was as good as another.

'Deal,' she said, flashing one of her man-eating smiles. 'It's time for two gorgeous Old Roedeanians to go bonk Hollywood.'

As always, I admired her confidence. I took her hand and led her to the bar, mentioning that our Hollywood sexual shenanigans were sure to be a first for our august old school.

'Maybe they'll put up a blue plaque in our honour,' Jane grinned.

When I introduced her, I felt for once that I wasn't in her shadow. She needed me. Luckily, Sam and Jez didn't seem to mind. Straight away, I could see Jez was interested. Jane's cleavage was prominently displayed thanks to a push-up bra and his gaze wasn't straying far from there.

Sam saw what was going on and, without warning, took my hand. 'Why don't we disappear?' Then I felt the delicious touch of his other hand on my bum.

****

Next morning, I was having a continental breakfast with Sam in the hotel restaurant. There was no sign of Jez or Jane. I was quiet, waiting for some signal from Sam that he'd enjoyed last night. He was the hottest lover I'd ever had by far. His body was every bit the godlike creation I'd dreamt of. I couldn't believe how energetic he was. He kept putting my body in all sorts of crazy positions and he definitely liked having me on all fours. His tongue seemed laser-guided, hitting every sweet spot. But, by the end, my limbs were sore and exhausted. We'd used up his four-pack of chocolate-flavoured condoms. The whole thing was a kind of ecstatic blur.

Best of all was how he kissed me. He had this way of French-kissing really passionately and then, just when I was almost struggling to breathe, he'd slow down. His kisses became gentle, tender, the most exquisite things you could imagine. All the while he caressed me, and several times he held me so tight it was as if he never wanted to let me go. He made me feel so safe, so loved, so *precious*.

Yet he was indifferent to me now. He hadn't made a single comment about last night and was so distant he was scarcely in the same room. I hated it when men did this to me. I could never work out if it was a deliberate snub, or some 'man thing' where they tried to avoid any acknowledgement that anything intimate had happened.

'I'm going to see a movie at lunchtime,' he said matter-of-factly. '*Prohibition A* – it's about a Manhattan nightclub where all kinds of weird shit happens.'

'Sounds great.' I waited for an invitation that never came. 'Can I tag along?' I held out my hand to take his, but he immediately pulled it out of reach.

'If you want,' he replied.

Why was he being like this?

Jez appeared, minus Jane. Grinning, he said Jane had gone home 'to recover'.

'How was she?' Sam asked.

I couldn't believe he was talking like this in front of me.

Jez didn't miss a beat. 'She was hot. That gal sure knows a few tricks. When she talks dirty, you gotta spend a month cleaning out your ears.'

'Are you going to see her again?'

'Get real.'

Sam looked straight at me. 'Yeah, no girl can expect to get serious with a guy if she sleeps with him way too soon. It's like the worst thing she can do.'

I felt sick.

My mobile phone bleeped and I turned away to read the text that had arrived, trying not to look too tearful. The message was from Jane. It said, 'Out of this world. Can't wait to see Jez again. How was it with Sam?'

14

Droogs

All through the movie, I dwelt on the awful truth – Sam had dumped me after just one night. Jane didn't know it yet, but Jez had done the exact same thing to her. To them, we were just two more groupies sliding notes under toilet cubicles.

Sam's arthouse movie went on for three hours and it was 6 o'clock in the evening when we finally emerged. Sam and Jez, both in hoodies, seemed quite taken by the strange film. I didn't have much to say and let them ramble on about the acting and direction.

They asked me to take them to a bar and I unenthusiastically selected *The Big Blue* – a luxury venue designed to make it seem as if it were a transparent cube suspended in the middle of the Pacific Ocean. Ambient ocean sounds played in the background while on every wall, and even the floor and ceiling, colourful aquatic scenes were projected. It could easily have been naff but somehow it got away with it and you could genuinely believe you were submerged. It probably helped that the owners had employed the services of a prestigious London studio that provided state-of-the-art special effects to Hollywood.

Jez and Sam grudgingly approved of the venue and settled down on a 'coral reef' sofa to drink Hawaiian beer. Keen on getting wrecked as quickly as possible, I gulped down two large glasses of white wine. I felt lost. There had been no word from Mencken and I seemed to be distinctly surplus to requirements. Sam was as distant as he'd been all day. As for Jez, he spent most of his time eyeing up the talent with that unwavering male gaze of his. I wondered how many women he'd slept with and guessed it must run into thousands. I remembered reading somewhere that he'd spent several spells at *The Meadows* rehab clinic in the Arizona desert, being treated for sex addiction. He was obsessed with strippers, lap-dancers and porn stars by all accounts. No surprise there then.

Soon the drinks caught up with me and I was loo bound. When I returned, I noticed three strangers standing at the bar. Strangers? Hardly that. Jez and Sam had left their seats and were lurking near the newcomers. While Jez was laughing, Sam was observing them like a gunfighter. Three beautiful girls were dressed as characters from *A Clockwork Orange*. They had all the great gear from the classic movie: black bowler hats and boots, white shirts, trousers, braces and codpieces. Their eye make-up was spot on too, with the right eye adorned with extravagant false eyelashes. The cocktail they were drinking looked like milk but when I asked later, the bartender said it was a *White Panther*; a mix of rum, vodka and coconut milk. *Yuk*.

The three girls talked in the strange language that had featured in the movie. I strained to listen and I heard something like: 'We gave this devotchka a tolchock on the litso and the krovvy came out of her mouth.' Two words were repeated over and over – lubbilubbing and gulliver. I recalled that 'gulliver' was slang for head. One of the girls began humming Beethoven's Ninth Symphony.

Jez was obviously finding it a hoot, but whenever he tried to start a conversation with the girls, they talked gibberish to shut him up.

'Grahzny bratchny,' they chanted in unison. Then one said, 'Oh my sisters, gullywuts sore. No pretty polly.'

'Listen, girls, you can't fool me,' Jez said. 'I know all about *A Clockwork Orange*. Alex and his droogs, and all that. They spoke some kind of Slavic language, didn't they? Did you know the title comes from a Cockney phrase: *as queer as a clockwork orange*?'

'Oh, my sisters, horrorshow rozz golly crark,' one of the girls said and the other two sniggered.

Sam took me to one side and whispered in my ear. 'Our Oxford stalkers aren't giving up, huh?' He scanned around, as if checking for others.

I understood his concern. These people were showing an unhealthy interest in us and were worryingly well informed about where to find us.

I leaned forward to say something then pulled back, resenting the fact that Sam was suddenly treating me as a confidante after freezing me out all afternoon. On the other hand, maybe there was still a chance for me. 'What are you going to do?' I asked.

'Bring it on.'

'You can't be serious. You don't know these people. It might be dangerous.'

'Exactly.'

Did he want to invent trouble for himself? Was that where I'd gone wrong? – I'd committed the cardinal error of making it too easy.

'We're going to follow them,' he said.

I frowned. He was playing a game and so were they. Trouble was, I wasn't sure it was the same one.

'Do you think that's a good idea? If they're on your case, the last thing you want to do is walk right up to them and tap them on the shoulder.'

'Earth to Sophie,' Sam said, 'Jez and I have saved the world several times over. Haven't you seen any of our movies?' He winked. 'Besides, don't you want to find out what they want with us?'

'I'm in,' Jez said when Sam explained his plan, then sauntered over to the three girls and offered to buy them a drink. Without a word, they put down their White Panthers and left. We waited a few seconds before tailing them.

The girls made their way towards the mansion, humming *Singing in the Rain* as they pretended to kick each other in choreographed slow motion, as in the movie. The same ceremony that we saw before then took place. The glamorous students came out, formed parallel lines and began clapping and cheering one of the girls in particular. Elvis was among them and clearly aware that we were watching, but he gave no sign that he intended to do anything about it.

I remembered Mencken telling me that a *goddess* was in charge of the Oxford students. What if Sam or Jez fell for her? Forget Jez – it was only Sam I cared about. I just couldn't get him out of my head. I was gutted that I'd lost him almost before I'd even had him. Already, I was convinced I was rubbish in bed and that's why I'd been given the boot. Was I too fat? Too inhibited? Didn't know enough bedroom tricks? I mean, I only found out a few weeks ago that 'tea bagging' meant sucking a guy's balls, or, to be more precise, letting him dunk his scrotum in and out of your mouth like, er, a tea bag. It had honestly never occurred to me to do something like that.

I anxiously looked around amongst the students. The girls were all very pretty, but none was what I would call a goddess. I was so relieved.

'Come on,' I said. 'We've seen all this before. Let's go somewhere else. I can get you into a fancy-dress charity ball with wall-to-wall models and debs.'

'We don't want to rain on your, parade,' Jez said, 'but the best party in town is the one going on behind that door.' He jabbed his finger towards the mansion. 'Those dudes are full on and we want some of the action.'

'Yeah,' Sam said, 'forget the tourist junk in that little brochure of yours. Right from the start we said we wanted something wacky. Well, *this* is it.'

'But what game are they playing?' I asked. 'They follow us, but don't let us speak to them. We follow them and they slam the door in our faces.'

The boys shrugged.

'He's your mission impossible,' Jez said. 'We want you to get us an invite to that place. We'll give you a five grand bonus if you can pull it off.'

Inwardly, I sighed, but part of me was intrigued. Could I do something like that from a standing start?

'We want to hear some good news by tomorrow,' Jez said. 'Get on the phone, pull in favours, do whatever needs doing to get us in there tomorrow night.'

'We'll meet you for breakfast tomorrow,' Sam said. 'Don't disappoint us.'

'I'll see what I can do,' I said, but I didn't have a clue where to begin. 'What are you guys doing now?'

Sam winked. 'Some surveillance stuff.'

****

I went back to my apartment. Surveillance? *Fuck.* I was dreading reading about it in the papers the next day. It was vital to find out if these students were serious players. I made calls to all of my contacts and, for the second time, tried to discover if they knew anything about a group of eccentric Oxford University students. This time I was able to add the detail that they were extremely rich and holed up in an amazing mansion in Green Park. Still no joy.

Peter Henson, my murky former business mentor, had put me in touch with a dodgy policeman from the Met a year before – Sergeant Jim McCann, 'a useful guy to know', Henson had told me. And he was right about that.

I'd call him whenever I wanted someone checked out. It's amazing what info you can get from someone inside New Scotland Yard; for a small consideration, of course. He wasn't available when I first called, so I left a message.

He got back to me at around 3 am, after he'd finished his shift. He ruined a lovely dream I'd been having about Sam, so I was a bit tetchy at first. He told me the students had come to the attention of the police on more than one occasion. They called themselves the Top Table.

I pictured the card Sam had swiped from Lawrence Maybury. The gold lettering, the One Button and Top Table references, and that strange quote along the bottom. So, now I'd found out about one of the cryptic statements. They weren't the Millionaires' Death Club after all, it seemed.

McCann said the Top Table was an exclusive drinking and dining club for super-rich Oxford University students. Each summer they made the short journey from Oxford and took up residence in their Green Park mansion. They got themselves involved in all kinds of trouble, but everything was always hushed up thanks to their influential connections. They liked cruel stunts and practical jokes. Humiliating celebrities was their speciality, but their pranks never made the media because they never attempted to publicise them.

I realised the student Mencken had met at the Beverley Hills party wasn't there by accident: he'd been sent on a mission to lure Sam and Jez to London so that the Top Table could play a trick on them. Exactly why was a different matter. I couldn't imagine they'd had any previous contact with Sam. Maybe they were targeting him because he was the ultimate celebrity and therefore probably everything they despised. In a way, I was relieved. There was no doubt in my mind now that these were the people who'd taken out the contract on Sam. If they were nothing more than student jokers there couldn't be anything to fear. Well, except embarrassment.

When I asked McCann if there was any chance of getting two friends and myself an introduction to the group, he laughed.

'Absolutely no chance. They never let in outsiders.'

'We'll see about that,' I said, then cringed as the sergeant laughed even louder.

15

Clues

I slept badly that night, unable to get the Top Table out of my mind. I considered them the worst type of snobs, laughing at everyone, and laughing all the harder when their joke went way over everyone's head. But Lawrence Maybury was dead and there was nothing funny about that.

As I walked into the Sargasso hotel that morning, part of me was certain I couldn't help Sam and Jez with the Top Table. But another part hadn't given up on the fifty grand Mencken had offered for NexS, and the five grand Sam promised for an intro to the Top Table. That was serious money; money I urgently needed. Also, I had professional pride. I felt bad about letting clients down, and it would be like admitting I didn't have much clout in London if I had to confess I'd made no progress. I hadn't worked out if I was going to come clean or plead for more time.

I trudged to the breakfast area, trying not to trip over my long face.

Déjà vu.

Sam and Jez were sitting in exactly the same positions as they had on Royal Ascot day and were again absorbed with what was on the TV. Lying in front of them was an intricately designed, colourful piece of paper that looked like a page from a medieval illuminated manuscript. The marvellously ornate gothic lettering on the page was embellished with bold yellows, greens, blues and reds that appeared to have been painstakingly applied by some ancient monk. I was about to pick it up and read it when Sam spoke.

'You won't believe this. Quick, take a seat.'

On the TV was the same newsreader who'd made the announcement about Lawrence Maybury. The picture switched to an eerie black balloon floating over the Thames.

The newsreader spoke over the pictures: 'In an extraordinary sequel to Thursday's suicide of brilliant Oxford student Lawrence Maybury, his close friend and fellow philosophy student Chloe Sanford has now also been found dead. She was wearing a T-shirt with the words 'Lady Lazarus' printed on it. As with Mr Maybury, two unopened bottles of rare champagne were found lying next to Ms Sanford. An amateur cameraman shot the pictures you are now seeing of the hot-air balloon in which her body was discovered just after dawn this morning. The balloon travelled over twenty miles and was sighted by numerous eyewitnesses before drifting to the ground on farmland in Surrey.

'A note was found on the body. It said: "Lawrence has found the exit from the Lazar House. It's time for me to join him. NexS delivers us all from this prison. *Dying is an art, like everything else. I do it exceptionally well.*"

'Those last words are from the poem *Lady Lazarus* by the American poet Sylvia Plath. Plath, a heroine of Chloe's, gassed herself to death in 1963.'

'That girl,' I blurted, 'isn't she…?'

'Yeah,' Sam said, 'one of the *Clockwork Orange* girls.'

'Listen, two people are dead now. We have to finish with the Top Table right away.'

'But they have NexS,' a voice said from behind me – Mencken.

'You won't *believe* what's been going on,' I said.

He ignored me and picked up the strange parchment. 'What's this?'

I couldn't believe they were all behaving so casually about two deaths.

'Come on, guys. This is serious. What would the papers say if they found out we knew anything about this?'

'Screw the papers,' Sam said. 'Anyway, no one's finding out anything. We're the guys who do the finding.'

'What do you mean?'

Sam nodded at the parchment Mencken was now clutching. 'We found that in the mansion last night.'

'You're not telling me you broke into someone's property?' I spluttered. I looked at Mencken expecting him to be equally outraged, but he seemed intrigued.

'It was easy,' Sam said. 'The mansion has a courtyard at the back. We climbed over the wall and found a tradesmen's entrance.' He grinned. 'The door was a cinch. I learned all about how to pick locks in *The Jericho Conspiracy*.'

'We found the paper lying on a photocopier,' Jez added. 'We'd planned to have a good look around, but we heard noises and got out.'

'You guys are mad,' Mencken said. 'I can't have my stars getting arrested just before we start shooting my picture.'

'We're really into this,' Jez said. 'It's like something from one of our movies, but for real. Besides, you're the one who keeps going on about NexS.'

'I know, but please try to remember who you are and where you are.' As Mencken read the parchment, his eyes widened. 'Wow, this is terrific.' He waved it in the air before handing it to me.

The ornate page was entitled *The Fourth Protocol*. 'Of the gathered,' it said, 'one is selected as the chooser by receipt of the knave of hearts in the dealing of the cards. The chooser selects the Chosen One and presents him with the Substance. The Substance is always contained in a black capsule. The attenuated Substance is always contained in white capsules. In the ceremony, the gathered take the white capsules while the Chosen One receives the black capsule.'

'Are you getting it, Sophie?' Sam asked.

'I'm not getting anything.'

'Here's our theory,' Jez said. 'The mansion in Green Park is the Lazar House. The Substance described in this "Fourth Protocol" is a designer drug of some kind, maybe NexS itself.' His eyes gleamed.

'What about the black and white capsules?'

'Different concentrations,' Sam answered. 'The black is much stronger. The person who takes it has special status. We think Lawrence Maybury was chosen on the first night and Chloe Sanford last night. That ceremony at the mansion is part of it, the moment when someone is made the Chosen One. That's why everyone cheers.'

'So those stunts they do are some sort of initiation or selection ceremony?'

'Yeah, I reckon,' Jez said.

'But why do they kill themselves?' Mencken asked.

'We were thinking about that,' Sam said. 'Maybe once they've taken the black capsule, life is downhill from then on. They check out while they're at the top.'

'A devil's deal, huh?' Mencken remarked. 'The price of ultimate pleasure is death.'

'Only if you take the black capsule,' Sam said.

Mencken gazed at each of us in turn. 'Well, we said we'd go anywhere and pay any price for the perfect high.' He turned to Sam. 'How far are you willing to go?'

'All the way,' Sam responded without hesitation.

I was shocked. Did he really mean that?

Mencken's face betrayed the slightest of smiles. 'If you're not in, you're out, right, Sam?' When he turned to me, I felt queasy. 'Are we *all* in?'

'I don't like this,' I said. I explained what my sergeant friend had told me about the Top Table. I mentioned how the students had got a reputation for targeting celebrities, and my theory that they'd been following us all along, probably luring us into some spectacular prank. I even mentioned the contract on Sam, and the sinister gesture Elvis made in the nightclub.

'It was no accident they came into the Hexenhaus on the first night,' I said, 'no accident they found us at Royal Ascot, and again last night.'

'Well, I don't care,' Sam said. 'We've got the drop on them now.'

'Yeah, fuck their contract,' Jez added. 'We'll take one out on them – but ours will be serious.'

'They're weird intellectuals with a sadistic sense of humour,' I protested. 'You can't second guess people like these.'

'Listen,' Mencken interrupted, 'maybe these people *have* targeted us, but they obviously didn't know we were looking for them anyway. Let's just focus on what I told you before. They're a secret society that performs a pleasure ceremony based on NexS. That's all we're interested in.'

He'd omitted one detail – the goddess. I pictured her as a deadly Siren, luring my men away from me. I prayed I was right that she didn't exist, or that her goddessness was exaggerated.

'They're just like the Skull and Bones secret society at Yale,' Mencken went on.

When he saw that we were staring at him blankly, he explained himself.

'*Skull and Bones* is reserved exclusively for the ultra-rich and powerful,' he said. 'Members are recruited from one place only – Yale University. Many American presidents, CEOs, CIA directors and Supreme Court judges have been members. Membership is for life. Rumour has it that the society practises occult rituals. They see themselves as a super-elite destined to rule the world. In fact three of the last four presidents were Skullsmen.'

For me, that confirmed just how dangerous these people were. 'We should forget we ever heard about the Top Table,' I said.

'No way,' Sam said.

'We've been doing some digging,' Jez said. 'You know the card Sam swiped from Lawrence Maybury, the one that mentioned Hyperboreans? I Googled it.' He pulled a printout from his back pocket. 'Listen to this. The Hyperboreans were a mythical people who lived in a paradise beyond the north wind, where the sun shone twenty-four hours a day and gold lay heaped on the streets. The Greek god Apollo spent his winters there. That line on the card is from a poem by some ancient Greek guy called Pindar.'

'It's a perfection cult,' Mencken commented. 'They're chasing the rainbow. NexS is their passport to paradise.'

'You mean they're all going to kill themselves?' I said.

Before anyone could respond, my mobile phone rang.

Clues

'Hi, Sophie.' It was Sergeant McCann. 'Bit of a coincidence you were asking about the Top Table,' he said. 'I hear the top brass are getting interested in them.'

'What do you mean?'

'You've seen the news, haven't you? The two Oxford students who killed themselves were both members.'

'Yeah, I sort of knew that.'

'Well, here's something else. This case isn't as straightforward as people are making out. Something was found on each body.' He hesitated. 'No one's supposed to talk about it.'

'How much do you want?'

'Five hundred.'

That was twice McCann's usual rate for good snippets, but I agreed.

'OK, here's the thing. Black calling cards with silver writing were found on the bodies…'

I gulped and stepped back from the others.

'This is what the cards said,' McCann stated. '"Congratulations, you have been selected by the Millionaires' Death Club."' He paused. 'You know what that means, don't you?'

I knew, all right. The two deaths weren't suicides. *They were murder.*

And I also knew who else had been given one of those cards.

16

Alphabet Love

Later on that evening, just before midnight, I found myself standing outside the Top Table's mansion with Sam and Jez. I was hoping the revelations about the cards might have changed things, but the others seemed even more intrigued now, and keen to get to the bottom of the whole thing. Mencken insisted that the whole Millionaires' Death Club thing was a Skull-and-Bones-type stunt done purely for effect. Jez, more cautious at first, had eventually agreed.

I was still trying to work out where the Top Table ended and the Millionaires' Death Club began. Were they the same thing? Perhaps a club within a club. As Mencken said, the Millionaires' Death Club might be nothing more than an elaborate joke, but I didn't think so. It was dangerous for the simple reason that two people were dead. The police were certain to begin a serious investigation of the Top Table. Sergeant McCann had implied that much already. Then the media would get hold of the story and if they found out there was a connection with Sam and Jez it would hit front pages all over the world. But there was no talking to them. They were determined to get their hands on NexS. End of.

This evening's cooked-up plan was to wait until dark, knock on the Top Table's front door and then for Sam and Jez to try to use their star status to get us an invite to the 'party'.

As we stood there, I could hear someone playing Beethoven's *Moonlight Sonata* inside the mansion. Sam was staring at the black door, at the huge silver doorknocker. He seemed mesmerised for some reason. Jez ignored the knocker, and loudly rapped on the door. It opened almost immediately. A six feet plus, gaunt young man – surely one of the Oxford students – peered at us. He was dressed casually in a black fleece and stone-coloured combats. With his fair hair and clear blue eyes he was definitely my type, much to my annoyance. Why did I always seem to fancy the wrong guys?

'Who are *you*?' he said in a plummy accent that was several notches up from my own. Eton, I suspected. I'd never quite perfected my Roedean accent, but I could do upper class. Not like this, though. This was pukka posh. The young man peered even more. 'No way,' he said then slammed the door shut.

Jez knocked a second time. The door opened again, more slowly this time.

Sam stepped forward, holding up the Fourth Protocol.

'Where did you get that?' the student snapped.

'We want to talk,' Sam said.

'You know what? You're pissing me off.' He turned round and shouted something I couldn't quite make out. A moment later an even taller student appeared. He had longish, flowing hair and was handsome in that pale, vampiric way so characteristic of elite English public schoolboys. A blond, blue-eyed version of Lord Byron, I thought. Wearing jeans and a white T-shirt, his casual clothes didn't match the arrogant glint in his eyes. There was a whispered conversation and then the newcomer gestured at us to come in. All the time, Beethoven's beautiful music wafted from somewhere further inside. Abruptly, it changed to one of my father's favourite pieces – Liszt's *First Mephisto Waltz*, a virtuoso piano solo. He always claimed it was so difficult that it took a genius to play it properly. He'd never mastered it, but whoever was playing it now certainly had. It was a stunning rendition.

The two students stood there in the large entrance hall, with their arms folded, glaring at us. A spectacular chandelier hung over their heads, a grand staircase behind them and a row of black doors further back, presumably leading to the ground floor's interior rooms. Gloomy paintings of apocalyptic scenes hung on the walls while large, ornate mirrors, full of eerie reflections, were perfectly positioned to capture the strange light being cast by two solid gold Venetian lanterns. My gaze flicked to a couple of marble statues of winged, demonically handsome angels – two of Lucifer's fallen angels, seemingly – and I wondered if they were modelled on the two students.

They were probably a couple of years younger than I was and yet there was something about them that made them seem older, *much* older.

'Well?' the second one asked.

'We want to know – why are you following us?' Jez asked aggressively.

I was amazed that he'd come out and said it so bluntly.

The two students glanced at each other.

'If *we're* following *you*, how come you're standing on our doorstep?' the first one said. 'Logically, you must be following us.'

'Look, we were outside last night and we're intrigued,' Sam said. 'We want to join whatever kind of thing you've got going on here. We'll give you whatever you want.'

'You're not welcome,' the taller man said. 'Our club is particularly exclusive. We accept only the best.'

'The best?' Jez blurted. 'So what the hell are we? Bums?'

'You're dramatis personae, I understand,' the man said, almost spitting with contempt.

'What?'

'Very well – *actors*. Or should I say impersonators.' He stepped forward, towering over Jez. 'Isn't that right? – you do impressions of real people.'

'You don't like our movies, huh?' Sam said quietly.

'You know what,' Jez said, 'for ninety-nine percent of people on this planet it would be the biggest honour of their lives if we showed up on their doorstep.'

'We're the one percent,' the man responded with total disdain. He turned his gaze towards me, giving me a look that suggested I might be something he'd picked up on the sole of his shoe and accidentally tramped into his house. 'I'm asking myself why two American impersonators and their *fluffer* have come to our house and why they're in possession of a stolen document.'

I was immediately indignant. *Fluffer*?

'Shall I call the private security firm, Charles?'

'How about *we* call the *cops*?' Jez said.

'We've just spent two hours answering their plodding questions,' the taller student said, 'and I don't think they'll be anxious to come back for more. Now, I think it's time you left.'

So, the police had shown up, just as I expected. I shuffled nervously.

'These people aren't worth it,' I said. 'Let's get out of here.' I realised I couldn't hear Liszt any longer.

A moment later, one of the rear doors opened. A stunning woman appeared. When I say stunning, I mean…*Jesus*. There was absolutely no doubting who it was – the no-longer-mythical goddess. Shit!

Tall and slim with exquisite high cheekbones, shining skin and a perfect jaw line, this Glamazon sauntered across the hall towards us. Her blonde hair was cut in dramatic spikes, punkish style. Her eyes were an astonishing shade, a kind of electric blue. When she looked at you, it was like having high intensity lasers trained on you. She had a kind of lustrous, supernatural beauty.

Bitch.

Wearing tight blue jeans and a fabulously trendy denim cardigan buttoned at the belly button, it was obvious she had no bra on.

'Now, gentlemen, we don't wish to be rude, do we?' she said in an incredibly posh voice, the plummiest of the lot. 'After all, these men have travelled an *ocean* to see us.' Infuriatingly, she didn't bother to acknowledge my existence. 'And they know something about us,' she continued as she promenaded over to Sam and stopped in front of him. I couldn't help noticing that her fingernails were painted with black varnish. 'What *is* it you think you know?' she purred.

Sam stared, mouth open, and *kept* staring. I knew what that look meant – I was never getting him back. I glanced at Jez. He was just as bad. *Christ Almighty*. Two Hollywood megastars, struck dumb in an instant. I wanted seriously bad things to happen to this woman.

'They know that this is where the action is,' she said, answering her own question. She flashed a heart-stopping smile. 'They want entry to the greatest show on earth.' She patted Sam's cheek as if he were a pet dog. 'Isn't that right, Mr Sam Lincoln?'

'You *know* me?'

'Of course I do. I've seen *all* of your movies.'

'Are you a fan?' he asked, hopefully.

'Hardly. But I *think* you're one of mine,' she said, eyes twinkling.

Sam's eyes were glued to her as she turned round. Her jeans had a rip over the top of her bum. No underwear. Sam's gaze was drawn there as if attracted by the world's most powerful magnets. Jez's too.

Wake up, you clowns, I thought. *You can't be falling for this*. Forget goddess, this woman was a witch, pure and simple.

She hadn't finished her introduction. 'As you always like to say, Sam – if you're not in, you're out. That's right, isn't it?' She turned round again. 'You want to be in, don't you? You have to know the secret.' Her smile was lethally alluring. 'You'll die if you don't.'

Sam stared back, smitten beyond repair as far I could tell. Jez too.

'Oh *dear*, our glittering stars are tongue-tied,' the witch said. 'No scriptwriters, you see. No one to put the words in their mouths.'

'Shut up,' I yelped.

'Aha,' the witch said, 'an intervention from the loyal *secretary*. Did you know the word derives from the Latin *secretus* meaning "secret"? So, *secretary*, are you holding secrets, or are the secrets holding you?'

'Get over yourself.' It wasn't a clever reply but I felt better for it.

The witch smiled and turned to Sam. 'You're here because your greatest desire is to join us. There's nothing you wouldn't give to make it happen.'

Sam didn't contradict her.

'Well, here's a challenge for you, *Sam Lincoln*.' She smiled, her eyes twinkling. 'We'll let you join the Top Table. All you have to do is work out how to do it. You have all the facts at your disposal. Just put the jigsaw together.'

I didn't think Sam was capable of speaking given how beguiled he was.

Eventually he roused himself, but only managed to say, rather feebly, 'You think you're so clever, don't you?'

I watched as the witch deliberately moved slinkily towards Jez, giving him an übersultry smile.

'I *know* so.' She held Jez in her gaze while speaking to Sam. 'The question is, *are you*?'

'Who the hell do you think you are?'

'Why, I'm all your dreams come true.' She put her hand on Jez's muscular arm, and his eyes sparkled with triumph.

'You're nothing special,' Sam grunted, shuffling forward as he futilely tried to make her look at him. 'Marlon Brando said a woman's "honour" is half an inch from where she shits from. Don't ever forget that.' He flashed an angry glance at Jez.

'But that half inch is *everything*, isn't it, Mr Lincoln?' the witch retorted. 'You know as well as I do that it might as well be a thousand miles. Or *infinity*.'

I was flabbergasted by how cool she was.

Sam just gazed at her, a helpless snake fatally mesmerised by its cruel charmer.

'Oh, I haven't properly introduced myself yet, have I?' she said teasingly. 'My name's Zara.' She paused. '*That's Zara with a Z.*'

17

Pictures

The only subject I really enjoyed at school was art. It took me away from the dreary voices of the teachers and transported me to other worlds, just like my magic bus. Sometimes, I went to Sotheby's to watch art auctions. There was something about that whole process that fascinated me – the buying and selling of beauty, of human imagination. Mostly I went to art galleries. After all the goings on of last night, I was in need of an art overdose, so I headed for one of London's finest art havens – the National Portrait Gallery off Trafalgar Square.

After our encounter with Zara – the supreme bitch of the worldwide grand bitches' coven as far as I was concerned – everything had gone crazy. Jez had crowed gleefully about Alphabet Love. The winner would be the one who slept with Zara, and that was obviously going to be him.

'Did you see the way she touched my muscles?' he had bragged. 'Man, that babe's so hot the frigging sun can't keep up.'

Sam was having none of it and insisted Zara was interested only in him. That's why she'd given him the challenge and not Jez. If he succeeded, she'd sleep with him, he was certain. I felt so small when he said that. I pretended not to care but I was miserable. There was no chance of him coming back to me now – not unless I could get Zara out of the picture just as fast as she'd entered it.

I couldn't believe how a brief encounter with this woman had got both men so frothed up. They were more like teenagers than world famous seducers. I read somewhere that it takes us just four or five minutes to form an enduring opinion of any new person we meet. With Zara, apparently, it took less than a second to turn Sam and Jez into her dribbling slaves.

I was disgusted with the whole thing. OK, jealous too. Who wouldn't want to look like Zara? Not just the looks either. So well bred, so smart, so sassy. Above all, she had a kind of aloof coolness, or was it cool aloofness, that, annoyingly, intrigued even me.

So, what now? I needed Mencken's fifty grand to relieve my financial worries. That meant getting NexS from the Top Table. If Sam *did* pass Zara's test and was allowed to join the Top Table, maybe they'd give it to him free. Then Mencken wouldn't pay me a penny. But somehow I felt membership of the Top Table wasn't the whole story. I was convinced there was another, deeper layer – the Millionaires' Death Club.

Whatever the case, I couldn't believe that only a small group of Oxford students had access to NexS. Others had to know about it.

Occasionally, some of my clients asked if I could get them designer drugs and I'd discovered that almost anything could be had in Brixton or Camden Town, for the right price. Could my contacts help me now in my hour of need?

That morning I'd gone south of the Thames to Brixton, but none of the dealers had ever heard of NexS. Some thought I was playing a dumb joke and one just about threatened me for wasting his time.

Then things took a distinctly weird turn. Big Pat, a major drug dealer originally from Glasgow, called me on my mobile when he heard I'd been asking about NexS. I'd done business with him on a couple of occasions, but he had one of those scary Scottish accents that made me anxious to stay out of his way. In ten minutes, he was there in front of me. Wearing his trademark green-and-white-hooped Celtic football strip, he took me into an Irish bar, sat me down and bought me a double Glenfiddich. Like Mencken, he wasn't the sort who wasted time asking me to choose what I'd like to drink. The whisky was so strong it made my whole body shake. *Yukeo max.*

He said that if I discovered anything about NexS I was to pass on the info to him immediately. This was becoming surreal. Not only did I know nothing about NexS, I was now being asked by others to pass my non-information on to them.

Big Pat claimed NexS was the Holy Grail of drugs, describing it as one of the *Four Riders*. I wasn't wrong in thinking that he was referring to the Four Riders of the Apocalypse.

Big Pat said that a Nazi scientist in the Second World War had discovered a set of four extraordinary linked drugs. They belonged to a new class of drugs called transpathics that apparently allowed users to have direct access to others' feelings. The Nazi scientist hadn't been able to manufacture them in any significant quantities and it was thought that none of these experimental drugs had survived the war.

Big Pat admitted he didn't know whether the whole thing was an urban myth. What he did know was that if NexS were real then whoever supplied it would become rich beyond dreams. And he intended to become that person.

I told him that if I heard anything, he'd be next in line. Secretly, I thought his story was bonkers. Surely NexS, if it actually existed, was a brand new designer drug, not something from the dark ages. It was hard to believe Big Pat had swallowed such a whopper, but I guess anyone can be suckered.

So, back to the drawing board. Maybe I should seek out chemistry students at UCL; see if they'd heard anything about a miraculous new drug. What about consulting a private investigator? Man, I was getting desperate.

Around lunchtime, Sergeant McCann phoned me to say that autopsies on both suicide victims had revealed no signs of anything indicating foul play. Both had died from heart failure after swallowing a capsule of atropine. There were no marks on the bodies, no traces of illicit substances other than the seemingly self-administered poison that killed them. McCann explained that atropine was a commonly used poison centuries ago, but was hardly seen nowadays. Apparently it could cause delirium and maybe that could account for the tone and intensity of the suicide notes. The police had interviewed every member of the Top Table and there was no evidence of anyone else being involved. As far as the authorities were concerned, the case was closed.

Was there really no trace of anything unusual in the bodies? What about the reference to the Substance in the Fourth Protocol? But if they didn't have a test for something then they weren't likely to find it, right?

I needed to take my mind off the whole puzzle for a while, and wandering around an art gallery was the closest I ever got to meditation. I pushed through the revolving doors of the National Portrait Gallery and picked up a brochure from the desk.

I always found it relaxing to stare at people's faces in paintings and wonder what quality the artist was trying to capture or the image the subject was hoping to project.

As I walked through one of the rooms, lost in my own little world, I abruptly froze. The breath left my lungs and I wondered if I was seeing things. I hurried over and stared at one of the pictures. *Not possible*. But there was no mistake: looking back at me was a face I recognised instantly.

Wearing a breathtaking blood-red dress and a black choker was none other than the grand witch herself, her head crowned by a dazzling diamond-studded tiara. Underneath the portrait, it said: 'Lady Zara Hamilton, painted on the occasion of her twenty-first birthday.'

I stared at it, flabbergasted. *Lady Zara Hamilton*?

'Well, well,' a voice whispered in my ear. I spun round and there was the student who'd first opened the door to us at the mansion last night.

'Christ, you startled me.' I used my hand to fan my face, sure I was turning red.

'I didn't introduce myself yesterday. I'm Marcus Gorman. You're Sophie York, of course. I saw you on that charming TV show a while back.' He was several inches taller than me and was almost literally looking down his nose at me.

My forced smile was so half-hearted it was probably dribbling off the side of my face.

'You took us by surprise turning up on our doorstep like that,' he said.

'Did you have to be quite so rude?'

'It's part of the game.'

'The game?'

He smiled and took a step towards Zara's picture. 'The mansion belongs to her, of course. It's been in the family for generations. We stay with her for a few weeks each summer.'

'Are you going to explain this Lady Hamilton thing?'

'She intrigues you, doesn't she? Everyone falls under her spell. I guess it's in her genes.'

'What is?' I sniffed.

'Come off it. You can see her natural authority, the way people are willing to follow her. It's all there in the portrait, isn't it?'

'Where do genes come in?'

'Zara's father is Earl Brigham and her grandfather Viscount Catesby. She can trace her family tree all the way back to James II. She's the rightful heir to the throne if you ignore the so-called Glorious Revolution.'

'The rightful heir to the *throne*?' I blurted. No, Marcus was spinning a yarn. Hadn't he just told me that he and his friends were playing a game?

'Very clever,' I said, smiling. 'This is one of your scams. You planted this picture, didn't you?'

'I beg your pardon?'

'You put this portrait on the wall yourself. The attendant's probably in on it with you. Did you slip him fifty?'

Marcus stared down at me. 'I don't care for your opinions. If you think this is a fake why don't you try removing it and see what happens?'

When I did nothing, he sneered.

'Zara's a remarkable woman,' he said after a moment. 'Every man who meets her falls for her. Even your Hollywood friends.'

There was a telltale wistfulness in his voice.

'And what about you?' I asked.

'I got over it.' He glanced away. 'There was no chance she was ever going to be interested in me. She only goes for…'

'What?'

'*Hyperanthropos*,' he said at last.

'And they are…?'

'I suppose "supermen" would be the more familiar term.'

'Like Sam and Jez?'

'They're pathetic *little* men,' he snorted. 'The only surprise about them is that they occasionally dare to venture out without their protective carapace of helpers. I assume they're normally surrounded by an entourage of long-tongued cheerleaders, personal assistants and arse-wipers, not to mention the back-slappers, assorted flunkies and ego massagers.'

Whoa, bitter or what? 'But Zara rates them, doesn't she?' I said. 'Or at least she sees them as more worthy suitors than most.'

No response.

'So, why is she giving them a hard time?' I tried again.

Gazing at her portrait, Marcus mumbled, 'A terrible beauty is born.' He walked away then turned and gestured to me to follow him. I hesitated.

'Don't you want to see Zara's favourite painting?' he asked.

My curiosity got the better of me and I set off to follow. What sort of painting would someone like that enjoy? We left the National Portrait Gallery and went round the corner to the National Gallery. In silence, we walked through several rooms before Marcus came to a halt.

'Voila.' He indicated a large canvas.

It was a famous Titian entitled *Bacchus and Ariadne*. I'd seen it several times, but it had never done much for me and still didn't.

'I believe it's the subject matter rather than the artistry that interests her,' Marcus said.

I couldn't remember much about the story of Ariadne, but Marcus promptly obliged. Ariadne was the princess in the story about Theseus slaying the Minotaur in the Labyrinth. She gave him the golden thread that let him find his way out. She thought they were in love, but having taken her to the island of Naxos, Theseus seduced her before callously dumping her. The god Bacchus found her there, fell in love and wed her.

I wondered what personal resonance it had for Zara. Did some guy ditch her, leaving her heartbroken until she found someone much better, or did she have no interest in mortals, only in gods? Frankly, I couldn't imagine Zara with a broken heart. She'd be the one who did any breaking.

'Do you agree with Francis Bacon that it's the task of the artist to return the onlooker to life more violently?' Marcus asked.

I shrugged and looked again at the painting. 'Why do you think she likes it so much?'

Marcus seemed to hesitate. 'Bacchus is the god of intoxication.' There was a curious look in his eye. 'He makes people go mad.'

'What are you saying?'

'I've said too much already.'

'What about your two friends, Lawrence and Chloe? Did they kill themselves? Why so dramatic? Why the unopened champagne bottles?'

I think I saw a flicker of doubt – or regret – cross Marcus's face, but it quickly passed. 'Everyone needs a drink on their final journey, don't they? Did you know that Chekhov's doctor prescribed him champagne on his deathbed?'

I frowned. All I knew about Chekhov was that he was a dead Russian who wrote plays.

'Chekhov smiled,' Marcus went on, 'drained the glass and said, "It's been a long time since I last had champagne." Then he died. The perfect way to take your leave of this world, don't you think?'

'So Lawrence and Chloe's champagne was deathbed champagne?'

'Only the best will do for us. Zara bought a caseload recovered by divers from a sunken ship in the Baltic. It dates back to the early 1800s.'

Already, I knew that was a 'Zara' thing to do. Always a touch of the dramatic.

As we made our way towards the exit, Marcus mentioned that his favourite painter was Caravaggio. 'I love the way he handles light and dark. He had a dramatic private life that Bacon described as a "gilded gutter life". What an epitaph, huh?' There was a far-away look in his eyes. '*The Raising of Lazarus*,' he said. 'That's his masterpiece. It's so appropriate.'

'For what?'

No answer.

'Do you think Sam Lincoln has the nerve to play the game?' he asked eventually. 'Zara says he'll surprise us.'

'You haven't told me what the game is yet.'

Marcus glanced at his watch. 'It's been interesting chatting to you, Sophie.' He gazed down at me. 'I doubt we'll meet again. *Goodbye*.'

18

The Great Gatsby

My blouse was clinging to me thanks to the sweat rolling down my back. I think my make-up had begun to melt. The afternoon had turned into the hottest day of the year. I made my way back to the Sargasso, convinced it was no accident Marcus had found me in the gallery. Was I supposed to go running back to Sam and let him know Zara was royalty? And what did Marcus mean by that final comment of his? Was he suggesting one of us wouldn't be around for much longer? I wondered if I should go to *Captain Toper Records* and try to get John Adams to explain about the contract, but he'd probably deny all knowledge of it. Or had I swallowed too many paranoia pills?

I was furious that a bunch of arrogant Oxford students were having a laugh at our expense. They wanted to humiliate Hollywood's brightest stars, with me as collateral damage. Even worse, we were actively helping them.

When I reached the hotel, I went straight to Sam's room, knocked and said it was me. The door opened, and I heard Sam saying I could come in, but I couldn't see him.

'What are you doing?' I asked when I realised he was standing behind the door.

When he stepped out, I gasped. Wearing an immaculate cream suit, a pale pink shirt and silver silk tie, he was Jay Gatsby reincarnated. His shoes were covered with stylish black and white spats. My eyes tracked back to his gorgeous face. I stood there opened-mouthed, sucking in every feature.

'Wow, you look fabulous.' Having seen him dressed so casually so often, I was almost orgasmic seeing him like this.

'You like?'

'I *like*,' I purred, attempting to sexily sashay closer. 'If you're all dressed up you must be going somewhere.'

'I've worked it all out. It's simple, really,' he said, excitedly.

Ah, not for me then; all for the witch's benefit. My body sagged. I felt like *Frumpelstiltskin*.

'Here's how it works,' he said. 'If you want to join the Top Table you have to go through an initiation ceremony. You recreate a scene from a movie. Those guys with the cakes – my guess is that was in some old English movie. As for the *Clockwork Orange* girls, we've all seen the film. So, my idea is to do a scene from *The Great Gatsby*.' He rubbed his chin. 'Only one person is initiated at a time. Two others have to be witnesses. That's why we saw three people each time and why only one of them got the cheers at the mansion.'

It made sense, I suppose. 'Who are your witnesses going to be?'

'I was just getting ready to make the arrangements when you knocked.' Sam smiled and held up the card he'd swiped from Lawrence Maybury. 'Remember this?' He pointed at the phone number on the card. 'I'll ring this and ask for two witnesses to come along and watch me do my stuff.' He picked up his mobile phone from the table and tapped in the number. 'You know who this is,' he said firmly after a moment. 'I'll be at the south side of Green Park at eight o'clock tonight. I want my two witnesses ready and waiting.' He winked at me and put the mobile down.

'Result,' he said then went to the window and stared out. 'Those bastards thought I was a no-brain jackass. Who's laughing now, motherfuckers?'

He snatched up a grey fedora hat and a pair of old-style sunglasses from a side-table. 'I have to go and collect something. I'll see you later.' He snapped his fingers. 'Don't forget, eight pm – you can watch all the fun.'

I wanted to tell him what Marcus had revealed about Zara, but he obviously wasn't in a listening mood.

'I'll show *her*,' he said. 'There's only one class act in this town and that's me.'

'She's got under your skin, hasn't she?'

'That bitch thinks she's "A No.1" with that fat ass of hers.'

I smiled feebly, but if Zara's ass was fat, what did that make mine? I wanted to shake Sam and make him tell me exactly what he was thinking about Zara. Was he angry with her because he was in love with her? Or was she just an überconquest, with no real purpose except to help him prove he was better than Jez?

'What about Jez?' I asked. 'Where is he?'

'Haven't seen him. Don't need him.'

'Do you think you'll win Alphabet Love?'

'That rich ho can't get enough of me. I'll fuck her right up that posh English ass of hers, the bitch.'

I was shocked by how crude Sam had become.

He stared at himself in the mirror. 'Boy, are you looking good, my friend.' He grabbed some breath freshener and sprayed it into his mouth then pointed me towards the door. 'Let's rock and roll.'

Watching him step out of the room, all I could think of was what had happened to Jay Gatsby at the end of *The Great Gatsby*. I pictured Gatsby floating face down, dead, in his swimming pool, destroyed by the fatally alluring woman he loved so much. *Don't go near any swimming pools, Sam,* I mouthed as I followed him out.

19

Old Sport

He was signalling to me. I squinted across the park and tried to work out who it was; my eyesight isn't the greatest. Seconds later, he was close enough for me to recognise him: Marcus Gorman. He'd changed into white jeans and a black T-shirt. The man beside him wore the exact opposite: black jeans and white T-shirt. I realised the second man was the other obnoxious student we'd met at the mansion, the Byron wannabe. I figured that if anyone could hope to match Zara, he was the one. He had that same super-arrogant vibe, and he even looked quite similar. With their blonde hair and piercing blue eyes, those two would be invited right to the front of the queue of the Aryan Master Race.

'I thought you said we wouldn't be seeing each other again,' I said as Marcus approached.

'That call from your Mr Lincoln…it changed things.'

'We weren't introduced yesterday,' Marcus's companion said. 'I'm Charles Leddington.' He nodded with cold politeness.

I shook his hand and felt myself recoiling at the clammy touch. I hadn't liked him yesterday and not a thing had changed.

'So, is Mr Hollywood going through with this?' Leddington asked. 'Zara said he would, but I can't believe he's that dumb.'

'What do you mean?'

'There are some games you should play only if you know what's at stake.'

'And what *is*?'

'That's him now.' Marcus pointed at a fabulous old car motoring along the road. It was the Franklin coupe from our day at Royal Ascot.

'Nice car,' Leddington said grudgingly.

We watched as the car made its way towards us, with Sam in the passenger seat waving at all the passers-by and tourists gawping at the car.

'Neat, huh?' he shouted at me through the open window as the chauffeur parked. He jumped out and strolled over with supreme Hollywood cool.

'So, it's you two again.' He shook hands with Marcus and Leddington. 'How am I doing so far?'

Leddington said nothing but Marcus nodded. 'Not bad.'

'That's just swell, *old sport*,' Sam said in a mock Oxford University accent. He went back to the car and grabbed something from the back seat: a stack of beautiful silk shirts in various colours. Leddington scowled at Marcus.

Sam approached some of the people standing around his car and offered them a free shirt. Most accepted while a few politely declined. With two shirts left, he tried his luck with two pretty girls sitting in bikinis on deck chairs at the edge of the park, absorbing the last of the day's sunshine.

'Help me out here, dolls.' He handed a shirt to each of them. 'Give these to your boyfriends.

The two girls giggled and one of them said, 'Is this one of those hidden camera things?'

'This is a free shirt,' Sam responded, deadpan. 'Just a gift from a Yank, that's all.'

One of the girls nudged the other and squinted at Sam. 'You're a dead ringer for Sam Lincoln.'

'I get that all the time,' Sam said, winking, 'but I'm much better looking.'

The girls giggled, accepted the shirts and watched curiously as Sam returned to the car.

After a whispered conversation between Sam and the chauffeur, the car drove off. Sam rejoined us, carrying a book he'd retrieved from the glove compartment. In pristine condition, it looked like a collector's book, maybe a first edition.

'This is a fake,' Leddington said when Sam gave it to him.

Sam smirked. '*And*?'

Marcus snatched the book from Leddington. 'Look, you can tell no one has ever opened it. It's perfect.'

I smiled as I realised how clever Sam had been. In *The Great Gatsby*, Gatsby possessed dozens of beautiful silk shirts that he never wore. He had a library of expensive books that he never read; they were all untouched, the pages never opened. They might as well have been fake for all the use they were.

'Do I pass the test?' Sam asked as Leddington flicked through the blank pages of the phoney book.

Leddington hesitated for a moment then reluctantly nodded.

Marcus slapped Sam on the back. 'Well done, old sport.'

That was something Gatsby liked to say, claiming to have picked it up when he was studying at Oxford University of all places. How appropriate.

'I'm not surprised you chose Gatsby,' Leddington remarked. 'After all, he was a conman, a bootlegger, and a scammer.' He sniggered. 'Let's see now – an opportunist fake, living in a counterfeit world. I guess Gatsby's life reminded you of Hollywood, a bad simulation of reality?'

'Brideshead, actually,' Sam shot back.

Marcus burst out laughing. 'Touché.' He gave Leddington a nudge.

'You must agree that Gatsby was a curious man,' Leddington rasped. 'He threw parties he never attended. He watched from a distance, hoping a certain beautiful woman would show up.' He practically snarled his next remark. 'Are you waiting for a certain beautiful woman, Mr Lincoln?'

Sam's mouth opened, but nothing came out.

'Gatsby's beautiful woman destroyed him in the end,' Leddington said. 'She drove a fatal yellow car.' He gestured towards where Sam's antique car had been parked. 'We're all making fatal journeys, aren't we?'

When we reached the mansion, Leddington rudely stopped me at the gate. Then he ushered Sam towards the great black door and told him to knock.

I glumly watched from behind the iron railings as the door opened and the strange honour parade took place once more. Sam received the usual applause and cheers, but I could tell he was desperately searching for Zara. There was no sign of her. A deliberate snub? Sam didn't seem at all euphoric; subdued, if anything. He trudged inside and the door slammed shut.

I stood there on my own, fighting back tears. I felt so lonely. Did this mean it was over? I turned and walked away. I couldn't help thinking that the last two people who had enjoyed that honour parade were now dead, but surely Sam couldn't be in danger. Not a Hollywood superstar. *Surely*. I felt sick and fanned my face.

I had only taken a few steps when the door opened again and I heard Marcus's voice.

'Sophie, where do you think you're going?'

20

The Toast

I couldn't believe I was inside. We'd spent so much time working out how to do it that it was absurd that, finally, I'd simply been invited in.

Outside, it was warm and bright, but in here the opposite. I shivered. Every object in the entrance hall cast long, creepy shadows. Marcus seemed to be studying me as I stood there. I was unsure what to do with myself. Everyone else had disappeared and I had the ridiculous idea they were playing hide-and-seek with me.

'I suppose you'd like the guided tour,' Marcus said with a smile, his voice transformed into a baritone by the hall's acoustics. He started by showing me the ground-floor rooms. Each one had a small plaque describing its function: *Morning Room*, *Library*, *Ante Room*, *Palm Room*, *Painted Room*, *Dining Room* and so on. The *Music Room* was dominated by a magnificent grand piano. Each room looked as elegant as any in England's finest stately homes. The furniture and décor were mostly based, so Marcus told me, on the designs of Charles Rennie Mackintosh. 'He championed the Art Nouveau style, of course,' Marcus said. 'It works fantastically well, don't you think?'

I nodded politely. I loved Mackintosh's famous chairs, but I wasn't sure if he was also the inventor of the waterproof raincoat, or if I'd got completely the wrong person. I felt too embarrassed to ask.

I gave a feeble smile then scuttled away, hoping to drag Marcus to the Great Hall, the room I most wanted to see. When I reached the door, he stopped me.

'*Later.*' He put his hand against the small of my back and steered me towards the grand staircase. 'The mansion has one forbidden room,' he announced, leading me up the steps to the upper floor.

When I asked which one, he shook his head.

Upstairs, all of the main rooms were magnificently grand bedrooms, all ensuite and with sumptuous four-poster beds. Each room contained a large painting showing a scene from the notorious adventures of the *Hell-fire Club*. When Jane and I got drunk at Roedean one night – our first contact with alcohol, actually – we fantasised about setting up a girls-only version of the club. We knew all about Sir Francis Dashwood and the obscene ceremonies his club conducted at Medmenham Abbey. The Top Table's paintings, full of ravishing nudes and rakish men, showed all the debauchery in graphic detail. I suspected the Top Table had provided the models for the figures in the paintings.

The only room I wasn't shown was the one in the far left-hand corner. From its position, it clearly commanded a superb view over Green Park. I was desperate to find out what was in there.

'At least, tell me why it's forbidden,' I asked as Marcus attempted to lead me the opposite way.

He gazed at me, the light from a stained-glass window laying oblongs of colour over his face, making him resemble a jigsaw man. Beckoning me to follow, he strode towards the prohibited room, halting outside its black-varnished door. It had a small silver plaque on it, engraved with a Latin motto: *Sunt lacrimae rerum et mentem mortalia tangunt.*

Immediately, I remembered that odd phrase from Lawrence's suicide note.

'It's a quotation from Virgil's *Aeneid*,' Marcus explained. Speaking almost in a whisper, he translated. '*These are the tears of things, and the stuff of our mortality cuts us to the heart*.'

'This is Zara's room, isn't it?'

'You can feel it, can't you?' Marcus said.

'Feel what?'

He slapped his hand onto my arm. 'Don't worry, those words get to everyone.'

'Is that why Zara chose them?'

'It's her bedroom. No one's allowed in, unless she invites them.' I noticed that his hand was trembling. 'It's time to get ready,' he said.

'For what?'

He smiled and took me to a small room that appeared to be a cloakroom. Reaching into a wardrobe, he handed me several items: a dark suit, a white shirt, white waistcoat and white silk tie. It seemed it was a requirement of Top Table events that everyone had to wear this 'uniform'.

Marcus stood there watching me, the nerves he'd shown outside Zara's door gone. Did he expect me to strip in front of him? He seemed to read my mind and pointed at a two-fold Japanese screen.

I went behind it and started changing. I was distractedly gazing at the beautiful designs on the screen when I started to squint and saw that they formed part of a bigger picture. When I peered hard, I thought I could make out the faint image of a butcher chopping sausages. Slowly I realised what it really was: a Samurai warrior disembowelling himself.

The Toast

I hastily finished dressing and queasily stepped away from the screen.

'What do you think?' Marcus directed me towards an antique, full-length mirror.

I tried to forget the horrific image I'd just seen. Gazing at myself, I was convinced I looked different. My eyes were darker, my face more gaunt. I wondered if crossing the threshold of this mansion altered people in some strange way. I started to button up my waistcoat but Marcus stopped me.

'No buttons,' he said, before explaining the Top Table's rules regarding the waistcoats. Every member or guest was obliged to wear one on formal occasions. Guests weren't allowed to do up any buttons. Anyone who had been invited to join the Top Table could do up one button, those who'd passed the initiation two buttons and senior members all three. As a guest, I wasn't entitled to any buttons, but Sam, having passed the initiation, was now a fully-fledged two-button man.

'OK, I guess I'm ready,' I said.

Marcus took my hand and I was surprised to feel some warmth there. 'Come on, let's eat.'

As we headed for the staircase, I realised there were many more members of the Top Table than there were bedrooms. When I asked if all the students slept in the mansion, Marcus said there was a large cellar area. Half of it had been given over to the Top Table's extensive wine collection, a state-of-the-art kitchen, various storage facilities for food and so forth, while the rest had been turned into a dormitory like something from a particularly Spartan public school. All the no-button, one-button and two-buttons slept there. The luxury upper rooms were reserved exclusively for the senior members.

Marcus escorted me downstairs again. When we reached the door of the Great Hall, he stopped and put a white glove on his right hand. 'On special occasions, we dine in here rather than the Dining Room,' he said. He knocked on the door and a moment later it swung open. A pony-tailed girl wearing a black designer blouse and matching trousers silently welcomed us in.

We stepped into a huge, plush room with a gleaming wooden floor and spectacular vaulted roof. A long oak table set for an elaborate meal took pride of place in the centre, a crystal chandelier overhanging it. About twenty gorgeous-looking men and women dressed in identical style to me were seated at the table. They were like supermodels and sparkled as if their skin were covered with an exquisitely fine layer of cut diamond.

Six waiting staff, dressed like the girl at the door, were standing in a neat row behind the table, watching attentively.

Seated next to the head of the table was Sam, wearing the regulation Top Table uniform and looking at home amongst the other shining people. He waved at me and I smiled back.

It was when I looked at the paintings on the walls that my mood changed.

'They make you feel more alive, don't they?' Marcus whispered.

'But they're all about death,' I said, '*every one of them*.'

'That's the point.'

We walked slowly round the room, Marcus allowing me time to study the silver nameplates beneath the paintings. They gave the artist's name, the title and the year the original was completed. As I read each one, I felt increasingly uneasy. *The Death of Chatterton* by Wallis was the first painting, followed by the *Burial of Count Orgaz* by El Greco then *Expulsion from Paradise* by Masaccio.

Marcus said that Zara had paid a young artist fifty thousand pounds to paint the reproductions. Other paintings in the collection were *Pieta* by Botticelli, *Last Judgment* by Signorelli, *Crucifixion* by Grunewald, *Death of St Bonaventure* by Zurburan, *Death of Sardanapalus* by Delacroix, *Salome with the Head of St. John the Baptist* by Caravaggio.

The final painting was *Death of Marat* by David. Marcus said it was his favourite. 'It's almost erotic,' he commented. 'Look at how the light bathes Marat's naked body. It makes him so beautiful, like a lover, though in reality he was hideously ugly with a debilitating skin condition. It's as if David is showing death as a sensuous, orgasmic experience.'

I turned away, repulsed.

'It doesn't take much to make you uncomfortable, does it?' Marcus said as he showed me to the seat opposite Sam.

I couldn't argue with that. I was acutely aware of all the others peering at Sam and me. Half way down the table, staring intently, was blond Elvis.

Everyone stopped speaking. The waiting staff stood to attention and the members of the Top Table got up from their seats. I followed everyone's gaze to see Zara gliding into the room. She wore a suit like my own, except in her case it fitted perfectly, and her waistcoat was fully buttoned. Taking her seat at the head of the table, she nodded politely at Sam and me while everyone else resumed their seats.

Scores of candles were lit as the chandelier lights were turned off. In the shadows and flickering light, the waiting staff busied themselves with serving the food. Marcus whispered that a nine-course meal had been prepared.

A man in a white tunic announced in a booming voice what we would be having. 'Sabayon of Pearl Tapioca with Kumamoto Oysters and Iranian Ossetra Caviar,' he said, 'followed by terrine of fresh duck foie grois with cooked apples and quinces. Savoy cabbage soup with braised chestnuts, Granny Smith apple charlotte and caraway mousse, followed by celeriac with grated black winter truffles. Mango pâte de fruit and sweet garden cilantro sorbet, followed by grilled Scottish lobster with frisée salad. Young pigeon with head on, feathers and feet off and gut out, followed by pig's trotter braised in red wine, accompanied by cubes of whale meat. For dessert, we have milk chocolate crémeux with hazelnut streusel and poached Asian pears accompanied by hot whisky cream and frozen blueberries. Assorted friandises and gourmandises are also available.'

'We enjoy the services of *Tmolos's* ex-head chef,' Zara said to Sam when the announcer had finished. 'He was the one who got it its third Michelin star. We doubled his salary, halved his hours, gave him the best kitchen in the world and told him to create the finest food humankind has ever enjoyed. He hasn't disappointed.'

The announcer then assumed the role of sommelier and listed which wines had been provided from the cellar; five bottles of each, some sixty in total, displayed on a side table.

'Château Lafite Rothschild Pauillac 1996,' he intoned, 'Château Margaux 1995; Château Haut Brion Pessac-Léognan 1982; Château Mouton Rothschild Pauillac 1986; Château La Mondotte Saint-Emilion 1996; Haut Brion 1982; Château Valandraud Saint-Emilion 1995; Château Latour Pauillac 1990; Château Le Pin Pomerol 1999; Pétrus Pomerol 1998; Dom Romanée Conti 1997.' He coughed before introducing the final offering. 'Pétrus 1947' he said, as if he were praying in the Sistine Chapel.

'Bring me all of the Pétrus '47,' Zara said, snapping her fingers. She smiled at Sam and me. 'You must let me treat you to the wine of the gods.'

I knew a bottle of Pétrus 1947 could easily cost over ten thousand pounds. Just how rich *was* Zara?

There was an awkward silence as the sommelier poured our wine. Sam seemed tongue-tied and I wasn't any better. Zara told us not to start drinking until she said so.

'Perhaps you'd like to hear about this corner of London,' she said to Sam, before launching into a potted history of Green Park. I realised I knew none of its history even though I lived so near. Apparently, it was once part of Henry VIII's hunting grounds, and in the seventeenth century Charles II made it into a royal park.

'This was the favourite haunt of duellists in the eighteenth century,' Zara went on. 'Then the balloonists made it their base of operations. It was also famous for firework displays. Handel wrote a special piece of music for one particular event.'

It got the name Green Park, she explained, because in the beginning there were acres of grass, but no flowers and, even now, centuries later, there were precious few plants.

Policemen and security guards were always in evidence because of the proximity of Buckingham Palace and other royal residences.

It occurred to me that the reason Zara lived so close to the royal family was that she wanted to keep an eye on the 'usurpers', as she no doubt regarded them. I half expected her to refer to herself as Princess Zara, perhaps even as Queen Zara I. The footpath outside her front door was called *Queen's Walk* of all things. How appropriate. She probably imagined that if she surrounded herself with enough queenly things, she'd become one.

While Zara spoke, Sam's expression didn't change. It was obvious he wasn't listening to her, just staring at her blue eyes and sensuous lips. Even my eyes lingered too long on her whenever I looked her way. I wanted eyes like hers – eyes that could freeze men – and lips like hers – lips that would scorch their hearts.

Her eyes suddenly sparkled like sunlight on water and those lips parted to reveal her perfect white teeth. I'd never seen such a seductive smile.

'I haven't congratulated you yet, Mr Lincoln,' she said. 'There were doubters, but I knew you'd come through.' She leaned towards him. 'I admired your *Great Gatsby* theme. Where did you find that delightful car?'

'A friend of a friend sorted it out for me.'

'Well, it was perfect. Now, tell me – where's that sexy friend of yours, this evening?'

'*I'm* here,' Sam replied. 'That's all that counts.' Even by candlelight, I could see how irritated he was by the reference to Jez.

When everyone had charged their glasses, Zara stood up and clapped her hands.

'Welcome one and all to the Top Table. As ever, only the finest, only the best. Neither by land nor by sea shalt strangers find their way to Hyperborea. It is *ours*, ours alone.'

Everyone stood up, raised their glasses and waited for Zara's toast.

'There are none we would rather be,' she said. 'To the Top Table.'

'The Top Table,' everyone repeated and drank the toast. For a moment, I thought they would turn and smash their glasses against the walls like Greeks or Russians, but they simply sat down again.

The taste of the Pétrus overwhelmed me, lingering on every part of the palate. I was no connoisseur, but I could tell how special this was. I glanced at Sam and he seemed every bit as appreciative.

'Tonight we welcome a new member to our ranks,' Zara announced. 'Mr Lincoln from…' She turned to Sam and raised an eyebrow. '*…Hollywood.*'

Everyone clapped, and some even banged the table with their hands. There was some cheering too. Zara motioned to Sam to stand up. He got to his feet and gave an embarrassed bow.

'Well, Sam,' she said, 'The Romans spoke of the *theatrum mundi* – the theatre of the world. That's our stage and I'm sure you'll agree we're putting on the best show of all.'

I thought Sam would tell her where to get off. He was Hollywood's biggest star, after all. His movies had been seen by hundreds of millions all over the world. If anyone were an actor in this theatrum mundi, it was him, not these people.

But he didn't say a word.

Zara held out her hand and made a half-hearted gesture in my direction. 'Sam is accompanied by a guest. Ms…York, I believe, of…where?'

'Mayfair,' I said sullenly.

She didn't condescend to look at me, and no one clapped. Only Marcus made me feel welcome, reaching out and supportively clasping my hand.

'This week, the first of our sacred band reached the Promised Land,' Zara said. 'Their funerals will be held in the next few days, but their families have led me to understand we won't be welcome. The truth is we were their *real* family, the ones who gave them true friendship and love. As for these others, they were mere incubators. They can keep their desiccated ceremonies and their shambling, mumbling priests. As Nietzsche said, "The higher we soar, the smaller we seem to those who cannot fly."

'Please charge your glasses once more and let us toast Lawrence and Chloe. Polymaths, explorers, adventurers – where amongst hoi polloi could you find people of that calibre, individuals with that exquisite combination of intellect and artistry?'

Again, everyone stood up and raised their glasses in salute.

'To Lawrence and Chloe,' Zara said. 'Lacrimae rerum.'

'Lacrimae rerum,' everyone echoed, except me.

While the rest of us took our seats again, Zara remained standing and began reciting a poem:

Those who have crossed
With direct eyes, to death's other Kingdom
Remember us – if at all – not as lost
Violent souls, but only
As the hollow men
The stuffed men.

With that, she sat down. I hoped Sam found it as ridiculous as I did, but instead he seemed swept up in the whole thing.

'What was that?' he whispered to Zara. 'It was so haunting.'

I could see her face shaping to deliver one of her put-downs. She talked incredibly slowly. '*The Hollow Men*…it's a poem…by one of your compatriots…Mr T.S. Eliot…it's quite long, so I quoted just a few lines.'

'Don't speak to me like that. I'm not stupid.'

The smile on Zara's face was sarcastic enough to strip paint. 'Then I must remember to get your opinion on why Wagner didn't resolve the Tristan chord,' she said. 'What do you think of Baudrillard's treatment of the *simulacrum*? Perhaps you could give us your thoughts on whether *perspectivism* may be considered as Nietzsche's version of epistemology. I hear they talk of nothing else in Hollywood.'

Sam bowed his head and stared at his plate. The silence was deathly.

21

The Sermon of the Dead

The dinner was bizarre, almost frightening. Not the food, though. The portions may have been tiny – much to the relief of my *Body Fascism Index* anxieties – but each dish was mouth-watering, even the pigeon, pig's trotters and whale meat. It was the dinner-table conversation going on around me that was so scary.

The topics ranged from snippets about 'gunshot orgasms' to thoughts of slitting your wrists in a warm bath after finishing a thousand-pound bottle of Remy Martin Louis XIII Grande Champagne Cognac. The students talked of Edward II having a red-hot poker rammed into his bowels via a tube inserted into his rectum, leaving his body free of visible wounds; about James Connolly, critically wounded in the Irish Easter uprising of 1916, being tied to a chair to allow a British firing squad to shoot him. I couldn't keep up with all the grisly details. There was a story about the axeman at the execution of the Duke of Monmouth making five hacking attempts to remove the Duke's head. As the head and body were about to be buried, someone realised that no portrait had ever been painted of the duke. Since he was a member of the royal family, protocol demanded that a portrait be made. So, his head and body were sewn back together and the corpse dressed in clothes fit for a prince. Thus he sat for his one and only official painting.

The sick catalogue went on and on, quite turning my stomach. I think the vilest contribution was from a raven-haired girl, so pale she reminded me of Snow White. I overheard her saying she loved bukkake. Apparently, this was a sexual practice in which a circle of masturbating men showered a 'receiver' with sperm; or they filled up a dish with spunk, which she then had to drink.

No one seemed remotely shocked by her story and I started to think I'd led a sheltered life. Snow White gleefully explained that bukkake had its origins in ancient Japan. An unfaithful wife would be publicly humiliated by being tied to a stake in the centre of the village while every man ejaculated over her face to show their contempt for her. In more extreme versions, the woman was buried up to her neck and, after she'd been sprayed with sperm, she was decapitated.

About half way through the evening, just after the fifth-course dishes had been cleared away, Zara turned to Sam, eyes gleaming.

'Mr Lincoln, the Top Table has a tradition of asking new recruits to describe something that's of interest to everyone. As you may have noticed, *death* is what fascinates us. The night before he was assassinated, Julius Caesar was asked at dinner what he considered the best way to die. "Quickly", he said, "and amongst friends."' Another of her irritating smirks surfaced. 'We like to add to that a little...*sexual* charge. So, what can you offer us, Sam?'

I leaned in so as not to miss anything.

'When I was a kid I heard that there was an adult sex ring in LA where all the members had sex with ducks,' Sam said. 'Just as they were approaching their climax, the men shouted out to the master of ceremonies, and he came along and chopped the heads off the ducks while the men were wedged to the hilt. Apparently, this produced the most incredible contractions through each duck's body, making it grip the guy's cock like a vice. Add in the adrenalin rush of seeing a lethal blade so near your manhood…Well, they say it's the best male orgasm money can buy. Word on the street has it that Marlon Brando particularly recommended it.'

Of all the things I expected to hear, that wasn't it. I thought *fuck a duck* was just a figure of speech, not an actual sexual peccadillo.

'That always stayed with me,' Sam said. 'Sometimes I think there can't be anything more powerful than the combination of death and orgasm.'

'Well, of course, the French call the orgasm *la petite mort*,' Zara said. 'The little death.'

'Maybe autoerotic asphyxiation is the best way to go,' Sam said.

'Excellent.' Zara's eyes sparkled bluer than ever. 'You should read Yukio Mishima. I think you'd find him a kindred spirit, though he preferred disembowelment to hanging.' She gave a little laugh. 'Death is nature's way of telling us we've had too much fun, right?'

'What about you?' Sam asked. 'How would you like to die?'

Zara's answer came with a slow smile, twisted to fit. 'For me, you can die well only if you've tasted ultimate pleasure. Then you'll have nothing to regret.'

'And what *is* ultimate pleasure?' I asked.

'It's a release from everything that's holding us back. It's about breaking taboos, achieving the impossible. One thing in particular fascinates me.'

I watched Sam, completely sucked in, willing her to continue. I was sure he'd forgotten I existed.

'The perfect murder,' she purred. 'That's what I dream of.'

Sam tipped his head to one side but said nothing.

'All you have to do is select the right victim. After that, everything else follows.'

'And who is the right victim?' I blurted.

'I wasn't speaking to *you*,' she said, barely turning her head.

'Tell me,' Sam said.

'Isn't it obvious? – someone who wants to die. If they commit a very public suicide, no one will believe they were murdered. That doesn't mean they weren't, of course.' She laughed, and Sam started laughing too, albeit nervously.

After a few moments, she smoothed out her napkin and turned again to Sam. 'So, you like Robert Louis Stevenson.'

'Who?'

'Ah,' she nodded to herself, 'the *Clockwork Orange* re-enactment was your clue, I see.'

'I thought that guy with the cakes must be from some English movie,' Sam said.

'I think they did make it into a movie,' Zara replied. 'The cake scene was actually borrowed from Robert Louis Stevenson's *The Suicide Club*.'

Hearing that, I almost choked, and the young man on my left had to slap me on the back.

Zara turned sharply to face me. 'Do you have any idea how fortunate you are? Every member of the Top Table is either a millionaire or an heir to millions. Normally, every prospective member, even guests, have to meet that requirement. You plainly don't qualify. You're way out of your league.'

'Yet here I am.'

'Indeed, here you are. But don't forget, we invited you in.'

'And when do we get into a Millionaires' Death Club dinner?' Sam intervened. 'I must be rich enough for that.'

'Excuse me?'

'And when do we get our NexS?'

'I don't know what you're talking about.'

'Oh, come on. They both put it in their suicide notes: your cake guy and the Clockwork Orange girl.'

'So try asking them.'

Sam shrugged but I got the impression he thought he'd scored a point.

'On the subject of *A Clockwork Orange*,' Zara said after a pause, 'did you know the protagonist's name was carefully chosen. "Alex" literally means "without law". Like all truly great people, Alex was a law unto himself.'

One of the waiters dropped a plate and it broke with a great boom. He started apologising and desperately tried to clear up the mess.

'So, Sam, now that you're in,' Zara commented, without the slightest reaction to the commotion, 'how far are you going?'

'You know the answer to that.'

Zara ran her hand through her hair. I had to confess she looked fabulous, even in men's clothes. Sam's pupils were dilated, sucking in as much light from her face as possible.

'So. Be. It.' The slow, emphatic way she said those words…like a threat.

Turning to me, she said, 'Did you know there's a special part of the brain that's dedicated to working out what faces tell us.'

I squinted, trying to work out what she was talking about.

'There's nothing more important than knowing what another person is thinking. And the face is the biggest clue we have.'

Sam edged his chair closer.

'Did you know that severe autistics can't read faces,' Zara continued. 'They can't even recognise their own face if they see it in a mirror or on video. They treat it as an inanimate object, like a table or a chair.'

'What's your point?' I snapped.

'I'm sorry if I'm taxing your pretty little head.'

'So,' Sam interrupted, 'you mean that if some people can't read faces at all, there must be others who can read them *too well.*'

'Clever boy,' Zara said. 'Some of us are blessed, or perhaps cursed is the right word, with superior sensitivity to facial movements. We can read every nuance, every flicker of doubt, every trace of attraction or dislike.' She put her hands together, as if in prayer, and pointed them at me. 'You don't get on with your father, do you? You latch onto strong people because you're searching for a daddy substitute.' She stared right through me. 'How does it feel to be so weak?'

I sat there, speechless.

'And you can't hide for even a second how much you loathe me.'

Well, she didn't need any special powers to see that. Anyway, she was a good one to talk. Her face was contorting with her dislike for me.

'You're just another book that I'm dipping into,' she said, 'and not a very good one at that. It's poorly written with a tedious middle and a bad ending.'

I'd heard enough. I began to push back my chair to stand up.

'Leaving?' she smirked.

'You know what, I'll go when I choose,' I said. 'As for you, yes, you're absolutely right, I can't stand you. You're a stuck-up bitch. Talk about delusions of grandeur.' I turned to Sam. 'This woman thinks she's descended from royalty. She claims she's the rightful Queen of England. Her main ambition is to move into Buckingham Palace down the road there.'

Sam put down his glass and turned to Zara. 'The Queen?'

'Does that get you going?' Zara asked. 'Want to fuck me up the arse? That's usually what Yanks tell me they'd like to do to me when they find out about my royal connections. Pardon me, I mean fuck me up *my nice, tight ass*.' She pronounced those last words in a perfect American drawl. 'Somehow, the American version hits the spot so much better, don't you think?'

'Oh, how daring of you to mention anal sex,' I snapped. 'I bet you never do it the normal way.'

'The natural way?' she echoed. 'Whatever you do, you can be sure I *don't*.'

I fantasised about strangling her. 'This is all about creating your own little kingdom, isn't it? You want to pretend you're the Queen. This is your court and these sad students are your fawning subjects.'

'An interesting fantasy. Believe whatever you like. Stupidity, as ever, is free.'

I scowled.

'Both of you are free to go any time you like,' she said. 'This isn't the Tower of London.'

I hoped Sam would want to leave, but it was clear he was staying put.

'Tomorrow we're performing,' Zara announced.

'Performing?'

I could see the hook was back in Sam's mouth.

'It's when we go out and inflict ourselves on the locals.'

'You're playing games just after two of your friends have died?' I said incredulously.

'What better way to celebrate death than with acts of life?' Zara said. 'That's what the divine comedy demands, don't you think? Anyway, as I said, you needn't come. We dislike anaemic sorts, those who *flee* from life.'

'What have you got in mind?' Sam asked.

Zara gave another of her smarmy smiles. 'Come with me.' She pushed back her chair, stood up and made a signal to the sommelier. Sam bounded after her as Zara wandered through the Great Hall, while I glumly trailed along at the rear.

Zara led us to the *Painted Room* where she showed us two works by Hans Baldung Grien. One was called *Three Ages of Woman and Death* and the other *Death and the Maiden*. Each showed a beautiful naked woman gazing into a mirror while a horrific skeletal figure lurked behind her.

'Have you ever noticed,' Zara said, 'how often you see this type of composition in medieval art? Mirrors, skulls, skeletons, Death and female beauty. These were called *Vanitas* paintings. Do you know why?'

Sam shook his head. I stared straight ahead, not wanting to participate in this.

'*Vanitas* is the Latin for vanity, of course,' she said. 'These paintings were allegories to show how fleeting beauty is, how fickle and ephemeral the glories of this world are. Everything decays and dies in the end.'

'Where's this heading?' I asked impatiently.

Zara ignored me. 'I have a gift for you,' she said to Sam, 'a special prize for solving the puzzle I set you – a two-hundred-year-old bottle of champagne.'

Zara looked at me. 'You're shivering, Ms, uh…sorry I've forgotten your name.'

'Miss *York*,' I snapped.

'Of course,' she said, and put her hand over mine.

Now I really did shiver, but it wasn't the cold causing it.

She clapped her hands and the sommelier stepped into the room holding an ice bucket containing the beautiful old bottle of champagne Sam had been promised, and three glasses.

Zara flicked her gaze in my direction and for a second I imagined she felt sorry for me. 'It's yours to do with as you please,' she said to Sam, presenting him with the bottle.

Sam didn't think twice, quickly opening it and filling the three glasses.

'You first,' Zara prompted.

Sam took a sip. 'Not bad. A bit sharp, but…'

Without touching a drop, Zara tipped her glass and emptied the contents into the ice bucket.

'But you haven't tasted it,' I spluttered. 'You didn't even smell it.' I took a sip and instantly spat it out.

Zara's face crinkled with malicious glee. 'It would be a miracle to find drinkable champagne more than a hundred years old,' she cackled. 'When I bought the stuff it was for the *idea* of it, not the actuality.'

Was Sam thinking this was the last straw? I prayed he was. But he just stood there.

That was when I got a text on my mobile. It was from Harry Mencken. It said: 'See u at hotel 10 am tomorrow. Art gallery.'

'Harry's back,' I said to Sam.

'Ah, your master has summoned you?' Zara mocked. 'Do you roll over and let him rub your belly after he throws you a bone?'

'Oh, fuck off!'

22

Narcissus

'So, where's my NexS?' Mencken said as he strolled into the Sargasso's subterranean art gallery, constructed beneath the hotel's car park.

I'd been waiting for him for over ten minutes, using the time to look at some of the exhibits and wishing I could have stayed in bed longer. The previous night, things had fizzled out after Zara's stunt with the champagne. When I took Sam back to the Sargasso, he didn't speak other than to say he was 'going to get her'. I wasn't sure whether he meant get revenge, or shag her.

'I thought you would have it by now.' Mencken was dressed in cream trousers and a white polo shirt that showed off his Californian tan to perfection.

'I haven't found a single trace,' I confessed. 'No one in the Top Table – well, no-one *living* – has ever mentioned it.'

'What did you expect?'

Mencken walked over to a piece of modern art – a bust of Narcissus – exhibited on a polished silver pedestal in the centre of the room.

It was a striking work. The artist had used a circular mirror to represent the water. Narcissus's head was made from white clay, with pieces of mirror set in the mixture before it hardened. The bust's eyes, lips and nose were all mirrored, and its hair was made from mirrored strips. A circle of gleaming mirrored roses surrounded the water, with Narcissus's head reflected back from every petal. I think the idea was to show that beautiful people live in a mirrored world, always gazing into mirrors, or the lenses of cameras or human eyes. Maybe they ceased to be real and just became reflections.

It could easily have been a sculpture of Mencken or any other Hollywood big shot. He crouched down and read out an inscription beneath the sculpture: *If my eyes were mirrors, what would I see when I looked in the mirror*?

'NexS means everything to me,' Mencken said. 'I must have it.' He sounded weary. 'When you're young, with everything ahead of you, you're sure pleasure will always be waiting for you. You grab it in handfuls as you go along. You don't understand that one day it turns to sand and runs through your fingers. Time *kills* pleasure. Every dream fades in the end.'

He stared into space for a few moments. His usual self-confidence seemed to be temporarily deserting him. He resembled a past-his-sell-by-date playboy searching for the kicks he realised were now beyond him. I actually felt a little sorry for him.

'You can't go through life without messing things up,' he went on. Then, quietly, as if to himself, he started to recite poetry:

The eyes are not here
There are no eyes here
In this valley of dying stars
In this hollow valley
This broken jaw of our lost kingdoms

'Isn't that from *The Hollow Men*?' I blurted. For some reason, I stopped myself from mentioning that Zara had been spouting from it just last night.

'How…' Mencken shot me an astonished look. Then he laughed. 'Hell, that poem is so famous Marlon Brando used it in *Apocalypse Now*.'

'I've never seen that film,' I said defensively.

Mencken smiled, wandered over to a green leather sofa and sat down, beckoning me to join him.

'*The Hollow Men* is one of my favourite poems,' he said. 'Your favourite things say a lot about you, don't you think? I bet I can tell everything about you from a single item.'

I gave him a puzzled look.

'Tell me your favourite line from a movie or a book, the thing that spoke to your heart.'

I gave him the first thing that popped into my head. 'It's *Off with her head*, as said by the Queen of Hearts in *Alice in Wonderland*.'

'Nonsense, that's not your favourite line, but…' Mencken raised his finger. '…let's run with it.' He glanced at the Narcissus sculpture. 'My theory is that everyone chooses a line relating to some cherished fantasy about themselves, a fantasy that's usually the precise opposite of who they really are. So, your fantasy is of someone in total control who can get rid of anyone who opposes you.' He rubbed his chin thoughtfully. 'According to my theory that means you're actually someone who doesn't feel in control at all. You're threatened by others, particularly rival women.'

I winced.

'Bang on the button, huh?' Mencken smiled. 'It's one of my party tricks. If you love Edith Piaf's song *Non Je Ne Regrette Rien*, it's because your life is full of regret. If *My Way* is your favourite it means you've always done it someone else's way. If you like *It's Raining Men*, you're having a date drought. When your life is so depressing that you're contemplating suicide, you'll be at a karaoke night with your friends belting out *I Will Survive*.'

'You're getting carried away.'

'You're sore because I did a ghost job on you.'

'A what?'

'I saw right through you.' Mencken winked. 'I call it the *Suckers' Fifth Amendment* – the Law of self-incrimination. It explains so many things, like why fat people are fat – because something's eating them. Smokers? – someone lit a fire under their ass. The people who rush around so much? – they're running from themselves. Druggies? – they're so low they have to get high. People are always shouting out to the world what's wrong with them. You just need to read the signs.'

'So, your favourite line is from *The Hollow Men*?' I asked.

Folding his arms, Mencken chuckled. 'It's my theory, so obviously I can beat the system. Actually, my line is, "What I'm out for is a good time – all the rest is propaganda." It's from an old black and white British movie called *Saturday Night and Sunday Morning*.'

'So, that must mean you're *pretending* that all you care about is pleasure, when, really, it's *work* you're obsessed with.' I peered at him to see his reaction.

Sunlight streamed through a small circular window in the ceiling, capturing a funnel of dancing dust particles in its path.

'Maybe that's why I need NexS.'

It was impossible to miss the sadness in Mencken's voice. I got up from the sofa and went over to another of the sculptures – a giant clown's head with glass tears dripping down its cheeks into a vortex of unsmiling faces cut out from magazine pictures. Some of the faces had been arranged into a sentence saying, 'This joke isn't funny any more.'

I saw my face, my *life*, reflected back in the clown's huge tears. For a second, I wanted to pick up a hammer and smash it.

'So,' said Mencken, standing up, 'I hear you and Sam have been, how shall I put this delicately, *involved*?

'Who told you?'

'You should be careful with someone like Sam. Remember what Borges said: "To fall in love is to create a religion that has a fallible god."'

'Was it Sam? He's such a jerk.'

'Jez mentioned it, actually.'

'Jez?' I rolled my eyes. 'What's he been saying?'

'It must be hard for you, seeing Sam lusting over that woman at the mansion. Jez is into her in a big way too from what I gather. He seems to think he's in with a better chance.'

'Oh?'

'He tells me Alphabet Love is as good as over.'

'Why are men so obsessed with that woman?'

'I hear she's stunning.'

'But you should see the way she treats Sam. She's humiliating him. I mean, he's one of the most famous men in the world. He doesn't have to take shit from anyone, but he does from her. I don't understand.'

'Well, that's the whole point.'

'What are you talking about?'

'Let me tell you something, Sophie. I'm the person who first spotted Sam. I plucked him from the gutter. His father walked out on him when he was a kid. His trailer-trash mum was involved with a succession of drive-by men. He was bullied at school. All the guy had going for him were his looks. Everything else was a disaster zone. No one had it as tough as Sam Lincoln.'

'What's that got to do with Zara?'

'Don't you see? She's become the symbol of all the things that hurt him in the past. She's a strong, dominant character – just how Sam imagined his dad. She's smart and that makes Sam remember his shit time at school when people laughed at how dumb he was. He thinks that if he can beat Zara, he's beating the dad who rejected him, beating the school bullies who tormented him, beating everyone who ever did him down. Let's face it, everyone wants to beat their past.'

'But he loves her.'

Mencken shook his head. 'Trust me, he detests her.'

'You haven't seen them together.'

'I don't have to. Sam will take everything she throws at him. He'll pass every test, meet every challenge. Why? – because he's got nowhere else to go. If he admits defeat, he'll hear the laughter of the bullies all over again; hear his dad slamming the door on him for good.'

'That's mumbo jumbo.' But the more I thought about it, the more I believed it.

'Freud said that every psyche has a bullet in it,' Mencken went on. 'If you want to heal someone of whatever's making them sick, you have to remove that bullet. Sam's is his childhood. He's never come to terms with it.'

'And if someone keeps reminding him about it?'

'Then the bullet goes in deeper, maybe fatally deep.' He seemed to enjoy the way I had started to fidget. 'Coming round to it now, aren't you? When it comes to Sam and Jez, expect the unexpected. I was astonished when Sam found out about Jez. I still don't know how he figured it out.'

'Found out what about Jez?'

Mencken waved his finger at me, smiling. 'Your job is to get me NexS. Forget everything else.'

'Don't you want to be in on it next time?' I asked as he walked towards the door. 'Don't you want to meet Zara?'

Mencken stopped then turned, half smiling. 'Perhaps I already have.'

23

Telling Tales

I'd arranged to meet Jane for a quick lunch in the West End. As I hurried along to the *San Cesario* restaurant in Leicester Square, my mind was buzzing. What had Sam discovered about Jez? As for Mencken and Zara, maybe Mencken wasn't teasing and he really *had* met her.

That wasn't all I had to think about. I hadn't seen Jane since our mutual debacle with Sam and Jez, but I knew she'd be feeling as sore and miserable as I was.

She was sitting at the bar, gulping down a large glass of white wine. Her last text said she had 'mega news', so I was curious to discover what was so important.

We found a corner table and ordered a bottle of Sicilian white wine to accompany a light Caesar salad for each of us.

'Anyway, he was shit in bed,' Jane snarled as soon as the waitress had served our food. So much for her initial take that Jez was fantastic. 'I had to do all the work,' she said. 'I faked every orgasm.' She gave me a twisted look. 'You know, the only difference between real orgasms and fakes is that men *prefer* the fakes.'

I felt strangely pleased that she was so bitter. It had always irritated me then she never seemed to suffer man trouble. Until now, men were always the ones in trouble when Jane was around.

'I gave him every orifice,' she went on, almost muttering to herself, 'and if I'd had any more I'd have given him those too.'

After giving her a good chance to bitch, I managed to steer the conversation onto her mysterious news.

Her eyes gleamed. 'Well, I was chatting with Nadine, one of the girls in our New York office, and giving her a blow-job-by-blow-job account of my encounter with Mr Jez right-up-himself Easton.

'Nadine told me I'd got off lightly, then gave me this story about some scandal that Jez was involved in a couple of years ago. Apparently, his publicists hushed it up and his legal team threatened to sue if anyone leaked it to the media, but every PR person in Manhattan got the low-down anyway.'

I listened in astonishment as Jane passed on what she'd heard. Weeks before their infamous MTV bust-up, Sam had let Jez and Mencken use his penthouse apartment overlooking Central Park in Manhattan while he was out of town filming. They'd had a raucous party that ended abruptly when a girl fell to her death from the balcony outside Sam's bedroom. According to the autopsy, she'd taken a large amount of cocaine and alcohol.

Mencken's PR people spun the whole thing as a tragic accident, and the police played along. But it came out that detectives were concerned about conflicting witness statements from the people who attended the party. What was for sure was that Jez was alone with the victim just before she jumped. Some of the partygoers claimed a strange ritual took place in Sam's bedroom half an hour beforehand. Those who were allegedly in the bedroom, including Jez and Mencken, denied involvement in any ritual and said they were simply chilling out.

The upshot was that the case was closed with a non-committal open verdict. When Sam returned he was furious, and from then on things became strained between Jez and him, culminating in that MTV low point. There were rumours that Sam had secret surveillance cameras in his bedroom and that the events of the night in question were taped. Sam rubbished those claims, but the speculation persisted.

When I asked Jane what the bottom line was, she said some people wondered if the girl had been pushed rather than jumped. Alternatively, they thought it was possible she'd been given something that made her take a leap. More colourful theories speculated that she was possessed by a demon following a black magic ceremony to summon the Devil.

Jesus, first I'd heard from Big Pat that NexS was a miracle Nazi drug and now I was learning that Jez and Mencken were Satan worshippers. The whole thing sounded stupid and I wasn't surprised the NYPD didn't give the claims any credence. Jane was lapping it up purely because she had the hump with Jez. Then again, perhaps I'd now discovered the cause of Jez's recurring dream. Was guilt the burden he imagined he was always dragging around with him?

'Well, do you think Jez is a psycho killer?' Jane asked.

I was shocked to realise I was beginning to find her rather low grade. I'd been in awe of her at Roedean and for years afterwards because I thought she was incredibly sophisticated. That impression was rapidly draining away. In comparison with Zara, she was like some Essex slag, giving knee tremblers to cheap tricks up back alleys at midnight.

I didn't want to admire Zara. In fact, I wanted to hate her for stealing Sam from me, but more and more I found myself thinking of how I might emulate her. I stared at the clock. It was almost time for today's Top Table event.

I shuddered when I realised how much I was looking forward to it.

24

The Pov Parade

I found the Top Table sitting on black deckchairs on their front lawn. It was another sweltering day, but it would be stretching things to say the students were sunbathing. They were dressed in black paramilitary uniforms like riot police, and had black helmets equipped with full-face tinted visors lying within easy reach. None of them spoke. All of them had their noses stuck in a book. I soon realised it was the same one – *Poetry of the First World War*. There was no sign of Zara, Leddington or Marcus. Sam and Jez were missing too.

It was hard to recognise one student from another in their uniforms. They were all slim, good-looking and somehow bland. Their individual characters had vanished, had been *assimilated*: the *Zara* effect. Then I saw the bukkake girl, still looking as pure as Snow White. I went over to ask her what was happening, but as soon as I spoke she stood up, walked to the front gate, opened it and strolled out onto Queen's Walk. All the others filed after her one by one.

As I watched them go, I wasn't sure if I detested them or longed to be one of them. Wouldn't I be better off if I stopped resisting and just bathed in Zara's glory. I slammed the gate behind me and tried to catch up. They walked quickly, attracting a lot of attention from tourists.

At the foot of Queen's Walk, there was a parking area with a large *Reserved* sign overlooking it. Nine scarlet Lamborghini Diablos with black windows were parked in a line. The Top Table drivers pressed their key fobs and the hi-tech scissor doors of their supercars simultaneously swung upwards in flawless synchronisation. The tourists who were milling around filming with camcorders let out a collective gasp. Separating into couples, the Top Tablers took up position beside each car.

I felt a tap on the shoulder and turned to find Sam standing behind me. He was looking all sexy in his tight white jeans, with a black hoodie pulled forward to hide his face.

'Hi! How *are* you?' I said.

'Nice cars, huh?'

'Do you know what's happening?'

'Leddington told me to be here at two pm, so here I am. I *guess* we're going for a drive.'

'Have you…um?'

'What?'

'I thought after what happened at the mansion, you might not be too keen…'

'Don't sweat it,' Sam replied. 'Last night's history.'

'Yeah?'

'Yeah!'

'What do you drive in the States, Sam?'

'A Maserati MC12,' he sang, his eyes lighting up. Twelve cylinders, top speed of 205 mph, nought to sixty-two in 3.8 seconds. Cost me a million dollars and I still think it was a bargain. A thing of beauty.'

'Is that the best car in the world?'

'Well, here's the thing. The MC12 is really a downgraded version of the Ferrari Enzo, but only fifty MC12s were ever manufactured whereas there are four hundred Ferrari Enzos, so the MC12 is actually more expensive, even though the Enzo is the superior car.'

'So, you really want an Enzo?'

'I must have the best, you know that, Sophie.'

'What's stopping you?'

Sam smiled. 'The whole stock of Enzos was sold years ago to existing Ferrari customers who put their names on a waiting list years earlier. And no one who's got one ever sells.'

'And what about these Lamborghinis lined up here?'

'Same deal. Generations of these kids' families have probably been loyal customers of Lamborghini. Automatically, our Top Table friends get on a privileged customer list for any new Lamborghinis. The only list I'm on so far is Maserati's. All the rest are fucking snobs.'

A tenth identical Lamborghini Diablo arrived and I saw Sam staring at the driver's door as it scissored open, no doubt hoping Zara would appear, but it was Charles Leddington who climbed out. A moment later a passenger appeared – Jez.

'What the fuck's *he* doing here?' Sam growled. 'Well,' he said, fidgeting with his hood, 'I guess this means *Game On*.'

Jez gave us a little nod but made no attempt to come over and speak. He and Leddington remained with their car, chatting conspiratorially. They were both wearing the same black uniforms as the others, but Jez had added a black baseball cap and black shades. I'd always thought Leddington held Jez in contempt but now it was like they were the best of friends. Had they been secretly meeting up over the last couple of days? All around me, relationships were shifting, shape-changing. Zara and Mencken, Jez and Leddington, Marcus and me, Sam and me, Sam and Jez. I couldn't keep track.

'How *are* things between you and Jez?' I asked Sam.

'He does his thing and I do mine.'

'Aren't you supposed to be bonding?'

'What makes you think we're not?' Sam said gruffly.

Was he joking?

Some of the throng of tourists began to point at something. Following their gaze, I saw a spectacular jet-black car cruising along The Mall. Just when it seemed it would drive past, it swept into the parking zone, making several tourists scamper out of the way, and came to a dramatic dead stop.

'Fucking hell,' Sam yelped.

Instantly, I realised we were looking at a Ferrari Enzo. No need to ask who was driving. Both doors opened at once, but these were no ordinary doors. I found out later they were called gullwings. They swung high into the air and came to rest on the roof. They looked like a fly's bulbous eyes. In fact, the whole car resembled some huge sleek and scary insect.

Zara emerged and flashed a radiant smile. Wearing a fitted pink leather jerkin, complete with soft leather helmet, goggles and tight black jodhpurs, she looked irritatingly glorious. I glanced at Sam and saw that familiar look in his eye: lust beyond all reason.

'Glad you could all make it,' she said loudly, standing opposite the row of Lamborghinis and ignoring the tourists who were enthusiastically taking her picture. 'Pov Parade is here again. For those of you who haven't done this before, you have a unique treat in store.' She glanced at her watch. 'Come on, the povs need their annual entertainment. Let's hit the road.'

Pov Parade? I looked at Sam and he shrugged. Jez and Leddington got back into their Lamborghini and all around us pairs of students disappeared into the other cars. I began to worry that Sam and I might be left behind. Then I saw Marcus signalling to me.

As I climbed in beside him, I noticed that Zara's Ferrari was the only other car left. She slipped inside and sat there smiling. A black widow spider, I thought, awaiting her prey. A moment later, she beckoned to Sam and he sprang forward and leapt into the passenger seat. I took a deep breath and began to fumble for my seat belt.

A Smart car pulled up nearby. A guy with a goatee beard, clutching a huge, professional-looking camera, got out and started snapping away. Zara would *hate* that.

Seconds later, I heard police sirens. Jesus, were we all going to be arrested? I looked in panic at Marcus. 'Shit, what are we going to do?'

Four motorcycle cops appeared and flashed their headlights at Zara's car.

'Time to get moving,' Marcus said, with the cheesiest of smiles.

I gazed at him, my mouth gaping.

Marcus continued to grin.

We set out in convoy, with Zara's car moving to the front, behind two of the police motorbikes. The other two motorcycle cops dropped to the back.

'I love Pov Parade,' Marcus commented.

'And what is it exactly?'

'Just sit back and enjoy the ride.'

****

'So,' Marcus said as we drove fast through west London, 'having yourself a *time*?'

'I think my head's going to burst.'

Marcus smiled. 'Well, we like to provide lots of surprises. Every day is a rollercoaster ride with the Top Table. You aren't that much different from us, you know. I'm sure you want to avoid the flatliners as much as we do.'

'The flatliners?'

'You know who I mean – the white noise, the static…' We were on the Hammersmith flyover and Marcus waved his hand in a great arc over the whole city. '*Them*.'

'You mean Londoners?' When he didn't react, I offered another suggestion. 'Chavs?'

'Chavs! I'm talking about Mr and Mrs Average doing their average couple thing then their average family thing then their average holding down a tedious job to pay off their tedious mortgage thing while sending their children to private school thing. Those people are dead already; they flatlined when they were about fifteen years old.'

'Is that what the Top Table saves you from?'

'There's one question you'll never catch flatliners asking,' Marcus said. 'Is…life…worth…living?' He laughed. 'Why would *they* ask it? I mean, it's not as if any of those cunts were ever alive in the first place.'

I thought about Mencken's back-to-front theory. According to that, Marcus was revealing that the thing he feared most was that he might be just another Mr Average. It seemed spot on.

The convoy accelerated as we reached Chiswick, where our police escort parted company with us.

'A few people in my year are getting ready to join City firms after graduation,' Marcus said. 'I see them looking in mirrors, continually checking that all the blood hasn't drained from them, that they still actually possess a reflection. They're husks, zombies with fatter wallets than the other flatliners, but slowly fading away just like the others.'

He shook his head. 'One time, Zara took us along to a City recruitment fair and gave each of us a mirrored mask. When the recruiters asked what we were doing, she told them we were making life easy for them. "After all," she said, "all you do is recruit in your own image." Afterwards, we stood in a circle facing outwards, with our arms folded, staring at the others. We must have spooked a lot of people. Someone called security to move us on.'

Marcus's eyes shone with approval. 'I was so impressed with Zara that day.'

'You really admire her, don't you?' The word I wanted to use was 'love'.

'*Eyes I dare not meet in dreams,*' he responded. '*In death's dream kingdom.*'

'Don't tell me – T.S. Eliot.'

'That's right. Zara told us how much she loved *The Hollow Men* and we all decided to learn it by heart so we could recite it to her on her 21st birthday.'

I couldn't make up my mind if that was one party I was delighted I'd missed, or if I'd have given anything to be there.

'I want to do something special,' Marcus went on, 'something Zara will appreciate.' He tapped his fingers against the driving wheel. 'It's hard to think of anything that's up to her standard. I mean, she's so imaginative it's frightening – how can I come up with something that won't seem dullsville in comparison with the things she dreams up? One day, she got us all to stand outside the Houses of Parliament. We wore masks with question marks on them, like *The Riddler* in *Batman,* and held up placards with nothing on them but even larger question marks. No one made a sound; the police were baffled. When an MP asked Zara what we were doing, she replied, "Questioning things." It was so funny.'

I turned away. I didn't want to admit I was impressed.

All through the journey, our convoy attracted attention. Cars going the opposite way regularly tooted their horns. Every time we travelled along a high street, pedestrians stopped to gawp.

The Pov Parade

After an hour's drive, I noticed towerblocks in the distance and signs for Feltham – *Chav-central.* Why on earth were we going there?

****

Feltham was everything I expected: run-down housing estates, grim high-rises, litter strewn everywhere.

Marcus opened the car windows. 'Listen to this.'

I heard a loud ticking sound. If my ears weren't deceiving me, it was coming from Zara's Ferrari.

'Tic tock,' Marcus shouted. 'Tic tock.'

'What's going on?'

Scores of people on the high street stared at the luxury cars. The volume of the ticking clock had been turned right up. The sound abruptly altered to a deep chime. A few minutes later it changed again, this time into a Big Ben *bong*.

'Last year we hired open-top Pink Cadillacs for the Pov Parade and we drove along Brick Lane,' Marcus said. 'We wore dark suits and shades and played Elvis. That was a blast. This year we've planned something more dramatic.'

'The clock?' I asked.

'It's inspired, don't you think? Zara's idea, of course. Horrendously cruel, but that's Zara for you.' He sniggered. 'Not that the morons out there would ever understand it. That's part of the joke.'

'I don't understand.'

Marcus smirked. 'Zara calls poor people *povs*. Poverty, right? Each year we do this parade in some scumbag part of town to show them how rich we are and how poor they are…to demonstrate the natural order of masters and slaves.'

'That's sick.'

'Yes, horrible, aren't we?'

'And the clock?' I prompted again.

'It's the sound of the povs' lives ticking away.' He threw his head back in laughter. 'How's that for bad taste?'

'Zara's a real people person, isn't she?'

'If you think that's bad, listen to this for her idea for next year's parade. It's our graduation year, so Zara wants to go out with a bang. She's planning a Roman Triumph in Streatham.'

I listened in disbelief as Marcus explained the details. He said the Metropolitan Police had already okayed the plan and traffic cops would be on hand to supervise the parade. Zara would ride in a gilded chariot led by white horses. A 'slave' would stand behind her, holding a golden crown over her head. Using a megaphone, he'd repeatedly chant a warning: 'Remember, thou art mortal.'

With her face painted silver, Zara would wear a purple toga lined with gold. On her head would be a laurel wreath, on her feet golden shoes, in her hand an ivory sceptre topped with an eagle. The rest of the Top Table, dressed in red robes, would follow the chariot, some holding long incense sticks, some garlands of flowers, while others threw chocolate coins in gold foil to the spectators. Several of them would act as trumpeters to herald the arrival of the conqueror.

'That woman's a nut,' I said.

'She's a genius. I think she's like Mozart. They say that before he'd even lifted his pen, he'd worked out complete symphonies in his head: he could hear *every* note of *every* instrument. He knew precisely where everything fitted in. Zara's the same – she can see the big picture and all the detail too. She's always several jumps ahead of the rest of us.'

When he saw I was looking dubious, he shook his head.

'I wouldn't expect someone like you to understand.'

'What do you mean by that?' I huffed.

'No offence, but you're not one of us.'

'Arrogant know-alls from Oxford University?'

'Look, we're students heading for starred firsts, and, with all due respect, you're a party girl. We might listen to your ideas on a night out, but when it comes to intellectual matters, you're simply not there.' He looked me straight in the eye. 'You're nowhere at all.'

'Well, I thought Sam and Jez were up themselves but they have nothing on you lot.'

Marcus snorted. 'Sam and Jez wouldn't listen if you lectured them about acting. Why should we be any different? You have no idea what Zara is all about. It's her ambition to inspire the world. She wrote a dissertation called *The Theatre of Cruelty as the Sublimation of Mister Kurtz's Dark Heart*. It's extraordinary.'

'Mr Who?'

I could see his facial muscles moulding themselves into an outright sneer.

'Dr fucking Who,' he said.

I felt so small and ignorant. I could never compete with these people.

'Some people think there's nothing clever about what we're doing,' Marcus went on. 'They say we're nothing but self-proclaimed intellectuals playing infantile pranks. Those sad fucks haven't a clue. Sticking your nose in a book doesn't entitle you to call yourself an intellectual. You have to take your ideas to the street, confront the stupid wherever you find them, that's what Zara says. You must force them to think, to see the power of ideas. Those withered academics hiding away in universities aren't fooling anyone. They can't hack it. They don't encourage *thought*. They kill it. Zara wants to challenge every professor. That's what her dissertation says. It's a rallying call for true intellectuals. Intellect is a savage thing, not some cosy, peaceful pet to be shut away in institutions for the mild-mannered.'

'Am I one of your thick guinea pigs then?'

'You can define yourself how ever you like.'

As the car took a corner, I noticed a sign for Feltham Young Offenders Institution.

'We're not going *there*?' I spluttered.

'Where better?' Marcus put on a CD and flicked to a particular track, and turned it up extra loud. I'd never heard it before, but it was quite good. I think it was some old eighties thing. The chorus was *They'll never take me alive*. I found out later it was by *Spear of Destiny*. It told the story of some criminal desperado phoning his mum just as armed cops were closing in.

'Prisons are full of people who love this song,' Marcus shouted over the music. 'Ironic, huh? Shouldn't they all be fucking *dead* if the lyrics mean so much to them?' He turned down the music. 'HM Inspector of Prisons will be there today, in a safe area. He doesn't want to get too close to the action.'

'What do you mean?'

'Oh, I wouldn't want to spoil the surprise.'

25

It's a Riot

The security gates swung open for us, and the convoy swept into the car park. Hundreds of inmates in prison-issue orange jump suits were assembled at the far end, flanked by warders in full riot gear. The visors of the warders' blue helmets were pulled down, and they were carrying long Perspex shields.

'Talk about a captive audience,' Marcus sniggered as we parked.

'What's happening?'

'A poetry reading, that's all.'

Since when, I wondered, did a poetry reading require a riot squad? I got out of the car, shielding my eyes from the glare of the sun. The cars were all parked in a perfect row, with Zara's on the far left. As they gleamed and glinted in the sunshine, they looked like part of a glamorous shoot for supermodels.

A row of microphone stands had been set up and the Top Table took their positions in front of them, one microphone for each. They placed their helmets on the ground and started doing stretching exercises.

Marcus told Sam, Jez and me to stand to the side, and said we should run for the guardhouse if things got out of control.

'What are you talking about, man?' Sam asked. With his hoodie up, he didn't look much different from the chavs we'd passed in Feltham High Street.

I glanced at the hundreds of sullen, shaven-headed inmates lined up twenty metres away and started to feel apprehensive. There was so much testosterone in the air.

'Officially, we're here to give a talk to the inmates about the benefits of higher education,' Marcus said. 'You know the kind of thing – an inspirational pep talk, something to show these scumbags the path to virtue. We'll be rounding off with a poem to light their benighted minds.'

'And unofficially?'

'To have a riot.' He strode away.

As we watched him go, Sam nudged me, his eyes wide. 'Did you see his holster? He's got a Taser.' He shook his head. 'They all have.'

Students armed with electronic stun guns? – *Jesus.*

A short man with nondescript grey hair and a dark blue suit switched on a microphone and tapped it a couple of times to check it was working.

'Good afternoon, everyone,' he said to the inmates. 'I'm Edward Megson, HM Inspector of Prisons. The Governor and I have assembled you here today because we have a special treat for you. A number of Oxford University's most promising students have agreed to give you a talk on university life. We hope you'll find it as inspirational as those beautiful cars they drive. It's not too late for some of you to become students and enjoy the fruits of a good education too. The door to opportunities never closes on you unless you let it.' He cleared his throat. 'I believe there will be an element of performance art involved in the students' presentation. I'm sure it will be unforgettable.' He turned and gestured to Leddington, before striding fast in the direction of the guardhouse.

Leddington came to the microphone, folded his arms and stood for several seconds without saying or doing anything. He stared silently at the inmates and they stared back.

'It's strange, don't you think,' Leddington said slowly, 'how people spend all their time avoiding the one terminus they're sure to reach. They put so much thought into their summer holidays and none at all into their final destination. The Christian missionaries sent to Africa carried their belongings in coffins to show they were prepared to die for their beliefs. Shouldn't we all be dragging coffins behind us?'

His expression was an odd mixture of contempt and craziness.

'The Greeks called the god of death Thanatos,' he went on. 'When Freud identified a death instinct in human beings, that was the name he chose for it. It drives us remorselessly to destruction.' There was a curious look in his eyes. 'It's associated with an energy called mortido, the opposite of libido. 'What it means is that we're as tuned into death as we are to life. War, violence, hatred, crime – they're all manifestations of mortido. You here are all high on mortido. Your blood is full of it. You long to destroy, to wreck, to smash everything in your way. You want annihilation, an end to everything...perfect apocalyptic destruction.'

A huge cheer erupted from the inmates.

Leddington allowed himself a sardonic smile. 'Humans are death machines,' he said. 'The very moment we're conceived our journey to death begins.' He stretched out his hand. 'Death is the purpose of life. To have children is to create death. At the start of the last century, the world's population was one and a half billion – all of them in various stages of dying. At the start of this century, six billion people were at various points along the path to death. Do you see? – in just one century, four and a half billion extra deaths were generated. Death has quadrupled and the rate is increasing all the time. Soon there will be nothing but death. Life is a lethal virus, spreading death wherever it goes, infecting the whole universe.'

He paused, and gazed at the horizon. 'In the ruins of Berlin days before the city fell to the Red Army, the Nazi High Command knew they were staring catastrophic defeat in the face. Do you know what they did? They went to one last performance of Wagner's *Gotterdamerung*. Can you imagine *that*? With bombs and shells dropping around them and savage house-to-house fighting taking place within a mile or two, they went to the opera.'

He turned away. 'The performance at the end of the world,' he said, his voice full of emotion. When he recovered his composure, he clapped his hands. 'Let's do this thing.'

All the members of the Top Table, apart from Zara, stepped forward to their microphones. With impressive synchronisation, they read out Wilfred Owen's poem *Futility*:

Move him into the sun —
Gently its touch awoke him once,
At home, whispering of fields unsown.
Always it woke him, even in France,
Until this morning and this snow.
If anything might rouse him now
The kind old sun will know.

Think how it wakes the seeds —
Woke, once, the clays of a cold star.
Are limbs so dear-achieved, are sides
Full-nerved, — still warm, — too hard to stir?
Was it for this the clay grew tall?
— O what made fatuous sunbeams toil
To break earth's sleep at all?

There was a pause and then, in unison, the Top Table began chanting one line over and over again, as many as thirty times, until I was certain it would be imprinted on my brain forever: *Was it for **this** the clay grew tall*? All the while, they pointed straight at the inmates, swinging their arms backwards and forwards as their pointing became ever more aggressive. I'd seen some surreal things in the last few days, but this beat them all. The inmates began to shuffle ominously.

Zara, minus her leather helmet, took up her position in front of her microphone. I wondered how she'd trump that.

She didn't get a chance. A voice rose up from a fat guy with a broken nose right at the front of the inmates. 'Show us your cunt!' he yelled savagely. All of the inmates cheered. They began to chant 'cunt' over and over and pointed at Zara, just as the Top Table had pointed at them.

For a moment, Zara seemed flustered, and I couldn't stop a smile crossing my face. I looked at Jez and he seemed to find it funny too, but Sam was ashen-faced.

Zara made a hand signal to the chief of the prison warders and he nodded back. She strode towards the fat troublemaker and, with each step she took, the chant of '*cunt*' got louder and louder until it was practically deafening. When she reached the ringleader, everything fell quiet.

She leaned forward and whispered something to the fat man. Moments passed while they simply stared at each other.

'What did you call me?' the fat inmate bellowed suddenly. 'If I'm a lard ass, you're a fucking posh dyke.'

She said something into his other ear before quickly retreating.

The ringleader seemed momentarily stunned then screamed, 'Get her. *Get them all.*'

Shouts of primal aggression exploded amongst the inmates and they surged forward, forcing Zara to run. I thought the illusion she'd painstakingly constructed around herself would shatter if she had to do something as uncool as fleeing in panic, but not only did she not look flustered, she ran like an athlete, with incredible grace.

Cunt.

She withdrew behind the Top Table and I watched them all drawing their Tasers. At the same time, the prison warders raised their riot shields and charged into the inmates, batons flailing.

The Top Table, now wearing their helmets, used their Tasers to expertly drop the whole front row of charging inmates. Simultaneously, the warders fired tear gas canisters and baton rounds into the mass of bodies.

As clouds of gas drifted over the car park, the Top Table high-fived each other. For the first time today, they had big smiles on their faces.

'Job done,' one of them said as everyone hurried back to the cars to escape the tear gas. I saw Zara exchanging a few words with the Inspector of

Prisons and shaking hands with him. He leaned forward to kiss her on the cheek.

Marcus signalled to me and I joined him at the car.

'What did you think?' he asked, out of breath and grinning.

'Zara arranged all of that, didn't she?'

'Naturally.'

'But didn't you say she was aiming to be some kind of revolutionary? Why doesn't she want people to see what she does?'

'We never photograph or film any of these events. Zara says it's easier for them to be transformed into mythological happenings if there's no record. She wants rumours to spread that no one believes, with eyewitnesses being forced to insist they're true. These are the stories that become urban legends. This is how they're born.'

He switched on his CD player and *The Ride of The Valkyries* came on. 'Man, we should have played that during the riot. It would have been like that moment in *The Shawshank Redemption* when Tim Robbins put on that opera track.'

The convoy set off and soon we were in Hanworth – yet more concrete, greyness and litter. But suddenly the scenery improved dramatically. We went past a picturesque cricket ground, a lovely tennis court and reached a park with a shimmering blue lake at its centre. A sandstone castle with a moat stood near the edge of the water. Marcus said it was a luxury hotel – the *Aggiornamento.*

'This is Bushy Park,' he said. 'We're not too far from Hampton Court Palace.'

'What happens now?'

'It's a beautiful summer's afternoon. We're having a picnic, that's all.'

26

The Lake

The convoy parked near the edge of the lake, every car taking its place in a neat line, with the Ferrari Enzo at the centre. We all got out and sat on a grassy mound with the lake in front of us and an idyllic little wood behind. I lay on a blanket that Marcus had brought from the car, and let the sun beat down on me for a few minutes. No matter how much I tried, I couldn't get comfortable. And I could still smell tear gas on me from earlier. I sat up and watched Zara talking to Marcus. He was hanging on her every word, and at one point he burst out laughing, even wiping a tear from his eye.

Marcus joined me on the blanket and pointed out an ugly redbrick building on the far side of the lake. It looked like some old Victorian mental asylum. 'We go there sometimes,' he said. 'On special occasions.' He didn't elaborate.

'What did Zara say that sparked the riot?' I asked.

'That's what she was just telling me.' Marcus stretched out on the blanket and folded his arms over his chest as though he were a laid-out corpse. 'She said, "L'audace, l'audace, toujours l'audace." It's a quote by Frederick the Great. It means *boldness, boldness, always boldness.*'

'How did that cause all the trouble?'

Marcus smiled. 'The prisoner misheard her. He thought she was calling him "lard ass". As you saw, he wasn't a happy bunny. So, she whispered to him, "What I asked, lard ass, was whether it was your turn to stick your fat cock up your boyfriend's arse tonight, or is he doing the honours?"' Marcus began sniggering. 'I guess that would start a riot just about anywhere.'

His eyes followed Zara everywhere. She was such a bloody magnet, while every other woman had to endure a nuclear winter of lack of attention from the opposite sex.

'Where's the food?' I asked to make him look at me.

'It should be here any time soon.' He gestured in the direction of the tennis court we'd passed on our way in. 'Ah, look, dinner is about to be served.'

A gold Rolls Royce swept into the park. It parked about fifty metres away and two men in black bowler hats and frock coats got out. They went to the boot, brought out a huge wicker hamper then walked towards us over the grass in some sort of ceremonial march, each holding a handle of the hamper.

'Fortnum and Mason's?' I spluttered. No expense spared, obviously.

When the two men arrived, they put down the hamper and threw back the lid.

'Voila,' one of them said. 'Twenty-four fish suppers, twenty-four cans of Barr's *Irn-Bru*, and assorted sachets of condiments. Bon appetit.'

The men took off their bowler hats, gave a little bow, then turned and went back to the Rolls. I got to my feet to look inside the hamper. I was amazed to see a mound of newspaper-wrapped packages. One of the servings even came wrapped in the unmistakable pink paper of *The Financial Times*.

Zara sauntered over, immediately plucking the pink package from the hamper. She also collected a can of *Irn-Bru*, much to my surprise.

'Look,' she said, pointing at an article on the newspaper, 'the proles have found a new Pied Piper. Someone called Ligger.'

'I *know* him,' I blurted, grabbing the newspaper wrapping from Zara's fish and chips. I'd never forgotten meeting Ligger outside *Ballum-Rancum* all those months ago. I still had his hat somewhere at home, and he was right that whenever I pulled my ear I automatically thought of him. I'd read somewhere that his band was getting rave reviews for their live performances and being tipped for mega success. According to *The Financial Times'* article, it had now arrived – big time. Their newly released album was the fastest selling in UK history, the article said.

'Why does that not surprise me?' Zara said. 'I bet your contact book is full of all the classiest names,' she sneered. 'Low class, I mean, naturally.'

'Well, you're in it,' I retaliated.

'I can't be held responsible for your fantasies,' she said and turned away.

I wanted to throw my chips at her, but I didn't have the nerve. Besides, they smelled great.

I vowed only to have a few chips and just a small corner of the fish, but once I added salt and vinegar and poured a blob of brown sauce on the edge of the paper, I felt like a crack addict and compulsively stuffed my face.

'You have to hand it to the Povs,' Marcus said as he ate greedily. 'Their food is the best.'

I let him talk on, nodding politely as I dipped a chunk of my fish into the brown sauce.

'Last year was good too,' Marcus said between mouthfuls. 'Like I said, we were in Brick Lane. We rounded up a bunch of homeless people and took them back to the mansion. We treated them to a fabulous meal with our usual full waiter service. We stood behind the vagrants in complete silence for the whole evening, studying them as if they were zoo creatures. We wanted to see if their dignity outweighed their hunger. There was no contest, of course. I think they hardly noticed us. They certainly didn't show any signs of feeling insulted even though we were aiming to be as insulting as possible. In the end, Zara led us in a round of applause for them. Later, we drove them back to Brick Lane. Of course, we had to have the cars and the whole mansion fumigated afterwards.'

I scowled, but said nothing.

'Not crazy enough or too crazy?' Marcus asked, taking a sip of *Irn-Bru.*

'Can't you tell the difference any more?'

He gazed towards the lake. Zara and Leddington were chatting at the edge of the water as they ate their fish supper. Zara laughed and Leddington put his hand round her waist. He leaned forward and kissed her on the cheek.

Marcus turned away.

'Are those two…?'

'Let's not talk about it,' Marcus huffed.

Why did that woman inspire all this slavish male devotion? She was no messiah, just a spoiled diva.

'They say that Medusa turned men to stone because she was so ugly,' Marcus said wistfully. 'I think the opposite was true: Medusa was beautiful beyond imagining. Her beauty paralysed men. It was because they became so still when they saw her that people believed they'd been turned to stone.'

'So is Zara Medusa?'

'*Heart of Darkness* is her favourite book,' Marcus said. 'She loves Mister Kurtz. He was terrible and demonic but also brilliant and charismatic. I think that's how she sees herself. In the book, Kurtz's assistant says, "You can't judge Mr Kurtz as you would an ordinary man." That's how I feel about Zara.' He shrugged. 'I'm not sure if I'm Marlow searching for Kurtz, or one of the savages who worshipped Kurtz.' He gazed at the grass. 'Aren't we all searching for something to worship? Bataille said, "Love is based on a desire to live in anguish in the presence of an object of such high worth that the heart cannot bear to contemplate losing it."'

I leaned over, took his hand and clasped it for a moment. I wanted to kiss him. I couldn't believe what was happening to me. He gently pulled his hand away.

I turned and looked at the beautiful water, shimmering and sparkling as though the bed of the lake were encrusted with diamonds. Zara and Leddington were still at the edge of the lake, inches from the water. I noticed Jez strolling over to them. He said something that made the others laugh, then patted Leddington on the back and sauntered away. When did they all become such good friends?

I scanned around for Sam and saw him standing alone under one of the trees in the small wood.

Marcus must have followed my gaze. 'So what's going on there?'

'What do you mean?'

'You have the hots for him, don't you?'

I picked at my skirt glumly.

You seem curious about Zara and me,' Marcus remarked. 'Is it any different from you and Sam? But he's not extraordinary like she is. He's just an actor.'

It was odd hearing a Hollywood megastar being reduced to the status of a non-entity, but I didn't contradict Marcus.

'I used to be contemptuous of Sam,' Marcus went on. 'Now I pity him. I think he believes Zara is waiting for Mr Right – for *him* – but he's read her all wrong. She's not some demure lady counting the days until her true love shows up. She's a terrible goddess, who can tear men apart.'

'What was Zara's initiation into the Top Table like?' I asked, picturing her all young and eager.

'Now you've entered the land of myth,' Marcus laughed. 'I've heard two versions of what happened. One says she served herself up as a surprise dish at a banquet in Balliol College's main hall. Six men in tuxedos carried in a huge silver soup tureen. They laid it on the High Table where the master of the college was discussing, over a fine dinner, future funding with the Secretary of State for Education, the Minister of State for Higher Education and the Economic and Financial Secretaries of the Treasury. With a grand flourish, Zara's men removed the lid. There was no soup, of course, just Zara lying on the dish, stark naked.'

I didn't believe a word of this. Even by Zara's standards, it was preposterous. I rolled my eyes. 'And what did the master and his guests do?' I asked sarcastically.

'They were shocked, of course. I don't know if anyone made a formal complaint, but apparently there was talk of *rusticating* Zara. It didn't come to anything. At the disciplinary meeting, she read the opening chapter of her thesis. It was a searing denunciation of conventional academics. She said they were frauds, traitors and saboteurs, poisoning the wells of intellectual life. It made her sick, she said, whenever she encountered timid university lecturers who were more interested in paying their mortgage than leading an intellectual insurrection. The master was all too aware of how well connected she was, how she could cause all kinds of trouble, so he simply buried the whole thing.'

Marcus poured another blob of HP sauce over the last of his chips. 'Anyway, she was just repeating a stunt performed by Lady Caroline Lamb – you know, the crazy blueblood who sent a clipping of her pubic hair to Lord Byron. She's one of Zara's favourites.'

'I thought you had to recreate a scene from a movie or a book?'

'Well, maybe you'd prefer the other version. According to this one, Zara attended a garden party for professors of Classics visiting Oxford for an international conference. They were standing around an ornamental pond, sipping champagne and admiring two swans that had been supplied for the day. Zara announced that, for the professors' delectation, she would perform *Meretrix to Imperatrix*, based on a recreation of Procopius's infamous account of a performance by the Empress Theodora in the early years of the Byzantine Empire. Theodora was a highly skilled and amazingly smart prostitute who caught the eye of the Emperor.

'The professors smiled and applauded, no doubt imagining they were about to be shown some anodyne version of the story. That's not what they got. Zara stripped naked in the middle of the lawn, lay on her back and smeared honey over her, um, pudenda. One of her attendants scattered some barley grains on top of the honey. Immediately, the two swans waddled out of the pond, went over to the honey-trap and picked up the barley grains with their bills.'

'Heavens!'

Marcus laughed. 'Well, no one in the Top Table actually says they saw it, not even Leddington. We heard about it second-hand.'

'What about the two official witnesses everyone's supposed to have? Can't they confirm what happened?'

'They're not part of the Top Table any more,' Marcus said quietly

There was an awkward silence as we both sat looking at the lake. 'When she first met me,' he went on, 'she put her hand on my shoulder and said, "Bring down the curtain, the farce is over." It was a quote from Rabelais. She was saying it was time to be reborn. That's the opportunity Zara gives all of us.'

He munched on his final chip.

'She's my *beau idéal*,' he said, his eyes tracking to where she was standing, animatedly pointing at the redbrick building. As he gazed at her, he recited a couple of lines of poetry.

I have spread my dreams under your feet;
Tread softly because you tread on my dreams.

His adoration unnerved me and our conversation tailed off. I excused myself and wandered away to be on my own for a while. I hadn't gone far when Leddington strolled up to me. Raising his hand, he shooed away a wasp flying erratically near his head. He reached into his pocket and brought out a pair of sunglasses.

'Hello, enjoying yourself?' he asked. 'I must say you're looking particularly pretty today.'

I saw exactly where his eyes were directed and instantly blushed, feebly trying to cover my chest by waving my hands in front of me.

'Is that a designer dress?' he went on. 'It fits you perfectly.'

'That, er, building across the lake…' I stumbled.

'Curious, aren't you?' He put on his shades. 'We use it for…' I saw myself reflected in the blue-mirrored lenses of his sunglasses. '…special occasions.'

When I tried to find out more, Leddington held up his finger to his lips then walked away. I went over to Zara's car and sat down with my back against the front wheel. I sipped some wine and tried to shut out the world.

'These people are whacko,' someone said, not too far from me. It was Jez? 'Let's split,' he went on. 'We could go visit Scotland. I've always wanted to see all that Braveheart stuff. Did you know the sword of that William Wallace dude was almost six feet long? He was one huge motherfucker.'

'I'm staying,' a voice replied – *Sam*. 'The Top Table is something else. Zara…I've never met anyone like…'

'Forget it, man. That bitch is sick. She won't sleep with me and she'll definitely never sleep with you. Can't you see? – she's laughing at you. You're her freak-show for the year, a gas for when she goes back to Oxford. "Hey, everyone, I made a giant ass out of a Hollywood megastar."'

'Garbage, man. This is a much bigger gig than that. These people…'

'They're fucking Nazis. The Klan would welcome them with open arms.'

'Yeah, and what about us? I remember I was at a premiere with you when you said, "Watch out, *Eyes* approaching; let's move to cleaner air."'

Jez raised his voice. 'You're totally gone, man.'

I heard scuffling feet and I sat up to watch as they walked off in opposite directions. I got up and scampered after Jez.

'Long time no see,' I said when I caught up with him. He was standing in the middle of some bluebells.

He smiled. 'London's a big city.'

'Things not going too well between you and Sam?'

'Sam's nuts,' he whispered. 'I think Zara's put a hex on him.'

'So, what are you doing back in the fold? I thought you had bailed.'

Jez looked around. I presumed he was checking to see if Sam was nearby.

'Well, confidentially,' he said, 'I called Mencken. I told him what was going down – not too many details, of course – and he said I should check up on Sam from time to time. So, here I am, being a good boy scout.'

'Very noble of you.'

'*So*. I'm surprised you're still here, Sophie – haven't you been weirded out by everything that's happened?'

'Does that mean *you're* weirded out? I have to say I thought you and Leddington were getting on pretty well. And I had the impression things were even better between you and Zara.'

'I don't know what you mean. I was just being civil with Leddington' His voice crackled. 'As for *her*...she scares me to be honest. She gets off on mind games.'

'She *scares* you?' I repeated.

'I don't know.' He stared out across the lake and seemed to shudder. 'When that woman's around...people end up dead.'

27

Zero Night

As Jez made his way back to the group, I couldn't help staring at Zara. She was standing on her own, seemingly deep in thought. I was shocked by what Jez had said about her. He was right – she had a deadly presence, if there's such a thing, or maybe it's just that beautiful women always cause trouble. Don't the French say *cherchez la femme* whenever a dead body shows up?

As we drove back to Green Park, Marcus put on the radio and a report came on about the riot at Feltham Young Offenders' Institution. There was an interview with the Inspector of Prisons who denied he'd deliberately engineered an incident to test new riot control techniques. He said he'd told the inmates a few home truths and they'd reacted violently. There wasn't a single mention of the Top Table.

Marcus winked at me and remarked on how effectively the Top Table maintained their secrecy. 'If we wanted, we could be the most famous people on earth, but that's not Zara's bag.' He started blabbering on about how Zara was an authority on some French philosopher called Baudrillard and she was exploring his concept of the *hyperreal*. She was fascinated by simulation and simulacra, whatever that meant.

We didn't speak for a while after that. I was too busy thinking about Zara. At Roedean, the Chaplain told us about the angel of death flying over the homes of the Egyptians to take the lives of their firstborn. I could easily picture that angel with Zara's face.

That was the end of things for the day because the Top Table were having what they called a *zero night*, when they stayed in and chilled. They made it clear that Jez and I weren't welcome. As for Sam, as a two-button member he was entitled to remain, but he had decided to spend the evening on his own.

I went back to my apartment and zoned-out for a while in front of the TV, then spent a fruitless couple of hours searching the Internet for any mention of NexS. Finally, I collapsed into bed around two.

When I stepped into the reception of the Sargasso the next morning, I discovered Mencken and Jez chatting at the desk. I hung back as Mencken pulled Jez towards him and the two men embraced. After a moment, Mencken turned, saw me, quickly let go of Jez, and began brushing some imaginary fluff from Jez's collar. *Strange*. What was *that* all about? Mencken whispered something to Jez and then left him talking to the woman on the desk as he wandered over to me.

'All good things come to an end,' he said.

I looked blankly at him. What was he on about?

'I think Sam's going to be staying on for a few days,' he continued.

It took me a moment to realise he was telling me Jez was checking out.

Jez finished his business at the desk then came over.

'Going back to the States?' I asked.

'I've done everything I had to.' He grinned. 'It's been a blast.' Leaning forward, he kissed me on the cheek. 'Sorry if we gave you a hard time. I think you did swell. I'll definitely look you up when I'm next in town.' He glanced in a mirror and smoothed his hair. 'I'll mention you to my friends.'

When I started this whole business, those were the words I prayed I'd hear. Now they were empty. 'What about NexS?' I asked.

'We're leaving that to Sam and you. Don't let us down.'

'There's your car,' Mencken said as a black Mercedes pulled up outside the hotel. He gestured to a bellboy to take Jez's luggage out to the limo.

'I guess that's everything,' Jez said.

I couldn't let him go without asking the question that had been at the back of my mind for ages.

'What did Sam say to you at the MTV awards? It must have been bad to make you throw a punch.'

Jez glanced at Mencken.

'There are some questions you should never ask,' Mencken said sharply.

Jez gave me one last smile. 'Oh, pass on my best to your friend Jane. She was one hot babe.'

Yeah, but not worth more than one night or a civil word to tell her it was over. I felt like giving him the finger as he left.

'Jez is a good boy,' Mencken said quietly as we watched Jez stroll out of the front doors.

What a curious thing to say. Was I missing something? 'Does Jez have to be somewhere?' I asked.

'The shooting schedule has been moved forward a few days. Jez is needed immediately for some scenes.'

'And Sam?'

'He can stay a while longer.' Mencken abruptly gripped my arm. 'Just make sure you get our NexS. I don't care what it takes.'

And with that he stalked off, leaving me standing there, open-mouthed. I went to Sam's room to check up on him. I told him I'd just seen Jez leaving and was amazed when he said he knew nothing about it.

'Jerk,' he snarled. 'I knew he'd do something like that. He was always a quitter.'

'The shoot's been moved forward, that's all.'

'Garbage. He knows he can't win Alphabet Love. He's saving face.' Sam rubbed the back of his hand. 'You know, sometimes I think Mencken planned this, to get us at each other's throats. Some sort of method-acting ploy.'

Their new movie – *The Fatal Past* – was apparently about two elite CIA agents who'd once been close friends but who'd fallen out over a beautiful woman. She dated both of them at different times. On a vital mission, they allowed their personal rivalry to cloud their judgement and tried to sabotage each other's efforts. In the end, despite their mutual loathing, they had to cooperate or a nuclear bomb would be detonated in Washington DC.

Apart from the nuke, it sounded spot on.

Sam picked up a slim book lying on the cabinet next to his bed. 'This is that book by Robert Louis Stevenson.'

I read the title: *The Suicide Club*. My heart raced.

'It's brilliant,' Sam said. 'It's about the Prince of Bohemia who enjoys travelling in disguise to mix unnoticed with ordinary people. He and his bodyguard go on a vacation to London. They're in a bar looking for some excitement when they see a young man handing out cakes, just as we did that night in the Hexenhaus. He's giving away all of his possessions because he doesn't need them any more. He detests himself for squandering a fortune and losing the woman he loved. Suicide seems the only way out, but he's too cowardly to actually do anything about it.'

'So, what happens?' I said, leaning closer.

'He uses the last of his money to join a club that will perform the service for him – *the Suicide Club*.

'The members play a card game. Only two cards are important – the ace of clubs and the ace of spades. Before dawn, the holder of the ace of clubs must kill the person who has the ace of spades.

'In the story, the prince and his bodyguard join the club, with the help of the young man. They pretend they're ruined businessmen looking to end their troubles.'

'The prince gets the ace of spades, right?'

Sam nodded. 'Long story short, his bodyguard manages to save his life and they beat the bad guys. The Suicide Club is closed down permanently.'

'Interesting…'

Sam smiled. 'So you're thinking that *if* the Millionaires' Death Club exists then it's modelled on the Suicide Club, right?'

'The Fourth Protocol,' I exclaimed. 'There's a card game in *that*, isn't there? What were the rules again? Do you still have that sheet of paper?'

'Yeah, there's a card game and it's very similar,' Sam said.

'So, are we saying Lawrence and Chloe were murdered?'

Sam shook his head and laughed. 'Get real. If people are showing up dead, it's because they want to be. Simple as that.'

I didn't think there was anything simple about it. 'What happens now?' I asked.

'Leddington phoned me,' Sam said. 'They're having some traditional student fun tonight: a toga party.' He smiled. 'Crazy, isn't it? Here I am, reading Stevenson, and about to go to a party with masterminds from Oxford University. If only my schoolteachers could see me now.'

'I'm sure they're already proud of you, Sam.'

He ignored me. 'So, tonight's the night!' He rubbed his hands together. 'Anything that starts as a toga party always ends in an orgy.' His eyes shone. 'Then I'll bag the bitch.'

28

Toga Party

The Great Hall was transformed and now resembled a scene from ancient Rome. The attention to detail was incredible, apart from the distinctly unRoman Marilyn Manson music playing in the background.

There were many unfamiliar faces, making me wonder if tonight's shindig was some sort of recruitment event. Everyone had been colour coded. Guests wore white togas, while senior members of the Top Table were in purple, ordinary members, including Sam, red, and potential new recruits sky blue.

We were all handed a laurel-wreath to wear as we entered the room. Sam's arrival created an audible gasp and a flurry of furtive glances. He grinned, and winked at me. I noticed Leddington scowling and whispering forcefully to several guests.

Sculptures of huge phalluses and vaginas, *Caligula* style, were positioned at various strategic points around the room. I overheard two pretty blondes pointing out that the sculptures were made of marzipan.

One of them giggled and playfully shoved the other. 'Not even you could deep-throat that.'

The other grabbed a chunk of the penis tip and teasingly began to eat it.

There were ornate Roman vases, Mediterranean fig and olive trees and several fake stone columns like those from a ruined temple. An ornamental pond took pride of place in the centre of the hall and was full of disgusting black eels, each about five feet long.

The death paintings had been removed from the walls and replaced with vast photos of scenes from an old *Julius Caesar* movie, with a young Marlon Brando as Mark Antony prominently featured. The back wall was dominated by a strange symbol that looked like a black mushroom with both a long and short stalk. I discovered later that it was called *amenta* and it was the Egyptian symbol for the Land of the Dead – so no escape from the Top Table's favourite subject.

An empty velvet-cushioned throne draped in imperial purple was positioned just beneath the sign. I wondered when Lady Muck would make her appearance.

I couldn't help noticing how slim and attractive everyone in the room was. It was impossible not to overhear their clever-clever conversations.

Brilliant young things, without a doubt. Many were reclining on Roman-style couches and eating from a wide selection of fruit, meat, sweets and savouries. There were bronze basins in which they could rinse their hands. Waiters dressed as slaves were always on hand to refill everyone's glasses.

'Great party, huh?' Sam nudged me in the ribs. His toga allowed him to show off his muscular torso, perfectly toned and buffed. As for me, my hair was piled up in what I hoped was an elegant bun. Beneath my white robe, I had on a G-string and nothing else. I think most of the other girls had made the same choice. There was lots of flashing going on as everyone got increasingly drunk. There were definite signs that an orgy was brewing.

On one side of the room were glass statues of a handsome man and beautiful woman, holding hands. Both were naked. By pressing the belly button of either, a stream of alcohol poured from their genitals.

A girl placed a glass beneath the penis of the male statue and watched, transfixed, as red wine flowed through tubes from a stainless steel barrel behind the man. The wine passed through a coil in the statue's stomach then passed down through its bladder, out of the penis and into the girl's waiting glass. The female statue had a similar set-up, but this time white wine rather than red flowed through her. It was a surreal spectacle.

Throughout the evening, Leddington strutted around holding a flail and crook, symbolising – as Marcus explained to me later – majesty and dominion. Sometimes it was difficult to work out who was madder – Leddington or Zara.

Leddington came over to me at one point while I was looking at the repulsive creatures in the ornamental pool.

'They're moray eels,' he said. 'The Romans loved them. Whereas we have nice little goldfish in our ponds, the Romans chose these. They have a certain beauty, don't you think?'

'They're hideous.'

'And lethal,' he smiled. 'According to Pliny the Elder, Vedius Pollio liked to fatten his eels on human blood. Disobedient slaves were thrown into the pond to be eaten alive.'

'Always first with the funny stories, aren't you?'

'*Always.*'

After an hour, there was still no sign of Wonder Woman. Sam continually flicked his gaze towards the door, waiting for the moment when she'd make her grand entrance. I was already imagining her as a Cleopatra or Helen of Troy, perhaps even the goddess from *She*.

I tried a few nibbles from the silver food trays then washed my hands in one of the bronze bowls. It was filled with perfumed water and I splashed some onto my neck. Still no sign of the main event. Fashionably late, or a no-show from the hostess?

Without warning, the music changed. Manson's cheery *Suicide is Painless* gave way to *Right Here Right Now* by Fat Boy Slim. I heard a collective gasp, even louder than the one that greeted Sam. I looked up and there she was, standing in the doorway. Sam, lounging on a sofa, sat bolt upright and stared in disbelief. I couldn't blame him.

Zara was dressed like an Egyptian queen, her lithe body draped in a golden robe that caught the light and threw out sheets of glinting light. A gold snake-bracelet wound its way round her upper left arm. I'd never seen shoulders so elegant or such a graceful neck. Her face was perfectly made-up, with dramatic black eye shadow and eyeliner, defining her eyes in that distinctive Egyptian way.

She was wearing a majestic sapphire necklace and fabulous gold earrings in the shape of the Egyptian *ankh* symbol. As far as I recalled, it was the symbol of eternal life, so it was odd to see her wearing it. Her fingernails and toenails were painted gold and looked sensational. On top of her sleek head, she had the same flat-topped blue headdress that I'd seen in paintings of Queen Nefertiti. With her intense blue eyes and exquisite cheekbones, it was hard to imagine that anyone could be more beautiful.

With the faintest of smiles, she walked into the room with a supermodel's poise. Taking her seat on her throne, she surveyed her little kingdom with a suitably haughty expression. The rightful queen? There was no denying that if there were such a thing as a royal look, she had it.

Marcus wandered over to me. It was obvious he was every bit as captivated as Sam. 'She looks stunning, doesn't she? Did you know that Nefertiti means *The Beautiful one is come*? So appropriate.'

Everyone in the room paid court to her. They were all permitted a few minutes with the Sun Queen before she grew tired of them and despatched them with a wave of a shining, jackal-headed gold sceptre.

Halfway through the evening, she called for quiet. She stood up and declared that she was making an offering to the gods. Raising up a small crystal flask, full of what looked like blood, she closed her eyes for a moment, then, with a flourish, poured it into a gold dish.

'With this libation, we call on the gods to favour our endeavours,' she said in that intimidating cut-glass voice of hers. 'As Nietzsche, *our* philosopher, declared, "We are the new, the unique, the incomparable, those who impose on themselves their own law, those who *create* themselves." None are more deserving than we. Through our veins flows the ancient blood. We are the original nobility, the first masters, the lost kings and queens.'

Each time I tried to speak to Sam, his gaze drifted past me towards her, yet he never went near her.

At last, it was Zara herself who made the move. 'You,' she said, pointing at Sam with her sceptre. 'Have you come to praise Caesar or to bury him?'

Sam stood there, not knowing what to say.

'Did you burn the topless towers of Ilium?' she asked.

Still nothing.

'Ambition should be made of sterner stuff.' She was practically jeering.

Leddington went over to Sam and whispered something in his ear.

'Make me immortal with a kiss,' Sam said hesitantly a moment later.

Zara sniggered. 'If you have tears, prepare to shed them now.'

She walked over to Sam and prodded him in the chest. 'Your dreams have stretched too high, Mr Lincoln. Your vanity blinds you to your folly. The words of Shakespeare and Marlowe are unknown to you. You're a microscopic man, a pygmy in a sea of learning.' She jabbed him again, and, judging by the expression on Sam's face, it was as wounding as a dagger thrust. 'You have no class, no breeding. In fact…' She paused. '…what *is* the *point* of people like you?'

Sam stared at her incredulously. 'I'm one of the most famous men in the world.' His voice was so quiet it was barely audible.

The others in the hall tittered. A few turned away in embarrassment. I kept my head down, not wanting to catch Sam's eye.

'Sic transit Gloria mundi,' Zara said.

'And what the hell does that mean?' At last, Sam managed to raise his voice and show some defiance.

'It means you're way out of your league.' Zara turned her back on him.

'Why are you doing this to me?' Sam said, but Zara simply ignored him and returned to her throne.

I hurried over to Sam. 'Come on, let's get out of here.'

He didn't look at me, his eyes refusing to stray from the witch. 'I'm never giving up,' he whispered. 'Do you hear me? – *never*.'

He'd lost it. He really had. People go to a strange land in their head sometimes. Some never come back. I wondered if I was watching the meltdown of a Hollywood megastar.

Someone turned the music back on, much louder than before. Marilyn Manson's version of *Tainted Love* was all too appropriate.

'Let's get this party pumping,' Zara said, winking at Leddington.

Soon people were dancing, kissing, chatting excitedly, having passionate discussions. All except Sam and me. It was the most awkward situation I'd ever been in.

At midnight, Sam walked up to Zara even though she was deep in conversation with Leddington.

'Tomorrow night, it's my turn to throw a party,' he said.

Zara gave him a sly look. 'The ancient Egyptians believed that at the moment a baby was born, seven gods decided how and when it would meet its death. What do you think the gods have decided your fate is, Sam?'

'I couldn't care less. My party tomorrow night – yes or no?'

Zara winked at Leddington. 'Do you think it will be a spectacle worthy of Trimalchio?'

Leddington guffawed.

'Fuck off.' Sam was like a cornered rat. 'Just give me a goddamn answer.' He grabbed Zara's arm and she recoiled as though a leper had touched her.

'Sure, Sam,' Leddington intervened. 'Tell us when and where and we'll be there.'

'You'll definitely come?' Sam ignored Leddington and stared at Zara.

'Of course.' Her eyes sparkled malevolently. 'I wouldn't miss it for the world.'

29

Casanova

Sam was in the Sargasso's breakfast area, sipping orange juice. He told me he'd been up since seven o'clock. As for me, I'd needed a long lie in after the debacle of the toga party and I didn't reach the hotel until eleven.

'I want this to be good,' he said. 'You know, up to their standard.' His eyes were puffy as though he hadn't slept. 'I *have* got class,' he muttered. 'All those MBA jerks from Harvard and Yale…they don't know jack. Oxford doesn't scare me either. They're all the fucking same.'

'Why do you care so much, Sam?'

'Don't you get it?' He looked at me wildly. 'If you're not in, you're out.'

'That's just a catchphrase from one of your movies.'

He shook his head and scrawled furiously in his notepad. 'No, it's life. It's winners and losers; success and failure. That bitch is telling me I'm a piece of shit.'

'You're letting her. You have to stop playing her game.'

'Winners can succeed at anything. She thinks she's better than me, but I'll take everything she's got.'

'Let it go, Sam. You're famous, a superstar. People all over the world love you. Zara could never achieve anything like that.'

'That's all bullshit. It doesn't impress her and it doesn't impress me.'

I knew there was no point in trying to talk him out of it. Damage limitation was the name of the game now.

'When I was a kid, I once ran away from home,' Sam said, staring forlornly at the single slice of brown toast on his plate. 'It was raining and I tried to find some shelter. I sneaked into the porch of a house and stared through the window. I saw a family inside, sitting in front of a fire, with the TV on. They were eating candy and laughing. The coldness I felt vanished. I wanted to be in that house with those people, to be part of their family.'

He massaged the back of his head like a little boy who'd just had a bump. 'I never belonged anywhere. No one wanted me, not ever. I dreamt of being in a little cocoon, protected from all the shit, but shit was all I ever got. You know, sometimes I stand behind a door and scream as loudly as I can. I have this picture of happiness – that family around the fire – but happiness never featured in my life. It never happened. Not once.'

I didn't know what to say. It was so hard to believe that the greatest star on earth was so unhappy. 'OK,' I said, attempting to lift his mood, 'what type of party do you want to throw?'

He held up a brochure showing a man and woman in sumptuous eighteenth century clothes emerging from a black gondola, their faces concealed by silver masks.

'I was planning a trip to Venice in February for Carnival,' he said. 'That gave me the idea – I'm putting on a masked ball.' He tapped the brochure. 'I'll be playing a special role: *Casanova*.'

When he told me, I tried not to groan. Did he seriously think that by putting on the costume of the world's most famous lover, he would seduce Zara? Wasn't that what they called magic thinking? Casanova himself might not have succeeded with Zara.

'You'll need a lot of help,' I said.

'Already taken care of.' He explained that he'd hired the *Aggiornamento* – the castle hotel by the lake where we'd had our picnic. A costume supplier was providing the period outfits while the hotel would take care of the food and drink. There would be music too – he'd hired a small orchestra to play Vivaldi throughout the evening. As a final touch, a gondola would patrol the castle's moat, full of water diverted from the lake, allowing guests to go for a romantic trip round the castle.

I was impressed he'd done so much work in such a short time, and all without a PA, manager or agent.

****

We arrived at the *Aggiornamento* at 7.30 pm and were met by an excited manager who immediately requested an autograph from Sam for his daughter. All of the staff were buzzing. The orchestra had already arrived, set up their equipment on the stage in the ballroom and were busy now tuning their instruments.

The ballroom had wonderful oak panelling, several glittering crystal chandeliers, and a red carpet fit for royalty. A throne was prominently positioned at the side of the ballroom. No doubt Sam wanted to give Zara a taste of her own medicine, but I feared he'd be the one swallowing it.

We went outside and listened to the gondolier practising his scales. It was an ideal evening for punting – sunny and cloudless – but I felt queasy. Sam was planning a moonlit gondola ride with the witch, wasn't he? They'd travel round the moat, under the castle's great stone battlements, and Sam would probably imagine himself as a noble knight about to tremulously receive his beloved Lady's favour.

'Perfect,' Sam said, clapping his hands.

His plan was that Zara and the others would arrive for a champagne reception. A feast would be served at 9 o'clock, then there would be a masked ball, and guests could pop out at any time for a gondola trip.

The costume I'd chosen for the evening was a Venetian courtesan's, which managed to make my boobs look surprisingly voluptuous. I don't know what Casanova looked like but I could well believe it was something like Sam. In his rakish cavalier hat and blue satin coat with white frills, he was simply mind-blowing.

When he glanced repeatedly at the clock, I asked him exactly what time the Top Table had said they would be here.

'Maybe traffic's bad,' he said.

Half an hour later, still nothing.

'Plenty of time.' Sam forced his mouth into a rigid smile.

The manager spoke to him and I overheard something about the chef being worried about the food.

'Everything's paid for,' Sam snapped.

Several times he grabbed his mobile phone and punched in a number.

'Any luck?' I asked.

'No answer. I've left messages.'

Nine o'clock came. Nothing. No sign of anyone, apart from some hotel guests wandering in and out and staring curiously at everything. At least the orchestra was playing, the music vaguely drowning out the misery.

I went outside and gazed at the entrance to the park, searching for any sign of the Top Table. I shouldn't have bothered. I imagined them in the mansion laughing themselves hoarse at the increasingly pathetic messages being left by Sam.

Back inside, Sam was slumped on his throne, gazing at the orchestra, a glass of red wine dangling precariously in his hand. I'd never seen anyone so dejected, a king without a kingdom. I don't think the waiters and bar staff could believe what they were seeing. The gossipometer was off the scale, the whispering like the sound of locusts.

I went over and held Sam's hand. He seemed close to tears.

'She gave her word,' he said. 'She fucked me right up the ass.' He groaned. 'Why does she hate me so much?'

'We can turn this around, Sam.' A crazy idea had come to me. It was nuts, but I had to try. 'I'll be back soon.'

I hurried over to the manager and told him what I intended to do. He was reluctant, but I think he felt he owed Sam a last chance. I told him to have the chef serve the feast in thirty minutes and to get the bar ready for business. Then I drove to the largest pub I could find nearby. Unfortunately, it was slap-bang in the middle of a grim housing estate.

The Dog's Bollocks looked like…well, it wasn't where ladies went, shall we say. I pushed open the door and everyone at the bar turned round. I expected to hear pigs squeaking and see a retarded kid in the corner expertly playing a beaten-up banjo.

'Hey, isn't that the posh cow off that dumb TV show?' someone muttered.

'What the hell kind of dress is that?' another voice said.

I ignored the abuse and tried to maintain my dignity despite being dressed as an eighteenth century prostitute. 'Listen, everyone, spread the word,' I said. 'There's a fancy-dress party at the *Aggiornamento*. Free food, free bar, free costumes. And a superstar will be there. I can't tell you his name. It's a surprise.' I don't know why I said that last bit. It sounded good, I guess.

'Will we be on telly?' a shaven-headed man shouted from the pool table.

His friend slammed down his cue. 'Come on, let's see what's doing.'

'Make sure you bring your girlfriends,' I shouted as I left the pub, praying for some kind of civilising influence.

I drove back to the *Aggiornamento* and asked the manager to let in anyone who turned up. I guaranteed that Sam and I would cover all expenses, including the bar bill that was likely to be huge. The manager hesitantly agreed.

When I went inside the hall, the waiters were busy laying food on the tables that had been set earlier for the Top Table. Sam was still on his throne. He had a crazed look in his eye as he listened to another depressing classical piece and I thought he was on the verge of vomiting. He alternately grinned and grimaced, then began chewing his fingers. Finally, his head slumped against the back of his throne, his hand covering his face.

'I should have known she wouldn't come. She's *so* far out of my league.'

I was incredulous that one of the most famous men on the planet, as handsome as any Greek god, adored by millions, could be talking this way.

Moments later, the manager came in carrying a black envelope addressed to Sam. 'A motorcycle courier just delivered this,' he said, handing it over.

Sam tore it open and snatched out a card. I saw his hands trembling then he let it drop to the floor as though it had scorched his fingers.

I picked it up and was instantly livid. A cartoon showed Sam dressed as the Pope, riding on an ass that had a photo of my head stuck on it. Along the top it said, 'Vanity of vanities, all is vanity.' A caption at the bottom said: 'The Pope of Fools makes his annual pilgrimage to the Feast of Asses.'

I tore it up and scattered the pieces over the floor. 'Come on, Sam, get up. It's time to party.'

'What do you mean? They're not coming.' His head lolled backwards. '*They'll never come.*' Unsteadily, he got to his feet. Two empty bottles of red wine were lying beside the throne.

I took his hand and dragged him into the toilet. 'Come on, splash some water over your face.'

'What's the point?' Sam's voice had faded to a pathetic croak.

There was a commotion outside. Instantly, Sam was alert. He rushed out, his eyes wide.

'It's not Zara,' I yelled.

He stared in confusion as the hordes from the housing estate swept into the banqueting hall, a whirl of cackling and guffawing. Everything they said was 'fucking hell' and 'I don't fucking believe it.' Some of them sat down to eat while others just grabbed whatever they could lay their hands on. The food was devoured within minutes. Then they hit the bar. The staff seemed stunned at what was happening. The manager tried to stay calm but couldn't conceal his agitation.

Sam watched with a kind of perverse fascination as the locals swarmed around him, slapping him on the back, saying things that I'm sure he couldn't understand because of their strong accents.

I had wondered how ordinary people would deal with a Hollywood megastar in crazy circumstances. Now I knew. They get really excited for a while, stare like they've forgotten how to blink, rush around like buzzing bees and then, finally, totally ignore him. Apart, that is, from the women who have a crush on him, who always stay within a couple of feet, too frightened to get close, too starstruck to move too far away, like porcupines huddling together in the cold.

One of the locals told me he was a DJ and knew how to operate the music-desk standing unused behind the orchestra. There was also a drum kit, guitars and several other instruments. I went onto the stage and told the orchestra to stop playing and pack up their gear. They were welcome to stay for the party, but we were having a change of music.

'Listen up, everyone,' I yelled into a microphone. 'Can we all give a big London welcome to our very special guest – Hollywood's finest, Mr Sam Lincoln.' I waved at Sam. 'Come on up here, Sam.'

He stepped forward amidst a raucous cheer, climbed onto the stage and took the microphone from me.

'Am I the best dressed guy in here or what?' he said. Already, he'd recovered some of his Hollywood sheen. Maybe it was a reflex response to being in the limelight.

This time there were loud jeers from the men in the hall. Sam smiled. 'And what do the lovely ladies think?' Huge cheers and wolf whistles drowned the catcalls.

'Well, I'll tell you what,' Sam said. 'I'll give twenty dollars, uh, pounds to everyone who puts on a costume. There's a stack of this gear at the back of the hall. And a hundred pounds goes to the girl with the best costume.'

More cheers then a frantic change of clothes. People just stripped off and slipped into the costumes. In seconds, everyone was striding around like characters from a TV costume drama, clutching their twenty-pound notes. All the time, more alcohol was guzzled.

'Let's get this party started,' the DJ shouted. Within seconds, he had club music pumping out, and the dance floor was jammed with eighteenth century party animals.

Sam and I were still on stage, watching in amazement. Not for long. A young guy grabbed me and swung me down onto the dance floor. Two girls took Sam by his arms and launched him into the midst of the revellers.

I could see that Sam was starting to enjoy himself, or think less about Zara, and maybe those amounted to the same thing. We danced like crazy for about an hour until I noticed that someone had discovered the guitars and the rest of the music equipment. Soon, we'd collected a band – a bass player, a guitarist, a saxophonist, two fiddlers, a drum machine, and a pretty singer. The DJ handed over to the band and a moment later we were being treated to a hi-energy mixture of country, folk, rock, and jazz.

At one o'clock in the morning, Sam was good-naturedly manhandled onto the stage. 'Sing us a song,' everyone roared.

'I have something to do first,' he said, taking the microphone. 'I promised a hundred pounds to the lovely lady with the best costume.' He turned to the singer, gave her a kiss and handed her a bundle of notes. It was a popular choice. The girl blushed furiously but managed to give an extravagant curtsey.

Sam applauded along with everyone else. 'You people have been fantastic.' There was no mistaking his sincerity. 'You know, people like me…sometimes…well, we find ourselves in a bubble where the real world stops showing up…we, um, get disconnected from regular folks.' He hesitated, struggling for the right words. 'I guess what I'm trying to say is that you guys have given me the best night I've had in a *long*, *long* time. I really mean that.' His voice cracked with emotion. 'I can't thank you enough.'

There was a mighty cheer as he whispered something to the makeshift band. A second later, I heard the opening bars of *New York, New York*. Doing a good impersonation of Sinatra, Sam got everyone singing along with his hometown anthem. They formed into lines and kicked their legs into the air in perfect synchronisation.

I'd never seen Sam looking so relaxed and happy. After what I'd witnessed in the last few days, it was a miracle. His tortured body language had vanished and he was back to the charismatic star we all loved.

He was lifted shoulder high and carried in triumph round the hall. Everyone slapped him on the back and told him how cool he was. Then they put him back on his throne. This time, he actually looked like a king.

Just then, the hotel manager made an appearance. He told me it was time to wrap everything up. The houselights came up and I went onto the stage to thank everyone for coming along and making it such a special night. I asked them to leave their costumes at the side, and wished them all a safe journey home. They trooped out, laughing and joking, no doubt already putting this night at the top of the roster of local legends. I'd never forget it either.

I changed back into my clothes. Sam was still on his throne, but now he was asleep and snoring. His hat had fallen off and I couldn't help smiling. I cleaned him up, wiping some dribble from the corner of his mouth. I brushed his hair and wondered how many women would give anything to be doing this. I wished so much that things had turned out differently between us.

I nudged him awake and managed to get him to his feet. We both staggered off upstairs. 'Good party,' I whispered, as we swayed back and forth.

'Yeah,' he replied, 'that was a party, all right.'

****

When I went to Sam's room next morning, I was surprised to see that he was clean-shaven, looking neat and tidy in his regular clothes. He'd made his bed and his costume was folded on top.

'Some Casanova, huh?' he said.

'Everyone *loved* you, Sam.'

'Thanks.' He sat down at the edge of the bed. 'That was a unique night. It would never have happened without you.'

'Just doing my job,' I said, smiling broadly. I was *so* proud.

'Christ, what did I become?' he said, rubbing his temples. 'I was as much of a snob as *her*.'

'Not any more,' I said.

'Those people last night...' He gave a big smile. 'It was great fun, wasn't it? I've had it with fakes. It's time to get back in touch with real people.'

'So, what's your plan?' Even as I asked, I knew the answer.

'I'm going home,' he said. 'I'm getting a flight tonight.'

He came over and gently clasped my face before giving me a tender kiss on the nose. 'I really do like you. It's just that…'

'I know,' I blurted, and turned my head away. But I didn't know.

He picked up his costume. 'I guess there's going to be a helluva dry-cleaning bill.'

As he headed for the door, I was thrilled in a bittersweet way. For all I knew, he was walking out of my life forever, but at least he was safely out of Zara's clutches. *You're back to your old self again*, I thought, as he gave me a final, twinkling smile.

A Hollywood star.

30

Soul Auction

Sam flew home that evening. In the following days, everything went quiet. I had no further contact with the Top Table, and The Millionaires' Death Club didn't put in any mysterious appearances. As for NexS, there wasn't a whisper. The strange thing was that Mencken didn't contact me about it. There was nothing from Jez or Sam either. I put no effort into finding out anything more.

At a further meeting with *Far Havens Financial Services*, I was able to persuade Graveson that good times were about to roll. He had seen stories about Hollywood's hottest stars and me in the newspapers and grudgingly acknowledged that the publicity had raised my profile big time. So, I was now gleefully clutching the slack he'd cut for me.

Frankly, I cashed in on my time with the stars, using it in my promotional material. Well, I figured Sam owed me that much. I wasn't the only one making hay in the sunshine, or whatever the expression is. The bellboy at the Sargasso turned out to be an aspiring journalist and he wrote an article on the behaviour of celebrities at the hotel, mentioning Sam and Jez in particular. It wasn't flattering, but it didn't do them too much damage either, making them seem more complex than how they were normally portrayed. He said that sometimes they were extrovert and chatty and at other times so shy you'd think they were terrified of people. 'They skulked around a lot,' he said. 'They were unreal, not like normal people at all. I couldn't connect with them.' His last remark was the most telling: 'The funny thing was that the look-alikes were much easier to get on with. They were far more believable than the real thing.'

One of the Paris Hilton look-alikes couldn't resist spilling what had gone on at the lap-dancing club, and managed to rustle up some dodgy digital pictures. Again, it didn't do the actors any harm; just added to their sexy bad-boy reputation.

So, business picked up dramatically. I went back to showing a good time to financiers and rich tourists, eager to hear my tales of Hollywood and to enjoy some kind of weird, second-hand contact with the stars, while I awaited the arrival of bigger, more glamorous fish. But in a strange way I felt as though I'd reached the top and the only way from here was down.

Lawrence Maybury said something along those lines in his suicide note. It was odd, but I felt I could understand him now.

Weeks went by. I read in gossip columns that Sam and Jez were constantly feuding on the set of their movie, but Mencken was reported to be delighted. Every scene crackled with tension – perfect for a thriller.

As far as I knew, the members of the Top Table went back to their studies at Oxford. I pitied their poor lecturers.

I continued with my occasional habit of going to Sotheby's. One day, there was a particular buzz thanks to a previously unknown Boucher painting, discovered in some eccentric French aristocrat's chateau, coming to market. It was estimated that it would sell for about five million pounds. I'd been a fan of Boucher ever since I decided one of the nudes he liked to paint looked a bit like me. He made their bottoms look fantastically sensuous. I thought this newly discovered painting might reach as high as eight million given that it was a particularly good example of Boucher's over-the-top Rococo style.

The bidding had got to six million when I felt something nudging my shoe. I glanced down and noticed an auction programme wedged between my feet with something scribbled on it. I picked it up and squinted at it.

'I bet you're a fabulous fuck,' it said.

Appalled, I twisted round. Leddington was sitting behind me, wearing a ridiculous white suit like some sort of pimp, and wraparound black shades. I scowled at him with as much distaste as I could muster, but he didn't move a muscle.

I faced forward again, fuming. I figured it must be half term at Oxford: the inmates had been allowed out of the asylum.

'The bid on the phone is six and a half million,' the auctioneer said. 'Do I see seven?'

I heard a gasp behind me, and looked round once more. Leddington was just bringing his numbered card down, to the obvious excitement of a middle-aged woman with a prominent pearl necklace sitting two along from him. I couldn't believe it. Was he here on Zara's behalf?

The auctioneer gave the phone bidder a fresh opportunity to raise the stakes.

Again, something nudged my feet – another auction programme, another obscene note from Leddington. 'Do you give good head?' it said. 'I bet you're a screamer in bed. Want to see my joystick?'

'Seven and a half million on the phone,' the auctioneer said.

At that, Leddington got up and walked out. I stalked out after him, catching up with him in the hall outside.

'How dare you say those things to me,' I yelled.

He smiled slyly. 'You really are very attractive, you know.' He licked his lips in a disgusting way.

'Get away from me. I can't stand you.' I stared at those ridiculous shades of his, futilely trying to see his eyes.

'I wouldn't have had you down as a Sotheby's groupie,' he said. 'I suppose you were one of those kids with a weird interest in the *Antiques Roadshow*.'

Well, he was right about that, but I ignored his comment. 'How could you afford to bid on a Boucher? Were you taking the piss, or is Zara bankrolling you? Besides, isn't Boucher a bit too chocolate box for someone with your morbid tastes?'

'You think *I'm* a fraud, huh? Are *you* the expert these days? You're the FakeFinder General, right? It must come from all that experience you have of looking into the mirror. Will the real Sophie York please stand up?'

'Go screw yourself,' I spat and stormed off towards the exit.

'Don't you love me any more?' he shouted after me. His voice sent a shudder through me. I confess I found him quite good looking, but he was utterly repellent in every other way. I carried on walking.

'You're not in the same league as your sister,' he said as I reached the door.

I stopped dead. '*What*?'

'Zara told me she met your sister once. Ophelia, wasn't it? She was a real quality act by all accounts. Such a shame class doesn't run in a family.'

I ran.

Outside, it was raining hard, and people were sheltering in doorways and fiddling with umbrellas. I found myself in the teeth of the downpour.

My head throbbed. Was it really true – *had* Zara known my sister? The thought repulsed me. I fumbled in my handbag for my purse, grabbed it then dropped it again. The purse had a photo of my sister in its back compartment. I always kept it close, and every day I longed to look at it, but it was just too painful. I'd never once managed to open that rear compartment.

Ophelia. She was three years older than me, and the Headgirl at Cheltenham Ladies' College. She was in a school mini-bus returning from a trip and there was a head-on collision with a truck. They said afterwards that the truck driver was three times over the drink-drive limit, and taking medication for depression. He walked away without a scratch. The mini-bus driver and my sister were killed instantly. Five other girls were injured. The truck driver got a three-month jail sentence. *Causing death by careless driving whilst under the influence of drink*, the newspapers said.

My parents practically worshipped my sister's memory. She was little short of a saint in their eyes. They were convinced she had been destined for greatness. In fact they'd sent me to a different school so that I couldn't cause her any embarrassment. Effortlessly brilliant academically, she was eagerly accepted by Oxford. She was *so* beautiful. People said she could have been a model. Stylish, funny, charming, with loads of friends. Everyone who met her loved her. The girl who had it all. And me? I could never do anything right. Always in her shadow, always suffering by comparison. I was the stupid one, ungainly, the one without the natural grace and razor-sharp mind. *The big letdown.*

I couldn't help wondering what Ophelia would have made of Zara. Would they have been best friends? Would Ophelia have regarded Zara as a much better sister than I was?

I dabbed my eyes. Even if Zara did know my sister, so what? It wasn't as if our paths were ever likely to cross again. *Thank God.*

31

Most Likely to Succeed

On a frosty morning in late October, I was having a mocha coffee in Starbucks. I enjoyed chilling out on my own, sipping my drink. I'd taken to reading a quality newspaper rather than a tabloid. I guess I was trying to educate myself. Life was back to normal, even slightly dull. I didn't mind. I'd had my share of excitement for quite a while.

It was the same Starbucks where, two months ago, I'd met Francis Hamlin, the HR Director of Sotheby's. He recognised me from my trips to the auction house and we got chatting over our cappuccinos. I was able to throw in all the stuff I'd learned from the Top Table. I must have impressed him because he said he'd be happy to offer me a job as a trainee auctioneer since they were always looking for people with the right qualities. That meant the right look, the right accent, a friendly personality, an interest in art and an ability to mix easily with wealthy people. It was a glamorous job, quite well paid and the working environment was superb. I'd get regular trips abroad to take part in foreign auctions and they'd pay for me to a take a part-time degree in Art History.

I couldn't see myself studying at university. Nor did I think the pay could sustain me in my current lifestyle, but Francis had left it as an open offer, which I appreciated. He hadn't come in that day, so I concentrated on my newspaper. The front page was devoted to a murder trial at the Old Bailey. Nothing so unusual about that, but when I flicked over, my mouth fell open. At the top of page three was a headline that made my hands tremble. 'Millionaires' Death Club?' it asked. I read the article in amazement…

Following the tragic suicides of two Oxford undergraduates in the summer, another of their classmates has now been found dead in his rooms in Balliol College.

Marcus Gorman was the only son of Steven and Hayley Gorman, owners of a successful London publishing company. Neighbours reported that Marcus's parents were too distraught to comment.

Police confirmed that a cleaner discovered Marcus's body lying in a black coffin with two unopened bottles of rare champagne clutched in his hands. He was surrounded by fake gold coins and had an astronomical photograph of a dying sun over his heart. Cause of death was reported to be atropine poisoning. This was also the cause of death in the cases of

Lawrence Maybury and Chloe Sanford. A spokesperson for the college issued a statement saying that Marcus had struggled to cope with the loss of his two friends and had been depressed for some time.

A suicide note was found that ended with the last words attributed to the French comic writer Rabelais: 'Bring down the curtain, the farce is over.'

In a bizarre twist, police said that a stack of cards was found near the body, bearing the message: 'Congratulations, you have been selected by the Millionaires' Death Club'. It appears that Mr Gorman himself had designed these cards. The template was found on his computer together with an essay about his favourite book: The Suicide Club by Robert Louis Stevenson. Police revealed a previously undisclosed fact that cards of this type were also found on the bodies of Lawrence Maybury and Chloe Sanford.

It has been speculated that the three had a morbid fascination with death and created a secret club to pursue their interest.

My eyes filled with tears. Of all the Top Table's weirdos, Marcus was the only one I'd got close to.

The article contained a final revelation. An incomplete poem was found on Marcus's computer. It was called simply *You*, and said:

The enchantment of summer soon fades
You told me
Dreaming of death we die of dreams
You told me
I love you
I never told you
I think of you and thinking of you I dream
Of summers fading and sunlit dreams dying
You are my summer dreaming
You are my death in the sun
You are...

I silently filled in the missing final word: *Zara*. Did he plan to show it to her one day? It's never healthy to fly too near the sun. Coming so close had fatally scorched him. It could have happened to Sam too if he hadn't recovered his senses.

So, the mystery of the Millionaires' Death Club had finally been solved, it seemed. But what about the card Sam received in the lap-dancing club, and the reminder he got at Royal Ascot? The Elvis look-alike had planted those cards, not Marcus, Lawrence or Chloe.

The article went on to discuss if suicide was now fashionable. Apparently, online suicide clubs were springing up in alarming numbers. In Japan, police had been forced to restrict access to certain beauty spots because so many youngsters were killing themselves there. In Germany, a man arranged his suicide by agreeing to be eaten by a man with a cannibalism fetish. Suicide by cop – where people contrived to be shot dead by armed police – was a growing phenomenon all over the world. There was even a website called *mysuicidespace.com* which morbidly listed all of the *MySpace* users who had committed suicide. There were thousands of entries.

The article then speculated about whether a suicide epidemic amongst Oxbridge students was likely, if suicide was contagious.

There was a reference to a satirical novel called *Zuleika Dobson: An Oxford Love Story*, written in 1911 by someone called Max Beerbohm, which told the story of the entire lovelorn male student population of Oxford drowning themselves during the collegiate boat races. As they dived into the rain-lashed water, each of them shouted, 'Zuleika!' She was a *femme fatale* with whom they'd all fallen hopelessly in love, and her other claim to fame was that she was an expert at conjuring. It all sounded worryingly like Zara. The most memorable line from the book was, apparently, 'Death cancels all engagements.' It was exactly the sort of thing Zara would say.

The article said that philosophy students might be particularly susceptible to suicide given that Albert Camus wrote: *There is but one truly serious philosophical problem and that is suicide. Judging whether life is or is not worth living amounts to answering the fundamental question of philosophy.*

Further on, the article reported that counsellors had been provided to all the students who'd shared classes with the three suicide victims. I found it hard to imagine Zara seeing a shrink. Whether I liked it or not, she'd been on my mind every day. I guess everyone wants to know how life turns out for someone like that.

A few days later, I got the phone call that threatened to drag me back into her world.

'Guess what,' Harry Mencken said, 'the biggest, baddest whales are back in town. Grab your harpoon and get your ass over to the Sargasso.'

As soon as I heard his voice, I was once more in that extraordinary, overheated atmosphere of the summer. My old worries flooded back. I was sure Mencken would quiz me about NexS and I'd still have no answers and even fewer clues. In any case, I knew what happened to Captain Ahab when he went chasing Moby Dick. Obsessive quests aren't good for your health.

At least I'd see Sam again. I'd missed him so much. In fact I hadn't had sex since that glorious Royal Ascot day.

I hurried over to the hotel, but I found only one familiar face in the foyer.

'Where are Sam and Mencken?' I asked Jez, trying to hide my disappointment.

'Mencken's gone out.'

'So, what brings *you* here?'

'Oh, this and that. I'm doing some promotional interviews.'

'Has filming ended?'

'Actually, that's what I wanted to talk to you about.'

He invited me up to his room. Already, I sensed the sole reason he was in town was that something was up with Sam.

'What's this really about?' I asked once we were alone in his suite.

Jez smiled awkwardly. 'Sam's gone awol. There's only a week left of shooting. Mencken's furious.'

'What makes you think he's in London?'

'We found these in his trailer.'

Jez handed me two pieces of paper. The first was a printout from an online edition of *The Sunday Times*. It was an article entitled, 'The next big things?' There were profiles of fifty up-and-coming under-25s, Britain's supposed future movers and shakers. A by-line said, 'Watch out for these people in ten to twenty years' time.' Scanning the list, I saw that at number two was none other than Lady Zara Hamilton. The only person deemed more likely to succeed was – I had to look twice – Charles Leddington. Seemingly, not only did Leddington have a brilliant brain, he was also the star of the Oxford University debating society, the owner of a thriving multi-million pound Internet business and a prospective parliamentary candidate at the next general election. 'A future prime minister?' the article asked.

Jesus, no wonder he could bid for the Boucher painting. I flicked to the second piece of paper. It was an e-mail Sam had printed out:

Dia de los Muertos – November 2nd.

Mr Lincoln, you are cordially invited to the Top Table's most special night of the year.

With much love,

Your devoted admirer, Zara.

'Bitch,' I exploded. Yet again, the siren had called and Sam couldn't shut his ears.

'So that's where he's disappeared to,' I yelled. 'She clicks her fingers and he runs to her like a puppy dog.'

'Mencken wants you to go over to the mansion and bring Sam back,' Jez said. 'We need to persuade him to finish the shoot. After that, I don't think we care what he does. We've had just about as much as we can take of Mr Lincoln.'

'I don't know what I'll be able to do. I doubt he'll listen to me.'

Jez put his hand on my arm. 'Try anyway? You'll be well rewarded.'

****

I knocked on the door of the mansion and a few seconds later Charles Leddington appeared. I felt intimidated, convinced I was looking at a prime minister to be.

Opening the door wide, he extended his hand in a pretentious welcoming gesture. 'Come in,' he said in that plummy voice of his then escorted me into the *Palm Room*, so-called because it had at its centre a magnificent gold sculpture of a full-sized palm tree.

Zara entered moments later, looking as perfect as ever despite wearing army-surplus camouflage combats and an olive green army vest. I got the impression she'd been working out because her face was slightly flushed.

I stared at her and Leddington as they stood side by side. The country's future? God help us all. What chance would normal people ever have in a society governed by those two? They were the sort who would go for *full spectrum dominance*, as the Americans liked to say.

'Where's Sam?' I asked sharply.

'He's where he wants to be,' Zara replied.

'Why are you doing this to him?'

'Doing what, exactly?'

'You know what I mean.' This woman sure knew how to wind me up. She had a gift for it, antennae that detected all the best sore spots. Did I really want to model myself on her?

'I have no idea,' she said. 'Whatever it is you have in mind I can assure you he's doing it to himself.'

'Bullshit.'

'Are you in love with Sam?' she asked.

I stood there, frozen. Was I? I mean, *really*. I'd always believed that if you had to think twice about it then you definitely weren't.

'I'll take that as a *no.*' Zara gave me a typically arrogant smile. 'You shouldn't feel so bad. After all, there's precious little difference between love and lies.'

'I can see how someone like you might keep getting them confused.'

'You can lie to someone only if you know their thoughts are different from yours. Love is exactly the same. They have the same source.'

'Yeah, your twisted mind,' I blurted. 'But for normal people, love is the antidote to lies. You never lie to the ones you love.'

Zara smiled. 'You obviously don't get out enough,' she sneered. 'Lovers are the biggest liars of all. They even lie to themselves.'

'I'm sure they lie to you,' I grumbled. 'It would be the only way to put up with you.'

'Did you know that severe autistics lack the ability to understand that others have different thoughts?' Zara went on as though she hadn't heard me, 'and it's a proven fact that they can't tell lies and nor can they fall in love.' She turned away and looked at herself in a circular wall-mirror. 'Maybe love is the biggest lie of all.' She tidied loose strands of hair with her fingertips. 'The grand deceit amongst all the petty deceptions.'

'That's the biggest crap I've ever heard.'

Zara spun round. 'But you love *me*,' she sang, 'and yet you lie to yourself that you don't.'

My mouth gaped open. I felt blood rushing to my face and I hoped it was anger and nothing else. 'You're nuts.'

Zara simply raised an eyebrow.

Leddington smiled. 'We like you, Sophie. You're welcome to join us for tonight's festivities.'

'We're celebrating Dia de los Muertos,' Zara said, making sure she held my gaze. '*The Day of the Dead.*'

My pulse raced. 'Why don't you let me talk to Sam?'

'You seem to think we're holding him prisoner. He's not here.'

'Where is he then?'

Leddington scribbled something on a note: a Mayfair address.

'I'm going,' I said.

'I don't see anyone stopping you,' Zara retorted. As I made to leave, she made another of her mystical remarks. 'The story moves on, Sophie. It always does. Only those who were part of it are left to remember.'

I slammed the door behind me.

****

The address I was given turned out to be an up-market costumier's. When I went inside, I saw Sam right away. He was deep in conversation with the old man behind the counter. As I closed the door behind me, they both turned to see who'd come in and Sam immediately gave me a typical Sam smile.

'Excuse me for a moment,' he said to the old man and sauntered over, planting a big kiss on my cheek. 'I was going to call you, Sophie. I've been really looking forward to seeing you again.'

I had no idea if he was being sincere or just talking the talk.

'Jez and Mencken are here,' I said. 'They're staying at the Sargasso.'

When Sam didn't answer, I put my hand on his arm. 'You must come with me.' I'd convinced myself that Zara's spell would be broken if Sam stepped outside with me. I just needed to make him take those few steps. 'Come on, you can't screw with your career.'

'I've set something up,' he said with a grin that was practically manic, 'something incredible. It's a gift, the most fantastic present.'

I didn't need to ask who it was for. Zara was *all* that existed.

'It cost me ten grand, and took ten artists,' he went on. It's so cool it needs refrigeration equipment. It's waiting for me at the *Aggiornamento* hotel.'

'What is it?'

'You'll see when the time's right.'

While we stood there, a man in a smart dark suit came in. He walked straight up to Sam and handed him a black envelope. Sam turned away to read it. A second later, he bolted for the door.

'What is it?' I pleaded, chasing after him. 'What did that man give you?'

Sam didn't answer. All of his composure had vanished.

'Don't go back to them,' I begged as he sprinted from the shop. 'There's still time. Go home to America.' I knew I was wasting my breath. 'I can't do this any more,' I shouted.

No response, nothing. As if I wasn't there.

'Fuck you!' I screamed as I came to a dead halt. 'Fuck *her* too.' My lungs filled with air, allowing me to hurl one final insult, the big lie that made me shudder with self-disgust. 'Jez has already screwed the bitch.'

32

Follow your Heart

Is it possible to have a perfect experience, a moment when everything feels just right, when not a single detail needs to be changed? I don't think I've ever had a time like that. I think I'm too anxious, always waiting for the incident that will ruin everything. Maybe waiting for the disaster is what makes it happen.

I'd ruined everything between Sam and me. I guess I'd never really come to terms with the truth that there was no 'Sam and me' and I'd simply been fantasising about a fairytale relationship between us. Before he went back to the States in the summer, I thought we'd genuinely connected. I hoped he'd spend a few weeks getting over Zara then realise I was the one he really wanted. How dumb can you get? Getting over Zara was something Sam, or any other man, wasn't capable of.

'We meet again,' a voice somewhere behind me said, making me jump.

I'd been walking aimlessly around Mayfair, not wanting to go back to my apartment to sit on my own. So, I was just staring at people, especially anyone who looked happy, wondering what their secret was. Now, I was outside a bar, gazing through the large windows at the dozens of smiling people inside having a cosy lunchtime drink.

I turned to see who had spoken. 'Hey, how are you doing?' I beamed. It was Ligger, my handsome pop star.

'Real good,' he answered. 'I think I have you to thank, don't I?'

'What do you mean?'

'I heard you put in a good word for us. It was *that* word that got everything started.'

'Well, delighted I could help, but I don't want to take any credit.'

'But you knew the whole thing was Scotch mist, didn't you?'

'Only because you reminded me of *me*.' I smiled again. 'I bet it makes a great story.'

He nodded. 'That night I met you outside the club, all I had was a drum-machine and a few songs in my head.'

'So, you made a few stickers and badges to prove you were real?'

'Yeah – the more you fake it, the more real you become, somehow.'

I understood perfectly.

'When they saw the stickers, professional musicians started taking me seriously and asked if I needed anyone. One was a keyboard player…'

'And you said your keyboard guy had just walked out and you were urgently looking for a replacement?'

'You're good at this.' Ligger's eyes twinkled. They were a striking blue, a bit like Sam's. Was he *flirting* with me? 'In no time, I had a complete band,' he went on. 'Then, out of the blue, what do you know? – the boss of *Captain Toper Records* gets in touch and says he met a beautiful girl at *Ballum-Rancum* who told him we were red hot. I knew it had to be you since you were the only person who took a badge from me.' He blushed. 'And you were the only beautiful girl. At least, the only one I noticed.'

I felt myself blushing too. 'Happy to oblige,' I said. It was odd to be taking credit for what was originally intended as a joke at the expense of an obnoxious record boss, but what the hey.

'He said he wanted to see us live and as soon as we mentioned his name, venues that had turned us down flat suddenly welcomed us with open arms. He came to one of our gigs…'

'And the rest is the birth of a rock 'n' roll legend?'

Ligger laughed – such an incredibly sexy laugh. 'You got it. We signed a megabucks deal. Our new single's about to come out.'

'That's fantastic.'

'Hey, come in and have a drink with me so that I can thank you properly.' He led me into the bar and showed me to a corner table. He bought me a glass of white wine, and a Vodka and Red Bull for himself.

'You seem a little down,' he said.

'It's a long story. Some people can get inside your head, you know?'

'And it's always the wrong people.'

I nodded. 'Some people know all the buttons to press, don't they?' I let him take my hand. It was so nice to feel physical contact with someone who seemed genuinely sympathetic.

'You're obviously in with the wrong crowd.'

'Well, it could be worse, I suppose. I could be in with that lot over there.' I gestured at a group of assorted hippies, crusties and bohos in the corner, nursing their pints of Guinness.

'They're with me,' Ligger said slowly.

'Oh, I'm sorry, I…'

He burst out laughing. 'Gotcha!'

I felt the blood rushing to my face, and giggled pathetically.

'No, those types aren't so bad,' he said. 'Always good for a laugh.' He told me a story about visiting the ancient stone circle at Avebury for the summer solstice. The place was full of hippies zonked out of their brains on skunk as they watched the flickering lights from hundreds of burning torches. A druid dressed in black robes stood in the centre of the circle. As the sun came up, he was pushed out of the way by white druids. At midday, a final druid, in red, appeared. Ligger could hardly control his laughter as he described how the druid made everyone have a 'dry orgasm'. Every person had to moan as loudly as they could while writhing around: basically doing a *When Harry Met Sally* routine. When he asked me if I'd go with him next year, I shook my head.

'Oh, you're still with someone?' he said quietly.

'Only in my head.'

'I see, it's a *thing*. They're always the worst.' He squeezed my hand. 'Whoever he is, he must be dumb if he's giving you a hard time.'

I should have been incredibly flattered. Ligger was a fantastic catch and he was coming on really strong, but I felt empty, and I just smiled sadly.

'Come on,' he said, 'give me a proper smile. That first night I met you, I thought you had the most beautiful smile I'd ever seen. I've even written a song about it.'

'Oh God, I'm mortified.'

'Bleak Mortified, huh?' He grinned.

'Er, what *is* a Bleak Mort, exactly?' I asked.

'Oh, it's old New York slang for a pretty girl. It turned out John Adams was playing the same game as us. Maybe that's why he loved us so much.'

'What do you mean?'

'*Captain Toper* means a smart highwayman in old New Yorkese. Adams was also the guy who gave *Ballum-Rancum* its name.'

'Good choice,' I said.

'Damn, got to go,' he said, glancing at his watch. 'Something I mustn't be late for.' He finished his drink and shrugged. 'Some other time?'

I nodded. 'I'd like that, but maybe after I've had a bit of a breathing space.'

'The *thing*?'

I nodded glumly.

'Well, let me give you my number and you call me when you're ready.' He scribbled it down and passed it to me.

As he got up to leave, I gave him as appreciative a smile as I could muster.

One of these days, you'll smile at me again just like you did that first time.' He pointed at his heart. 'Always go where this takes you, Sophie.'

When he said that, I realised a lot of my heart was pointing in his direction.

33

Apologies

Half an hour later I was slumped on the sofa in my apartment, wearing an oversized woollen jumper as I attempted to keep warm. In the last couple of days, the mild autumn weather had turned bitter. Now snow was falling and my central heating was taking too long to kick in. Snowflakes were melting on my windows. Some things fade away almost unnoticed while others vanish with a bang, leaving you gasping for air. With Sam and the Top Table, an emergency oxygen mask seemed like essential equipment.

I'd blown it. I should have gone along with Sam, put up with all of his crazy behaviour. He needed help to save him from that witch. He was world famous, loved by millions, yet no one cared, not really. There's such a gulf between the life people think stars are leading and the one they actually lead. I remembered Cary Grant's great line: 'Everyone wants to be Cary Grant. Even I want to be Cary Grant.' That summed it up. Sam desperately needed support and I wasn't there for him. Instead, I'd taunted him. Did I really say Jez had screwed Zara? What a bitch. But Zara would be proud of me, and wasn't that what I wanted above all? The more I resembled her, the more chance there was of Sam liking me again.

I stared at my telephone and wondered if I should yank the cable out of the wall. When I'm feeling down, the phone scares me. Each time it rings you have to stop whatever you're doing and leap up to answer it. You've become this puppet creature, being manipulated by people very far away. I'm uncomfortable even when a friend rings. I'm sure they're sitting at the other end of the line, pulling faces at me and making yawning gestures.

Jane's friend Becky let it slip once that she couldn't bear to make love to her boyfriend doggy style because she was sure he was laughing at her behind her back. I knew exactly what she meant. I always want to see people's faces, to see if their pupils are growing or shrinking, to study the wrinkles around their eyes when they laugh, the direction of their gaze, all the little things that betray whether they're genuinely interested or stringing you along. All the rest is propaganda.

It's crazy that I feel this way. After all, I spend most of my life in a world of pretence, where phoniness has been raised to an art form. In the kingdom of fakes, is it the most fake or the least who's the king? Shit, I was beginning to sound like *them.*

Apologies

I sat upright – someone was knocking on my door. I didn't want to answer it, convinced I looked ghastly. I'd been crying and my make-up was probably smudged. I rushed to the mirror to check if I looked OK.

'Parcel!' a man shouted. 'Need a signature.'

I put on a baseball cap to hide my messy hair and scurried to the door.

'Sign here.' The courier didn't even glance at me.

I took the package inside. It was wrapped in expensive gold gift-paper. Opening it, I found a beautiful pearly pink box containing champagne truffles. The attached card said, 'Sorry – Sam.'

I stared at the chocolates in amazement. An *apology*! I flopped back onto the sofa, opened the box and popped one of the truffles into my mouth.

Perfect.

As the first chocolate melted in my mouth and my hand automatically reached for another, my mobile rang.

I hesitated, not recognising the number of the caller. I hit 'answer.'

'You can't walk away.' *Sam.*

I felt light-headed as I listened to his voice. Had he come back to me?

'It would be weird without you, Sophie. Everyone's asking for you. Zara and Charles say they'd love to see you again.'

My heart sank. He was just the messenger boy for the unholy couple, wasn't he? They were probably standing behind him right now, sniggering.

'I thought you'd seen enough of me,' I said.

'Didn't you promise me a good time?'

'Is that what you call *this*?'

There was a long pause. 'No.' At least he hadn't completely lost his senses.

'But, despite everything, it's what you want, isn't it?'

There was an even longer hesitation. 'Yes.'

I could hear something in his voice. Despair, resignation, acceptance, I don't know what. It nearly made me cry. I didn't care about Zara and Leddington, I just wanted to help Sam.

'Years ago, my therapist told me I had to get rid of my anger towards my dad,' Sam said. 'He advised me to write a letter to him. Not one for sending. I was supposed to set it on fire and burn those bad feelings out of me forever.'

Somehow I could picture Sam gazing out of a window, fighting back tears.

'It was a good idea,' he said 'but you know how these things go.' His voice was so weary. 'In the end, the bad feelings were burned into me worse than ever.'

I think he was explaining to me that there was never any chance he could escape from Zara. When people get enough of a grip on you, it's impossible to shake free. There's no way out. Perhaps when it came to Zara I wasn't so different. I wasn't in as deeply as Sam, but I was in deep enough. One day, I would have to deal with it.

I wasn't going to abandon Sam this time, and I was determined to prove to Zara once and for all that I was worthy of her respect.

'I'm on my way.'

34

Day of the Dead

It was as if the intervening months had never happened. I was with Sam at the mansion, and my old worries were back, worse than ever. We'd been given the task of helping to redecorate the Great Hall. Zara's plan was to transform it into...well, she didn't say exactly, but I knew headstones were involved because about twenty of them had been lined up outside the hall. We took all the paintings off the walls, removed the dining table and put it in the middle of the entrance hall then began moving in lots of weird stuff: long black curtains, wheelbarrows of soil, wooden crates. It appeared we were reconstructing the set of *Nosferatu*.

I was banned from the room for the last half hour of the preparations, presumably while the others applied the Top Table's trademark touches. I sat alone in the *Palm Room* and sipped mineral water. I had been offered wine, but I wanted to keep a clear head.

By 10 pm, everything was ready. The girl I'd nicknamed Snow White led me upstairs to the changing room where all the other girls were getting ready. The men were nowhere to be seen. I was nervous about the costume we all had to change into or, rather, about the final item we had to put on. I tried not to think about it as I wriggled into a man's formal black morning suit, complete with black silk trim down the exquisitely cut trousers, and beautiful brand-new top hat. Before I could put on the hat, I had to force my head into the thing that had been terrifying me since I first saw it.

A *gasmask*.

Snow White ushered all of the girls, apart from Zara who was absent, down the staircase and into the Great Hall. As we descended, I caught a glimpse of our motley group in one of the hall mirrors. We were like a procession of alien creatures with black rubber faces, huge round glass eyes and strange protruding noses. We looked as though we were on our way to the wedding of some monstrous bride and groom. If so, who were the betrothed? I could only think Zara was marrying Leddington. Maybe that was how they intended to deliver the final humiliation to Sam. Perhaps they'd ask him to be Leddington's best man, or he might be forced to give away the bride.

As I walked into the Great Hall, my mouth gaped. It was now a vast graveyard, complete with headstones, freshly turned soil and dim lanterns.

Beautiful bright flowers, different-coloured candles and odd, skull-shaped loaves of bread covered the fake graves, assuming they *were* fake.

Three red skulls rested on pedestals in the middle of the graveyard, the forehead of each printed with a name. I leaned forward to get a better look: *Lawrence Maybury*, *Chloe Sanford* and *Marcus Gorman.*

We stood in a line on one side of the graves and waited for the men to appear. The doors swung open and in they trooped. I gasped when I saw them. They were dressed like doctors from London's Great Plague. They wore black circular hats, long brown coats and thick gloves. Their masks with bizarre curved beaks and strange inbuilt spectacles that made them resemble vultures entranced me. You'd know you were in big trouble if you ever looked up from your sick bed and found a doctor like that bending over you. When they lined up opposite us, it was easy to imagine they weren't human.

In the far corner of the hall, a mausoleum had been constructed, and the sommelier – resembling a corpse what with his face caked with white make-up and dark shadows round his eyes – was standing there surrounded by wine bottles and glasses. He pulled a lever and smoke belched from pipes located around the hall and inside some of the graves. In seconds, the room was full of swirling, thick clouds of dry ice. I imagined I could see ghostly faces appearing through the haze. Blue laser beams stabbed through the white smoke and began to move around at high speed. They were overtaken by strobe lights that sent shimmering flashes through the hall, like sheets of blue lightning.

That was when a stunning figure in a gold skull-mask appeared – *Zara.* No one else could make an entrance like that. In a beautifully-cut black dress with a slit all the way up her left thigh, and Viktor & Rolf crystal high heels, she strode in like a supermodel, accompanied by heart-stopping music: *Dies Irae* from Verdi's *Requiem.*

Zara was also wearing elegant long black opera gloves, and the sort of headline-grabbing *Bulgari* diamond necklace that Oscar-nominated actresses loved to flaunt. She took up position in front of the largest headstone at the front of the hall. A microphone stand had been prepared for her.

As she waited for the smoke to clear, she stood perfectly still, almost seeming to merge with the grave. She looked around the room and I was sure she was smiling to herself beneath her mask.

'Welcome to the Day of the Dead,' she said. 'This is our time for honouring the souls of the departed. Tonight, cemeteries are transformed.

They are no longer the abode of the cold dead; now they are the kingdom of the reawakened.

'On this night, the boundary between life and death disappears, allowing the dead to return. Tonight we will welcome back the most noble of us: our absent friends Lawrence, Chloe and Marcus.'

I felt vaguely queasy, as if some dark spirit were crawling inside me. There was a unique quality to Zara's voice, something piercing. You didn't so much hear the voice as feel penetrated by it. Her words reached much further into your head than anyone else's, as though they were sharpened arrows, aimed perfectly.

'We gather at the graves by candlelight and bring flowers and food,' she went on. 'But these are no ordinary flowers, and the food is a very special bread. These are the *Flor de Muertos* and the *Pan de Muerto*. All the time we are illuminated by *Lux Perpetua* – the perpetual light of sacred candles that stay lit day and night forever.'

There was enthusiastic applause as photographs of Lawrence, Chloe and Marcus were held up. Moments later, people began smashing the red skulls and eating them…*candy*!

'Long ago in Mexico,' Zara declared, 'the Mayans said, "We only come to dream, we only come to sleep. It's not true that we come to live on Earth." For Lawrence, Chloe and Marcus, the dream is over. Now they've started their true lives.

'Never forget, the life you lead is inconsequential. It's how you die that's important. That alone determines your rank in the afterlife.'

I wondered how Zara became so morbid, how she'd roped all these others into her death fixation. As I stared down the line of gasmasks on my side of the room, and across at the weird beaks of the plague doctors on the other, I realised I wasn't in the normal world any longer. This was the Top Table's greatest skill. With their odd costumes, strange talk and bizarre events, they succeeded in separating you from any sense of normality. Life was painted in brighter, bolder colours. Was that why Sam was so hooked? Whatever Hollywood could offer, it was nothing like this. This was Zara's realm, and there was no one on earth like her.

A spotlight picked out three ten-foot-tall skeleton puppets and we all turned to watch their strange disconnected dance at the other end of the hall. The music blared as all kinds of weird lighting tricks took place. As I watched, the puppets' skeletal faces morphed into those of Marcus, Chloe and Lawrence. I couldn't see who was pulling the strings: true of so many things when I was with the Top Table.

Zara clapped her hands and I followed the other women as they removed their gasmasks. At the same time, the men removed their plague-doctor headwear.

I picked out Sam and started edging across the graveyard to speak to him when I was stopped by a sudden scream. One of the girls pointed at three plague doctors who, for some reason, still hadn't removed their masks. Blood dripped from their beaks. Everyone backed away.

Zara raised her hands and made a calming gesture. 'No need to be alarmed. Our three friends have returned, as we always knew they would.'

I glared at the three figures, trying to make sense of them. Seconds later I felt a tap on my shoulder. I spun round. Zara was right behind me, still wearing her gold skull mask.

'Do it,' she said. 'Show me how brave you are. Go over there and greet the dead.'

'Alright, I will.'

I was acutely aware of how cold it was in the room. I drew in a deep breath and began to slowly inch my way towards the three figures. I stopped a few feet short.

'You can't, can you?' Zara sneered. 'You're just a frightened little girl.'

I took another long breath and stepped forward. The eye sockets of the figures' goggles were filled with luminous blue light. I raised my hand and reached towards the nearest figure's mask. As soon as I touched it, the figure collapsed; its hat, mask and coat sinking to the ground in a heap. The other two did the same without my touching them. I looked down at the empty costumes. It would be easy enough to prop them up as though they had people inside. Then someone simply had to pull a string and they'd fall down. The trouble was, as with the puppets, I couldn't see any strings.

'Looking for something?' Zara was still behind me.

'I...well...I...'

Zara nudged one of the costumes with her toe. 'Why don't you believe, Sophie? Is it really so hard?'

'I'll never swallow any of this nonsense.'

'Oh, but you will. The truth is always the last thing people accept, but in the end it's the only thing left.'

I stumbled away, making a beeline for the sommelier. I needed a drink. *Badly*.

Later that night, after an elaborate buffet amongst the graves, Leddington took me aside and showed me a small painting hanging near the door at the side of the hall. I recognised it instantly. I first came across it in the *Tate* about a year earlier. I gazed at the old man with a long grey beard hovering in mid-air over five despairing men on the point of death. On the right of the picture was the extraordinary figure that made it such a memorable painting – a muscular, hairless, naked man with green skin. The figure's head was bowed as though a great weight were pressing on it. In his left hand, he clutched a dagger.

'What do you think?' Leddington asked. 'Macabre?'

'Genius.'

'Oh, you're familiar with it?'

'It's *The House of Death* by William Blake.'

'Very good,' Leddington said condescendingly. 'Why don't you explain it to me?'

I knew he expected me to screw it up and make a fool of myself, but I straightened up and girded myself. I pointed at the old man and said it was Jehovah, or *Urizen*, as Blake liked to call him, looking down on all the death and decay he'd created. The green figure, I said, was the creature who killed humanity, hence the dagger. 'It's the personification of death,' I said.

Leddington stared at me.

For a second, I felt he was genuinely surprised me and I grinned, savouring the moment.

'Well, well, Sophie York,' he said slowly. 'To think I was only interested in you for your body. There I was, neglecting that dazzling mind of yours.'

'You just can't be nice to me even once, can you?'

'What's the alternative name of this painting?' he rasped.

'Alternative?' I couldn't avoid the glint of triumph in his eyes.

'It's *The Lazar House*.'

I bristled. 'Is this mansion the Lazar House?'

Leddington's eyes flicked towards Zara. 'No, but maybe you'll see the real thing one of these days.'

'So what *is* a Lazar House?'

'In medieval times, beggars afflicted with dreadful chronic diseases, usually leprosy, were called lazars. Where they lived was the *Lazaretto*, the Lazar House.' He reached out and took my hand. 'You don't like thinking of death, do you?'

'Who does?'

'Nothing teaches us more about life than death.'

'Yeah, right.'

'Why do people like you never want to learn? Does thinking nauseate you?'

I wanted to say *Fuck off, wanker*! but I knew that if I walked away he'd take it as proof that I was stupid, so I stood my ground.

'Everyone ends up in the Lazar House in the end, Sophie. Why not celebrate it?'

'I don't see anything cool about worshipping death.'

Without any warning, he roughly pulled me into him and kissed me full on the lips.

I shoved him away as hard as I could and ran the back of my hand over my mouth in disgust. I headed straight for the bar. I ignored the sommelier, filled a large glass to the brim with the strongest red wine I could lay my hands on and gulped it down.

After that, I tried to keep as far from Leddington as possible, but if I thought I was escaping, I was wrong. Zara now sidled up to me.

'Have you been upsetting Charles?' she said. Her next remark startled me. 'Take off my mask and hand it to me.'

'Take it off yourself.'

She placed her hands over mine. 'But you know you want to.'

Almost against my will, I lifted her mask over her head. We were so close our breasts were practically touching. She gazed into my eyes and, for once, I didn't notice the usual contempt.

'Everyone needs a little *strange* from time to time, don't you think?' she said.

I wanted to…I don't know what I wanted.

'Do you think you have a good personality?' Zara asked.

'Pretty good, yes.'

She took her mask from me and held it in front of her. 'The word personality comes from the Latin word *persona*, meaning mask. Don't you think that's incredible? The thing that makes us unique, our personality, is a mask, something designed to conceal. What's underneath? – that's what we ought to be asking.' She brandished the skull-mask in front of my face. 'The real individual is so well hidden we never see him.'

'Very interesting.' I was desperate for an escape route.

'Of course, it's right that some things should remain hidden,' she said. 'Take omerta: that's a powerful concept, don't you think?' Her eyes bored into me. '*The art of keeping your mouth shut*.' She leaned forward, as if she were about to rub noses with me, or even kiss me like Leddington. 'No one likes a rat, do they?'

'No,' I said, pulling away from her.

She smiled. 'That's right, Sophie. Honour is everything to us.'

'I told you already – I'm no rat.'

'Even if you were, we'd deny everything. We leave no traces so there would be nothing for your police friends to find. It would be your word against ours.' Her voice had become a sinister rasp. 'We're not in the habit of forgiving our enemies.' She stabbed a finger through one of the eye-sockets of the skull mask. 'And we never forget them.'

She brought to mind those terrifying blonde children with gold eyes in that old horror movie *The Village of the Damned*; telepathic aliens whose powers grew stronger every day. They'd have destroyed the human race if they'd been allowed to grow up. Except now, it seemed, one *had* reached adulthood and she had her full alien powers at her disposal. I had been well and truly warned. Jesus, *threatened.*

'You don't have to worry about *me*,' I said.

Zara smiled. She tipped her chin and looked into my eyes. 'Do you know what you must do if you want the answers to all of this?' She abruptly stepped behind me. Before I knew what was happening, she had reached round and cupped my breasts. I nearly screamed with the shock. 'You must come into *my* world,' she whispered, breathing softly over the nape of my neck, her voice simultaneously forceful and seductive.

The world of the damned, I thought. I was certain she was offering me the chance to find out what the Top Table's secrets were. I didn't know if I was brave enough. I couldn't even tell her to take her hand off my breasts. Did I want her to?

'You have a beautiful body,' she said. 'I don't know why you hate me so much. After all, you want to be me. I saw it in your eyes the first time we met.'

When I tried to respond, not a thing came to mind, nothing whatever. I was like a cow in an abattoir, dumbly awaiting the terminal bolt in the brain.

'Have you any idea how lucky you are?' At last she took her hands away. 'We plucked you from the ranks of the nameless, the ciphers, the flatliners to give you an opportunity you can scarcely conceive. Nothing comes close to what we have to offer.'

'*Plucked* me?'

She walked round me in a circle. I felt stark naked, like a new harem girl being inspected by the sultan. What the *hell* was happening?

'I'm the gateway, the door,' she stated imperiously. 'As Jim Morrison said, "There are things known and things unknown and in between are The Doors." Believe me, I can open the door to a world you never dreamt of. I'll show you every unknown thing. You just need to have the courage to follow me.'

My head was beginning to spin. I could scarcely bear her looking at me.

'Would you accept the greatest pleasure imaginable if it were offered to you, no matter the cost?' Her eyes drilled into mine. 'A perfect moment to echo in eternity?'

'I think I'm going to be sick,' I said.

35

Alone

My eyes sprang open. I didn't understand why I was so cold. Shit, where was I? I tried to move, but my limbs were reluctant to co-operate. My head felt fuzzy, as though someone was trying to force kitchen sponges between my brain and my skull. Slowly I began to focus. I was still in the Great Hall. Daylight was flooding in. Last night...*Christ Almighty*...I experienced that shiver of panic you get when you wonder if you've made a complete drunken arse of yourself, and realise the answer is almost certainly *yes*.

I was lying on a wooden floor in nothing but my bra and knickers. My clothes were neatly folded in the corner, next to my shoes. The mansion was eerily quiet. I dressed quickly and started searching each room, looking for signs of life.

Nothing. Plain walls and bare floorboards in every room: the mansion was deserted!

When I gazed out of one of the upper-floor windows, I was astonished to see that a *For Sale* sign had been erected in the middle of the lawn. Jesus, how long had I been asleep? Another Top Table stunt? I stared at the sign and it began to swim in front of my eyes. They couldn't vanish like this, they just couldn't.

I went back downstairs into the Great Hall. Somehow I'd slept through what must have been a massive removal operation to vacate the mansion. Had I passed out? I remembered helping myself to as much red wine as I could guzzle, like an alcoholic who'd just been told that the *Last Drink Ever* saloon was closing in the next five minutes.

Everything I wanted to forget about last night insisted on marching to the front of my mind. After my close encounters with Leddington and Zara, I'd spent most of my time dodging them and gazing at Sam. He planted himself in the corner of the hall and stood there all night, his eyes glued to Zara. He wouldn't let anyone come near him – except her, of course. Now and again, she stepped close to him, whispered something then moved away again without waiting for a response. The more she did it, the more beguiled Sam seemed. He was like one of those cult members whose attachment to the cult becomes stronger the worse they treat him. I couldn't bear to watch, yet found it even harder not to. The car crash syndrome, I guess.

Yet my eyes had occasionally strayed from Sam. More than occasionally, perhaps. I didn't like to admit who it was I had been looking at. It made me wonder if I'd taken off my own clothes or someone else had stripped me. Leddington – our nation's future glorious leader? I didn't dare contemplate the other possibility.

Even though no one was around, I felt myself blushing. I tried to concentrate on other things. I walked around the Great Hall, listening to my echoing steps, recalling all the odd things that had happened here, the strange paintings, the weird parties, the glittering students and their fascination with death. I could detect it all even now, somehow ingrained in the fabric of the building. Were the Top Table putting it all behind them? Was that why Zara was selling up? In a few months she and the others would graduate, but what could the normal world possibly offer them? They seemed far beyond the touch of everyday things.

I went upstairs again and stood outside the one room I'd never been allowed to enter. The silver plaque with the quote from *The Aeneid* had been removed from Zara's door, but I could still see it just as clearly as on that first night. I repeated aloud the translation Marcus gave me: *These are the tears of things, and the stuff of our mortality cuts us to the heart.* My voice rebounded off the ceilings and floors, reverberated from the walls of the deserted hallways, flew at me like darts from every direction. Just like they did that first time, the words made me tearful in a way I didn't understand. They were even more poignant now.

I opened the door and stood on the threshold of the empty room, trying to imagine Zara here. A palatial space, it was somehow anonymous, with a simple white ceiling, magnolia walls and gleaming maple floorboards. It had an old-fashioned bay window, no doubt commanding a wonderful panorama over Green Park.

I wondered how many men Zara had devoured in this chamber. Were their charred bones hidden beneath the floorboards; the mortal remains of the poor legions of previous Sams who approached too close to the flame? There was no flame quite like her, was there? I'd burned when she touched me, but, if she'd kissed me, I feared I wouldn't have pulled away.

When I tried to take a step inside, my foot froze in the air, powerless. This room had been explicitly forbidden to me on the first night and nothing had changed. Zara's perfume lingered in the room; the scent her lovers must have associated with heaven or – after she'd tired of them – hell. I hurried away, leaping down the staircase in my haste to get out of this place.

Alone

Outside the mansion, I felt nauseous. It was a freezing morning and the lawn was covered with frost. I walked across the terrace and down the steps onto the grass. I wanted to escape, but something held me back, as if the mansion were invisibly gripping me. I buried my face in my hands. I detested these people. I detested what they'd done to me, what I'd become.

I started crying. I don't know for how long. My head was aching, my body shivering and sweating, as though I were some junkie. I gazed at the mansion's black door and realised I'd never set foot in there again. It had become such a huge part of me, given me the most vivid memories of my life, yet now I was outside. *Forever*.

My eyes flicked up to Zara's window. Did she see me coming that first time? I remembered the spectacular flower display – all those lush, black tulips with their golden-orange flashes – on the lawn in the summer. Marcus told me they were a special variety of a tulip known as *Oxford's Elite*. Zara had got a horticulturist to breed them specially for her. There had been something magical about it all. But there were no flowers now. Just winter setting in.

I looked up even further, at the mansion's ornate roof, at the statues of the angels and gargoyles. I wondered what they were intended to symbolise. That beauty and ugliness are inseparable? That angels can become monsters? Did that sum up the Top Table – angels with hearts of darkness? To me, they'd always be the beautiful and the damned.

Dusted with frost, the mansion resembled a frozen palace from a fairytale. As I gazed at the white facade glinting in the morning light, I remembered that story I read as a kid – was it *Narnia?* – about the Snow Queen who seduced the little boy. I thought of the Snow Queen's palace of dead kisses and frozen loveliness, its white sparkling beauty, twinkling like ice crystals. But there was no happiness in the Ice Maiden's palace, was there? She stole laughter with her kisses that froze the heart. Had her icy fingers touched my heart, just as they had Sam's?

I trudged the half mile to my apartment, showered and changed into fresh clothes – skinny jeans, a fleece and cowboy boots, my default winter wear. What now?

I phoned Sam and Jez. Both had switched off their mobiles. I *did* get through to Mencken. He said Jez had gone out half an hour after me yesterday and never come back. They weren't at the Sargasso.

'They've both *vanished*,' he said.

Vanished? Part of me wondered if Jez and Sam were involved in a game of their own, or maybe another of their bets was in full swing. All through this thing, I'd been sure Sam was at the centre. Now I'd started to think it might be me. Someone was playing mind games with me. Right from the beginning it had been that way. Mencken started the ball rolling with his bizarre invitation to The Gherkin. Jez and Sam had taken up the slack and then the Top Table stepped in. I shook my head. I wasn't interesting enough. The truth was I was just the cheap-seats sideshow, and that's all I'd ever be.

I didn't know what to do with myself. I made myself a strong coffee and tried to clear my head. I took a couple of paracetemols then switched on the TV and watched the news, wondering if there would be anything about Sam. Part of me dreaded he'd show up dead somewhere with a convenient suicide note on his body. The police and the newspapers had explained away the Millionaires' Death Club, but I knew the stuff they'd found on Marcus' computer wasn't the whole truth.

I opened the fridge and reached out for a carton of grapefruit juice. As I stood there, my eyes drifted down to the freezer compartment.

Ice.

Sam said his present for Zara needed extreme cold, didn't he? He was keeping it at the castle hotel. I rushed out of my flat, jumped into my car and drove fast to the *Aggiornamento*.

A blonde at reception directed me to the lounge and said the manager would be with me in a moment. I sat staring out of the window at the moat where Sam had dreamt of taking Zara for the moonlit gondola ride that never was.

In the distance, the lake we'd driven to in the summer to have our picnic was different, faded, its vivid blue transformed into washed-out grey. When I thought of those sublime June days, everything was sepia-tinted, like photographs from another century. I was so young in June. I didn't understand anything. Now it was November and I was decades older.

When the manager appeared, he initially walked past me. I guess he didn't recognise me. Maybe I didn't recognise myself anymore. I waved at him to attract his attention.

'Mr Lincoln's suite isn't ready just yet,' he said apologetically. 'We weren't expecting him until later.'

'Er, he wanted me to check on his surprise.'

The manager nodded. 'Ah, that *is* ready. I was just having a look at it. I'm certain the lady will love it. Actually, when he first mentioned it to me, I thought...After all, you and Mr Lincoln in the summer...He's very taken with his new girlfriend, isn't he?'

I shrugged. New girlfriend, indeed. I wished so much he had been satisfied with me. If we'd stuck together maybe Zara would never have got inside our heads. Now that she was there, I had no idea how to get her back out.

The manager gave me a key and said, 'The pool's just as requested. Can you make sure you return the key to *me*?'

The pool room was freezing cold. I took a few steps inside then stopped, stock still, as if I'd gazed straight at Medusa. So *this* was Sam's present.

With all the water drained from the pool, I was able to walk down the steps and onto the black-and-white-tiled floor. Slowly, I negotiated my way around Sam's surprise. He had commissioned an ice sculpture, but it wasn't of swans, lions, cars or any of the other usual things – it was a group of life-sized human figures.

There were ten couples or, rather, one couple in ten different positions spread across the entire pool. The whole piece formed a narrative. The couple were at first apart, with their backs to each other. Then the man caught sight of the beautiful woman and began a pursuit. By the time I'd reached the fifth part of the sculpture, the woman had rebuffed her suitor with an outstretched hand. Three stages later the man's hand was accepted. In the final composition, the two were locked together, naked, in a passionate kiss like Rodin's famous sculpture, with the opaque ice taking on a sensual lustre, almost bringing the figures to life. The whole work had been sculpted exquisitely and it was unmistakable who it depicted: Sam and Zara, the enchanted boy and the fatal ice queen.

I wondered what the sculptors thought when Sam commissioned them to do it. Did they wonder who this beauty was? Did they fall in love with her too, with that frozen perfection, that ice-cold heart?

At the far end of the pool, a camcorder rested on a tripod. Did Sam plan to film the great moment when Zara arrived to see her present? Perhaps he hoped to make the ice doubles come alive, to take Zara in his arms for real.

Maybe the sculptures would appeal to Zara's massive ego, but I couldn't imagine her doing anything except mock them, as she did everything else connected with Sam. Above all, I was certain she'd laugh at the final one.

As I looked more closely at that passionate embrace, I saw that it wasn't exactly the same as Rodin's *Kiss*, after all. In Rodin's, the girl seemed dominated by her lover, with her head tilted backwards and the man's hand resting on her bare thigh. Here, there was no sense of the girl being submissive. Her lover's hand hesitated above her breast, above a beautifully carved erect nipple.

Maybe Sam intended that feature to show how attracted Zara had become to him, at least in his imagination. But to my eyes – and Zara's too, I was sure – all it revealed was that he didn't dare touch her. He was just the frightened little boy awestruck by the Snow Queen in all her wintry power, dreaming of her white sparkling kisses, her frozen caresses.

I stood there, transfixed by Zara's face. It had started to haunt me. I could only guess at how much it tormented Sam. What did he have in mind? To bring her here tonight, show her the surprise then propose to her? In the state he was in, anything was possible. Hollywood marries into royalty. It even had a suitably ludicrous ring to it. What was that word Marcus used? – *hyperreal*.

36

The Hospital

As I left the hotel and headed for the car park, I tried Sam's mobile again but still got nothing. Mencken and Jez were also incommunicado.

Leaning against my car, I watched my breath condensing in the cold air. Although the sun was shining for the first time in days, it didn't provide any heat. With a sun like this, the whole planet could freeze. The more time I spent in the world of the Top Table, the more I felt part of me was freezing too.

As I watched a beautiful swan skim the surface of the lake, I wasn't sure what was worse – being humiliated by the Top Table or ignored by them. I couldn't face going back to my apartment.

I trudged over the frost-covered grass towards the lake's edge. I wanted to dip my hand in the water and feel its coldness. It would comfort me somehow. As I stared off into the distance, I noticed the redbrick building on the far side of the lake. Marcus and Leddington had been so secretive about it when we picnicked here in the summer. Maybe…

I returned to my car then set out on the short journey round the lake. In minutes, I was outside the huge U-shaped building. It was in a dilapidated condition and all of its windows were boarded up. When I walked round to the side, I found five black people-carriers parked on a derelict gravel football pitch. *Bingo.* Marcus had once told me that the Top Table often used a convoy of people-carriers to transport them around.

I thought it might be easier to get inside the building from the rear, but all I encountered was an overgrown garden, choked with weeds and ferns, enclosed by the building's two wings. Its concrete paths had disappeared beneath the undergrowth.

Returning to the main entrance, I noticed a rusting plaque on the wall. 'St Benedict's Hospital,' it read, 'For the containment and treatment of contagious diseases of the infected poor.'

I tried to force open the door but it was firmly locked. I strained to hear any noise coming from inside. I couldn't believe this hospital had no part to play. It was exactly the sort of place the Top Table would love.

I skirted round the building, squinting at each boarded-up window, searching for any weak point. I picked up a metal pipe lying on a grassed-over path, planning to use it as a crude lever. I found a corner window with loose boards and dislodged them. I peered inside but saw nothing except thick darkness. I clambered through and jumped down onto the floor, my feet scrunching on broken glass. I stood there for a second, breathing the stale air. Beyond, there was only that deep darkness. When I heard a scurrying sound, my heart thudded. God, maybe the building was full of rats. I brought out my mobile phone and used the light from the display to get an idea of where I was. I seemed to be in a long corridor, apparently clean and tidy. I had that odd feeling you sometimes get in old buildings when you think that just yesterday it was in full working order, with hundreds of nurses and doctors streaming past. I could almost see them bustling past me discussing the latest cases.

I moved further into the building, trying to tiptoe to muffle my steps. I passed through several reception areas and empty wards where it was easy to imagine ghosts still lying in beds, waiting for the cure that never came. There was no sign of the Top Table.

I trudged on, depressed. At the far end of one wing, light edged out from the bottom of a black door. As I crept nearer, I stepped on something. Directing the light from my mobile phone downwards, I picked out a silver object – another mobile phone…an unmistakable *Vertu*!

I stuffed it in my pocket then pointed my mobile at the door, found a small hole and peered through. Shapes materialised. The room was completely white, even the tiled floor. The Top Tablers were sitting on two long white benches, all the men on one, all the women on the other. The men were in black tuxedos, the women in black cocktail dresses. They all had their faces chalked white, just as I'd seen that day at Royal Ascot.

No one was speaking. In fact, they were hardly looking at each other. They seemed scared. I scanned around for Sam and Jez. No sign of them. Zara and Leddington were also missing.

I strained against the door, trying to force my eye as close as possible to the hole to see if I could get a wider view.

A door at the far end swung open and Zara strode into the room. Wearing tight black leather jeans and a beige padded tunic, together with a gorgeous white fur hat, she looked every inch a modern Lara from *Dr Zhivago*. She took a few steps and positioned herself beneath a lamp. With her ice-cool blue eyes, she was indescribably beautiful. In her buttonhole was the blackest of tulips: *Queen of Night*. How apt.

She said something that I didn't catch and a second later another figure emerged from the back room. I gasped. Jez was gagged and blindfolded, his hands tied behind his back.

There was no sound, no movement from anyone. What was going on? Then I heard more shuffling steps. A second figure appeared, also gagged, blindfolded and with his hands bound. *Sam*! I pulled back my head. Only then did I notice circles of light dancing around me. I spun round to see who was behind me and was dazzled by several torch beams. Leddington's face materialised in the centre of the stinging light.

'Give her *the treatment*,' he said.

His two helpers seized me by the arms and forced a gag over my mouth. The door of the white room opened and the members of the Top Table filed out, pushing Sam and Jez ahead of them. A blindfold was slipped over my eyes. Something hard like a truncheon was pushed against my back.

'Keep walking until I tell you to stop.' Leddington jabbed me. Ahead of me, I heard someone opening a door and felt fresh air rushing in. I was pushed outside into the cold. I took a few steps then tripped. Someone's hand gripped my shoulder and steadied me. I heard a metallic scraping noise and something being heaved to one side.

'You're about to go down a manhole,' Leddington said. He gave orders for Sam and Jez to be untied.

I got a prod in the back and realised it was my signal to climb downwards. Someone helped me to locate the rungs of a ladder and I descended. At the bottom, I was roughly shoved forward. I heard shuffling feet and a cough. A door slammed.

'Take off their blindfolds and remove their gags,' Leddington said.

It took my eyes a couple of seconds to readjust to the light. I was with Sam and Jez in a concrete bunker painted lurid scarlet with a huge black skull logo staring out from one wall. This, I realised, was where the Top Table ended and the Millionaires' Death Club began.

37

The Bunker

Leddington pointed at a row of bunk beds at the far end of the room. 'Your accommodation,' he said. 'It's half past two. The games begin much later. I suggest you do the same as the rest of us and get some sleep. You'll need all your energy for tonight.' He gestured towards a small white bottle on a table. 'If you're not tired right now, I recommend the sleeping tablets. They'll knock you out fast.'

One of his colleagues removed the ladder we'd climbed down and then the three men left by a side door, locking it behind them.

'Jesus, what did they do to you?' I stared frantically at Sam. 'Did they harm you?'

He had the strangest, spaced-out look in his eyes.

'They didn't do anything serious,' Jez said. 'Just tied us up, shoved us in a corner and made sure we couldn't see or hear. You know, the usual stuff posh English people get up to at those private schools of theirs.' He scanned around, looking more bored than anything else.

'How come you're back all of a sudden, Jez?' I asked.

He ignored me, turned to Sam and laughed. 'Well, this is what we wanted right from the start. The answer to the big secret, right?'

I repeated my question.

'I couldn't leave you guys to have all the fun, could I? I'm taking Sam back with me when this is over. Right, Sam?'

I was certain Jez wasn't being straight. I wanted to grab him and shake his secrets out of him. 'Why are you really here, Jez?' I said.

'Just making sure I win Alphabet Love.' He gave me a cheesy wink.

'I'm taking the tablet,' Sam said. 'We have a long wait.'

I went along with Sam's example and hit the bunks after taking a pill, wondering what on earth would be waiting for us when we woke.

****

When I next opened my eyes, Leddington was standing over me. Sam and Jez were already on their feet, looking groggy.

'Showtime,' Leddington whispered. He handed each of us a white robe and a fresh blindfold. 'Strip naked then put on the robe.'

I panicked. I didn't want him seeing me nude.

'I'm not doing this,' I yelped.

'Suit yourself. You'll have to stay here until we're finished.'

'Hey, man,' Sam intervened, 'don't be a jerk. We'll turn our backs.'

Leddington glared at me. 'You know, you make me laugh. You stripped off on national TV and danced with monkeys. Now suddenly you're Miss Modesty.' He shrugged. 'In a few hours, it won't make the slightest bit of difference. OK, you have ten seconds.'

All of the men turned away while I got naked and pulled on the robe. 'Finished,' I said, mouthing a *thanks* to Sam.

After Sam and Jez changed, Leddington tied our blindfolds and warned us not to try to remove them. The door closed and there was silence. I took a deep breath of musty air.

'What happens now?' I asked, but Sam and Jez didn't answer.

Minutes passed in silence. Just when I thought the Top Table might be playing a joke on us, I heard several people entering the room. They gagged us, put hoods over our heads and tied our hands behind our backs. My heartbeat raced.

'For a mortal to become divine a sacrifice is required,' a deep voice said. 'There can be no rebirth without death.'

This was all wrong. They were going too far. I thought of Lawrence, Chloe and Marcus. Did they take part in this same ceremony? Did it push them over the edge?

'I am the conductor of souls,' the voice went on. 'My title is the *hierokeryx*. I am the herald of the sacred, the guide of the dead through the underworld.'

I heard a door opening and we were told to walk straight ahead. There was an odd smell of countryside that made no sense down here. I breathed slowly, trying to quell the thudding of my heart. After about thirty seconds, someone pressed their hand against my chest, stopping me. Several people jostled past me. I had an impression I was in a large room, surrounded by many people.

Someone played a tune on panpipes. When it ended, shouting began. The shouts turned into low, harsh voices, overlapping each other. *We'll kill you*, they said. *You're going to be cut up like a pig and fed to cattle. Your head will be cut off and sent to your parents.* The voices became more menacing, the threats more grotesque. *You'll be buried up to your neck and honey smeared around your eyes. Then we'll break open a hive of bees over your head. We'll make small cuts all over your body and pour ants, leeches and spiders over you. We'll feed your entrails to your pets, and send your kidneys to your lovers.*

Someone clashed cymbals together. The voices stopped. I began to sway then felt myself falling. Someone hauled me back to my feet and shoved me forward. I could hear crazy echoes that started out as laughter then mutated into screams. Sometimes the sounds were distant, at other times right beside me. I was sure I was being led through a succession of twisting passageways. A labyrinth? I had no idea if Sam and Jez were still with me, but I was aware of the deep breathing of several people. Occasionally they whispered to each other but I never quite caught what they were saying. Sometimes I thought they were talking in some ancient language. The air was increasingly stale.

The acoustics changed and at the same time the musty smell gave way to fresher air. The countryside scent I'd noticed before was much stronger, but I still couldn't place it. I was certain we'd moved into another large space.

I heard a grunting noise that sounded disturbingly non-human. Every other sound faded as my ears strained to hear what was making the noise. It became slow, rhythmic. Someone – or *something* – was breathing unnaturally heavily. I pictured the Minotaur standing there at the centre of its labyrinth, awaiting its sacrifice.

Someone shouted something, put their hand on my head and forced me down onto my belly.

'*Crawl.*'

I tried my best, but it was almost impossible with my hands tied behind my back. I edged forward using a combination of my left shoulder and right knee. My feet were grabbed and I was hurled forward. I rolled down a steep embankment, and landed in a heap, colliding with someone. I tried to work out what had happened. I thought I was in a pit.

I knelt up, nausea billowing in my stomach. A man shouted. The shout grew louder, turning into an ear-shattering yelp. Something grunted and snorted. I thought it might be a horse. A whooshing sound was followed by a bestial howl. Liquid, hot and sticky, splattered all over me. *Mother of Mercy* – what had they done? A tremor surged through me. Blood pounded through my ears. A second later, I was dragged out of the pit. Someone ripped off my hood and tossed away my gag and blindfold. *Sweet Jesus.*

I seemed to be in a slaughterhouse. My robe was drenched with bloody splashes. I thought Sam had been murdered, but then I saw him standing a couple of feet away, blood-soaked, staring madly. My gaze followed his. I wanted to run, but my legs were jelly. Some creature had been hacked to pieces on a lattice altar above the pit. It was only when I saw the horns that I knew what it was.

I stared at Sam and saw him blinking rapidly. His head swivelled around, and now mine did the same. We were in a cave, lit with concealed uplights so that everything was casting shadows. All round the walls, bulls' heads were staring at us from hooks they'd been placed on. I counted at least ten, many of them in an advanced state of decomposition. I stood there in shock. At least the peculiar smell now made sense, but I had no idea how they'd managed to drag bulls down here.

Around us, figures in red robes, hoods and masks began to emerge from the dark corners. The masks were like the faces of some forgotten race: huge circular eyes, noses placed at crazy angles, unsmiling mouths.

A hooded man in black stepped through the ranks of red.

'This is the masque of phantoms,' he said. I recognised the voice of the hierokeryx. 'Meet the creatures of the underworld. You know what they must do.'

I felt everything crowding in on me. I couldn't breathe. My mouth hung open as I desperately sucked in air.

The hierokeryx signalled to the phantoms and each of them picked up a long rod from a pile. 'Now I am become death, the destroyer of worlds,' the hierokeryx declared.

In silence, the phantoms struck us with their rods, almost in slow motion. As each hit my body, I imagined my flesh was being sliced into. I stared down at my robe, expecting to see it cut to shreds, with blood pouring from scores of slashes all over me. But there was nothing.

A man slapped me violently across the face. I saw a bucket being lifted and then a huge blur of red racing towards my eyes. I ducked. Too late. Blood was everywhere, running through my hair, streaming down my face. It was all over my hands, spilling down my back and over my breasts.

'Turn round,' someone barked from behind me. 'And see your future.'

Disorientated, I shuffled round to face the speaker. Three marble headstones confronted me with our names on them, and a date. *Today*.

We were dragged away. Upwards we went, up the long slope of a smooth brick tunnel, lit by flickering strip lights, until we reached a white-tiled toilet block. We were stripped of our robes, thrown naked into a shower and hosed down with freezing water. The next moment a huge blast of hot air hit us as though some industrial-scale hand-dryer had been switched on.

The warm air cut off after a few seconds and fresh white robes were thrust at us. We were hauled out and marched along a whitewashed corridor.

A huge painting covered one of the walls. It was a Caravaggio and I realised it must be *The Raising of Lazarus* that Marcus once told me about. Lazarus was reaching towards the divine light emanating from Jesus. The painting's significance was obvious: like Lazarus, we'd been raised from the dead.

A door swung open and we were bundled into a brightly lit white room, full of people in white hooded robes like our own. They were wearing smiling golden masks. They began to clap and cheer.

I suppose I should have been relieved, but numbness swept over me. I was breathless, exhausted, my head spinning.

One of the revellers stepped forward and removed her mask – *Zara*.

'Welcome,' she said, 'to the Millionaires' Death Club.'

38

The Cards

'Sacrifice means *making holy*,' Zara declared. She stood there in the middle of the white room, surrounded by her disciples, with all the glacial perfection that made her so infinitely beguiling – like the high priestess of an ancient cult. 'Tonight, one of us shall become divine,' she said, her voice echoing eerily. She turned to the hierokeryx. 'The cards, please.'

As I looked on, my heart pumped wildly. I'd barely recovered from the blood ceremony and I realised I was about to be plunged into something even worse. All around me, everyone took off their masks. Their faces were filled with excitement.

'There are fifty-two cards and twenty-six people,' Zara said, shuffling the cards. 'Two apiece.'

According to the Fourth Protocol, the knave of hearts was the critical card in the ceremony we were about to undertake, but I couldn't stop thinking of the fatal game in *The Suicide Club*.

We stood in a circle. Zara went round dealing two cards to each of us. 'Don't look until I say so,' she ordered. When she finished, she clapped her hands. 'Reveal the first card.'

I looked at mine: the nine of diamonds. The hierokeryx inspected everyone's cards before turning to Zara and shaking his head.

'Discard the first and show the second,' Zara said. Everyone threw down their cards into the middle of the circle.

This time I got the queen of clubs. I glanced at Sam. He had the two of spades.

The hierokeryx again went round scrutinising the cards then suddenly stopped. 'Fate has spoken,' he announced and raised Jez's hand.

'So, Mr Easton, you shall perform the selection.' A peculiar smile flitted over Zara's face. 'Provide us with the Chosen One.'

Jez hesitated for a moment and then his hand stretched out and came to rest on Sam's shoulder. In Sam's eyes I saw a look of...*wonder*.

'It's what you wanted, isn't it?' Jez sounded apologetic.

'You understand what this means?' Zara asked.

'Let's do it.'

Sam turned round and I realised he was looking for me. I pushed through the throng and grabbed his hand. 'Please don't go through with this.'

'My whole life has been about this moment,' he whispered. 'I'm glad you're here.'

For an instant, I felt incredible pride, but then I grew breathless. I couldn't move, couldn't think, couldn't do anything. I believed Sam had just been sentenced to death in some unknown way. Yet this was a Hollywood god. He probably thought he was indestructible like the action heroes he portrayed. Maybe I thought that too. Perhaps the other three wanted to die and this experience simply pushed wide a door that was already open. If anyone could beat the rap, it was Sam.

I shook my head. There were no movie cameras here: Sam was mortal just like the rest of us.

'Time to go,' Zara said.

39

NexS

Zara led everyone through a connecting corridor and into a large hexagonal room partitioned into six zones. The walls of the different zones were coated with thousands of exotically coloured synthetic flowers. One zone contained purple carnations, one red snowdrops, another blue orchids. There was an emerald zone of tulips and a zone of weird roses with petals of crystal veined with microscopic rivers of translucent blue liquid. Finally, there was a zone of black daffodils, in the centre of which was a huge holographic skull like the ones on the cards Sam received. The ceiling was made of thick glass, filled with an artificially generated electric storm that threw a continuously changing light into the room like some trippy, 1960s psychedelic experiment.

The hierokeryx moved through the room putting round everyone's neck a silver chain with a glass locket containing a pill-sized white sphere. So, I was finally seeing NexS. It seemed innocuous, almost pathetic.

Sam's chain was gold and his locket contained a black sphere. Somehow, this was much more majestic.

'The NexS ceremony begins at the twelfth hour,' the hierokeryx announced as several burning incense sticks were brought into the room, trailing fumes. 'Think of it as a poem. As Rimbaud said, "The poet makes himself a visionary by a long, immense and reasoned derangement of all the senses." We, too, are poets and Rimbaud's project is our own, our *Season in Hell*. The senses are bombarded, deconstructed, re-assembled in a new configuration open to all possibilities. But the final moment of transformation awaits. Only the Substance can deliver that.'

He stretched out his arms like a druid welcoming the sunrise. 'When every flower glows in our garden of earthly delights, everyone shall take their capsule.'

I'd never felt uneasier. Anything could happen down here. A huge, ornate Grandfather clock showed five to midnight.

Hypnotically sexy music began to play, a breathy female voice singing over a sensuous electro beat. Everyone started to dance, apart from Sam and me.

My head grew lighter and the room seemed to spin. I was sure the incense sticks were giving off narcotic fumes. I walked through the revellers, trying to think straight. Everyone was staring into space, as if their eyes had become glass, yet their arms were moving frenetically, some stabbing them back and forth as though they were the wildest of ravers in Ibiza, while others carved intricate patterns in the air like trippy hippies. Many had glow sticks and luminous bracelets that echoed the colours of the synthetic flowers all around us.

I had an extraordinary impression of sexual energy cruising through the room, touching people until they practically glowed with desire. Sparks shot from the ceiling to the floor. I imagined I was trapped inside a plasma globe. My hearing had become amplified. When Zara reached out to stop Sam, I swore I heard her whispering that she'd dance for him.

'*Better than Salome's dance...*'

I was hot and cold at the same time. I glanced at the clock. *God, time up.* Everyone stopped dead as the clock signalled midnight with booming chimes.

'Let the ceremony begin,' the hierokeryx said, throwing back his hood. I gasped. It was blond Elvis.

All around us, the synthetic flowers glowed, like a million points of rainbow light in the darkness. I felt as though I was wrapped in all the bright colours of the universe. It was breathtaking. I had a sensation of being in outer space, swimming through an ocean of changing colours, floating in liquid time.

The hierokeryx asked everyone to take their capsules from their lockets and put them in their mouths. He gestured to Sam to do nothing for now.

I took out my capsule and stared at it. What would it do to me? Could I get away with dropping it on the ground and crushing it? Around me, everyone else was swallowing their capsules. Jez didn't hesitate.

Leddington was watching me. I put the capsule in my mouth and reluctantly crunched on it. A sweet liquid oozed into my mouth.

Zara personally removed Sam's black pill from his locket and now placed it in his mouth.

'*Free* yourself,' she said.

Several people helped Sam into a high-backed chair in the middle of the room. The chair had a circular Caravaggio painting on it. It was *Medusa*, her hair made of writhing snakes, her eyes wild.

Everyone gathered around and the music changed. The dark, sinister tones of Marilyn Manson's version of *Sweet Dreams are Made of This* boomed around the room. If there was a darker, more sickly song, I'd never heard it. It was cruel and utterly perverse.

Zara began to move slowly, swinging her hips, working herself into a rhythm.

Sam's hand stretched out to touch Zara's thigh.

'I want you.' He half rose from his seat.

'I know.' She pushed him back.

'I must…' He looked pained.

Zara commenced the most sensuous of stripteases. Bit by bit, she allowed her white gown to slide over her shoulders. Soon, only her breasts were stopping the robe falling completely.

Everyone was swaying and moaning. They had closed their eyes and thrown back their heads. Their lips were trembling. A wave of pleasure swept round the room, intensifying as it moved, feeding from everyone it passed. *Devouring us*.

I'd never felt anything like it. I was dissolving, losing my identity, becoming united with everyone in the room. In seconds, we were a single organism, capable of feeling just one sensation. No other thoughts, no concerns, just *pleasure*. A *universe* of pleasure. Pleasure, most especially, in the perfect form of Zara, the goddess of sex. It was swamping everything, short-circuiting all inhibitions.

My perceptions were being rearranged, my senses reconstructed. I was sucking in unimaginable pleasures, new thoughts and feelings, an entirely different reality. A freeze-frame world, then monochrome then rainbow-coloured. Sights, sounds and smells merged. I could touch everyone in the room simultaneously. Distances vanished. Everything was connected, interlinked, the same.

At last, Zara let her robe slip over one breast and then the other. It fell to the ground. She stepped free, naked. Her body was perfect. Her pubic hair had been waxed into a sexy landing strip; her breasts were firm and capped with erect pink nipples. Every part of her was sinuous, toned, lightly tanned. All of us were drawn towards her, towards that phenomenal beauty. The light glinted off a Death's Head silver piercing in her belly button. With a ballet dancer's elegance, she moved past me towards Sam, her glorious long legs stretching up to a bottom to die for.

Sam stared at her with the look of a man who'd just set eyes on every Shangri-La ever conceived. Zara sat astride him and kissed his forehead. Sam threw his arms around her while she writhed on his lap. Up and down she moved, virtually riding him. I felt as if a bridge had opened between Sam and me and that everything he was feeling was rushing over the bridge and straight into me. It was incredible. I had the same desire, the same lust, the same love as Sam. I wanted Zara, wanted her like I'd never wanted anything in my life. I wanted to have her, to lick her, to fuck her, to spray sperm inside her then all over her body and face. I wanted to possess every part of her, every atom. I'd die if I didn't.

A blue strobe light started to flash. Sam reared up in the seat and tried to take off his robe. Zara pushed him back and got off him as if she were dismounting a horse. Everyone else was disrobing, including me, and in a moment we were naked. Every man was erect. I felt their lust so much I was convinced I had an erection too.

Zara grabbed Jez from the throng and jumped onto him, throwing her legs round his back to anchor herself. Jez spun her round, slammed her against the wall, and, without missing a beat, started pounding in and out of her. Zara moaned as if she were having the most intense orgasm imaginable. Then we all started moaning. I felt as if Jez was screwing me. It was unbelievable, fantastic, the best sex ever. We were all pairing off and fucking. All except Sam.

Or maybe especially Sam because, somehow, we were all Sam. And we were all Jez. We were all Zara. We were all the men in the room and all the women. We were all fucking and all being fucked. What sex were we? Male? Female? We were both and neither. We had become some new kind of human being, much more powerful, twice as conscious.

But, above all, Sam's feelings were pouring into us. He was taking us over. Jez had become Sam and because Jez was fucking Zara that meant Sam was fucking Zara. His pleasure was accelerating, gathering incredible energy as it spun like a huge whirlpool, sucking everything in. He wasn't laying a finger on Zara and yet he was. Or thought he was. And that was all that mattered.

My skull was pounding as though the whole world wanted to cram itself inside my head. Who was I? I couldn't tell any longer. And then I came, almost *screaming* with pleasure and I knew exactly who I was. I was Sam and I'd just had the greatest experience of my life.

And now I had nothing left.

40

The Lazar House

When I awoke, I was lying on the floor with a red blanket over me. Most of the others were asleep but some, in white bathrobes, were sitting up drinking coffee.

Sam! I looked around in panic and then I saw him, curled up a few feet away, sleeping. Not dead. No bizarre suicide note. Nothing. I almost laughed.

But I couldn't dismiss last night as any sort of dream, could I? Something incredible had happened to me, or maybe miraculous was a better word. Not an *out-of-body experience* but an *in-everyone-else's*.

'That was the best yet,' someone said. I turned my head and there was Leddington, smiling at me rather too warmly. He casually placed his hand on my upper thigh and gave it an intimate squeeze. God, I'd fucked him, hadn't I?

'I was afraid he'd kill us,' he said, glancing at Sam. 'He was so hot for Zara, I thought he'd make us vomit, piss, shit and come all at once: total fucking simultaneous evacuation of every orifice.'

'What happened?' I mumbled. Everything that happened last night seemed infinitely strange. It was as though I'd found myself in a secret universe where all the rules had been altered in some way. I had been left as someone who looked like me but definitely wasn't me. I could barely remember my name.

'God Almighty,' I said, 'what *was* that stuff?'

Leddington smiled. 'I forgot you were a NexS virgin.'

He lay back, resting his head on his hands. 'NexS gets its name from *nexus* and *excess*. It's a connection drug. What it does is allow everyone to come together to share the same experience, but it's not an equal experience because the Chosen One gets a much higher concentration than everyone else. They feed off his pleasure. But he can also feel their pleasure, and that increases his own. It ends in a kind of pleasure overload.'

'Where does it come from?'

Leddington shook his head. 'Zara has an arrangement with the supplier, that's all I know. She never talks about it and no one's allowed to ask.'

I looked away. I didn't know why but I wanted to cry. I was so lonely.

'*Post coitum omne animal triste est*,' Leddington remarked.

'*What*?'

'After sexual intercourse every animal is sad,' he explained. 'Don't worry about it, Sophie. When the show's over, you always feel empty. One second you're energised like you've never been in your life, the next it's all gone. My first time, I thought someone had grabbed me by the neck and plunged me into an ocean of hurt.'

As far as I was concerned, *hell* was more like it.

'You said you'd show me the Lazar House some time. It's something to do with this place, isn't it?'

Leddington gave me an odd smile. 'The old hospital up top was once the Lazar House for the whole of London. Before that, the lepers...'

'They lived down here, didn't they?'

Leddington nodded. 'This was the place Lawrence mentioned in his suicide note. It was originally a maze of underground caves. The MOD converted it into a nuclear command bunker in the early 1950s.'

'I need some fresh air,' I said.

Leddington found me a pair of slippers and a snorkel jacket.

'It's freezing outside,' he said.

He led me through a maze of neat, magnolia corridors. When we came to a staircase, he said we were almost there. At the top, there were two metallic doors with levers, wheels and buttons attached to them; everything except straightforward handles.

'When this place was operational, these blast doors had to be sealed gas-tight,' Leddington said. It takes minutes to open and close them.' He pressed a button and they swung open. 'We've had them modified, of course.'

Daylight flooded in, making me shrink like a vampire. We stepped outside and I heard birds twittering. There had been an overnight snowfall and everything was white. We were in the centre of the overgrown hospital garden. I glanced back and saw that we'd emerged from a thick concrete block painted in camouflage.

The daylight was feeble, almost sickly. I figured dawn had only just come up. The hospital, covered with snow, looked like a ghostly apparition.

'It was built in Victorian times,' Leddington said. 'They closed it at the end of the Second World War and it's been derelict ever since. Zara bought it a couple of years ago, mostly because of this bunker. It's a huge space. There are fifty rooms in total, including three decontamination rooms, a central control room, a canteen, a kitchen, dormitories, rest rooms and conference rooms. We've mothballed most of the complex but Zara has big plans for it. She intends to convert it into…' He glanced at me. '…a unique sex club for the super-rich.'

More weird nonsense, I thought. 'I'm exhausted,' I mumbled. 'I need more sleep.'

'Be careful,' Leddington said, 'the sleepy heads always miss the real action.'

41

Ice Heart

Shit, why had I gone to sleep again? Now I was in my car and driving fast towards the *Aggiornamento*, hoping I wasn't too late. I didn't know if I was in a fit state to be behind a wheel but I had no choice. They told me Sam had left with Zara over an hour earlier.

'He's not coming back,' the others said. Apparently, he'd asked to be dropped off at the hotel and wanted Zara to go with him. I tried to convince myself everything would be OK. He was a Hollywood legend, for Christ's sake.

When I reached the hotel, I leapt out of my car and ran into reception. The manager was there, talking to one of his staff.

'Is Sam here?' I blurted.

The manager nodded. 'He went to check his, er, *surprise*. He said he didn't want to be disturbed.'

'I need to see him right away.'

'Well, since it's you...'

I bolted for the pool. When I reached the double doors, I was almost too frightened to put my hand on the handle. It creaked and I managed to push it open a few inches. I couldn't see anything inside. There were no windows. All the light came from a few overhead strip-lights.

I stepped into the room, my head bowed.

'Sam?' I whispered.

Only my faint echo came back.

I said it again. Nothing. I knew, I *knew*. Why did you do it, Sam? Didn't you get what you wanted?

I inched my way to the poolside, my eyes practically closed. When I opened them…

Sam was lying face up on the floor of the pool in about an inch of water. *Not moving*.

I wanted to throw up. I felt so dizzy. I couldn't…

****

I had the strangest feeling I was outside, standing on the hotel's lawn near the edge of the lake. A woman was talking to me, asking if I was all right. I ignored her and stared at the blue sky. The sun was shining so brightly, even though it was November. A perfect day, the weatherman had said on my car radio that morning. Everything seemed different. All the colours around me had faded, except blue. That was all I could see – *blue* – like Zara's eyes, like the sky trapped inside ice, like kisses trapped inside the Snow Queen's palace. I heard more voices. They were asking if I'd been crying.

'*She's upset about Sam,*' one of the voices said. '*Did she know him? Haven't I seen her before somewhere*?'

I had to get away.

'*Come back, come back…we can help you.*'

I ran as fast as I could. Did Sam have any idea what he'd got himself into? He'd never met people like Zara. She was more than a beautiful woman: she was history, a bloodline, an accumulation of centuries of power and dominance. What chance did Sam have? He was just a movie star.

****

My eyes flashed open. I was sitting in a little ball at the edge of the swimming pool, with my knees pulled up to my chin. Maybe I'd blacked out. Did I hallucinate? I refused to look into the pool. Maybe I'd imagined that Sam was dead. You can't kill Hollywood legends. Everyone knows that.

Something made a sound, a low whirring. Perhaps I'd heard that noise all along and just not paid attention…Sam's camcorder.

Numb, I went over, picked it up off its tripod then sat back down at the side of the pool to play back the pictures Sam had recorded. I stared at the images on the little LCD screen. The first thing I saw was Sam just after he'd switched on the camcorder. He stared into the lens, his eyes struggling to focus. His hair hadn't been combed and his face was covered with stubble. I reached out and touched his face on the screen.

'Can you see?' he asked.

He gestured at the scene behind him, at the collection of ice sculptures in the swimming pool. Picking up the camcorder, he walked round every one of the ten sculptures, cataloguing the details of each of the ice couples, but rarely letting the focus stray from Zara's face.

'Who is she?' he babbled. 'I guess I knew all along. Could anything have stopped me?' He turned the camcorder onto his own face. 'When you meet her, you know the idea of stopping no longer exists.'

'What's her name?' He pointed at another of the Zara sculptures. 'We *all* know.' He continued to walk round, filming the different Zaras from every angle. 'At first, I thought she was just another beautiful girl, an English version of a spoiled Manhattan heiress. I've known enough of them. No big deal. How little I understood.'

He replaced the camcorder on its tripod, walked back into shot and smiled; such a sad smile. Then the smile became a grin, and then – what's that word? – *rictus*. It was fixed, rigid, *mad.*

'I asked her to come here to see my gift.' He was mumbling now. 'She refused, of course.'

He took something from his pocket – a piece of paper or card – and stared at it. He shook his head then said the word '*Belladonna*'.

'Why didn't I recognise her straight off?' He babbled to himself for a few seconds. 'Who is she?' he asked again.

He brought his face right up to the lens of the camcorder. 'I told you, we all know her name. We *all* meet her in the end.' Distractedly, he swept his hand through his hair. 'It was my destiny to be here like this. I guess it's what I always wanted.' He took a pen from his pocket and scribbled something on the back of the piece of paper. 'Even now I need a script.' He gave a sad chuckle. 'I suppose it's only fitting that someone else should provide an actor's last words.'

As he walked past one of the Zara sculptures, I noticed that it was melting. Raising his hand, Sam placed his palm against Zara's cheek. He was crying. 'I never realised death could be so beautiful.'

He walked into the middle of the pool. A puddle had started to form. Then he stepped behind one of the sculptures, blocking much of the view. I think I saw him putting something in his mouth, but I couldn't be certain.

He muttered some words, but the camcorder's microphone didn't pick them up. Then he just stood there, as frozen as the sculptures. They were melting quite rapidly now. He must have switched off the refrigeration equipment.

The rest of the video played out in silence apart from the dripping of water from the sculptures. Occasionally, an individual finger, hand or arm fell off. A couple of times whole heads fell off. All the time, Sam just stood there.

After fifteen minutes, he collapsed, clutching his heart. His breathing was shallow, then I couldn't hear it at all. Just that dripping sound. More and more water filled the pool. Then there was nothing, until the camcorder showed me entering the room.

I tried to feel something, but I couldn't. I might as well have been stone. Maybe that's what you had to become to survive in this world. Look at Sam.

He craved Zara, but never got her, except through the touch of his rival. He'd lost Alphabet Love and yet for a while he must have been able to delude himself that he'd won. Then the truth cracked his mind. His feelings were fake, stolen from Jez. All he'd done was taste Jez's absolute victory.

Maybe if my name started with Z instead of S some of the trouble could have been avoided. Alphabet Love…how much of a role did it play, or was it just a sideshow? I think Zara could have been called anything and not a thing would have changed.

I'd got so close to Sam, but perhaps it was no more real than how close he got to Zara. I didn't want to talk to the police. Sam was dead. I had no doubt he killed himself. What else was there to say? I agreed with Zara about omerta. I wouldn't say a thing and I knew that's why I'd been allowed to play the game in the first place. I liked to think I had what Zara had – class, breeding, loyalty. It's a question of doing the right thing. If you don't have honour, what are you?

I wondered what was in the letter Zara sent to Sam that day in the costumier's in Mayfair. Words? A picture? It might as well have been a death warrant. I realised the answer was right here – the item Sam had stared at in the pool. I scrambled down the steps and into the pool. I splashed through the thin layer of water, frantically searching for it, but I didn't go anywhere near Sam's body.

The piece of paper was floating on the surface of the water, a few feet from Sam's body. I snatched it up, my hands shaking. It was sopping wet but I could still make out the image: a photograph of Zara wearing a designer white raincoat, her hands provocatively placed on her hips so that the raincoat was pushed back to reveal what she had on underneath. In fact, she was stark naked apart from six-inch transparent high heels.

I flipped it over, to see what Sam had written.

"*This is the way the world ends*
Not with a bang but a whimper."

I suppose it was inevitable that Sam's last words would be the final lines of Zara's favourite poem, but all I could think of was a remark he'd made months ago. When Jez asked him how he wanted to die, he'd replied, 'I'd like to drown in a pool of women's tears.' As it happened, he drowned in his own, dying in a swimming pool, just like Jay Gatsby.

****

The next hour passed in a haze. I think it was the hotel manager who found me. He must have called the police. They took the camcorder away and made me hand over Sam's photo of Zara. They asked me lots of questions but I can barely remember any of them. Some part of me wanted to make sure the truth came out about the Top Table and what they did to people, but I didn't reveal anything. I couldn't have looked Zara in the eye if I'd broken my word. Somehow, now that Sam was dead, I was taking on his troubles. I needed some kind of closure with Zara and I had no idea how to do it. I loathed her, yet, in some weird way...*God.*

The police knew I was lying to them. 'Where are your feelings?' one of them yelled at me at one stage. It was the only thing that made an impression. 'Is there nothing inside you?' he bellowed. 'Are you all hollow?'

That last word startled me. Was that why Zara and the others liked that poem so much? Was I becoming like them? Truth was I didn't know anyone who wasn't hollow. If we really *felt* – I mean, *really* – we couldn't live with the things we've done, the people we've become. It was never meant to be this way but what other way could it be?

Over the last few years, I'd gone from being a teenage wannabe on the party circuit to an entertainment consultant taking advantage of rich middle-aged men, to someone who'd lived intimately in the highest circles with top A-listers. I'd been plunged into a world where I was exposed to as much fame and glamour as I'd ever desired. All the way through I'd been a fraud, defrauding even myself. I used to have so many illusions about A-listers. I thought I'd be saved if I could share their lives.

But they were the most fucked up people of all.

42

Belladonna

It shouldn't have finished the way it did, but life doesn't do happy endings, does it? It took months for the scandal to fade. I heard that the American government was keen to send over an FBI team to investigate Sam's death. It seemed no one could accept that such a huge star had committed suicide. Maybe they thought that if the man who has everything kills himself, what's to stop the rest of us?

The post mortem revealed that Sam died in the same way as Lawrence, Chloe and Marcus: atropine poisoning. It wasn't established where he got it from. One interesting detail that came out in the newspapers was that atropine was extracted from a plant called deadly nightshade, or *Belladonna*. It meant 'beautiful woman' in Italian. That's exactly what Sam died from.

The police never discovered anything about how and where Sam spent his last night. I was interviewed, as were Jez and every member of the Top Table, but none of us told the police anything. Unofficially, the police complained of a lack of cooperation. There was little they could do. After all, there was no doubt Sam killed himself. When a policeman leaked Sam's camcorder film to a cable channel, it became the most publicised suicide in history: the whole world watched it. Sam's photo of Zara was also made public. At first, she was referred to as a 'mystery supermodel.' I think she would have preferred something rather grander, reflecting her class and supreme intelligence.

Commentators queued up to offer opinions. Unrequited love was the favourite theory. They said Sam was a hopeless romantic who died from a broken heart. Others said he became disillusioned with the falseness of Hollywood and the pressures of being a star. A philosopher claimed Sam was consumed by his own hyperreality, and that we'd all be sharing his fate unless we found our way back to the real world. One cynical commentator declared that a deluded snob met even more deluded snobs, with fatal consequences.

Psychiatrists described him as an 'eggshell' personality. They said he had fundamentally low self-esteem that he'd spent years trying to hide, and he was ready to crack at any time. An arrogant egotist on the outside, deep down he was cripplingly insecure because of his deprived background, they claimed. When he encountered the Top Table, his greatest fears about himself were exposed. Everywhere he went, people flattered him and pandered to his every whim, but he was never comfortable with it. When he met Zara, he came up against someone who had no interest in him as a star and unconcealed contempt for him as a person. Her evaluation of him matched his own true opinion of himself.

Maybe some elements of that were right, but I know what the bottom line was when it came to Sam's suicide. NexS killed him. I have no idea what it actually was, but I'd never experienced anything like it. It allowed me to feel what other people were feeling. It was the most exhilarating experience of my life. They say we're made of stardust. Maybe it was like going back to the stars, where we all began.

Sam took a much higher concentration than the rest of us. He must have felt as though he were flying. When you've soared as high as you can go, can you ever return to earth?

Someone anonymously sent me an article from a science magazine. It was complicated and I didn't understand most of it, but the gist was clear enough. It said that the pleasure and pain parts of the brain are linked and anything that affects one also affects the other. The worst lows follow the best highs – isn't that what people have always said? Apparently there was now scientific proof that it was true. A hugely pleasurable experience also triggers the pain circuits in the brain. Eventually when the pleasure has gone all that's left is the pain. The author of the article speculated that someone could have a pleasure overload that would ultimately trigger so much pain that the person might become suicidal.

I think that whoever sent the article was trying to explain what happened to Sam and the others. Was it Zara? I suspected Leddington. After all, he was the one who blabbered on about Thanatos, mortido and all that weird stuff. Death by pleasure? Just more speculation, really. I guess suicidal lows can follow ecstatic highs, but it doesn't seem likely. Surely lots more people would kill themselves if it were true. Then again, I'd never experienced a drug like NexS. Who knows how much something like that could screw with your mind? Four people took concentrated NexS and all four were dead. Maybe others took it and didn't die. There was no way for me to tell.

Nothing more was ever said about NexS. Mencken claimed to have lost all interest in it after what it did to Sam. I could understand that coming from anyone but him. Wasn't he the one who said he was prepared to go all the way for ultimate pleasure? Sam had taken that final ride; shouldn't Mencken have been burning with curiosity? For God's sake, Jez and I had both done the NexS trip. At the very least, Mencken should have wanted to go as far as we did. It didn't add up. But Mencken refused to explain himself, and that was that.

I confess that sometimes I wondered if NexS really existed. Maybe I had an incredibly powerful hallucination that night. A super strong dose of LSD might do that to you, perhaps. If NexS were real, where did it come from? Who supplied it? I couldn't believe that something as potent as that could stay underground forever. It had vast commercial potential. If it ever hit the streets, it would become the most popular drug the planet has ever known. The supplier would become a trillionaire, just as Big Pat said. That's how huge it was. But there were no answers. Zara was the only one who knew, and she wasn't saying.

It didn't take long for journalists to identify her as Sam's femme fatale. Overnight, she became the most famous woman in the world. She and Leddington appeared on countless chat shows offering their opinions on almost every subject. I think many people were in awe of them, intimidated by how clever and glamorous they were. They admitted what I'd always suspected – that they were boyfriend and girlfriend, though in a very 'open' sense, as I'd already discovered. Somehow, no hint of scandal attached itself to them. Many details about the Top Table were revealed, but it was all regarded as just over-spirited student fun. Their reputations weren't damaged in any way by their links to the suicide victims. Enhanced, if anything.

The Millionaires' Death Club was never mentioned by anyone. There were no more mysterious suicides. I could never work out if Zara and Leddington had ever genuinely been at risk from the whole thing. Would they have taken concentrated NexS if they'd been chosen? I didn't think those two had any kind of death wish. I suspected the card game used to select the victims was rigged. They made sure that only those who were attracted to suicide – and I'm including Sam in that – were chosen. If, somehow, it had been their turn, I think they would have got out of it.

Zara, Leddington and the others were the strangest, most compelling people I've ever met. I didn't doubt for a second they were smart and brilliant, and that great achievements would soon be associated with their names, but I also suspected they were capable of anything in pursuit of their ambitions. Nothing would be allowed to stand in their way. Did I envy them? Well, who wouldn't? I could understand why even a superstar was in awe of them. They represented something much higher, much more inspiring than the fools' gold of Hollywood. Class, breeding, history – they had it all. In a way, they were, as a besotted broadsheet journalist lovingly said about them, 'immortal, a representation of a timeless quality of elite humanity.' It didn't surprise me that their favourite philosopher was Nietzsche. I read that he was a mad, syphilitic German who wrote about an ideal human whom he named the Übermensch – the 'superman'. That was their game, all right. They saw themselves as masters of creation, the best that humankind has to offer.

As for me in my humble little world, I'd actually become quite famous because of my association with Sam, especially in the States. I soon went back to my old routine, with much more interesting clients than before. I was in constant demand, and was able to make regular healthy payments to *Far Havens Financial Services* that kept the miserable Mr Graveson more than happy. The only problem was that I wasn't the same person any more. My dreams had changed. I was planning to make big alterations in my life, but something still held me back. I guess I still hadn't come to terms with everything that happened. Above all, I needed something from Zara before I could move on. I wasn't sure what, exactly. I didn't even know if I'd ever see her again.

Sam and Jez's new movie was finished using a look-alike and CGI. The only downside was that because the movie was successfully finished and not abandoned, the terms of Mencken's insurance policy stipulated that he could only collect half of the hundred million he thought he was getting. Not that he was worried. They say it's the most successful movie ever. Everyone wanted to see Sam's final screen appearance. He's right up there now with James Dean, Jim Morrison, Jimi Hendrix and the rest. The glamour of young death.

Jez gave several press conferences saying how devastated he was by the loss of his 'close friend' and that he was thinking of retiring from the movies. Word on the street is that he's already signed up with Mencken for three new blockbusters.

As for Alphabet Love, a year ago it was a cheesy, sleazy underground game. Now you'll find people playing it in every country of the world. It has become the latest 'must-do before I'm thirty' activity. Thousands have claimed it changed their lives. A shop-girl married an A-list celebrity thanks to it. Of course, not everyone approved of the game. The Pope called it, 'Unfettered promiscuity; the latest abomination of a depraved and godless society.'

In a way, everyone came out of it OK. I miss Sam, of course. Did I really love him? I guess not. If you can recover from someone's death in a few weeks, they can't have taken up permanent residence in your heart. Maybe if I'd spent more time with him and got to know him better things might have been different.

Belladonna

When I think hard about what happened it makes me uncomfortable. All along, I knew Sam was in some kind of danger, but I never tried to talk him out of it, not really. I stood by, more or less, while he hurtled towards his fate. Not only did I allow it to happen to him, I allowed myself to be part of it. Sometimes I ask myself how I can square my almost casual acceptance of his death with the deep feelings I had for him. When he needed me most I wasn't there.

I didn't confront Zara even though she was the maelstrom sucking Sam in. Why was I so ambivalent? I think something broke inside me when Sam threw me aside so lightly. Also, I believed that whatever happened I had to go along with it. I knew Sam couldn't be talked out of it, so I didn't make any serious attempt. Above all, I was curious to see what would happen.

Maybe there was something else. I remembered Marcus's unfinished poem about Zara. 'My death in the sun,' he wrote. Sometimes I thought Zara actually *was* death. Leddington's William Blake painting might as well have shown Zara clutching the dagger instead of that strange green figure. 'Who is she?' Sam kept asking throughout his video. He never gave an answer, but it was obvious anyway. Zara is Death, is what he meant.

She herself said that medieval paintings often showed a beautiful woman standing next to a skeleton representing death. Perhaps the experts were wrong. Maybe it wasn't the skeleton but the woman who symbolised death. *Beauté du Diable* – even before I met her, was I thinking of Zara? If anyone had the devil's beauty, she did.

Sam said he never realised death could be so beautiful. That will always stay with me. Now, when I think of Death, it's not the Grim Reaper I have in my mind, it's Zara. She was the new gold dream that killed everyone who dared to pursue it.

I know one thing for sure – it was the ride of my life, the magic bus trip I'd always dreamt of taking. In some way, the whole thing began with that newspaper article I featured in: *Extreme Pleasure: the Search for the Perfect High. (Adventures of modern city girls seeking their personal Xanadu.)* I can now say I've had the extreme pleasure part of the equation. NexS, whatever else it was, was certainly that. Did I find Xanadu? It doesn't exist – not for anyone. Just look at Mencken, Jez, and Sam. As for the perfect high, I can't say for certain. What I know is that those few days I spent with Sam will be forever like a glittering dream when life seemed, briefly, to have been painted in more vivid colours. But every bright colour fades in the end.

43

All the World's a Globe

I was amazed when Mencken phoned me a month later and invited me to attend a performance of *Macbeth* at the Globe Theatre. He said he was back in London on business and had an 'opportunity' to discuss with me. I wasn't sure I wanted to meet him, but I persuaded myself there was no harm in listening to what he had to say.

I'd never actually visited the Globe, but it was certainly a striking building: timber construction, three-storeys high, full of authentic *olde worlde* touches, supposedly an accurate reconstruction of the Elizabethan theatre where Shakespeare worked. Open-air, circular, with a thatched roof, it really brought old London to life.

We stood close to the stage, with a view so good I could see the sweat on the actors' foreheads. Three scary witches were on stage, cackling as they threw frogs into a cauldron. The words of the play kept distracting me. They seemed so eerily right for everything I'd experienced at the hands of the Top Table.

Fair is foul, and foul is fair.

I fidgeted when I heard something that reminded me of Sam.

Nothing in his life
Became him like the leaving of it.

I thought that if every time I substituted the word *Zara* for *Macbeth*, I was getting close to the heart of the matter.

Methought I heard a voice cry, 'Sleep no more!
Macbeth does murder sleep,' the innocent sleep.

The play even seemed to express the Top Table's casual attitude towards Sam's death.

A little water clears us of this deed.

All the World's a Globe

Mencken made me a business proposition; a truly fantastic opportunity, as he kept repeating. He seemed to believe I wouldn't need to think twice about it, despite everything that had happened between us. His idea was that we'd massively expand my set-up, creating a network of entertainment consultants in every big city in the world. Everything would be put on a much more professional basis than I'd ever managed. We'd become *corporate*. Anywhere on earth, if an event were legitimate and entertaining we'd know about it and would guarantee to get our clients in. High rollers would love our operation. We'd even incorporate Top-Table-type events into our programme. Mencken said he was a natural at the entertainment game, whether it was movies or anything else.

Double, double, toil and trouble;
Fire burn and cauldron bubble.

It was such a strange experience for me. It was a particularly dark night, and light rain was falling. I kept expecting thunder and lightning to erupt overhead to reflect what was happening on stage, and in my mind. The play was all about the madness that ambition works on susceptible people. Now, here I was, being given a blueprint for how I could make all my dreams come alive. Everything Mencken said to me was what I'd once prayed I'd hear. I ought to have said *yes* instantly.

By the pricking of my thumbs,
Something wicked this way comes.

'What is it you *want*?' Mencken asked when I stayed silent. 'I thought I was giving you all the things you desired. Why aren't you happy? Is it Sam?'

A deed without a name.

'Don't you know what your dreams are any more?' Mencken peered at me, but I kept facing forward, staring at the stage.

All the perfumes of Arabia will not sweeten this little hand.

I sneaked a glance at Mencken. Did his ambition come before everything else? The Hollywood Macbeth.

Canst thou not minister to a mind diseased?

'I…I need time to think about it,' I stammered.

Mencken smiled. 'Sophie, you're a sweet, charming young lady. Don't spoil it by taking life too seriously.'

On stage, Macbeth had become as serious about life as you could get.

Life's but a walking shadow, a poor player,
That struts and frets his hour upon the stage,
And then is heard no more; it is a tale
Told by an idiot, full of sound and fury,
Signifying nothing.

Was that Sam's life? My own? I felt like crying. 'I'm sorry,' I said to Mencken, 'I'm not feeling well. I need to go.'

'Sorry to hear that. Get better soon, won't you?' He lifted his hand and made a phone shape. 'Call me.'

I fled outside.

A film crew was positioned near the Globe's front entrance, filming an interview with Julie Regan, one of London's hot new starlets, brilliant lights falling on her beaming, beautiful face. Paparazzi were swarming in the background, ready to pounce.

I came to a halt and stared in morbid fascination. I could see that familiar hunger in Regan's eyes, that addiction to fame's bright dream. You could see she was convinced she'd made it, that she only needed to stretch out her hand and she could take whatever she liked from life.

Did I used to be like that?

I heard her saying, 'This is everything I ever wanted. It's what you work for during all those hard years at drama college. You don't think it's ever going to happen to you, but then you wake up one day and you think you've won the lottery. I'm so excited, so lucky.'

I felt cramping pains in my stomach, and staggered over to a bin. Under the dim night-lights, I could make out insects swarming over a discarded, rotten banana. The smell was appalling. I was convinced I was going to collapse. I bent over double and threw up. No one offered me any help. I fished around in my handbag for tissues to clean myself up.

'Are you OK?' an American voice said.

I looked up and saw a young man and woman staring at me.

I didn't answer.

'You're Sophie York, aren't you?'

I nodded dumbly. Did they want my autograph? To slag me off? I didn't need any hassle. I just wanted to get home, crash out on my bed and throw the covers over my head for days.

'Sorry to catch you at an awkward moment,' the young man said, 'but we'd like a word with you.'

I squinted at them.

'We're from the FBI.' They held up impressive gold badges.

'FBI?'

'We'd like to ask you a few questions.'

I felt light-headed. 'What about?' I croaked.

'*Zara.*'

44

Secrets

I'd never heard of the Behavioural Analysis Unit. Special Agent Thomas Carson said they profiled criminals: murderers, terrorists, rapists and serial killers. As for his colleague, Special Agent Hannah Levrov, she didn't speak. She was standing near the window, arms folded over her slim body.

I was perched uncomfortably on a red plastic chair in front of a Formica-topped table in a whitewashed interview room in the American Embassy, wondering why I'd been stupid enough not to insist on having a solicitor with me. The digital clock on the wall proclaimed 21:00. *Jesus*. So much for snuggling under my duvet.

'We've come a long way for this,' Carson said. 'We had to get special permission from your Home Secretary.'

'I don't know how you think I can help.'

'You can start by telling us about the Millionaires' Death Club. You're a member, aren't you?'

'There's no such thing.'

Carson smirked. 'The London CID were scared of Zara and her creepy boyfriend, but those two don't worry us.'

I almost smiled when he said that. He'd obviously never met Zara and Leddington.

'You all seem to think that because you've been on the TV and in the papers you're something special,' he went on. 'Think we can't lay a finger on you? You couldn't be more wrong. I don't give a rat's ass about celebrities. My job is to catch criminals, whoever they are.'

He lifted a brown folder from the table and thumbed through several pages.

'Everything you told the police before was bullshit from beginning to end, wasn't it?'

'Listen, if this is yet another investigation into Sam's death, all I can say is that the whole world knows what happened. They watched it on TV.'

'You can't walk away from this. When one of the most famous men in the world dies, no one forgets.'

No one forgets. The words made me shudder. The memories were in my bloodstream, circulating all the time. Sometimes when I looked in the mirror I thought I saw the ghosts of the four who died. Above all, I remembered

Zara's Day of the Dead and I wondered if they could come back to this world just as she claimed.

'I know what the murder weapon was.' Carson crouched down so that his head was level with mine. 'Zara's gang killed him with NexS.'

'That's a fantasy. There's no such thing.'

'We both know you're lying.'

'Like I said, Sam's death was filmed. Everyone saw it. No one else was there. There was no murder. No one found any trace of this NexS.'

'That's what it seems like, but you know what they say about appearances being deceptive.'

I tried hard not to look at him: a smug Yank who thought he could understand the Top Table. They were light years beyond his comprehension. He'd probably come in his pants if Zara ever spoke to him.

Carson waved his folder at me. 'It's all here, the full story. All the motives. The whole shitty shebang.'

'What are you talking about?'

'How's this for starters? Mr Harry Mencken went to Yale as a student and joined an elite secret society called the Skull and Bones. It's safe to say the Millionaires' Death Club would have been right up his street.'

I tried not to react. Mencken himself had told us all about the Skull and Bones society, merely omitting that one detail that he was a member. OK, he'd deceived us, but the more I thought about it the less I cared. I was sure he had many secrets, some harmless, some unsavoury. I had no desire to find out what they might be.

Carson tried again. 'In the end, we discover everyone's secrets. Did you know that when Sam was eighteen he got his girlfriend pregnant? The baby boy was two months premature. He was so sickly the doctors couldn't do anything for him. His mother and Sam were allowed to briefly hold him, but he died minutes after being born.'

I flinched. Poor Sam. Now his recurring dream made perfect sense.

'I see I finally got your attention,' Carson said. 'Want to know what Lincoln said to Jez Easton at that MTV ceremony? An FBI sound engineer managed to isolate his words. It gives us a clear motive for Easton wanting Lincoln out of the way.'

I pretended I had no interest but I was desperate to find out what it was. It had always intrigued me.

'Ah, here we are,' Carson glanced at his notes. '"You're some actor, aren't you, Jez?" Sam said. "Shall we show the world what you're really like, *asshole*? I have the whole thing on video."'

I remembered Jane's story about the party in Sam's penthouse when a guest jumped to her death and suspicion fell on Jez; the rumour that Sam had a secret camera that recorded exactly what happened.

'Easton made light of Lincoln's comment,' Carson continued, 'saying it related to a home sex video he'd accidentally left in Lincoln's apartment. We never did find any video, sexual or otherwise. That doesn't mean it's not out there somewhere. It will fetch up one of these days. Then we'll know for sure.'

'I can't help you with any video,' I said.

'But the mere mention of it riled Easton, didn't it? You have to wonder why.'

Was it possible that Jez threw the woman out of the window and Sam's camera recorded the murder? Maybe Jez gave the victim something that made her jump. I was already familiar with a substance that could induce people to kill themselves. *Did Jez know about NexS long before his trip to London*?

Sam was definitely right about one thing – Jez was some actor. He'd fooled everyone, especially me. He had a recurring dream of his own, of course, and now I knew precisely what it meant. The weight he dreamt he was dragging around with him was neither fame nor guilt – it was the knowledge that Sam held damaging evidence against him.

'Jez and Mencken have a close relationship, don't you agree?' Carson said. 'It must have tortured Sam, what with him treating Mencken like a surrogate dad and all that. Did he ever tell you how he found out?'

'Find out what?'

'You don't know, do you?' Carson's eyes gleamed with malicious delight. His next words slammed into me like punches. 'Jez Easton is Harry Mencken's son.'

I stared straight ahead.

Carson couldn't keep the sneer off his face. 'He's not the only Mencken bastard, of course. Simon Meade is Easton's half brother.' He took a photo from his folder and slapped it down in front of me.

'Blond Elvis!' I blurted.

'Pardon me?'

I shrugged. 'I never knew his name.'

'You weren't a big cog in this machine. I'm sure you weren't party to any of the major decisions. It was probably like a jigsaw for you, with key pieces missing. Is it all beginning to fit together now?'

Was it?

'I can't help you,' I replied. I knew that if my headteacher at school could see me now she'd shake her head and say, 'I told you so. A strangely amoral creature, not fit for Roedean.' But maybe my dad would still give me some credit. I wasn't ratting and I never would. Didn't that make me moral?

Carson was frustrated. 'This isn't over,' he growled. 'One day, one of you will crack. It might be a year, it might be twenty, but one day someone's conscience won't stay quiet any longer.'

'There's nothing to tell,' I insisted. I knew everyone's loyalty to Zara was much greater than any notion of obeying something as remote as the law. 'Well?' I asked when Carson's questions dried up.

He folded his arms and glowered at the floor.

'Get out of here,' a new voice said – Special Agent Levrov. Why had she chosen to speak now, just as we were finishing? She walked to the door and edged it open a few inches.

I got out of my seat and moved towards her. Manoeuvring past, I squeezed myself against her. I smiled as sexily as I could. I don't know why I did that. Or perhaps I knew exactly.

Levrov reached out and grabbed my arm. 'Come on, Sophie, why don't you stay and tell us about Zara? You must be dying to.'

She leaned into me, invading my body space, just as I'd done to her. 'Perhaps you think some cupboards should stay locked. You never know what might fall out, right?' Reaching into her handbag, she brought out a glossy colour photograph that showed Zara and me. I was shocked because I didn't know such a picture existed, and I had no idea how the FBI had got their hands on it. In it, I was standing side by side with Zara. She looked as perfect as ever while I was staring glumly at the ground.

'She's extraordinarily pretty, isn't she?' Levrov pressed her mouth so close to my ear I could feel her hot breath. 'But you seem a bit down.' She raised her eyebrows.

I froze. Everything started to flood back. That *face*.

'I don't think it was Sam Lincoln you loved,' Levrov said. 'Was Zara everything you aspired to be? All of your dreams come true?'

That last remark cut right through me. Last summer had started as a dream, but the flip side of heaven is hell. Tears pricked the corners of my eyes.

'Oh, here's something you might like to read.' Levrov pulled a book from her handbag. 'It's an advanced copy of Jez Easton's autobiography. Ghost-written, of course, but none the worse for it, I'm sure.'

I didn't want to look at it.

'I like the pictures,' she whispered, 'especially the one on page ninety-eight. There's one thing about it – I can't work out what it's showing me. Is it *everything*, or nothing? Have a good look. One of these days, maybe you can let me know what you think.'

I reluctantly took the book and walked out into the corridor. I should have been relieved to be out of that grim interview room, but I felt nauseous. The book was so heavy in my hand. I didn't want to open it, but I knew I had no choice. Sooner or later you have to confront your demons.

I went to the loo and locked myself in a cubicle. With my hands shaking, I opened the book at the section full of glamorous celebrity photographs. As I flicked through them, I saw picture after picture of Jez surrounded by famous friends, meeting presidents and royalty, jamming with rock bands on stage, opening nightclubs, sitting at the wheel of racing cars, sipping champagne on yachts with beautiful models, living the glitzy highlife of a superstar.

Then I reached page ninety-eight. I stared at the photograph and kept staring. It was a picture from almost two years ago, long before my first contact with Jez. He had made an appearance as a celebrity speaker at the Oxford Union and afterwards he went to a party with the sponsors of his trip and the leading members of the Union.

He was pictured standing amongst three of the students, with his sponsors on the right of the photograph. One sponsor was Harry Mencken, another John Adams of *Captain Toper Records*, and the third was my former business mentor Peter Henson. As for the tall students on Jez's left wearing tuxedos, Jez was paying no attention to them. He was preoccupied with passionately kissing a beautiful blonde in a blood-red cocktail dress.

There was no room for doubt, no possibility of error. The students in the tuxedos were instantly recognisable. One was Simon Meade, Mencken's son and Jez's half brother, as I now knew. The other was Charles Leddington. As for the young woman being kissed…Zara was as alluring as ever. Every time I looked at that picture, I knew the truth.

I had been an accessory to the perfect murder.

45

Bridge of Sighs

People talk about 'the shock of their life.' Maybe everyone needs one or they'd stay stuck in their rut forever. Wake-up calls didn't come any bigger than the one I'd just had. No court could ever prove the Top Table killed Sam, but they *did*. It was exactly what Zara had bragged about at dinner on that first night in the mansion. The fact that she'd openly discussed it with Sam no doubt made it all the more delicious.

Why had I ever got involved with people like that? There was no point in denying it – I'd been on a self-destruct course all of my life. I'd always admired the wrong people, chased the wrong dreams, aspired to everything that was wrong for me. I guess I'd been running from the one thing I never wanted to confront – *myself*. I was achingly, embarrassingly ordinary. There was nothing special about me, nothing at all. I could never be in the same league as Mencken and Jez and, especially, as Zara and the Top Table.

I phoned Mencken and arranged to meet him at the Millennium Bridge, exactly in the middle. He laughed when I said that.

We met on an overcast afternoon. The Thames was grey and cold, and I was wearing a red Puffa jacket to keep out the chill. I didn't say a thing about what Carson and Levrov had revealed. I knew that whatever I said about Sam, Mencken would put a spin on it. He would claim that he was doing Sam a favour, providing him with the same service that Stevenson's *Suicide Club* offered its clients. But I was convinced that Mencken's main motivation was to protect Jez and himself from being exposed over whatever it was that had happened in Sam's apartment. Sam was a loose canon who had to be silenced.

Anyway, I didn't want to argue. There was no point. I just wanted to tell Mencken in person that there was no chance I'd ever be joining him in any kind of business enterprise.

'So, this is where the adventure ends?' Mencken said. 'I suppose you want me to leave the bridge in one direction while you go in the other?'

I nodded.

He smiled. 'I see you've picked up a few tricks. Here we are, poised over the river of life, so to speak, confronted by a choice of which direction to take. Not terribly subtle, I have to say, but quite effective.'

'When I look back on this moment, I'll know exactly what was at stake,' I answered, 'and why I did what I did. There was a time when I'd have bitten off your hand for what you've offered me. It's everything I want, but it isn't what I *need*. I've only just worked out that the two are totally different.'

'You want to show the world the *real* you?'

'Something like that.'

'But whenever you hear celebrities saying things like that, what they're really confessing is that they're faking it the rest of the time. You never hear them admitting that they're professional phoneys.'

'Well, I'm admitting it. I'm a fake, a phoney, a fraud, whatever you want to call it. I don't want to be like that any more. I want to be myself.'

'Good for you. You've overcome your obsession with your sister.'

'Pardon?'

'Hey, come on, you've always known what this is really about. Your sister was the absent presence.'

'I don't understand.'

Mencken smirked. 'Didn't it ever occur to you how you ended up in the middle of all this? Did you seriously think it was coincidence, or some whim on my part? I didn't know a thing about you. I'd never heard of you. *Zara picked you.* She was fascinated by what Ophelia's sister was like. Of course, you were never able to compete with a ghost, immortalised by a tragic death hours after giving a divine performance. *Frozen perfection.* In a way, Zara was much harsher towards you than anyone. Everything about you seemed to her like an insult to the memory of your deified sister.'

'How do you know this?'

'Zara told me the whole story. I wanted to know how she came to be the way she is.'

'What are you saying? You must tell me.'

I listened in silence as he told his story. The Headgirls from several of England's most prestigious private schools were invited to Wycombe Abbey, the most elite girls' school of them all, to take part in a public speaking contest. The theme was 'Inspirational Heroines from Literature'. All the Wycombe Abbey girls, including Zara, who was just thirteen at the time, went to the great hall to watch the contest.

The usual suspects cropped up in the debate – Jane Eyre, Elizabeth Bennet, Scarlett O'Hara, even Bridget Jones.

According to Mencken, my sister was the last to speak. She began by giving a spellbinding recitation of *The Hollow Men*, starting with the quotation from *Heart of Darkness* that precedes the poem: '*Mistah Kurtz –*

he dead.' Then she launched into a scathing attack on the heroines chosen by the other competitors. One by one, she deconstructed them, exposed their anaemic, man-intoxicated, twee souls. She condemned them as glorified *Mills and Boon* heroines who infected women with the disease of defining their existence in terms of their relationships with their tiresome suitors. No, she declared, what women needed was a *Ms Kurtz*, a modern woman for the modern age, unafraid to journey to the darkest destinations, determined to wrestle with the great questions of the mind and soul rather than the trivial issues of the heart. Modern women ought to be fiercely independent and validated by their own merit rather than by the men in their lives.

Every girl at Wycombe Abbey was awestruck. My sister got a standing ovation, and a unanimous victory; even the other speakers cheered her. She was garlanded with flowers.

It was on her way back to Cheltenham that she was killed.

I vaguely remembered some of those details, but over the years I'd tried to blot them out, to forget. But any deliberate act of forgetting simply creates the ghosts that haunt you.

When Mencken had finished, he gave me a curious smile. 'You see, Sophie, Zara is trying to make your sister's vision a reality. She's chosen that as her mission in life.'

I couldn't believe it. My own sister was Dr Frankenstein. Trembling, I reached into my handbag and brought out my purse. I fumbled for the photograph of my sister. I hadn't looked at it since I put it there the day she died.

'Why do you have a picture of Zara?' Mencken asked, looking over my shoulder as I drew out Ophelia's photo.

I stared at the beautiful face, with the striking blue eyes, and the dramatic short blonde hair. With tears streaming down my face, I tore it up and scattered the pieces into the Thames.

'That was my sister.' I practically choked on the words.

'Ah, now I understand.'

I sobbed as I watched the current taking away the fragments of the photo, the picture of my personal ghost. I refused to live in my sister's shadow any longer. I missed her terribly, and I'd never stop admiring her, but she was a different person from me and I couldn't keep trying to do the impossible and emulate her in some feeble way of mine. I just wanted to be happy on my own terms.

Mencken put his hand on my shoulder and gave it a comforting squeeze.

'Keep it real, Sophie.' He gave me his Californian smile for the last time before heading off towards the Globe. I watched him for a few moments. Then I walked away in the opposite direction.

Epilogue

(Five Months Later)

If I'd gone along with Mencken's plan, I could have made quite a business of it. In fact, I'd have earned a fortune. As it turned out, Jane was the one who profited. Somehow, she managed to hook up with Mencken and now I hear she's well on her way to her first million, and loving every moment. Jez was only too happy to give her his priceless celebrity endorsement, particularly after she threatened to expose his kinky sexual practices. Love and war, huh?

I'm starting to discover the real me. Not any kind of great person for sure, but not as bad as I feared. Mencken and the Top Table showed me what extraordinary people are like and the word that sprung most readily to mind was *monsters*. I could accept my ordinariness now. In fact, I liked it.

Now my life has gone in a whole new direction. I've stopped being an entertainment consultant, given up my Mayfair apartment and moved to a small rented flat in Clapham. I've managed to pay off my entire debt to *Far Havens Financial Services* thanks to a number of lucrative appearances on prime-time American TV chat shows. Now I have a job at Sotheby's, courtesy of Francis Hamlin. The company has sponsored me to do a part-time degree in History of Art at university. I never thought I'd be a student, but I'm loving every second.

I even received a letter from my mum after years of silence. She and dad were no longer watching my career with dismay, she said, but with hope and optimism. If I could keep it up, they'd be glad to see me again. I'd like that so much.

I read that Zara and Leddington both graduated with starred firsts in Politics, Philosophy and Economics. I think the newspaper that predicted they were the people most likely to succeed was right. Already, they were well on their way.

****

One day, I was at work at Sotheby's main auction house in New Bond Street. I was nervous because, for the first time, I was taking charge of an auction unsupervised. I had been assigned a low-value auction of a number of trinkets from early twentieth century, pre-revolutionary Russia. Few people were in attendance, just a handful of collectors of Tsarist memorabilia. I noticed that all of the front seats were reserved, but no one was sitting there.

The auction began and went on uneventfully for an hour. The last item to be auctioned was a Russian Doll that may or may not have belonged to Anastasia, one of the daughters of the last Tsar. Its suggested price in the catalogue was a modest £400.

As I was getting ready to present it to the bidders, the doors of the hall swung open. I peered in disbelief. The Top Table marched to the front of the hall, all of the men in dinner jackets, the women in beautiful white ball gowns, just as I'd seen so many times before. Their faces were chalked white, apart from Leddington and Zara's. Zara wore the same gorgeous blood-red dress and black choker that she had in her picture in the National Portrait Gallery and in the photograph at the Oxford Union with Jez. Every one of the Top Tablers was carrying a black motorcycle helmet with black visor. As soon as I saw those helmets I realised something I guess I'd long suspected – Zara was the statuesque motorbike courier in Trafalgar Square last summer who gave me that gold envelope that started this whole thing.

All of the men sat on the left-hand row of seats, with Leddington beside the aisle. On the other side was Zara, with the women to her right. All of them stared at me. Flustered, I reached out for a jug of iced water and poured myself a glass. I took a long sip then, speaking into my microphone, read out the catalogue entry describing the Russian Doll.

'Can anyone get us started with a bid of three hundred and fifty pounds,' I said and glanced around the hall, praying I would get this wrapped up fast. There was no reaction from any of the collectors. None of them took their eyes off the Top Table. I saw myself reflected in a mirror at the back of the hall. I was sweating profusely. I took a tissue from my handbag and dabbed my brow. All the time, the Top Table gazed at me as though they were trying to burn holes through me.

There were no bids for the Russian Doll, not one. I stood there, baffled. I could declare the auction over, but I knew that would be like admitting defeat.

'One penny,' Leddington declared without warning.

I tried not to look rattled. Jesus, they were messing with my mind again.

'We have a bid of one penny at the front of the room,' I mumbled. I wondered if I should say Leddington's bid wasn't a serious one, but I suspected that's what he wanted. 'I'm sure you'll agree that this item is worth considerably more.'

The room was unnaturally quiet.

Epilogue

'Ten thousand pounds,' Zara said.

Whaaaaat???

'A new bidder,' I stated hesitantly. 'Uh, any advance on ten thousand pounds?' I felt so idiotic saying that. 'All done?' I asked, after taking another long sip of water, trying to buy time. What a futile question. I was so angry with myself. Yet again I was letting her humiliate me. Had I learned nothing?

'Selling for ten thousands pounds, then.' I tried to sound assertive as I held my gavel at the ready, pathetically praying some miracle would happen and someone might outbid Zara. Of course, no one did. I brought the gavel crashing down, much harder than normal.

'Sold,' I said, though I felt that the only thing that had been sold was me.

Zara came over to my table with one of her male minions. The man placed a slim silver attaché case on the table and flicked it open. It was full of crisp, brand new fifty-pound notes.

'Do you want to count it?' Zara asked.

'I'm sure it's all there.' I shakily handed her the Russian Doll.

She opened it there and then, revealing one figure after another. When she reached the smallest figure, she lined it up next to the others. 'You just can't get to the bottom of things, Sophie, can you?' She signalled to the rest of the Top Table and they all stood up and began to leave. As I watched her follow the others up the aisle towards the exit, I felt as much of a victim as ever. She'd even left the Russian Doll behind to mock me.

I rushed after her and grabbed her arm. 'Listen to me, Zara.' She turned round and we stood face to face. 'Have you ever listened to anyone in your life?' I scarcely knew what I was saying but, somehow, I had to settle things right here and now.

'One or two,' she replied in that appallingly arrogant way of hers.

'Well, you should try it more often. You might learn something.'

'That depends on to whom I'm listening, don't you think?'

'This isn't over.' I was becoming desperate. I had to do something to turn this around, but I couldn't think of anything clever. I needed more time.

'You've had your chance,' she said as though she knew what I was thinking. 'You're a fan of F Scott Fitzgerald, aren't you? Then you ought to know he said there are no second acts in American lives. What makes you think you're any different?'

'I'm *not* American.'

'Touché,' she said with a wry smile.

Jesus, I'd scored a point. 'Wait there,' I said, 'I want to give you something.' I darted back to my table. Making sure that Zara couldn't see what I was doing, I thrust my hand into the iced-water jug and grabbed several ice cubes.

All of the Top Table had stopped in front of the exit. Zara was gazing at me curiously, with Leddington a few steps behind her.

I hurried back to her and asked her to hold out her hand. 'I have a memento for you.' She looked at me expectantly, no doubt wondering if poor, simple Sophie could ever surprise her.

I thrust my right hand against hers, pushing the ice cubes hard into her flesh. This was absurd – I was giving ice to the Ice Queen.

She instantly tried to pull away but I swung my left hand across to reinforce my grip and stood there clutching her hand as tightly as I could.

'To remind you of Sam,' I said, staring directly into her eyes. I was shocked by what I saw there – a terrible blankness, a deadness. After a moment, light flickered inside them and her pupils began to dilate. Something amazing happened. I could tell she was seeing me for the first time, seeing *me*. A tiny, almost imperceptible smile crept over her face.

When the ice cubes had melted, I let go of her hand.

'Thanks, Sophie,' she said. Unfazed, she waved her hand to dry it then went over to Leddington and whispered something. They both turned and, simultaneously, gave me the slightest of nods.

The other members of the Top Table filed out, followed by Leddington. As Zara reached the exit, she stopped, turned and gave me the most vibrant, gorgeous smile. Then she was gone.

I wrapped things up in the auction room as fast as I could, locking the money and the Russian Doll in my safe. I'd never been so elated in my life. I rushed out into the street, hardly knowing what I was doing. It was a beautiful sunny day without a single cloud in the sky. I was intoxicated. The way Zara had smiled at me was unmistakable. She had acknowledged me, approved of me, shown me *respect*.

Dizzy, exhilarated, I raced up New Bond Street without a clue where I was going. An open-topped red double-decker tourist bus came towards me. It was called 'The Magic Bus.' I gaped at in amazement then started waving like a crazy person at the tourists on the top deck. As it drove past, I saw a huge advert on its side. 'Straight in at Number One: *Sophie's Smile*, the fantastic new single from *The Bleak Morts'* brilliant debut album *Always Follow Your Heart*.' The girl pictured in the advert looked exactly like me.

I started laughing and I couldn't stop. I'd give Ligger a call and let him know that the *thing* that had been holding me back was well and truly over. I might even tell him that if I'd been honest with myself, I'd fallen in love with him the very first time we met. Isn't it strange how we run from what we really want to chase dreams that have no connection with who we truly are?

I ran after the bus and jumped on at the next stop. 'How far ya goin'?' the driver asked.

When I heard that, my smile was one hundred percent authentic. I realised the fake feeling I used to get had vanished completely. My reply was the only one it could be.

'All the way,' I said.

THE END

Also available:

THE ARMAGEDDON CONSPIRACY

by Mike Hockney

When an SS officer commits suicide at the end of WWII, he leaves behind a document called *The Cainite Destiny* that hints at an incredible link between the Nazis and the Bible's greatest pariah…Cain. Only one person – Cambridge professor Reinhardt Weiss – appreciates the document's significance. His research is ridiculed when he claims he has begun to uncover an unimaginably dangerous conspiracy going all the way back to Adam and Eve. All of history's best-known conspiracies, he insists, are different aspects of a single *superconspiracy* that directly connects the Nazis to the Knights Templar, the Cathars, the Alchemists, the original Freemasons and the early Gnostic sects. His work unfinished, Weiss dies in obscurity.

In 2012, the fate of the world hinges on whether *The Cainite Destiny's* ultimate objective, which always eluded Professor Weiss, can be discovered. Adolf Hitler supposedly attempted to perform the final cataclysmic act, but failed for reasons unknown. Now the members of America's most elite Special Forces unit have deserted en masse and they appear to be the latest inheritors of history's oldest and deadliest secret mission.

When their backgrounds are checked, an extraordinary fact emerges. All of them are grandsons of American intelligence officers who, at the end of the Second World War, interrogated senior officials responsible for the treasure hoard that the Nazis had looted from all over Europe.

The deserters carry out a coordinated set of daring robberies, targeting holy sites associated with the three greatest religious icons of the Western World: the Ark of the Covenant, the Holy Grail, and the Spear of Destiny…the Roman lance used to pierce Christ's side at the Crucifixion, and which was coveted by Hitler.

It seems the American soldiers are the instruments of Cain's ancient revenge. Are they planning the greatest crime of all?

To kill God.

ISBN: 978-1-84799-474-5

Also available:

PROHIBITION A

by Mike Hockney

She's their best agent. Now they've given her a new mission. Sarah Harris must kill presidential candidate Robert Montcrieff on his wedding day in St Patrick's Cathedral in Manhattan. There's just one problem: Sarah is Montcrieff's bride.

She has one week to persuade them they've made a terrible mistake. To find some answers she must crack a top-secret project codenamed *Alice Through the Looking Glass*. She doesn't know it, but she's about to look into her own past...a past containing the US Intelligence Services' deadliest secret, and a shattering personal revelation.

Her frantic search will bring her face to face with Sin for Salvation, an ancient cult with murderous rituals. Its members aspire to commit an ultimate sin known as *Prohibition A*.

The cult preaches a hypersexual creed that has seduced Wall Street's highest flyers. New recruits are enlisted in the world's most exclusive nightclub, revolving around a sado-masochistic fantasy journey through Dante's nine circles of hell. But when its wealthy clientele leave the club, it's neither lust nor lucre they have on their minds.

It's murder.

ISBN: 978-1-84799-477-6

ABOUT THE AUTHOR

www.meritocracy.org.uk

ormation can be obtained at www.ICGtesting.com
he USA
534200112
LV00001B/181/P